THE CLONE WARS
WILD SPACE

THE CLONE WARS
WILD SPACE

KAREN MILLER

Based on the groundbreaking TV series
from Lucasfilm Animation

arrow books

Published in the United Kingdom by Arrow Books in 2009

16

First published in the United Kingdom in 2008 by Century

Arrow Books
The Random House Group Limited
20 Vauxhall Bridge Road, London, SW1V 2SA

Addresses for companies within The Random House Group Limited can be found at:
www.randomhouse.co.uk/offices.htm

The Random House Group Limited Reg. No. 954009

www.randomhouse.co.uk

A CIP catalogue record for this book
is available from the British Library

ISBN 9780099533184

Penguin Random House is committed to a sustainable future for
our business, our readers and our planet. This book is made from
Forest Stewardship Council® certified paper.

MIX
Paper from
responsible sources
FSC® C018179

Printed and bound in Great Britain by Clays Ltd, Elcograf S.p.A.

To Ewan McGregor, a fine actor who brought young Obi-Wan Kenobi so perfectly and heartbreakingly to life

ACKNOWLEDGMENTS

My thanks to:

George Lucas, who literally shaped the course of my life with the release of *Star Wars* in 1977.

Shelly Shapiro, for giving me this extraordinary opportunity.

Sue Rostoni, for her wonderful support and encouragement.

Karen Traviss, who made sure I didn't fall flat on my face. You rock, mate.

Jason Fry, with the eagle eye.

My friends and family, who cheered from the sidelines and agreed that yes, this was Seriously Cool.

The fans, who have helped to keep the galaxy far, far, away alive and vibrant for more than three decades. We may not always agree, but we know what we love.

THE CLONE WARS
WILD SPACE

ONE

———●———

THEN: THE BATTLE OF GEONOSIS, AFTERMATH

GEONOSIS, HARSH RED PLANET. DUST AND ROCK AND PITILESS HEAT, wind and sand and a sky full of shards. Tenacious life. Capricious death. All moist green beauty long burned away. No second chances here, no soft place to fall. Secrets and sedition and singular minds. Ambition and gluttony and a hunger for death. Refuge for some. Graveyard for others. Blood of the Republic seeping into dry soil. Faint on the ceaseless wind, sorrow and grief. Gathered in the arena, a weeping of Jedi . . .

Who wept their tears on the inside, where they would not be seen. To weep for a fallen comrade was to display unseemly attachment. A Jedi did not become attached to people, to things, to places, to any world or its inhabitants. A Jedi's strength was fed by serenity. By distance. By loving impersonally.

At least, that was the ideal . . .

Weary and heart-sore, Yoda stood in silence with his fellow Master and friend Mace Windu, watching as efficient clone troopers swiftly, methodically, and not unkindly loaded the last of the slain Jedi onto repulsorlift pallets, then pushed them one-handed out of Poggle the Lesser's brutal arena to the Republic transport ships waiting beyond its high walls. They were supervised by those few Jedi who had survived the slaughter and the military engagement that followed it . . . and who were not as serenely detached as Temple philosophy might dictate.

The Battle of Geonosis was over, the Separatist droid army dealt a crushing setback. But its leader Count Dooku had fled, the traitor, and his underlings from the Trade Federation, the Techno Union, the Commerce Guild, the InterGalactic Banking Clan, the Hyper-Communications Cartel, and the Corporate Alliance had fled also, to safety. Fled so they might continue to plot the downfall of the galaxy's great achievement, its Republic.

"I do not regret coming here," said Mace, his dark face darkened further by shadows. "We've dealt a serious blow to our enemy, and in doing so we've seen what this clone army is capable of. That's useful. But Yoda, we have paid a heavier price than I imagined, or foresaw."

Yoda nodded, his gnarled fingers tight about his ancient gimer stick. "The truth you speak, Master Windu. Nothing gained, there is, without some loss also to balance the scales." He breathed out slowly, a long, heavy sigh. "Foolish indeed would we be, to think we might escape such a confrontation unscathed. But this loss the Temple will find difficult to overcome. Into Jedi Knighthood too soon must we thrust our oldest Padawans, I fear."

Padawans like Anakin Skywalker, so bright, so reckless . . . and now so hurt. On his way back to Coruscant already, with Obi-Wan and the determined, brave, and equally reckless young Senator from Naboo.

Trouble for him, and for her, I sense. If only clearly could I see. But a shroud the dark side is. In smothering folds it wraps us all.

"What?" said Mace, frowning. Sensing his disquiet, as he always did. "Yoda, what's wrong?"

Talia Moonseeker, a young Argauun only four months into her Jedi Knighthood, was kneeling beside her fallen former Master,

Va'too, head bowed. With an effort Yoda pulled his gaze away from her grief, away from the monstrous arena, still searing in the daylight. A Geonosis day lasted so long. There were yet many hours before the sun would set on this stark vista.

"Answer you plainly I cannot, Master Windu," he replied heavily. "Time for meditation, I require."

"Then you should return to the Temple," said Mace. "I can oversee the cleanup operation here. You are our only beacon in the darkness, Yoda. Without your wisdom and foresight, I doubt we can prevail."

He meant the words kindly, a declaration of confidence, but Yoda felt the weight of them settle into his bones with a cruel finality.

Too old am I to be the last hope of the Jedi.

He watched as Talia Moonseeker withdrew to a discreet distance, so the body of her slain former Master might be decently carried from the arena by the tireless clones who had fought this day, and died this day, so utterly single-minded and fearless that he thought of droids, not men—droids of flesh and blood, bred and drilled to be perfectly disciplined, perfectly lethal. Bred to die so the people of the Republic might live. Commissioned under the most mysterious circumstances, the truth of which might never be unraveled.

Remembering the Kaminoan cloning facility, its bright white sterility, its impersonal care for the creatures it created so efficiently, so remarkably, so wholly without compunction, he repressed a shudder.

Deep questions of morality and ethics do these clones raise. But answers, are there? Know that I do not. Override ethics our desperate need for them might.

Mace dropped to one knee. "Is it Dooku, Yoda? Is he what's troubling you?"

Bitter pain, pricking deeply. *Dooku.* Yoda thrust the name, the shock, aside. There would be time later to think of that fallen man.

"To the Temple I shall now return, Master Windu. Follow me as soon as you can. Important matters there are for the Council to discuss."

Accepting the gentle rebuff, Mace stood. "Travel safely, Yoda. I'll see you on Coruscant once matters here are properly concluded." With an abrupt snap of his fingers he summoned a nearby clone trooper. "Master Yoda is returning to Coruscant. He requires an escort to his ship."

The trooper nodded. "Yes, sir."

Watching the lethal asteroid belt fall away behind them, watching cruel red Geonosis smear and streak as the ship's hyperdrive kicked in, Yoda released the lingering grief of the recent past in another long, slow sigh. Grief was but a signifier of attachment. It had no useful purpose to serve. If he was to serve the light, as was *his* purpose, then must he rediscover that perfectly poised place within himself, whereupon he could stand and know he stood upon firm ground.

For once he reached Coruscant, the hard work of saving the Republic would truly begin.

The Jedi Temple's Halls of Healing were beautiful. They had lofty ceilings and enormous windows that spilled golden light over the blue and green and rose-pink walls and floor. Imbued with the Force's most gentle aspects, with love and nurturing and peace, they were full of perfumed flowers and green growing things, with the music of running water and the vibrancy of life renewed. They were the perfect retreat for those who were broken in body and mind, a place where the ugliness of suffering was washed away.

Oblivious to the serenity around her, Padmé glared at the elderly, elegant Twi'lek Jedi healer standing in her way. "I don't need long, Master Vokara Che. Just a few moments. But I really do need to see Anakin Skywalker."

Twin head-tails gently twitching, the Twi'lek clasped her hands before her. "I am sorry, Senator Amidala, but that's not possible." Her voice had that familiar Twi'lek huskiness, but her Basic was flawless. "Anakin is gravely injured. He has been placed in a deep healing trance and cannot be disturbed."

"Yes, I *know* he's gravely injured. I just traveled back from Geonosis with him." Padmé gestured at her ruined white bodysuit, heedless of the hot pain any movement caused. "See here, Madam Jedi? This is his blood. Trust me, I know exactly how badly he's been hurt!"

To underscore that claim she could show the Temple's senior healer her crushed and bone-bruised hand, the hand Anakin had clung to as the waves of agony from his monstrous wounding burned through him without cease or mercy.

But I'd better not. He isn't supposed to be holding anyone's hand . . . least of all mine. It's bad enough that Obi-Wan was a witness.

The Jedi healer shook her head. "Senator, you are injured yourself. Let us help you."

"Don't worry about me," Padmé said, impatient. "I'm barely scratched, and anyway, I'm not in pain."

Vokara Che gave her a reproving look. "Senator, do not think you can hoodwink me. I'm not even touching you and I can feel your discomfort." Her head fell back and her eyes drifted closed. "Some kind of creature attacked you, yes? And you fell from a great height. There is head pain. Your ribs are bruised. So is your spine. It's a wonder no bones were broken." The Twi'lek's eyes opened, her cool gaze uncompromising. "Shall I continue?"

Aching from head to toe, the nexu's claw marks across her back burning, her battered ribs throbbing with every breath, Padmé gritted her teeth. "There is nothing wrong with me that five minutes with Anakin won't fix. Master Vokara Che, you don't understand. I really *must* see him. Anakin's my bodyguard. My responsibility."

And this is my fault. I bullied him into going to Geonosis and he nearly died, so if you think I'm abandoning him now—

"Anakin Skywalker is not your responsibility," the Jedi healer said sharply. "He is a Jedi and he is safely home among his fellow Jedi, who know precisely what to do for him. Please, let us treat you so you might leave the Temple in good order." A faint hint of censure crept into the Twi'lek's eyes. "Indeed, I must point out that it's not entirely proper for you to be here, for you to—"

"And where else should I be?" Padmé demanded, not caring that her raised voice was attracting the attention of three apprentice healers scurrying about their mysterious Jedi business. Not caring that she was perilously close to making a scene, behaving in a manner unbecoming to a former Queen of Naboo, a member of the Galactic Senate, a politician with a very public face.

I am not leaving this place before they let me see him.

Vokara Che's expression hardened. "If you're not comfortable with receiving Jedi treatment, Senator, I can see you escorted to a medcenter or—"

"You're not escorting me *anywhere*! I want—"

"*Padmé*," said a quiet voice behind her.

Master Vokara Che hurried forward. "Master Kenobi! What are you doing?"

Heart thudding, Padmé turned. *Obi-Wan.* Still in his slashed and burned Jedi tunic. Unhealed as yet. Standing with difficulty in the doorway of a small chamber, clinging to its framework so he didn't fall down. His face was pale; his eyes were darkened with fatigue and pain and something else.

Despair? No. It can't be. Jedi don't feel things like that. At least . . . not this Jedi.

"I'm sorry, Vokara Che," he said quietly. "But I need a moment alone with the Senator."

"I don't think that's wise," said the Jedi healer, one hand clasping his shoulder, unrepentantly aggravated. "You are a whisper away from collapse, Obi-Wan. I don't understand it; you should have been healed by now. I *expressly* sent—"

"And I sent her away," said Obi-Wan, apologetic. "I'd rather not be sunk in a healing trance until I've seen my Padawan."

"You're as bad as she is." Vokara Che clicked her tongue. "Very well. You have a moment."

Padmé watched the healer withdraw, then looked again at Obi-Wan. After a moment's hesitation she approached him, feeling suddenly young and gauche, like a childish apprentice. She tilted her chin. "Vokara Che's right. You look awful."

"Do you truly think you're helping Anakin?" said Obi-Wan. His voice was tight; his eyes were glazed. "You're not. You don't belong here, Padmé. Let them treat you, then go home. Before Yoda returns. Before things get . . . complicated."

She stared at him, shocked. She wanted to shout at him. She wanted to weep. Instead, she turned to leave.

What else could she do?

Upon his return to Coruscant, Yoda put duty first. Instead of going straight to the Temple's Halls of Healing, he answered a peremptory summons from the Office of the Supreme Chancellor. Naboo's former Senator was clearly anxious to hear firsthand of Geonosis; the language used was barely couched in the protocols accepted and expected for such communications.

It wasn't a meeting he anticipated with any kind of pleasure. More and more of late it seemed the Jedi were being drawn into politics, into matters of legislation and legalese that had never been their province. The Jedi were sworn to uphold the Republic and protect its ideals, not entangle themselves in the fortunes of any one Chancellor. Political careers were not their affair. Personalities were supposed to be irrelevant.

But somehow Palpatine was changing that. Not by being a bully or imposing his will. Quite the opposite: he was constantly resisting the Senate's eagerness for him to assume more and more executive powers. He resisted, the Senate insisted, so reluctantly Palpatine agreed. And every time he acquiesced to its requests, he turned once more to the Jedi for advice.

It was hardly an ideal situation. The Jedi Council was *not* just another branch of the executive office. But how, in good conscience, could it refuse to aid a man who so humbly petitioned for their assistance? A man who championed them in the Senate at every opportunity? Who had worked tirelessly for peace since assuming the highest political office in the galaxy and was now faced with the daunting, terrifying task of keeping their vast Republic intact? How could the Jedi Council turn its back on such a man?

Clearly, it couldn't. Clearly, in the face of these extraordinary times, the Jedi must set aside their traditions and come to the aid of the man a galaxy looked to as its savior.

But that didn't mean they had to be happy about it.

With his ship safely docked at the Temple's private spaceport, Yoda transferred to an air shuttle that would see him speedily delivered to the Senatorial complex. His Padawan pilot, T'Seely, acknowledged him respectfully but had the good sense not to talk as he guided the shuttle into the ceaseless slipstreams of Coruscant air traffic and headed for the sprawling Senate District.

They reached the sector without incident. Directly ahead of them the Senate Building gleamed mellow silver beneath Coruscant's sun. Cradle and crucible of democracy, it stood as a symbol of all that was right and good in the galaxy. Born in the Republic's early years, able to remember, vividly, its growing pains and minor upheavals, Yoda treasured that symbol and all it represented as he treasured his beloved Jedi Order.

But now does the silver show a touch of tarnish. Never before in galactic history has democracy trembled as it trembles now.

It was a sickening thought. Not once had he dreamed he might witness the fall of this grand Galactic Republic. All things died, that was true . . . yet somehow he'd imagined the Republic would be spared. Believed that it would evolve, transmute, reinvent itself, *continue*.

The Jedi were oathsworn to see that it did. They were dying now to keep that sacred oath. No sacrifice would be too great to ensure the survival of peace and the Republic. It was unthinkable that those sacrifices might be in vain . . .

The air shuttle's transponder beeped as the Senate control tower's automatic guidance system locked on to their signal and took over the business of piloting them to their assigned landing platform and dock space. It was a new security measure, implemented by Palpatine in a response to the Separatists' increased bellicosity on planets less vigorously defended and patrolled than Coruscant. Not everyone was pleased by the move, claiming a curtailment of civic freedoms.

Trying hard, Palpatine is, to keep us safe and free at the same time. An easy road to walk it is not.

As their shuttle was swallowed by the Senate Building's cavernous docking complex, joining a long line of other entering craft, the Padawan T'Seely cleared his throat, and his red head-scales brightened to scarlet, a sign of Hasikian anxiety.

"Master Yoda?" he said, hesitant.

"Speak, Padawan."

"There is rumor, at the Temple. Much death on Geonosis."

Yoda sighed. It was only to be expected, with the injured returning home. "Not rumor, Padawan, but fact."

T'Seely's head-scales blanched white. "I was told—Master Kenobi—Anakin—"

"Not dead they are, but injured."

"Oh." T'Seely's voice was a horrified whisper.

Yoda frowned. It was not the Jedi way to laud one Jedi Knight above another, call one apprentice greater than the next, but in the case of Obi-Wan and Anakin accepted practice simply did not apply. Anakin Skywalker was proclaimed a child of prophecy. Obi-

Wan was his Master, his reputation formidable. Together they appeared invincible. Or they had . . . until Geonosis.

But he couldn't afford to think of that now.

"Die they will not, Padawan," he told T'Seely firmly. "Gossip about them *you* will not."

"No, Master Yoda," said T'Seely, chastened.

Their shuttle slid smoothly into its allotted docking bay. All around them, as far as the keenest sight reached, other shuttles docked and undocked, carrying out the endless business of the Republic. Yoda dismissed T'Seely back to the Temple, then entered the bowels of the Senate complex and made his way through the bewildering maze of swift-tubes and corridors to its administration quarter, and Supreme Chancellor Palpatine's executive suite.

As usual, its crimson opulence threatened to oppress. An unexpected choice of color scheme for such a humble man. Palpatine had laughed about it, embarrassed. *"When I think of my new responsibilities I grow cold with fear,"* he'd said. *"Red grants me the illusion that I am warm."*

Senator Bail Organa of Alderaan was waiting in Palpatine's otherwise empty office antechamber. He was dressed not in his usual lavish attire, but in a plain dark-hued tunic and trousers of a distinctly military cut. A sign of the times, perhaps. As he was a member of the Loyalist Committee, and a man closely involved with the debates over the Republic's security, it was not surprising that he was also summoned.

"Master Yoda!" he said, leaping to his feet. "What a mercy to see you safely returned from Geonosis." He hesitated, his relieved smile fading. "Is it true—I'm given to understand we were victorious, but . . . that you suffered many Jedi casualties."

Yoda nodded. "True it is, Senator."

"Ah," said Organa, resuming his seat. "I am very sorry to hear that. Please, accept my condolences."

He was a good man, genuinely moved. "Thank you."

Organa hesitated, then added, "The clone troopers, Master Yoda. They were effective?"

"Most effective, Senator. The difference, they made."

"Well, I'm glad of that, for the Jedi's sake, but even so it's troubling," Organa murmured. "Because now the Separatists know we have the means with which to hurt them. Defeat them. I fear Senator Amidala was right after all. They will interpret the formation of this Grand Army of the Republic as an outright declaration of war. Any attempt now to solve this crisis diplomatically will be seen by them as nothing more than a stalling tactic, a ruse to buy time so we can consolidate our new forces."

"Accurately have you summed up the situation, Senator," said Yoda, grimly approving. "All around us the shadows of war gather. Much suffering do I see in the months ahead."

Organa pushed to his feet again and began pacing the antechamber. "There *must* be some way to prevent it, Master Yoda. I refuse to accept that our great and noble Republic can just allow itself to slide without resistance into unchecked bloodshed! The Senate has to *act,* it has to stop this violence before it spreads. If we allow grief and anger over Geonosis to push us into retaliation, if we give ourselves permission to say *this* death justifies *that* one, then we truly *are* lost. And the Republic is doomed."

Before Yoda could reply, the doors to Palpatine's office opened and Mas Amedda stepped into the antechamber.

"Master Yoda, Senator Organa," he said politely. "The Supreme Chancellor will see you now."

TWO

—●—

PALPATINE WAS STANDING BY THE VAST TRANSPARISTEEL WINDOW behind his desk, soberly gazing at the endlessly complicated ribbons of traffic seething across Coruscant's cityscape. Hearing their entrance he turned, gravely smiling.

"Master Yoda. I lack the words to express my profound relief that you have survived the carnage on Geonosis. In truth, I never dreamed the Separatists would take their petty disagreements with the Republic to such extreme and heartbreaking ends."

"Surprised also am I, Supreme Chancellor," Yoda replied. "Unforeseen was this development."

Palpatine returned to his chair. "Unforeseen, yes," he murmured as Mas Amedda took his accustomed place at his superior's right hand. "And by the Jedi, no less. That must be a matter of some concern for you." He leaned forward, his expression intent. "Master Yoda, before we discuss the specifics of what transpired on Geonosis, I must know one thing: how fares my young friend Anakin? I was most alarmed to learn he's been hurt."

"Hurt, yes, Supreme Chancellor," said Yoda. "But dying he is not."

Palpatine sat back and passed an unsteady hand across his face.

"Truly, he is protected by the Force." His voice caught, and he shivered. "I'm sorry. You'll have to forgive my emotion. Anakin is very dear to me. Having watched him grow up from small boyhood, watched him develop into such a fine young man, so courageous, so powerful, such a credit to the Jedi Order, I take a close personal interest in his well-being. I do hope . . ." He faltered. "I hope you don't consider my concern for him—my affection—to be an intrusion, Master Yoda. Naturally I don't wish to do anything that might impede Anakin's progress as a Jedi."

Yoda stared at the floor, both hands grasping his gimer stick. There was no easy answer to that. Yes, he was concerned by Palpatine's attachment to the boy. No matter how well-meaning, no matter how genuine and heartfelt, the Supreme Chancellor's care for Obi-Wan's apprentice was problematic. The root cause of all young Skywalker's difficulties was his need for emotional connections. His friendship with Palpatine only complicated matters. But the man *was* Supreme Chancellor. And he meant well.

Sometimes politics had to take precedence.

"An intrusion, Supreme Chancellor? No," he said. "Value your interest young Skywalker does."

"As I value him, Master Yoda," said Palpatine. "I wonder . . ." He paused, delicately. "Might I inquire as to the exact nature of his injuries?"

Yoda glanced at Bail Organa, so far unacknowledged. Did it bother him? If so, he was masterful at concealing his feelings.

A good man he is. Discreet and loyal. Still, discuss Jedi business before him I would rather not. And yet refuse to answer Palpatine I cannot.

He tapped his fingers on his gimer stick, then nodded. "His right arm has young Skywalker lost. Cut off in a lightsaber duel."

"A *duel*?" Palpatine repeated, incredulous. "With whom? Who would be rash enough to draw a lightsaber on Anakin? Who in all the galaxy possesses the skill and knowledge to defeat a Jedi with his abilities?"

Again, unwelcome, the shafting pain of failure and regret. Yoda made himself meet Palpatine's horrified gaze, unflinching. "Count Dooku it was, Chancellor. True are the first reports we received from Master Kenobi. An enemy of the Republic has Count Dooku become."

Palpatine turned to Mas Amedda, whose hands were spread wide in shocked dismay. Then he looked back, his mouth pinched, his eyes brilliant with distress. "Master Yoda, I scarcely know what to say. Count Dooku has betrayed the Jedi Order. He has betrayed us all. I don't understand. How could he do something so wicked?"

Yoda frowned. He certainly wasn't going to talk of the *Sith* in front of Bail Organa. "Seduced by dreams of power is Dooku. A great tragedy this is."

Palpatine breathed out a pained sigh. "Tell me the rest, Master Yoda. Though I know it will break my heart, I must hear of Geonosis."

It was a tale told swiftly, without embellishment or emotion. When it was done, Palpatine removed from his chair once more to stand staring through the transparisteel window into Coruscant's teeming sky, hands clasped behind his back, chin sunk to his velvet-and-brocade-covered chest.

"Do you know, my friends," he said at last, breaking the heavy silence, "there are times when I begin to doubt I have the strength to go on."

"Never say it!" Mas Amedda exclaimed. "Without your leadership the Republic could not survive!"

"Perhaps that was true, once," Palpatine admitted. "But if I, as Supreme Chancellor, can fail so terribly that these blind and foolish Separatists are emboldened enough to deal us *such* a blow . . ."

"Supreme Chancellor, you are far too hard on yourself," said Bail Organa swiftly. "If there is blame here, it belongs to this treacherous Count Dooku and the leaders of the various guilds and unions that support him, who manipulate events and the weaker, more gullible systems to their own advantage. *They* are the ones who have failed the Republic, not you. The blood spilled on Geonosis stains *their* hands, not yours. From the very beginning of this dispute you have done nothing but strive to find a peaceful solution."

"And I have *failed*!" Palpatine retorted, swinging around. "Who knows better than I, Bail, how important it is for this violence to end? I, a man whose home planet was invaded, who was forced to stand by, helpless, as an impotent Supreme Chancellor and a dilatory Senate allowed the people they were sworn to protect die in the name of Trade Federation greed. Ten years have passed since that dreadful time, but how have my circumstances changed, I ask you? They haven't! Though I stand before you the Supreme Chancellor of this Republic, I am *still* helpless. We are facing the gravest threat in our history. Republic citizens are dying, *Jedi* are dying, because I failed to act in time to prevent this tragedy."

"Not true," said Organa. "The only person with the power to prevent this tragedy was Dooku. And he chose to perpetrate an atrocity instead. No blame falls to you, Supreme Chancellor. You're owed our gratitude for having the courage to take the difficult but necessary step of commissioning the clone army. Without it, Master Yoda and his Jedi would doubtless have been slaughtered to the last. And where would the Republic be then?"

Slowly, Palpatine sat down. "I confess you surprise me, Bail. Given your close relationship with Senator Amidala, I wasn't entirely certain you agreed with my decision."

Organa looked taken aback. "It's true I respect and admire the Senator from Naboo," he said. "Since serving with her on the Loyalist Committee I've come to appreciate her unique qualities. But I have always thought our Republic must be defended . . . despite the very real risks that entails."

"And I appreciate your ongoing support," Palpatine replied, his faint smile pained. "Especially as I must ask you to shoulder even more responsibility. Senator Organa, I feel the Loyalist Committee has served its purpose. We need a new committee now, one that can oversee all matters pertaining to Republic security. It should consist of yourself, as chair, and three or four Senators whom you can trust absolutely. Will you see to it? Will you take the lead?"

Organa nodded. "Of course, Supreme Chancellor. I'm honored that you'd ask."

"Excellent," said Palpatine, his expression serious. "And Master Yoda, once you've taken care of any Jedi business arising from the Battle of Geonosis, you, your fellow Councilors, and I must convene a formal war committee so that we might bring this unpleasantness to a swift and decisive conclusion. For the sake of the Republic we *must* win this conflict."

Yoda frowned. *Deeper* Jedi involvement with government matters? It was the last thing he desired. But Palpatine was right about one thing. "Agree with you, I do, Supreme Chancellor. Ended this war must swiftly be, and the peace well prepared for."

"Then I shall delay you no longer," said Palpatine, standing. "Thank you for coming so promptly to see me, when I know you must surely prefer to be with your wounded Jedi. Please, when you see him, tell Anakin he's in my thoughts."

"Of course, Supreme Chancellor," said Yoda. "And hesitate to send for me you should not, if of any further assistance I can be."

Palpatine smiled. "Do not doubt it for an instant, Master Yoda. Believe me when I say that you and the Jedi are never far from my plans."

Dismissed, Yoda and Bail Organa withdrew from Palpatine's office. Regretting the lack of his repulsorlift chair, Yoda contemplated the long walk to the docking complex and swallowed a sigh.

"I'm leaving myself now," said Organa. "Can I take you back to the Jedi Temple, Master Yoda?"

"A kind offer that is," Yoda replied, nodding. "Accept it I will. Much to do there, I have. With no time to waste."

And at the top of his list, regrettably, was what would surely prove to be a difficult conversation with Obi-Wan Kenobi.

Scant moments after entering the Temple's Halls of Healing, he was ushered to meet with Master Vokara Che in her private chamber.

"Master Yoda," said the revered Twi'lek, smiling gently with cool, watchful eyes. "It's a great relief to see you unharmed. I understand you dueled with Dooku. It has been a long time since you drew your lightsaber in battle."

He gave her a small, one-shouldered shrug. He was sore and weary, but those things would pass. "Unhurt am I, Vokara Che. Worry you need not. Of our wounded Jedi tell me. How do they fare?"

Most were healed, or healing. Anakin was the worst affected, but he was resting comfortably enough—all things considered. He remained in a deep healing trance, to counteract the shock of his injury, while the final adjustments were made to his prosthetic arm. Tragically, the lightsaber damage inflicted upon his severed forearm made reattachment of the limb impossible.

"But I anticipate he'll make a full recovery," Vokara Che concluded. "Although doubtless he'll struggle a little at first."

A prosthetic arm. Yoda felt his spirits sink, although he'd been expecting the news. A Jedi's connection with the Force flowed through the midi-chlorians in his blood. The loss of a limb had been known to affect a Jedi's powers. True, Anakin Skywalker possessed more midi-chlorians than any Jedi in history, but even so . . .

"See him now, I will," he said heavily. "And Obi-Wan also."

Vokara Che frowned, her head-tails gently twitching. "Yes. Of course. Master Yoda . . . about Obi-Wan . . ."

"Tell me you need not, Vokara Che. Himself he blames for Skywalker's hurt."

They'd both known Obi-Wan from infancy. Expression rueful, she nodded. "Should we expect anything less from him?"

They should not, Yoda thought. No Jedi could have undertaken the daunting task of training Anakin Skywalker more seriously than had Obi-Wan Kenobi. Burdened by his promise to a dying man, by the knowledge that he trained a child of prophecy, by the ongoing fear that he would make a mistake, let Qui-Gon down, not a day passed when Obi-Wan did not find a way to make Anakin's faults and failures his own.

Sighing, Yoda slid down from his chair. "Counsel Obi-Wan, I will."

Vokara Che smiled, relieved, and stood. "Good." Then the smile faded. "First, however . . ." She cleared her throat. "I'm not sure if you are aware of this, but Senator Amidala accompanied Obi-Wan and his apprentice here. We treated her, of course, but not before there was a certain . . . unpleasantness. She was very concerned about Anakin. Insisted on seeing him. Heated words were exchanged when I refused. There might be an official complaint. I am sorry."

Yoda felt his embattled spirits sink farther. *Senator Amidala.* Another problem, another mystery, another piece of the puzzle that was Anakin Skywalker.

With an effort, he wrenched himself free of worry. "Concerned you need not be, Vokara Che. Now, to see young Skywalker please take me. Then will I speak with Master Kenobi."

With the debilitating pain of his lightsaber wounds at last a memory, Obi-Wan paced the confines of his healing chamber and cursed the hard-won discipline that prevented him from finding the nearest healer so he could demand that he be shown to Anakin's room *at once.*

"Master Kenobi," said a stern, familiar voice. *Yoda.* He turned.

"Your Padawan sleeps," said Yoda, in the open doorway. "Safe from pain he is for now. Sit, now, so talk we may."

Disobeying Yoda was unthinkable. Obi-Wan sank cross-legged to the floor, hands folded in his lap.

"Forgive me, Master," he murmured. "I am not in full control of my emotions."

"Need you to tell me that, do I?" said Yoda. "I think I do not."

Though the reproof was cutting, still it contained an undercurrent of dry humor. Obi-Wan risked an upward glance, to see that Yoda's expression was not one of unmingled disapproval. A certain gentleness lurked in his luminous eyes.

"Forgive me," he said again. "I meant no disrespect."

"Hmmph," said Yoda, and again he tapped his gimer stick to the floor. "Pleased I am to see you are healed, Master Kenobi, for to your duties you must return. Much there is to be done, with war threatening."

Though it might earn him an even more stinging reprimand, Obi-Wan had to speak. "Master Yoda, my place is here with Anakin. He is wounded because of me."

"He is wounded because of *Dooku*," retorted Yoda. "And because disobey you he did. A child no longer is Anakin Skywalker. A man he is now, and a man he must be. His own faults must he accept and make amends for."

"I believe Anakin has already made amends, Master Yoda. He is maimed. He nearly died."

"And your fault that is not!"

It should have made a difference to hear Yoda say so. It should have eased the crushing burden of his grief and guilt. But it didn't. Nothing did. Nothing could.

Anakin is my Padawan. It is my duty to protect him.

"Protect him from himself you cannot, Obi-Wan," said Yoda gently. "Protect you from yourself, could Qui-Gon, when mistakes you made as his apprentice?"

Melida/Daan. So long ago now, and rarely thought of. Swallowing, he met Yoda's stern gaze. "No."

"Learn the error of your ways you did," said Yoda. "Learn, too, will your apprentice. A task for you I have, Obi-Wan. When it is completed, return here you can."

Obi-Wan nodded. "Thank you, Master."

But instead of detailing this task, Yoda began to pace the small chamber, the tapping of his gimer stick loud in its silence. "Know do you, Obi-Wan, why reluctant I was for Skywalker to become your apprentice?"

Did he know? Not for certain. And once he and Qui-Gon had prevailed over the Council, and Anakin had been made his Padawan, Yoda's objections had no longer mattered.

"Ah . . . no, Master," he said cautiously.

Yoda flicked him a skeptical glance. "Hmmm. Then tell you I will. Reluctant I was because the same flaw you share, Obi-Wan. The flaw of *attachment*."

What? "I'm sorry. I don't understand."

Yoda snorted. "Yes, you do. Melida/Daan, attachment that was. Your promise to Qui-Gon Jinn, that you would train Anakin? From attachment it sprang. Great affection you felt for him. Great affection you feel for Anakin Skywalker. Run deep your feelings do, Obi-Wan. Mastered them completely you have not. Mastered his own young Skywalker has not. Suspect I do that strict with him about attachments you have not always been."

It was true. He hadn't. Because Anakin wasn't like other Padawans. Anakin remembered his mother. More than that, he was *bonded* with her. Their ties were primal and could not easily be broken. But the Council had known that when it accepted him for training, so it hardly seemed fair to criticize him for it. Neither was it fair not to give him a little leeway because of it. So he had . . . because Yoda was right about one thing, at least. Attachment was something he did understand.

"Because of attachment to his mother," Yoda continued, his expression severe, "to Tatooine did young Skywalker go, defying your direct instructions."

Obi-Wan stared. "I don't—we didn't—he has not told me why he left Naboo. There was no time to discuss it. Events on Geonosis moved too quickly."

"To Shmi Skywalker has something happened, I fear," said Yoda quietly.

"*What?*"

"Sensed young Skywalker in the Force, I did. Great pain. Great anger. A terrible tragedy."

Oh no. "He's said nothing to me, Master Yoda. If something had happened to his mother, I'm sure he'd tell me."

He'd tell me, wouldn't he? Or wouldn't I sense it?

Except he'd been so angry with Anakin, so disappointed and frustrated. By the boy's rank disobedience. For letting himself be captured. For dragging Padmé down with him. So when they'd seen each other in that Geonosis arena, he'd been distracted, his senses clouded by emotion.

Attachment, interfering again.

"Hmmm," Yoda said, still pacing. Then he stopped, his eyes half lidded, his mouth pursed in the way that made every sensible Jedi wary. The gimer stick rapped once, hard on the floor. "*Senator Amidala.* Aware of your Padawan's feelings for her, were you?"

Obi-Wan dropped his gaze to his hands, still folded in his lap. "I . . . know he admired her greatly as a small boy. I realized when we were assigned to her protection that he hadn't forgotten that admiration, or her." He looked up. "I did remind him, Master, that the path he's chosen forbids anything but a warm cordiality between them."

Yoda's eyes narrowed farther. "Heed your reminder, Obi-Wan, he did not."

Obi-Wan felt his heart thud. *Yoda knew.* His desperate argument with Anakin in the gunship as they pursued Dooku to their doom. Anakin's wild insistence on abandoning duty to save Padmé. Yoda knew.

"While Anakin sleeps, to Senator Amidala you will go," Yoda continued. "Ended his relationship with her must be, before more trouble it causes. Know this better than most do you, Obi-Wan."

Siri. Old pain, swiftly pulsing, thrust swiftly aside. Another life. Another Obi-Wan. Yoda was right. Anakin's attachment to Padmé could not continue. It had already proven itself a dangerous distraction.

I survived the loss. Anakin will survive it, too.

The only problem was . . .

The way she ran to Anakin, so gravely wounded in that cavern. The tenderness in her eyes, her touch. Her fierce protection of him on the journey back to Coruscant. How she ignored her own pain for his. And how she fought to see him, here in the Temple.

"Master Yoda, I fear the matter is not quite so straightforward," he said carefully. "I believe Anakin's feelings are reciprocated. It's likely Senator Amidala will resent my intrusion into her private affairs."

"Private affairs?" Yoda's ears lifted, and his eyes opened wide. "Privacy there is not where a Jedi is involved. Of no importance are her feelings, Obi-Wan. This relationship you will end."

Obi-Wan nodded. "Yes, Master," he said, reaching for the perfectly self-disciplined and tranquil Jedi. Beneath the surface, doubts seethed.

"Go now, Obi-Wan," said Yoda. "Nothing to be gained there is by waiting."

"Yes, Master," he said again.

After all, he had no choice.

THREE

THOUGH THE NIGHT WAS STILL YOUNG, PADMÉ LAY IN HER DARK-ened chamber seeking the blessed oblivion of sleep. Unfortunately, sleep remained stubbornly elusive.

I told Anakin I loved him because I thought we were about to die. But we survived . . . and now there's no going back. He is my heart. We belong to each other for life.

Restless, she shifted beneath her light sheets, tormented by the memory of running into the cavern on Geonosis, seeing him so dreadfully hurt and lost. Seeing his severed arm, abandoned in the dirt. Such a wounding, coming so hard on the heels of his mother's brutal slaughter. Of what had happened afterward.

And because they hadn't been alone, because Obi-Wan was there, and the truly formidable Yoda, she hadn't been able to kiss him, or weep with him. A hug was all she'd been allowed. Yoda's clone troopers had moved her aside so they could support him, help him into the gunship, help him board the starship that had carried them home.

That had been the worst pain of all.

Her closed chamber door chimed. *What?* With a resentful sigh she pulled on a robe and answered it. "Threepio, I said I didn't want to be disturbed."

"Oh, Mistress Padmé, please forgive me," said the agitated droid. "I did try to convince him to go away, but he's insistent, almost rude, so unlike him, and—"

"Who is? Who's here?"

"Why, Master Kenobi," C-3PO replied. "And he says he won't leave until the two of you have spoken."

Something must have happened. *Anakin.* "Tell him I'll be there in a moment," she said, her mouth dry. "Offer him refreshments. I won't be long."

As soon as the door closed behind the droid she tore off her sleepwear and pulled on a simple but elegant blue dress instead. Clothes were armor. If he'd brought her bad news—if Anakin was—she didn't want to face him at the smallest disadvantage.

But Anakin's not dead. If he were dead, I would know.

Obi-Wan was waiting for her in the living room, neatly dressed in a fresh Jedi tunic and leggings. From the way he stood there, steady on his feet, his face no longer pale and twisted with pain, it was clear the healers had seen to the lightsaber wounds that had rendered him more helpless than she'd believed was possible.

"Obi-Wan," she said, joining him. "Have you come to take me back to the Temple? Am I permitted to see Anakin now?"

He bowed his head briefly, hands clasped before him. "No, Senator Amidala. I'm afraid that's not possible."

Senator. Not *Padmé.* And nothing in his manner but a stiff formality.

"I see," she said, guarded. "In that case, given recent events, can't your errand wait? I'm tired. I need to rest."

"I do appreciate that, Senator," he said. "And I am sorry to disturb you, but no. This cannot wait."

Really? Well, that wasn't for him to decide, was it? Her home. Her rules. She folded her arms. "Have you seen Anakin?"

If he was annoyed, he didn't show it. "He's resting comfortably. There's no need for you to be concerned."

So cool, he was. Positively indifferent. Anyone would think he spoke of a mere acquaintance. But she knew better.

C-3PO returned with Karlini tea. Obi-Wan shook his head. "No. Thank you."

She took a cup, for the distraction as much as anything, then nodded a dismissal at the fussy droid Anakin had built. "That's all. I'll call you if I need you again."

As the door closed behind 3PO, she turned back to Obi-Wan. "Why are you here?"

He hesitated, then sighed. Abandoned his nonsensical reserve. "Because we need to talk, Padmé."

She felt her heart thud. "I see. Well, if we're going to talk, let's do so in comfort." She gestured to the sofa and chairs. "Please. Be seated."

Another hesitation, then he nodded. "Thank you," he said, subdued, and folded himself onto a chair.

She chose the sofa opposite and considered him over the rim of her teacup. His spine was straight, his shoulders braced as though he expected trouble. Some kind of attack. And surprisingly, he seemed at a sudden loss for words.

All right, then. I'll make the first move.

She put the cup down on the small table beside her. "Even though you're concerned for Anakin—and I know you are, so don't bother with the stoic-Jedi act—I imagine you're not very pleased with him right now. But you should know, Obi-Wan, he did not disobey his orders lightly."

Startled, he stared at her. Then he pulled a wry face. "Which time do you mean? When he left Naboo for Tatooine, or Tatooine for Geonosis?"

"*Both* times. Obi-Wan, no matter what you might think, he takes being a Jedi very seriously. It's all he talks about. Being a Jedi, and not disappointing you. He—"

But Obi-Wan wasn't listening. He stared into the distance, his eyes shadowed, his expression grim. And then he looked at her. "What happened to Anakin's mother, Padmé?"

The question jolted her, unpleasantly. She hadn't realized he knew anything was wrong. "What happened? She died."

And that jolted him. *Good.*

"What do you mean, she died?" he said, sounding shaken. "How? And where was Anakin? What—"

She held up a hand, halting the spate of questions. It wasn't her place to discuss Shmi Skywalker's death with this man. Not her death . . . and not what had happened to the Sand People afterward.

"I'm sorry. If you want to know more, you'll have to ask Anakin."

And Obi-Wan didn't like that, but he was smart enough not to push. "I can forgive him going to Tatooine, if—if the decision involved his mother," he said. "But in going to Geonosis he was willfully disobedient, he—"

"No, Obi-Wan. That was my decision, not his."

"*Yours?*"

"That's right. Anakin wanted to save you from the Separatists *and* he wanted to obey Master Windu. Obviously he couldn't do both, so I made the choice for him. The one he wanted to make but was afraid to, because of the consequences. Because whatever choice he made, he would have been wrong."

Obi-Wan frowned at her. "Following a direct order from the Jedi Council is never wrong, Senator. *Disobeying* an order, *that* is the error."

"Qui-Gon disregarded the Council quite often," she retorted. "He told me so, on Tatooine. He said it was the height of folly to substitute someone else's judgment for your own, when *you're* the person best placed to decide." Picking up her cup again, she took a small sip of tea. "I'd be very surprised if he never gave you the same advice, Obi-Wan."

His eyes blanked. His expression froze. "I have not come here to discuss Qui-Gon Jinn."

She couldn't help shivering, his voice was so cold. This was the Obi-Wan who could reduce Anakin to chastened silence. Almost to tears. *But I won't be intimidated. He has no right to chastise me.*

She put down the cup again. "Fine. Then let's discuss this. If you had died in that arena because he didn't go to your aid, Anakin would have been devastated. Do you honestly think I'd stand by and let that happen?"

"*Your* actions are not the point, Padmé. The point is that *Anakin* shouldn't have let it happen. He is a Jedi. He is required to put duty before his personal feelings."

"And he did! He was prepared to do what Master Windu told him. *I'm* the one who decided to rescue you. And as my appointed bodyguard Anakin had no choice but to tag along."

That earned her a look tinged with bitterness. "Very creative of you, Senator," said Obi-Wan. "Qui-Gon would be proud."

She leaned forward, trying to reach him. To reach through that self-possessed, deflecting Jedi manner. "Anakin admires you so much, Obi-Wan. He needs to know you trust him."

He nodded. "He does know."

"Really?" She sat back. "I wonder."

"You don't believe me? Why not?"

"Because if he believed you trusted him, he'd be less uncertain."

"Less uncertain?" echoed Obi-Wan, incredulous. "Padmé, Anakin's problem is not a lack of certainty. Quite the opposite, in fact. It's his *overconfidence* that has proven his undoing. Had he not disobeyed me, not leapt in to face Dooku alone, he would not now be lying unconscious in the Temple, waiting for them to complete construction of his prosthetic arm!"

"So," she said, her heart pounding. "You blame Anakin for what happened."

Obi-Wan stood and half turned away from her. "I did not come here to rehash the events on Geonosis. That is Jedi business, not yours."

"Then get to the point or return to the Temple, Obi-Wan," she retorted. "I didn't invite you here. And I've permitted you to stay as a courtesy, no more."

Slowly he turned back to her. His face was pale, his clear blue eyes darkened with difficult emotions. "The point is there can be no hope for anything but a civil cordiality between you and Anakin, Senator. He has made a commitment to the Jedi Order. His life is with us. To dream otherwise is folly."

She felt a shimmer of rage in her blood, like heat haze dancing on the Tatooine desert. "I don't know what you're talking about."

"Don't take me for a fool, Padmé!" he snapped. "Of course you do. He has feelings for you. Strong feelings that cloud his judgment and make him disobedient to the Order. Are you going to pretend you don't have similar feelings for him?"

"My feelings are my own affair!"

"Not when they involve a Jedi!"

Breathing harshly, they glared at each other. If she could see pain in him, surely he could see it in her, too.

"This is why you came?" she whispered. "To tell me I must forget Anakin?"

"I came because I was told to," Obi-Wan replied, after a moment. "And because I'm trying to protect him. And you, though I don't expect you to believe that. But Padmé . . ." He dropped to the edge of his seat again, touched his fingertips to her knee. "It's true. You must know that to pursue this any further will only lead to heartbreak for both of you. If you do love Anakin, you *must* let him go. He can't love you *and* be a Jedi. And he was born to be a Jedi. He has a destiny greater than you or I can imagine. If he is not free to pursue it, a great many people may pay a dreadful price. Is that what you want?"

She blinked rapidly, banishing tears. "And do you love him so little you would have him condemned to a lifetime of loneliness, all in the name of some prophecy not a one of your precious Jedi Council can say for certain is true?"

Again Obi-Wan stood, and this time he walked away. "If I did not . . . love . . . him," he said, his voice unsteady, his back turned, "I would not be here now."

She leapt to her feet. "Then I think you and I define *love* very differently. I will never do anything to hurt Anakin. Can you say the same, Obi-Wan?"

He swung around, his eyes blazing. "That's a stupid, childish thing to say!"

"Obi-Wan, I am *worried* for him. Can't you understand that?"

He took a deep breath. Let it out, hard, regaining his composure. "Padmé, you're wrong if you think I don't realize what I'm asking. I do. The life of a Jedi *is* lonely. It demands of us the greatest sacrifices. The placing of our needs last, and those of strangers first. But how much suffering would there be if the Jedi abandoned their duty? Is that what you want? Is that what you think *Anakin* wants?"

He wants to serve the Jedi, and he wants to love and be loved. I refuse to accept he must be forced to choose.

"I have no authority over you," Obi-Wan continued. "I'm perfectly aware of that. But I would ask you—beg you—to do this one thing. Leave Coruscant. Return to Naboo. Give Anakin the time he needs to recover from his injury . . . and realize what you and I already know: that going your separate ways is the only possible remedy for this unfortunate situation."

She blinked back stinging tears. *You say you understand, Obi-Wan, but you don't. In every way that counts you don't know Anakin at all. But I do. I know him. I have seen his true heart. All of it. My love can save him.*

But she couldn't tell Obi-Wan that. He'd never believe it. And he would *never* turn a blind eye now that he knew she and Anakin loved each other. So she had to make him think he'd convinced her to abandon Anakin. The need for such a deception grieved her. She liked Obi-Wan, very much. And she knew he did love Anakin, in the pallid, self-contained way of the Jedi. But Anakin's love was like the heat of a supernova. In attempting to control it, the Jedi would destroy him.

I will die before I let that happen.

She lifted her gaze. "Do you truly believe my love can only harm him?"

"Yes, Padmé," he said, and had to clear his throat. "I do."

It wasn't hard to let the tears rise again. The simple sincerity in his voice hurt her, and she hadn't been expecting that. "I see."

"I am sorry," he said, sounding helpless. "I wish things could be different. I truly do. But you must understand . . . no good can come of this relationship, for either of you."

"Perhaps—perhaps you're right," she whispered, with just enough reluctance.

"I am."

She stifled a sob. "I don't want to hurt him."

"I know, Padmé. But better a small cruelty now than a crushing devastation later."

Now she let the tears flow without restraint. "He'll never forgive me."

Obi-Wan took a step closer. "Perhaps not," he said, his voice unsteady. "But could you forgive yourself if loving you destroyed him?"

"No. I'd die," she said simply. And spoke the utter truth.

"Then you know what to do."

"Yes," she whispered, still weeping. "I'll leave Coruscant. Spend some time with my family. And—perhaps I won't return. To be honest, I'm not certain I can make a difference anymore. I lost the battle against the formation of the army and now I fear the voices of peace have been drowned out entirely. I do need some time to decide what I'll do next."

Surprising her, Obi-Wan took her hand. His fingers were cold. "You're wrong. The Senate will need you now more than ever."

Gently, she pulled free. "Maybe. Obi-Wan . . . I should be the one to make the break with Anakin. If it comes from you, he'll be angry, resentful, and I don't want there to be trouble between you. Besides, if it comes from you he might not believe it, and then I'll just have to tell him anyway."

He smoothed his beard, thinking. "All right."

"Let Anakin escort me home to Naboo. Saying good-bye is going to be difficult. I'd like our parting to be private. *Please*, Obi-Wan," she added, seeing his reluctance. "You owe me that much."

He sighed. "I can make no promises, but . . . I'll do my best."

"Thank you."

"Padmé . . ." He shook his head. "You're doing the right thing. The only thing that can keep him safe. Anakin will need all his strength, his focus, for what is to come. You don't see it now but you will, in time."

He left her then. Welcoming the solitude, she stood on her apartment's veranda and stared across the Coruscant cityscape to the distant, imposing Jedi Temple where Anakin lay cradled in his healing trance.

Have no fear, my love. I won't let them come between us. And if we stand together, not even the Force will tear us apart.

Obi-Wan returned directly to the Temple, to Yoda. Duty before personal feelings, always. Seeing his injured Padawan would have to wait.

Shmi was dead? Oh, Anakin.

"Done, it is?" said Yoda, cross-legged on the meditation pad in his private chamber.

Feeling sick, feeling empty, he bowed. "Yes, Master."

"Good. Necessary this was. Necessary it would not have been, Obi-Wan, if closer attention you had paid." Yoda's eyes narrowed. "Disappointed I am."

And that was a lightsaber thrust between his ribs. "I am truly sorry, Master."

Yoda tilted his chin, his steady gaze implacable. "A lesson let this be, Master Kenobi. Attachment leads to suffering for a Jedi. School yourself. School your Padawan, while you still can. A Jedi Knight must he become, sooner than we thought."

What? No. "Master Yoda, he's not ready."

"Make him ready, you must, Obi-Wan. Your task that is."

Given Yoda's mood it was folly to argue. But he couldn't stay silent. "Master Yoda, is there really a need to be precipitate? Surely it would be unwise to rush Anakin, especially now. His injury . . . and Master, his mother is dead."

Yoda nodded, short and sharp. "Yes. But mothers die, Obi-Wan. Sad it is, but distract a Jedi death must not."

And that was true. It was true, but . . . *Not distract him? Yoda, Yoda, you don't know Anakin.*

"Yes, Master," he said with great care. "But while I know our lost Jedi must be replaced, our victory on Geonosis was decisive. Surely there's a chance Dooku and the Separatists will think twice before escalating this conflict? Now that they've seen the military might at our command, they must know it would be madness."

Yoda pursed his lips. "Madness, yes. Think Dooku is sane, do you? To the dark side he has turned. Insanity that is."

"So war is inevitable?"

Yoda closed his eyes and lowered his head. "Perhaps," he murmured. "Wait we must, to see what the Force shows us."

And what an agonizing wait it would be. "Yes, Master," Obi-Wan said. "In which case, while we are waiting . . ."

Yoda looked up. "To your Padawan you may go, Obi-Wan. Your support and guidance will he need through this difficult transition."

"Yes, Master. Thank you," he said, retreating to the chamber door.

"*Obi-Wan.*"

Chilled by the grimness in Yoda's voice, he turned. "Yes, Master?"

Yoda's stare was bleak. "Great are the challenges your Padawan will face. To be his friend your heart will urge you. But Obi-Wan, a mistake that would be. A friend young Skywalker does not need. A Master he needs, and a Master you must be."

"I understand," Obi-Wan replied, and took his leave. But as he made his long way to the Halls of Healing, he realized it wasn't advice he was prepared to take.

For ten years I have been a Master to Anakin, and all that got me was defiance. The more I criticize him, the more he turns away. The more I withdraw, the angrier he becomes. More criticism, more emotional distance, isn't the answer. He's not a typical Jedi. He never has been. Yet I have tried to turn him into one. I've tried to contain him. Control him. For his own good, it's true . . . but even so. If he's to be a Jedi Knight soon, that has to end.

Besides. With the struggle of physical rehabilitation before him . . . with the death of his dreams about Padmé to come . . . with the crushing, terrible loss of his mother to face . . . the *only* thing Anakin needed now was a friend.

Tangled in nightmare, Anakin despaired.

Mom, Mom, stay with me, Mom. So beaten, so brutalized. He'd failed her. *You look so handsome. I love you.* The pain in her voice, the blood, the shame. She breathed in, she breathed out, and then she didn't breathe again. *Stay with me, Mom . . . don't leave me . . .*

"Mom!" he shouted and opened his eyes. His face was soaking wet; he could feel the hot tears.

"Hush," said Obi-Wan. "Anakin, hush. Keep still. You've been badly hurt."

As if he didn't know that. As if he couldn't feel the gaping hole in his chest where his heart had been, where his heart was ripped out, where an ocean of acid turned his world to pain.

He looked at the man who'd been his mentor and friend for ten years, and all he could think of was what he'd just lost. What he'd given up by joining the Jedi. "My mother's dead," he whispered. *"And it's all your fault."*

Obi-Wan jerked back. "What? No. Anakin, no."

"Get away from me," Anakin said, as the edges of his vision rippled scarlet and black . . . and the rage that dwelled inside him drew its breath to scream. "I don't want you here. She'd be alive if you'd believed in my dreams. She'd be alive if I had freed her. Get away from me, Obi-Wan. Leave me alone!"

But Obi-Wan wouldn't. "I'm sorry. I didn't know, Anakin. You didn't dream she was in danger. You didn't dream she'd *die*. If you had—if you'd *told* me—"

Anakin looked down at Obi-Wan's hand on his shoulder and shrugged, trying to dislodge it. "Don't touch me. Are you deaf? I said *leave me alone*."

Still Obi-Wan ignored him. Of course. Because that's what he did. He gave orders, he never listened. "Anakin, you have to know it wasn't deliberate."

All he had to know was that this man had failed him. Sickened, trembling on the brink of losing self-control completely, he reached out to pluck himself free of Obi-Wan's grasping fingers . . .

In the chamber's warm, soft light, the golden armature gleamed.

"What?" he said, confused and staring. His arm? That was his arm? His hand? How was that possible? He wasn't a droid, he was flesh and blood. "What's that? I don't—"

And then it all came pouring back, a torrent of pitiless, excoriating memory. Kissing Padmé. The Geonosis arena. The slaughter. All those Jedi, murdered in the sun. The desperate chase after Dooku. The duel in the cavern. Obi-Wan cut down, heartbeats from death. And his arm—his arm—

As though the images were a trigger, as though remembering a thing was the same as reliving it, the agony of that saber cut burst through him like a storm.

And Obi-Wan held him as he wept.

FOUR

"No, Ahsoka! Not like that!" said Anakin, frustrated. "How come you don't *listen* to me?"

Glowering at him, Ahsoka stepped back. "Don't yell at me, Skyguy. I'm doing the best I can. If I'm not doing it right that's your fault, not mine. You're the Jedi Master and I'm the Padawan, remember? I'm not *supposed* to know everything yet."

Incredulous, he stared at her; then he turned and stalked away from his insolent apprentice before he got himself in trouble by uttering words more suited to the heat of a hotly contested Podrace than the hushed serenity of a Jedi Temple dojo.

Again, still, he was startled by the lack of a Padawan braid slapping his shoulder in time with his gait. He should be used to its absence by now: weeks had flown by since that brief, solemn ceremony in which Obi-Wan had cut him free of his past, handing him his childhood with a cautiously approving nod.

They might not have made me a Jedi Knight too soon . . . but I'm pretty sure I'm not ready for an apprentice. At least, not an apprentice like Ahsoka.

Glancing up, he saw his former Master standing on the dojo's observation balcony, arms folded across his chest in that particular way he had. He was hiding an amused smile in his beard.

Yeah, yeah, it's funny. It's a riot. You think this is payback, Obi-Wan, don't you? You think I'm getting my just deserts.

Well . . . and maybe he was.

He turned back to his apprentice. She hadn't moved a step, hadn't lowered her defiantly tilted chin, hadn't powered down her training lightsaber that zapped but didn't maim or kill. Instead she just stood there, dangerously close to pouting, tears of anger and frustration shimmering in her eyes.

He knew that look. Knew how it felt to be wearing it on his face. How many times over the last ten years had he stared at Obi-Wan just like that? Fought the urge to stamp and shout his rage and disappointment . . . not always successfully.

His own frustration died then, seeing Ahsoka's distress. He sighed and walked back to her, deactivating his own training lightsaber. "Look," he said, halting in front of her. "It's not that you're doing a *bad* job. You're not. But that's not the same as doing a *good* job, Ahsoka."

Her chin lifted a little higher. "I did a good job on Christophsis, didn't I? And on Teth, and Tatooine?"

"I never said you didn't. But you got lucky a lot, too. Luck can only take you so far, Padawan. Do you expect me to trust my life to you based on *luck*?"

Slowly, slowly, her chin came down. "No," she muttered. "Of course I don't."

"Good, because I won't do it," he said sternly. "Now, complete fifty repetitions of Niman form, level one. By yourself. And I want every stroke perfect, Ahsoka. Identical. Centered in the Force. Don't rush it. Don't try and get it over with. Dwell within each beat of the exercise." He reached into his tunic and pulled out a droid-cam. "I'm going to record you, so we can review your style and technique together later."

"You mean you're not going to stay and watch?" she asked, sounding disappointed.

"I'll be around," he replied. "But it shouldn't matter where I am. It's where you are that counts. Centered in the Force, remember?" Flicking a switch he activated the drone and tossed it into the air. Once Ahsoka moved, the droidcam would lock on and record her until she finished her task. "Now . . . *begin.*"

While she did as she was told, her training lightsaber humming, he turned his back and walked away. Feeling bad, feeling guilty, that he'd been so hard on her. That he hadn't let her know he'd been where she was now, very recently, and understood the overwhelming tangle of emotions all Padawans were forced to conquer.

But this isn't about me, it's about her. Every Padawan walks the same path differently. She has to find her own way, in her own time. I can't help her. She can only help herself.

Something Obi-Wan had told him, once—which of course he'd resented at the time.

Clipping his powered-down training lightsaber to his belt, he made his way up the stairs to the observation balcony where his former Master still stood, watching Ahsoka sink deeper and deeper into the Force.

"She shows great promise, Anakin," said Obi-Wan, glancing at him. "The small, scrappy ones often turn out the best, you know."

And was that a typical Obi-Wan compliment? Oblique. Offhanded. Never effusive. *I think it was.* "She'll do," Anakin grunted. "Though I still don't understand why Master Yoda sent her to me. Not when you haven't found a new apprentice of your own."

"There's no hurry for that," said Obi-Wan. Another smile was lurking. "I'm still recovering from the rigors of my last one."

Anakin rolled his eyes. "Ha ha," he muttered. "Didn't see that coming."

Obi-Wan chuckled softly. "Really? You should have."

"I *suppose,*" Anakin said, indulging in a little sarcasm of his own, "this is when I'm meant to say, *Wow, Obi-Wan, I never knew how tough you had it when you were training me. But I get it now. Now it all makes perfect sense.*"

"Something like that, yes," said Obi-Wan, his smile widening.

Anakin sighed. "Yeah . . . well . . . maybe I do."

A comfortable silence fell between them. Anakin welcomed it— the amusement, the banter, the easy camaraderie. In the immediate aftermath of Geonosis, when he was still recovering from his catastrophic injury, it had seemed their relationship was on the brink of unraveling. Only Obi-Wan's steadfast refusal to be pushed away had saved it. Only his willingness to accept his Padawan's rage, his grief, his blame, and not take any of it personally.

And there'd been so much rage. So much grief. Even now the echoes lingered. They always would. He'd never be free of that moment in the Tatooine desert when he'd watched his mother die. *Felt* her die. He'd never be free of what had happened next. The savage massacre under the stars.

Obi-Wan knew nothing of that. He never would. Obi-Wan was the perfect Jedi. He could never understand the overwhelming need to kill what had killed the person he loved best.

In the end, Anakin knew, the only thing that had saved him was Padmé, and the single perfect day they spent together after their secret wedding. Her love. Her patience. Her unquestioning acceptance of everything the Jedi demanded that he deny.

But Obi-Wan had helped him, too. With his blood-and-bone arm lost, his balance in the Force now irrevocably altered, he knew that without Obi-Wan he'd never have come to trust his skills, himself, again. Never would have found a way past the nightmares of Dooku, the harrowing, nightly reliving of their brief and shocking duel. His failure. His maiming. Never found his way back to laughter, and the joy that came with being a Jedi.

And there was joy. Oh, there was *such* joy.

"It was all my fault, Master," he had admitted to Obi-Wan on his return from Naboo, after he had completed the private task of constructing his new lightsaber. "My arrogance nearly got you killed. And my impatience led to my defeat. I wouldn't listen to you. I'm sorry."

He'd braced himself then, for the inevitable lecture. A dissection of his myriad shortcomings. Instead Obi-Wan had tried to smile, and failed. "I'll gladly forgive you that, Anakin, if you'll forgive me the dreams of your mother," he replied, his voice not quite steady. "I would have saved her for you if I could."

They didn't speak of either incident again. And what had often been a tense relationship between Master and pupil gently transformed into a simple, unpressured, and unexpected friendship, which deepened during the countless hours they spent on lightsaber practice, preparing for war. Even before he'd been declared a Jedi Knight. A Jedi Knight who had never undergone formal trials, just like Obi-Wan. He was starting to think they had a lot in common after all.

Of course, they still had their moments. Sometimes Obi-Wan forgot the "former" part of "former Padawan" and lectured, or scolded. Forgot they were both Jedi Knights now, both generals, with equal responsibilities. Men whose lives depended on their leadership. That was . . . irritating. Sometimes he did wonder if Obi-Wan would ever truly see him as an equal. But mostly he didn't let it bother him. If he let it bother him he might spoil things—and he didn't want that.

Seven weeks after the Battle of Geonosis—not quite three weeks after Anakin farewelled without regret his Padawan braid—Dooku's Separatist forces launched a brutal multipronged attack on the Republic. He and Obi-Wan fought side by side, defending first Anoth and then Bakura. That was when they got their first sour taste of the monster Grievous.

And then had come Christophsis . . . and everything changed. Looking back now, he realized that Christophsis, and the subsequent missions to Teth, then Tatooine, with Ahsoka, had been the catalyst he'd needed to complete his transformation from Padawan to Jedi Knight.

Glancing sideways at Obi-Wan, remembering his former Master's restrained but heartfelt praise of that mission, he felt a twinge of guilt.

I wish I could tell him about Padmé. The Jedi are wrong. Love doesn't weaken us. It makes us stronger. I wish Padmé and I could show him that. He's very alone.

"What?" said Obi-Wan. "Is there a fly on my nose?"

Anakin shook his head. "I was just wondering how much longer we'll be stuck here on Coruscant when every day Jedi and the clone troops and ordinary people are fighting and dying for the Republic. For freedom. It's been over a week, and it feels wrong to be safe here, when no one's safe out there. Not as long as Dooku and Grievous and the other Separatists don't care how much innocent blood they spill."

"I know," said Obi-Wan, and rested a hand on Anakin's shoulder. "If it helps, I'm anxious, too. The sooner we defeat Dooku and his cronies, the sooner we Jedi can return to our first, best purpose . . . safeguarding peace."

"So you don't know anything?"

Letting his hand fall, Obi-Wan cocked an eyebrow. "If you mean do I know where and when our next mission will take place, then I must disappoint you. But don't be in too great a hurry to leave, Anakin. The longer this war continues, the less frequent will our respites at home become. Enjoy Coruscant while you can, my young friend. Something tells me we'll become strangers to the Temple soon enough."

A shiver of apprehension ran down Anakin's spine. Leaving Coruscant meant leaving Padmé . . . and it seemed scant moments since they'd been reunited. When he closed his eyes he could smell her subtle perfume, feel her fingers on his skin, her skin beneath his fingers, taste her tears of joy. Missing her was agony, their separation torture.

Not that he resented the chance to do his duty. He meant every word he'd just said to Obi-Wan: he was desperate to see the Republic victorious against the Separatists. Already this war had brought him to despair. And the longer it continued, the deeper would flow the rivers of blood.

We should never have let it get this far. If we'd been stronger, the Separatists would never have become so bold. We should have stopped them. The blame is ours. What use are the Jedi if we refuse to use our power for good? Why have power at all if we're forbidden to wield it as strongly as we can?

Obi-Wan nudged him. "Your apprentice has finished her task, Master Skywalker."

Anakin winced. "Don't call me that. It doesn't sound right."

As Obi-Wan chuckled, Anakin looked down into the dojo to see that Ahsoka was indeed done with her fifty repetitions of Niman form, level one. She was panting, her tunic damp from her exertions. Training lightsaber still engaged, she stared hopefully at the balcony.

"Not that I wish to tell you how to school your Padawan," Obi-Wan added, "but I think she's had enough for one day. What say you and I give her a demonstration of some more advanced techniques, hmmm?"

Anakin smiled. *Sparring.* There was nothing he enjoyed more than sparring. Especially against Obi-Wan, renowned as one of the Temple's most accomplished and formidable duelists. They were so attuned to each other now, after years of crossing lightsabers in sport, that in many ways it was like dueling with himself.

"An excellent idea, Master Kenobi," he said. "Shall we?"

And with a shared grin, no further discussion needed, they leapt lightly over the edge of the balcony to land cushioned by the Force at a startled Ahsoka's feet.

"Your training lightsaber, Padawan," said Obi-Wan at his most polite, hand outstretched. "And then perhaps you should find a safe place to stand."

Clearly awed and excited, Ahsoka surrendered her training weapon. Then, with a cheeky glance at her Master, she Force-jumped up to the observation balcony.

"Tut tut," said Obi-Wan. "Such levity, Anakin. I wonder where she learned *that* bad habit?"

"I can't imagine, Master," Anakin retorted, the old honorific slipping out. But it didn't feel wrong. It would never feel wrong. He unclipped the training lightsaber from his belt, powered it up, and let himself fall thoughtlessly, instinctively, into the prowling assessment that presaged every dueling bout.

Eyes intent, that small smile lurking, Obi-Wan matched him step for step. "Ready?"

Anakin nodded. "Always."

And their dance began.

When Master Yoda told her she'd been apprenticed to Anakin Skywalker, Ahsoka didn't know whether to laugh or cry. No Jedi in the Temple cast a longer shadow than Anakin, was surrounded by more rumor, more speculation. The tales of his exploits grew more lurid with each retelling. Everyone knew him . . . yet no one knew him at all. Except for Master Obi-Wan, of course, and he was as inscrutable, it seemed, as his legendary former Padawan.

The Chosen One? The Chosen One is to be my Master? Oh no. No, that can't be right. There must be some mistake. They've got the wrong apprentice.

Except venerable Yoda didn't make mistakes.

So heart in her mouth, terror bubbling in her blood, she'd traveled to Christophsis to meet the man who'd guide her to Jedi Knighthood. One way and another they'd had an . . . interesting . . . time.

He was more human than she'd been expecting. Pretty much as brilliant, and as volatile. More impatient, yet somehow more tolerant. All right, she'd skated pretty close to the edge a few times. Asked for the reprimands he'd given her. That had been nerves. The desire to impress him. Show him he'd landed himself the right apprentice. But she hadn't acquitted herself too badly, all in all. At least he hadn't seemed disappointed. Hadn't run straight to Yoda on their return to the Temple and demanded another Padawan, *any* Padawan, just get that Ahsoka out of my sight!

So . . . it looked like they were together for the long haul. A proper team. Master and Padawan, fighting the good fight side by side.

Standing tippy-toe on the observation balcony, peering over the railing to the Jedi below, she felt in herself an unbecoming envy.

I'll never handle a lightsaber as well as they do, even if I train twenty hours a day.

In some strange kind of Jedi alchemy, other Padawans and Jedi Knights were drifting to the dojo, joining her on the balcony to watch Master Obi-Wan and Master Anakin play as they dueled each other in the demanding Ataru Form IV.

And it was play, even though they were deadly serious.

Watching her mentor Force-leap over Master Obi-Wan's head, graceful as a Tarchalian gazelle, she wondered if he thought about what had happened on Geonosis. About nearly dying. It had happened once . . . it could happen again. Was he afraid? If so, he never showed it.

Will I ever be that brave? I hope so. I can't imagine it.

She wondered if he thought about the part of himself that was machine, not man. If she hadn't known his right hand and forearm were made of metal instead of flesh, she would never have suspected it. Nothing in the way he carried himself suggested he was no longer . . . whole.

A Jedi could sense the Force in a lightsaber's crystal, sense the amplification of power, that barely controlled catastrophe of potential. A Jedi became one with it, formed a living link with the Force as it flowed through and through the rare prism. So how did it feel to have that link interrupted by a prosthetic hand? What was it like for a Jedi to lose part of his incredible living connection to the Force?

I want to ask him. I don't think I can.

The balcony was crowded now, and a constant excited commentary buzzed. Ahsoka frowned on the inside, where none of them would see. This was *her* training session. This was Obi-Wan and Anakin—Master Kenobi and Master Skywalker—dancing with their lightsabers for *her*. It wasn't fair, these others pushing in.

An unworthy thought, and she thought it anyway—just for a moment.

Below them, in the dojo, the sparring Jedi had begun to sweat. But sweat didn't stop them. The mock-fight carried on. Strike and counterstrike, blow and counterblow, leaping and spinning and slashing and evading. Running and jumping, as one with the Force. Every now and then, a sharp bark of laughter. A good-natured jibe. A clever hit acknowledged. Obi-Wan slapped his lightsaber across Anakin's backside, and Anakin pretended to howl. That made the crowd on the balcony laugh. Ahsoka laughed with them, and didn't mind so much that they were there.

Because, after all, she *was* Anakin's apprentice. No one could take *that* away from her.

Though it scarcely seemed possible, they were fighting so swiftly already, Master Kenobi and Master Anakin increased their speed. The training lightsabers moved in a blur too fast to see with ordinary eyes. She could still count the individual moves; her Togrutan heritage had gifted her with senses more acute than those of a human, and many other species besides. Holding her breath, amazed and humbled, she watched two of the Temple's finest Jedi put on a display of unmatched skill.

Strike—block—parry—evade—bind—counterbind—countermeasure—broken time—body-to-body and double release—Force push—Force pull—feint—backflip—recover . . . and start again.

When Obi-Wan ran up the wall and then *across the ceiling* and down the other side and Anakin *pursued* him everyone cheered, though it was hardly in keeping with Jedi reserve. She cheered. It was marvelous.

That's who I want to be one day. That's the kind of Jedi I want to become.

But not even Jedi like Obi-Wan and Anakin could keep up this kind of pace and power forever. Tired now, they finished their bout. Wringing wet, blowing hard, they bowed politely to each other. Then Obi-Wan reached out his hand and pressed his palm briefly to Anakin's cheek. Ahsoka saw his lips move. Saw him say: *Well done.*

And the look on Anakin's face, at those two small words, brought her treacherously close to tears.

The balcony was emptying swiftly, the Jedi Knights and Padawans returning to the business they'd abandoned for a short time. Soon she was alone again, waiting for an instruction from her Master. He was saying something to Obi-Wan in a low voice; she couldn't make out the words. Obi-Wan nodded, smiling, then glanced up.

"Your training saber, Padawan," he said, all perfect courtesy, and tossed the borrowed weapon to her. "My thanks for the loan of it."

As Master Kenobi left the dojo, Anakin retrieved the recording drone that had captured her earlier exercises and, to her surprise, because such things were frivolous, Force-floated it to the balcony so she might pluck it from the air.

"Find a private study chamber, Ahsoka, and examine your technique," he instructed. "Tomorrow morning be ready to detail the best and the worst five things that you did."

She tucked the drone into her tunic. "Tomorrow, Master? We're not going to discuss my performance now?"

He shook his head. "Now I have somewhere else to be."

Again. She thought he did that a lot, take himself off without explanation. Where did he go? He never said, and she knew better than to ask. "Yes, Master. What time tomorrow?"

He hesitated. "I'm not sure. Until I come for you, continue your training with a remote—and make sure to wear a blinder."

Blind remote training *again*? She wanted to train with *him*. But she hid her disappointment and bowed, the perfect Padawan. "Yes, Master."

"Good," he said, and withdrew.

Alone, and philosophical, she left the dojo. *Five good things and five bad,* she mused, heading for the Temple library. *Think I'll surprise him and find ten instead.*

They had a name for it in Coruscant's grimy underbelly: buyer's remorse.

In the aftermath of Geonosis, with the shadows of war deepening, Bail Organa truly understood what the term meant. He'd felt it first, a crushing hammer blow to the heart, standing on that private balcony with Palpatine and the others, watching tens of thousands of clone troopers marching with mathematical precision up the ramps of the great destroyer starships. Marching to their deaths, unquestioning, uncomplaining. Doing a terrible, inevitable duty, because that was all they'd been trained to do since birth.

He felt it again now, listening to Palpatine regale the Senate with the official report on the Battle of Christophsis and the rescue of Jabba's son. And try as he might, he couldn't imagine an end to that dreadful feeling.

Buyer's remorse.

The battle of Geonosis had been a blooding, nothing more. A teasing taste of things to come. Since then, so many clone troops had fallen, most recently on Christophsis and Teth, in defense of a Republic that hardly knew what to do with them. Whose citizens, truth be told, didn't care very much that they were fighting and dying, provided the war was kept far away from their lives. On Coruscant war was something to watch on the HoloNet news service, if there was nothing more entertaining to pass the time. Elsewhere, of course, things were somewhat . . . different.

He shifted in his Senate platform, restless, as Palpatine concluded his stirring address.

"And so, my friends, I ask you to join with me in congratulating the Jedi on their triumph. Their gritty determination to defeat our misguided brothers and sisters of the Separatist movement stands as a monument to this august body's commitment—*my* commitment—to bringing this tragic conflict to a swift conclusion. This war is a dreadful burden upon us all, but I have complete faith that the Jedi will not long let our suffering continue."

Under cover of the thunderous applause that followed, Bail leaned a little sideways. "He gets more and more inspirational, doesn't he?"

Startled out of reverie, Padmé turned. "What? I'm sorry, Bail. I was thinking."

"Not still brooding about that deal with the Hutts, are you? Because it's done, and we can't undo it."

She shifted her attention back to the Senate Hall, where their fellow representatives were disembarking from their platforms, streaming into the honeycomb of passages behind.

"I know," she said shortly. "But I still regret it. The Hutts are criminals and slave traders, trafficking in misery to make themselves rich. They don't care who they hurt, who they maim, who they kill. They'll do anything, no matter how heinous, if they think it'll gain them an advantage or fill their coffers. They'll help us today and double-cross us tomorrow, if there's a better profit to be made."

"But if doing a deal with them keeps the Outer Rim hyperlanes safe from the Separatists, well . . . I mean, we can't afford to lose any more. We *need* those hyperlanes, Padmé."

She sighed. "I know that. And the Jedi wouldn't have brokered the deal if there'd been another choice. This *alliance* offends them as much as it offends me. Nobody is more aware than they are of the suffering the Hutts cause."

He considered her. "There's not much you don't know about the Jedi, is there?"

"I wouldn't say *that*," she said, blushing. "I've just had a little more to do with them than most people, that's all."

She certainly had, he knew. Fighting with them on Naboo. On Geonosis. She was practically an honorary Jedi herself. "I suppose your experiences have given you a unique insight into them," he said thoughtfully. "Which is good. You can translate. Because I think the rest of us just find them . . . a little strange."

"Strange?" she said, indignant. "They're not *strange*, Bail. They're brave and resourceful and—"

"Well, well," said a drawling voice. "Look at the pair of you, cozy as can be. What have we here, then? An impromptu meeting of the Security Committee? Where are your colleagues? You two mustn't do *all* the work, you know."

It was Palpatine, drifted over to them in his official platform. Alone now. Mas Amedda must have bustled off to take care of more administrative detail.

"Chancellor," said Padmé, standing. "No. No, we were just chatting."

Bail, standing with her, nodded. "About the Jedi," he added. "And how much we owe them."

"Yes, indeed," said Palpatine, enthusiastic. "A debt I hope someday to repay in full. Well, I shan't interrupt any longer. It's getting late, and I have things to do."

"Late?" said Padmé as Palpatine drifted away. She looked at their platform's chrono. "Oh no. *I'm* late. Bail, I'm sorry. I have to go."

"Yes—of course—go," he said, bemused by her sudden alarm. "I'll see you—"

But he was talking to thin air. For a dignified woman, she could certainly run when she needed to.

Ah well. Grinning to himself, he departed the hall for his Senatorial office, where a mountain of datapads awaited his attention.

FIVE

MACE WINDU LEANED FORWARD IN HIS JEDI COUNCIL CHAIR, elbows on his knees, hands loosely clasped between them. "And you're convinced that this request is genuine?"

Obi-Wan nodded. "Yes, I am." He looked at each Jedi Councilor currently resident in the Temple—Yoda, Oppo Rancisis, and Saesee Tiin—then back to Mace Windu. "I trust Dex implicitly. If you recall, it was his information that led us to Kamino."

"Any hint did he give you, Obi-Wan, of what he has learned?" asked Yoda, his eyes half lidded and intent.

"No, Master Yoda. He wouldn't risk divulging any details, as we were speaking over an unsecured comlink."

"Then whatever he knows, he thinks it's dangerous," said Mace Windu. "Which means meeting with him might also be dangerous. Especially if this is some kind of trap."

Obi-Wan considered him. *He has changed since Geonosis. Dooku's defection to the dark side has changed him. And the deaths of so many Jedi, whom he could not protect. I have never known him so cautious, so suspicious. So willing to see danger in every shadow.*

"Master Windu, if you are suggesting that Dex would betray me, I must respectfully disagree. The Jedi have no greater friend."

The Councilors exchanged swift glances, then Mace sighed. "What do you think, Master Yoda?"

"That in these dark times no offer of help can we afford to ignore," replied Yoda. "Victorious we were at Christophsis, but defeated we have been at Selonia, Carida, and Garos Four. Another victory do we quickly require. Meet with Dexter Jettster you will, Obi-Wan. But precautions you will take, in case Master Windu's suspicions prove correct."

Obi-Wan bowed. "Yes, Master Yoda."

"Go now," said Mace Windu. "The sooner we know what your friend has discovered, the better."

Another swift exchange of looks between the Jedi Masters. Obi-Wan felt a shiver of apprehension. "Has something happened? Something new?"

Yoda sighed. "Word we have just received, Obi-Wan, that three more hyperlanes have fallen to General Grievous."

Obi-Wan felt the name run through him like a lightsaber. *Grievous.* Part machine, part sentient. All murdering monster. Sworn to the destruction of the Republic. The Jedi.

"That makes six in the last month," said Mace Windu. "It's very bad news."

Bad? It was devastating. "Which lanes this time, Master?" Obi-Wan asked.

"Crucial routes leading to Bespin, Kessel, and Mon Calamari."

"So supplies of Tibanna gas and Kessel spice are jeopardized. Which will lead to civilian suffering once the shortfall of supply is felt. And those Mon Calamari who are driven home to spawn will not be able to answer the ancient compulsion." Obi-Wan frowned. "A bold move. Tactically ingenious . . . and unspeakably cruel. Perfectly in character for Count Dooku and his henchman."

Above all things a Jedi Master was serene, never overruled by strong emotions. That was the ideal. But Obi-Wan sensed a sourness ripple through the Force as the Jedi Council recoiled from that name. The echoes caused by Dooku's willing fall were a long way from fading.

He bowed. "Masters, I'll find Dex and report back to you as quickly as possible."

He headed to the Temple docking bay complex and signed out a plain, serviceable citibike, one guaranteed not to attract undue attention. He couldn't help thinking what Anakin would say if he could see the dull brown paintwork, the dents, the scattered spots of rust. *That heap of junk, Master?* he'd demand, outraged and horrified. *You're going to scoot about Coruscant on that piece of junk? Where's your pride? You're a Jedi! This isn't right!*

Ten years in the Temple and still Anakin hadn't outgrown his passion for machinery, or fallen out of love with beautiful speed. Probably he never would.

"Pride has no place in the heart of a Jedi," Obi-Wan said aloud, earning a quizzical look from the requisitions droid on duty as it handed him the bike key. "The machine is functional, which is all I require."

"Fully functional, yes," said the droid. "That's correct, Master Kenobi. Please be so kind as to return it that way this time."

Obi-Wan touched two ironical fingers to his forehead. "I'll do my best."

Emerging from the docking complex's artificial brightness into the sunlit Coruscant morning, he waited in hovermode until he was given entry to the pitiless slipstream of traffic that would lead him in circuitous, circumspect fashion to the Galarb district. That was where Dex presided over his profitable diner, a slovenly and benevolent dictator.

He felt slightly foolish, not selecting the most direct route, instead heading obliquely across the cityscape, virtually going in the opposite direction from his intended destination. But Yoda had told him to take precautions, so he did. It was for that reason he'd taken a citibike. Anyone who knew him knew he much preferred tackling Coruscant's traffic in an airspeeder. Citibikes were so . . . exposed. No undercover Separatist thinking to follow him from the Temple—such an unlikely thought—would pay attention to this battered old bike. And to make doubly certain he wasn't recognized, the hood of his cloak was tugged well down over his face.

But even if these precautions failed and some nefarious individual did try to follow him, without question he'd be able to sense them before they could cause him any mischief.

I'm in no danger. We're allowing ourselves to become unsettled, that's all. Therein lies the true danger. We must resist the temptation to give our enemies such power.

Except . . . Dex had clearly been nervous. And that was an unsettling thought all by itself.

The citibike's transponder beeped, signaling his acceptance into the traffic. Thrusting aside this new, niggling worry, Obi-Wan swooped into the slipstream of private airspeeders, public transports, citibikes much grander than his own, barges and chopters and runabouts and maxitaxis.

And was compelled to admit, in the privacy of his own thoughts, as he gunned the engine, just a little, feeling the cool wind in his face and tugging on his cloak, that even though he did miss Anakin, there was a certain seductive freedom in speeding through Coruscant's crowded sky with no life depending on him but his own . . .

"*Obi-Wan!*" Dex shouted, spying him through his diner's kitchen hatchway. The Besalisk tossed aside his wipe-down cloth and emerged into the service area, all four mighty arms spread wide, ready to envelop him. "Hey, buddy! What are you doing down here? I thought you were too grand for the likes of us in CoCo Town!"

Bemused, Obi-Wan stared at him. "Too grand, Dex? I'm sorry, I don't quite—"

"That's right! Didn't you know it? You're *famous* now!" Vast belly quaking, Dex turned to his breakfast customers like a conductor to his orchestra. "Hey, everyone! Recognize this guy? You musta seen him on the HoloNet, his ugly face is *everywhere*! This is Jedi Master Obi-Wan Kenobi, the hero of Christophsis! And before that Geonosis and Anoth! Come on, you mooches, a round of applause!"

Good-naturedly enough, Dex's ragtag collection of loyal breakfast patrons abandoned their meals and mugs to snort and whistle and clap and slap their flippers on the tables. Obi-Wan bowed, awkwardly.

Well, this isn't exactly the low-key welcome I was expecting.

And then he grunted, hard, as Dex crushed his ribs in an enthusiastic hug. "Play along," his friend whispered. "You never know who's watching."

Play along. All right. He could do that. "What am I doing here?" he said, as Dex released his suffocating hold and stepped back. "I've come for a cup of the best chava chava in all Coruscant."

Dex laughed, a rich, infectious sound . . . but beneath his joviality ran a tight thread of fear. "Is that right?" He grinned at his curious patrons. "Hey, I thought you Jedi types weren't allowed to lie?"

Blast. What was Dex playing at? "Oh," he said, and conjured up an embarrassed smile. "All right. You've caught me out. The truth is I didn't think to check the charge levels on my citibikes power cell. I'm afraid it was either land here so you could give me a spare, or crash."

Dex's patrons snickered and giggled and made kindly rude comments in a handful of different tongues. "I take it all back, Obi-Wan," said Dex, making up to the crowd. "You're not a hero . . . you're a rollicking *noski*."

An idiot. That was nice. "Look, I hope you don't mind, Dex, but I've parked the wretched bike out front."

Another gravelly laugh. "No, I don't mind, so long as you pay the fine if an inspector notices it!"

"Yes, of course. No need to worry about that. But I don't wish to get you into trouble so . . . about the power cell?"

Dex hitched up his sagging trousers. "Sure, sure, I can spare you a power cell, Obi-Wan. But d'you mind waiting a little while? I'm still a bit busy."

"Of course," Obi-Wan said, all good-natured courtesy. "I'll stand outside with the bike, just in case an inspector happens by."

"Good idea," said Dex, the genial host. "Take a rest from your heroics and I'll be right with you."

By the straightest line, the Galarb district's CoCo Town was some forty-nine sectors distant from the Temple. The diner was located near the area's main transport hub, which guaranteed Dex a steady stream of hungry customers. Pedestrians and groundcars flowed past without a break, heading to and from the main transport interchange. Multistory buildings towered all around the strip, but the diner itself sat in full sunshine, offering a panoramic view across the city-planet.

Obi-Wan lounged against the diner wall, enjoying the sunshine and idly perusing the faces of the passersby. It wasn't long, however, before he realized he was being perused in return. And not just perused—recognized. Pointed at, whispered about, double-taked and noticed. Because, just like Dex said, he was a HoloNet star now.

It was all Palpatine's fault. An inevitable result of the Supreme Chancellor's relentless drive to put faces to the names of the Jedi fighting for the Republic's survival. A drive that had culminated in the continuous looped reporting of the war via the HoloNet news service. And since the Jedi were playing such a prominent role in the conflict . . .

Yoda and Mace Windu had spoken forcefully against the notion, but Palpatine had been charmingly obdurate. The Jedi were heroes of the Republic, selflessly fighting in the name of peace. People should know this. Besides, only by making the Jedi known to every sentient on Coruscant, in the whole Republic, could they be sure of consolidating the groundswell of support for the fight against the Separatists.

"People cannot love an abstract," Palpatine had said. *"But thanks to the HoloNet they will come to love the Jedi. Masters, you must trust me. In this matter I know precisely what I'm doing."*

Yoda and Mace Windu had not conceded the argument, but somehow they had lost it anyway. And as a result Obi-Wan Kenobi had lost his comfortable anonymity. Acutely aware of the attention he was attracting, he flipped his hood back over his face and tried to vanish within the Force. Unfortunately it didn't help much. He could still hear the whispering, the sound of feet slowing on the sidewalk as gawkers stopped to stare.

This is ridiculous. I should have insisted Dex meet me at the Temple.

In the faint hope that he could avoid further notoriety, he turned his back to the sidewalk and groundcar strips and began tinkering with the perfectly functional citibike. A few moments later a droid joined him, wearing a diner cap and carrying a fresh power cell and a clunky battered toolbox. "Dex says you need these," it said.

He nodded. "Yes, I do. Thank you. Just put them down where you are."

"Sorry," said the droid. "Dex says take your repairs around the back."

Away from passersby, where there was a hint of privacy. "Oh. Of course."

He guided the citibike to the rear of the diner, the droid clattering along behind him. It dropped the toolbox and the power cell on the ground and returned to work.

After a swift check of the surrounding buildings—no eavesdroppers within sight or sensing—Obi-Wan opened the toolbox and shook his head at its contents. A kind thought, to be sure, but since Dex's hands were at least four times the size of his own . . .

He used the Force to help him swap out the power cells. A twist here . . . a nudge there . . . the Force's might whispered through him, familiar as breathing. Sunk just below the surface of his surroundings, as he worked he became abruptly, acutely aware of Dex's tightly coiled unease. Besalisks weren't Force-opaque like Hutts and Toydarians, but they weren't as easy to read or manipulate as were so many other of the galaxy's inhabitants. Obi-Wan had long since accepted that, extreme circumstances aside, he'd never truly know what Dex was feeling unless Dex was comfortable with him knowing it.

Right now, though, Dex wasn't blocking him . . . and he wasn't consciously projecting, either. Instead he was *leaking,* an unpleasant muddle of fear and disbelief, oozing out of him like a noxious psychic sweat.

Without warning, Obi-Wan felt a shiver run through him, sickeningly familiar.

I have a bad feeling about this.

But he couldn't pinpoint its source. Yoda was right; the dark side swirled around them like rancid fog. All he knew for certain was that his instincts, his intuition, his link with the Force, were driving him to leap to his feet and stare around him, hand on the hilt of his lightsaber, expecting trouble, expecting—

"That's the breakfast rush over," said Dex's strained voice behind him. "I got a minute or three for you, Obi-Wan. Then I have to get back to the kitchen."

Releasing a hard-held breath, deliberately relaxing his hold on the lightsaber, Obi-Wan turned to face his friend. "Was all of this elaborate setup really necessary?"

Dex's deep-set eyes crinkled shut, then opened wide. His throat-pouch bellied, a sure sign of annoyance. "And when was I in the habit of wasting your time, Master Kenobi?"

Chastened, Obi-Wan nodded. "A fair point. I'm sorry, Dex. I hate to admit it, but I'm a little on edge."

Leaning against the diner's smooth back wall, Dex reached into his cook's apron pocket, pulled out an Ambrian cheroot and a striker, and lit up. He inhaled deeply, then breathed out the fragrant pink herbal smoke.

"Christophsis was bad, eh?"

Obi-Wan snorted. "What makes you think so? By all accounts the HoloNet news footage was positively stirring."

Dex squinted, considering him. "And so it was. I think they filmed it somewhere on Alderaan with a holovid company supplying the special effects."

Obi-Wan stared. "Since when were you such a cynic?"

"War brings out my better nature," said Dex, and stubbed out the butt of his cheroot on the diner's Dumpster.

"Not this time it doesn't. The footage was real enough, Dex. Those blasted droidcams were everywhere we turned. But I suspect what ended up being broadcast was heavily edited."

Edited so the only death and destruction people saw was the death of droids. The destruction of fear. Slaughtered clones weren't . . . photogenic.

"Of course it was," said Dex, his cynicism still richly flowing.

"I don't entirely disagree with the decision, you know," Obi-Wan said gently. "The edited footage didn't lie, after all. We were victorious. Eventually. But what's the point of frightening people? The Core Worlds must remain calm and stable. You know that. Panic is contagious, and it spreads fast. If we let it take hold in the heart of the Republic, a great many people could be hurt. Even killed."

"That's true enough," Dex admitted. "But if you make this war too neat and tidy, Obi-Wan, could be folks won't mind how long it lasts. Then again, maybe it's different for you Jedi. Being as how you're warriors, and all."

Stung, Obi-Wan shook his head. "That's not fair. We didn't ask for this conflict. It was thrust down our throats so hard we nearly choked. But we can't not fight. The Separatists are willing to use the most brutal tactics imaginable to force separation on planets that have no desire to leave the Republic. They must be stopped."

Sighing gustily, Dex nodded and scratched his chin. "You're right. Don't mind my crotchets, Obi-Wan. Seems you're not the only one on edge."

"You said you had some important information, Dex," Obi-Wan prompted.

"You'd best get on with swapping out that power cell," he replied. "Just in case we're being watched."

"We aren't," Obi-Wan said, but he went back to tinkering. "Dex, what's going on?"

Dex reached for another cheroot. Lit it. Inhaled. This time he swallowed the smoke. Then he rubbed a hand across his face. "Could be—maybe—I know where you can lay your hands on that piece of *chizk* Grievous."

Obi-Wan stared at him, heart racing. *Destroy Dooku's pet general and the war will be three-quarters won.* "Where, Dex? Where is he?"

"Right now?" Dex grimaced. "Don't know. But I know where he might be in the next little while."

"*Might* be? Dex . . ."

"Intelligence isn't a sure business, Obi-Wan," said Dex, temper simmering. "If you've come for guarantees, you've come to the wrong place."

"I'm sorry. But Yoda and the other Masters are going to ask me. I have to be able to say I asked you."

Dex puffed furiously on his second cheroot. "They don't trust me?"

"They don't know you. It's not quite the same thing." With a final twist and a click, Obi-Wan connected the replacement power cell. Standing, he unkinked his back, then plucked the cheroot from Dex's fingers. "You really ought to stop smoking these. They're not good for you." He dropped the herbal on the ground and pulverized it beneath his boot heel. "Now. About Grievous."

Defiant, Dex pulled out a third cheroot and lit it. "There's a whisper come to me," he said, wreathed in a cloud of pink smoke. "Grievous plans on capturing Bothawui."

Bothawui. Home to the Bothans, whose intelligence-gathering skills were legendary. Information was their greatest currency, and already their assistance had made a difference against the Separatists. Losing Bothawui to Grievous would make the stolen hyperlanes look trivial.

Let him be wrong. Let it be a mistake.

"Dex, are you sure about this?"

"My source is," said Dex. "And she's not new at this game."

"And you trust her?" Which was a polite way of asking, *Is she a liar?*

Dex's hands clenched. "I trust her."

So. Not a liar. He didn't bother asking for the source's name. He and Dex might be friends, but the Besalisk was fiercely protective of the beings who fed him their dribs and drabs of information. *What you don't know, you can't tell,* was his stubborn motto. And who was to say he was wrong? The Jedi had long since learned such wisdom the hard way.

"Do the Bothans know what Grievous plans?" he asked, then shook his head. "They must. They're Bothans. But why haven't they told us, why haven't they—"

"They don't know," said Dex. His eyes were cloudy, a sure sign of his deep concern. "There's a good chance I'm the only one who does. Me and my source. And now you. It was an accident she found out. And she only risked telling me to pay back a life debt. Obi-Wan . . ." Dex's voice had dropped to a whisper. "You Jedi can't let Grievous get his metal hands on Bothawui."

No, they could not. And now he understood why his friend was so afraid, why he'd refused to discuss this over a comlink. With such a prize at stake, the merest hint that this plan might become common knowledge would surely see Grievous slaughtering thousands to stop one . . .

"What else can you tell me, Dex? When is Grievous expected to make his move? What size battle group will he take to the Bothan system? Can we expect—"

"I'm sorry, Obi-Wan," said Dex, spreading all four arms wide. "I don't know. If I did, I'd tell you."

"I know you would." Obi-Wan ran a hand over his beard. "Dex, thank you for this. The Council will be most grateful. We owe you the debt of many lives."

Dex sighed. Suddenly he looked weary, and years older. "I wish I could tell you more, Obi-Wan. But I can't, so you'd best go. I've got the lunch crowd to think about, and you've got an invasion to stop."

Somehow Obi-Wan managed to smile. "Are you quite sure you wouldn't like to change jobs?"

Dex's answering smile was equally strained. "Obi-Wan, old buddy, not for a hundred million credits."

They embraced, quickly, two comrades in arms saying farewell on the eve of battle. Or at least that was how it felt. Stepping back, Obi-Wan looked up into Dex's somber face. "I doubt I'll be on Coruscant for much longer. Even if I'm not involved in finding and stopping Grievous, there will be other engagements. The Separatists are merely catching their breath after Christophsis. The fighting will start again, perhaps within days." He smiled. "So keep the chava chava hot for me, yes?"

Dex nodded. "And a seat empty, old buddy. May the Force be with you."

"And with you," Obi-Wan replied. Then, with a sober nod, he slung his leg over the citibike, kicked it into life . . . and shot into the Coruscant sky without looking back.

Abandoning circumspection, pushing the citibike as hard as he dared and exploiting without shame the special traffic privileges afforded him as a Jedi, he took the most direct route back to the Temple. Dodging and darting his way through the endless streams of traffic, plunging from one lane to the next, ignoring the shouts and horn blasts from those whose right-of-way he arbitrarily usurped, all he could think of was the implications of Dex's information.

If Grievous takes Bothawui despite its existing defenses, the Republic will be crippled. Without the Bothan information network we'd have lost Christophsis as well. The clone intelligence units show promise, but we have only a handful of them. And the Jedi aren't spies.

The trouble was, nobody knew where Grievous was at this moment. *Heading for Bothawui.* How helpful was that? Dooku's blunt instrument and his droid army could approach the Bothan system from half a dozen different hyperlanes, and the Jedi had no hope of patrolling them all. Even so early in the campaign against the Separatists, the Republic's clone army was already stretched thin. And Kamino couldn't speed up clone production because the quality of the troops it created, that crucial edge, depended on slower maturation.

We need more intelligence.

If for no other reason than Dex's warning was so vague. That frightened him, too. Because what if the Council didn't believe it? What if Dex's lack of specific detail meant they discarded the informant as unreliable? Did he carry enough weight with them that they would trust him as implicitly as he trusted Dex? Or would they demand that he return to his friend and pressure him until his source was revealed, so she could be apprehended and interviewed?

Please, no. Not that. I couldn't do it. I'd be betraying him. Please let them trust me. Let them not ask me to do that.

The trouble was, with Yoda one never knew precisely what he'd ask. The Order's most venerable Master was as much a maverick, in his own way, as Qui-Gon had ever been. And he was a thousand times less predictable. One moment kindly and comfortable, a friend. The next a coldly implacable and ruthless taskmaster. And the shift from one to the other could happen within the blink of an eye.

I'll just have to convince them. I'll have to make them believe.

He could see the Temple now in the distance, so beautiful in the bright sun. Despite everything, he felt the familiar catch in his throat that told him *you're nearly home.* Not a Jedi-like emotion, but he was quite sure he wasn't the only one who felt it on first catching sight of those four splendid, soaring spires and the dominant central tower.

Now he was racing through the administration sector, between rows and rows of offices housing the thousands of workers who helped keep the ponderous wheels of the Republic turning. That was when he felt it: a violent tremor in the Force, a lightning-strike of dark emotion: terror and hatred and triumph and rage. Abrupt, annihilating, it seemed to come from *nowhere.*

And then the explosions.

The light came first, a bright blossoming of scarlet and orange edged in black. Directly below him. Off to his left, then his right. Straight ahead. Hard on their heels came the shock waves, as though an invisible hand had seized the air and shaken it like a blanket. The waves blasted over him in scorching roils of heat, flinging his citibike end over end. Last of all the dreadful sound, a deep and rolling *boom boom boom boom,* the echoes multiplying and magnifying as they bounced from building to swaying, shuddering, disintegrating building.

And suddenly the bright Coruscant sky was full of metal debris and bodies, of airspeeders and maxitaxis and gracious air gondolas, tossed like leaves in an unforgiving storm.

Helplessly tumbling, Obi-Wan summoned the Force and wrenched his citibike aside just in time to avoid a burning two-seater . . . and was struck from behind by an out-of-control speeder bus laden with screaming passengers.

Pain. Surprise. A detached and baffled anger. This can't be right. No, no, this is wrong.

Yet still he was falling . . . and falling . . . and—

SIX

"MORE CHEE-CHEES, MY DARLING?"

Anakin looked at the stemful of luscious purple berries Padmé was dangling so tantalizingly above his lips.

"Mmmm," he said, then flung his arms around her. "I can think of something tastier than chee-chee berries!"

Squealing with laughter, she let him tumble her to the sheets, mock-protesting as his embrace crushed the fragrant fruit against her skin. Didn't protest at all as he savored the sticky juice, the fragrance of her, let himself fall headfirst into their shared, secret passion.

My love, my love, my own true love.

Only when he was with her did the ache in his heart ease. Padmé made sense of his life: without her all was chaos, violence, the agony of loss. Sometimes, often, he marveled that Obi-Wan never suspected anything. How could he love Padmé so greedily, yet keep that devouring love hidden from the man who knew him best?

I guess I really am a powerful Jedi.

He muttered a protest as Padmé pressed her palms to his chest, holding him back. "Wait. Wait."

"Don't want to *wait*," he muttered. "You made me wait yesterday. I waited too long."

She laughed, but didn't drop her hands. "Anakin, seriously. There's nothing I'd like more than to stay here with you all day, but I can't. I have a holoconference with Queen Jamillia in less than an hour. And don't you have an apprentice to train?"

"I am training her," he protested. "I've given her instructions and she's following them without question. That's very important training for a Padawan."

She pulled a mocking face. "Very important training I think you neglected."

"That's not fair," he said, though he had to grin. "I only ever disobeyed Obi-Wan when he was wrong."

"Apparently he was wrong a lot," she retorted, then giggled. "I wonder if your apprentice will hold the same opinion of you?"

"She'd better not," he said. "Not if she knows what's good for her, anyway."

"Oooh, so stern! Such a taskmaster you are, Master Skywalker!"

There was that unlikely title again. Except he didn't mind it so much when Padmé used it. He didn't mind anything when they were together.

With a regretful sigh she kissed him softly on the lips, then slid from the bed. "I'm sorry, Anakin, but I do have to go."

He loved her in every way, but best like this: eyes sparkling, cheeks flushed, hair riotously tousled around her slender shoulders. Framing the heart-stopping perfection of her face. She was so many women it was hard to keep track: the regal Queen, the feisty Senator, the fierce champion of peace . . .

My wife.

He only had to look at her and the burden of guilt he felt about living this lie, deceiving Obi-Wan, betraying the vows he'd taken with such solemn intent, eased almost to vanishing.

Because this is right. We belong together.

Grudgingly, he sat up. "Yes, you have to go, and so do I. If I return to the Temple too much later, Ahsoka will start a panic looking for me. And that's the last thing either of us needs."

The brilliance of Padmé's eyes dimmed a little. She rarely spoke of it, but he knew their secret burdened her, too. Even though she swore she had no regrets. Even though she'd felt no more compunction than he had in breaking the Jedi's uncompromising code.

It's knowing they're wrong and being unable to shout it from the top of the Temple's spires. That's what's hard. It's having to hide and pretend and only live half a life together. But it won't last forever. When the war is over, we'll come out of the shadows. When the war is over, everything will change.

"What?" she said, frowning. "You look so serious all of a sudden . . ."

He bounced to his feet. "Indigestion," he said. "Race you to the shower!"

Afterward, dressed and almost ready to take his reluctant leave of her, he stood on her apartment's veranda watching the hypnotic crisscrossing of traffic. There was something almost soothing in the steady, ceaseless movement. It had taken him a long time to get used to Coruscant. As a child he'd missed the desert terribly, missed its silence, its stillness. The breathtaking sweep of stars overhead. He'd dreamed so often of visiting them . . . setting foot on other worlds, a free boy. A free man. A Jedi.

That dream came true. Others will come true, too. Good dreams, not just bad. The future's mine to make.

Across the cityscape, dominating the skyline, stood the Jedi Temple. Padmé thought he didn't know how often she stood on this same spot and looked toward it, thinking of him, longing for him.

He did.

Every time she thought of him, he felt it. Every tear she shed for their separation, he wept, too. There was nothing she could feel that he couldn't—didn't—feel with her.

And that's what Obi-Wan will never understand. He thinks love can be discarded, like an empty cup. He thinks that it will pass, in time. He's a blind man saying that sight doesn't matter.

He felt Padmé behind him and turned, smiling. She was wearing her *Senator* face now, all laughing softness put away, that intoxicating fall of hair smoothed into neat discipline. The seductive silk robe had been replaced by a severely formal dark green dress that hid her completely, just as his Jedi tunic and leggings hid him. Turned them into symbols. Stole their individuality.

But we are more than what we appear to be, both of us. And what we have here, together, makes us better. Stronger. Invincible.

"When will I see you again?" she asked, smoothing his arm. "Tonight? I have a dinner with the Malastarian cultural commissioner, but afterward?"

He kissed her forehead. "A dinner? My condolences. Political talkfests like that are so—"

A stirring in the Force . . . a dark premonition . . .

"Tedious?" she suggested, and laughed. "Yes, but—"

He pressed his fingers to her lips. "Hush. Hush, Padmé. There's something not right . . ."

. . . terror and hatred and triumph and rage . . .

A flash of light—gouts of flame—a shocking series of *booms*. Traffic erupting, spinning, impacting—and cutting through the chaos, through the maelstrom in the Force—

"*Obi-Wan!*"

As he tried to breathe, tried to calm his mind enough so he could find his Master, his friend, Padmé ran to the farthest edge of the veranda and stared at the pluming smoke, the leaping fires, four separate explosions somewhere close by.

"The administration sector," she said, her voice taut. "The Central Court. The Court of Appeals. And I think—I think—the Senate overflow offices." She spun about. "*Obi-Wan?*"

Shaken, he nodded. "He's hurt. Padmé, I have to go, I have to—"

"Yes, yes, *go*!" she urged him. "I must go, too; I must get to the Senate. I'll be needed. Anakin—"

"Oh, Mistress Padmé, Mistress Padmé!" cried C-3PO, tottering outside. "What's happening? Is it the Separatists? Are we under attack?"

She ignored the droid, her face white. "*Go*, Anakin. *Be careful.*"

"You, too."

Then she was running to the open doorway and he was leaping for his airspeeder. Their outstretched fingertips touched, in passing.

My love. My love.

He fired up the vehicle's engine and wrenched away from the veranda, heedless of rules, of safety, of everything but the overriding need to reach Obi-Wan.

He's not dead. He can't be. I'd know if he was dead.

Scant minutes had passed since the first explosion, and now the city of Coruscant was reacting. The sky was full of halted and halting traffic, strident with the sound of sirens, screaming. Emergency vehicles converged on the blast locations from every direction, air ambulances and security and traffic control and disaster crews. He could see debris scattered and floating, the remains of ruined maxi-buses and airspeeders and the like, their repulsorlift units still working. The air was hazed and stinking with smoke. And almost lost within the racket of the sirens, desperate pain-filled cries of the people injured in this cowardly attack.

Anakin closed his ears and heart to them, narrowed his focus until he could hear only one voice. Feel only one jagged, thrumming presence in the Force.

Hang on, Obi-Wan. Don't let go. Don't you dare.

It was the race to find and save his mother all over again. He could feel Obi-Wan's pain, his semiconscious confusion, his fear. It shouted through the Force at him, scraping his nerves raw, waking his own fears, his own terror of loss. It summoned him like a beacon, like a bonfire in the night.

An emergency services shuttle dropped out of the sky beside him. *"All Coruscant traffic is in emergency lockdown!"* a metallic voice blared. *"You are ordered to power down your airspeeder. Repeat, power down your airspeeder or face arrest!"*

Incredulous, Anakin stared at the pilot. What? Okay, it was possible there was a problem with his shuttle's transponder, but was this guy blind? Couldn't he *see* he was shouting at a Jedi?

"This is your final warning! Power down your airspeeder!"

No, apparently not.

One hand on the controls, not lessening his speed, he unclipped his lightsaber, flicked it into life, and brandished it over his head.

"Transponder signal confirmed. Apologies, Master Jedi."

Yeah. No problem. See you later, *poodoo*.

On a deep breath, heart pounding, Anakin plunged his airspeeder nose-first toward the distant ground. Obi-Wan's presence was weakening . . . fading . . . the outline of his spirit was starting to blur . . .

No! No! I will not let this happen!

Oblivious to the organized mayhem surrounding him, the destruction, the teeming emergency responders and their blaring horns and amplified voices, he flew like a blaster bolt to Obi-Wan.

The stinking smoke was really bad now, thick and choking. It was harder to see. But he didn't need eyes, he had the Force. It guided him lower, prompted him to slow down, slow down, slow down again. To nudge his way left—more left—just a little more left—

There.

An open rooftop. Uncluttered. A few garden boxes, a fountain.

Some kind of office retreat. Low benches. Shade cloths. A single shuttle pad. And there—a broken citibike. Beside it, a broken Jedi.

Obi-Wan! A citibike? What were you thinking?

Anakin dropped his airspeeder to the rooftop as though it were a brick. Force-leapt from the driver's seat to land kneeling by his former Master's side.

"Obi-Wan! It's me. It's Anakin. Don't move."

So much blood. Too much blood. Jedi weren't immortal. Qui-Gon had told him that, then died to prove it.

Lying in a crumpled heap, awkwardly twisted, half on his side, Obi-Wan blinked slowly. His eyes were clouded, unfocused. His right cheek was deeply split along the bone. "Anakin . . . ?"

Anakin leaned closer, too afraid to touch Obi-Wan's burned, bloodstained hand. "Don't talk. I'm going to call for help, okay?"

"Anakin . . ."

"I'm right here," he said, even as he stood and backed away to the airspeeder for his comlink. "Don't worry, Obi-Wan, I'm right here."

Obi-Wan groaned. "Blast. I think I'm hurt."

No kidding. Anakin cued the comlink to the Temple's emergency frequency and activated it. "This is Anakin Skywalker. I need Master Yoda."

A mushy hiss, then: *"Master Yoda is in an emergency Council session and cannot be—"*

"Get him now, you idiot! Do you hear me? *Get him now!*"

Sprawled on the rooftop, Obi-Wan stirred. "Temper, temper, Anakin. No need to shout."

Somehow, though it nearly killed him, Anakin managed to smile. "Don't be a spoilsport, Master. You know I like to throw my weight around."

Obi-Wan exhaled, faintly smiling in return, and red froth bubbled along his pale lips. Seeing it, Anakin returned to his side.

"Anyway, I told you to be quiet," he scolded, kneeling. "I think it's about time you started listening to me."

"Don't be bossy," said Obi-Wan. Tried to move, gasped, and lay totally still. "There was an explosion . . ."

"There were four," said Anakin. "Please, Obi-Wan. *Shut up.*"

"I think I've broken something," said Obi-Wan, his gaze restless. "No. Make that several somethings." He glanced down at his charred, torn, blood-soaked tunic. "Well, that's not good."

Anakin reached out a hand, risked touching it to Obi-Wan's forehead. His skin was ice-cold. "You're fine, Master. You're going to be fine."

"Anakin Skywalker, Master Yoda this is."

Flooded with relief, he lifted the comlink. "Master Yoda, I need help. I'm with Obi-Wan. He's hurt. He's really hurt. The attack."

"Bring him to the Temple, can you?"

"No, I don't dare move him. I need a healer. I need lots of healers. Can you come? Can you hurry?"

"Where are you, young Skywalker?"

Anakin stared around him. "I don't know. The administration sector. On a rooftop."

"Your comlink leave open. Find you we will."

"Yes. Good. Now hurry, please!"

He clipped his comlink to his belt and took a deep breath. Sweat stung his eyes, slicked his spine. Fear gibbered round the edges of his mind.

"Liar," whispered Obi-Wan. "You said I was fine."

"And you will be," Anakin said fiercely. "But Obi-Wan, you need to save your strength."

"Yes," said Obi-Wan, his gaze now curiously introspective. "Yes . . ."

Not for the first time, Anakin cursed his lack of healing talents. How could he be the Chosen One and be so *hopeless* when it came to healing? It wasn't *fair.*

"Anakin . . ."

Despairing, Anakin stared at Obi-Wan's sickly-white face. What could be seen of it, that wasn't bathed in blood. There was blood in his beard, from the awful wound in his cheek. That bloody froth, drying on his lips. He was damaged inside. Must be. What if he stopped breathing before Yoda could reach them? What if he went into convulsions? There'd been a Podrace crash once, a real messy pileup on the home straight. Larbo Nelik had been thrown clear, thrown right into the barrier. Broke herself to pieces, then convulsed and died as Anakin watched. His mother had wept, seeing it, and begged him not to race again. But Watto was the boss of things like that . . . and anyway, he loved it.

"Anakin," Obi-Wan said again. "Listen."

Anakin leaned even closer. "No, *you* listen. Yoda's coming, with healers. You have to stay *quiet,* you have to—"

"Anakin," said Obi-Wan, his voice so weak. "It's important."

He looked down at Obi-Wan, fighting outraged disbelief. How could this be happening? How could he be on this rooftop, surrounded by debris, by the wailing of sirens, choking on bitter smoke, bitter tears, staring at his dreadfully injured friend? When only moments ago he'd been in Padmé's arms . . . and laughing . . . loving?

This isn't happening. This can't be happening.

"Anakin," said Obi-Wan. His voice was almost too faint to hear. "Tell Yoda that Dex's message was about Grievous. He's after Bothawui."

That shocked him. "*Bothawui?* No. If Grievous gets Bothawui—"

"I know," said Obi-Wan painfully. "Anakin, tell Yoda."

"You can tell him yourself, as soon as he gets here."

Obi-Wan looked at him, almost puzzled. "I don't—I'm not sure—" His eyes drifted closed, and fresh red froth bubbled onto his lips.

Anakin slewed about, searching the crowded, smoky sky for Yoda. Ten years of rigorous Jedi training were all that stood now between him and screaming.

Come on! Come on! Where are you? Come on!

And just when he was on the brink of risking everything, risking Obi-Wan's life by putting him in the airspeeder and heading to the Temple himself, Yoda and a team of three healers arrived. One of them was Master Vokara Che, who'd worked so hard on him after Geonosis.

"Stand back, young Skywalker," Yoda commanded as the healers set about saving Obi-Wan's life. "Done well you have. Die he will not."

There were tears on Anakin's cheeks, he could feel them. He wasn't ashamed. He wasn't going to apologize to anyone, not even Yoda, for caring enough about Obi-Wan to weep for him.

But it seemed Yoda was in a forgiving mood. "Die he will *not*," he repeated, and to emphasize the assertion rapped his gimer stick on the rooftop.

"How do you know?"

"It is not his time," said Yoda, softly. "Despite the dark side see that much I can."

Shivering now, the shock setting in, Anakin felt his legs give way. He dropped to the rooftop, dazed. "He gave me a message for you, Master Yoda. Grievous is after Bothawui."

"*Bothawui?*" said Yoda. And then he said something else, in a strange tongue, not Republic Basic. He sounded . . . perturbed. "Certain you are? No mistake there can be?"

He shook his head. "None."

The healers were clustered about Obi-Wan, everything about them urgent. Vokara Che murmured something, the other two nodded, and then in one swift, coordinated move they turned Obi-Wan fully onto his back. He cried out as they shifted him, a shout of terrible pain.

"Master Vokara Che!" Yoda said loudly.

The healer turned, her twin head-tails writhing with her agitation. "Master Yoda, I'm sorry, but can you give me a—"

"Return to the Temple at once I must," said Yoda. "Leave you here to help Obi-Wan I will. When returned to the Temple you are, and news of him you have, find me."

Vokara Che nodded. "Of course."

Anakin flinched as Yoda poked him with the gimer stick. "Your airspeeder that is, young Skywalker?"

"Yes, Master."

"Then back to the Temple you will take me. And attention to the speed laws you will not pay!"

He didn't want to go. He wanted to stay here, with Obi-Wan. He scrambled to his feet. "Yes, Master," he said . . . but he was staring at his friend.

Yoda poked him again. "Trust me do you, youngling?"

Startled, Anakin looked down. "What? Yes."

"Then safe it is to leave Obi-Wan! *Not* safe is Bothawui!"

Obi-Wan would tell him to go. Obi-Wan would be furious if he lingered, endangering lives. He and Yoda returned to the Temple.

Supreme Chancellor Palpatine, previously plain Senator Palpatine, for the better part of his life Darth Sidious, Dark Lord of the Sith, stood pensively in his luxurious office, benevolently smiling at the mayhem he had wrought.

Well, not *personally*. He wasn't the one who *personally* found the willing dupes, stirred up their real and imagined grievances against the Republic, supplied them with the explosives and the codes required to evade security, and left them to get on with things. No. That was the tedious footwork of some minion or other. Some other willing dupe cozened by his useful—if elderly—apprentice, Darth Tyranus. The one keeping a seat warm for Anakin, who was ripening so *nicely*. Really coming along.

There was something so *satisfying* about a plan brought to fruition.

In the cocooned hush of his office it wasn't possible to hear the sirens, the screaming, the shouting, the horror. But he didn't need to hear it. He could see it, and feel it in the Force.

The dark side was a wonderful thing.

He glanced away from the fruits of his daydreaming to the chrono on his desk. Ah. Nearly time. Turning from the vast transparisteel window, from the panorama of death he'd painted with such skill, he retrieved his dark hooded cloak from his private wardrobe, slid into it, and activated the narrow-band holotransceiver he kept for these . . . *special occasions.*

"Master," said Dooku's hologram, bowing. Really the man should be kneeling, but age did have its compensations. At least for a little while. *"You are aware of our most recent success?"*

"Yes, Darth Tyranus," Sidious replied. "I've been watching events unfold with some interest. Well done."

Praise from a Sith Lord was rare, and Dooku let his surprise show. *"My lord, you humble me."*

And you bore me, but let us not go into that. Not yet. "How stand matters with General Grievous?"

"He assembles his renewed droid army now, my lord. He is anxious to engage the Jedi in battle once again."

"The point of this mission is that he *not* engage the Jedi, Tyranus. Not until Bothawui lies firmly in his grasp. Once Bothawui has fallen to us, they will expend themselves thoughtlessly in the attempt to reclaim it. We seek the deaths of many Jedi, my apprentice. Remind Grievous of that. Remind him he is hardly indispensable."

Dooku bowed again. *"My lord, I will."*

Darth Sidious disconnected the hololink, returned the transceiver to his cloak's pocket and the cloak to its hanger in the wardrobe. He liked to keep his possessions neat and tidy. A place for everything, and everything in its place.

His desk holopad beeped, and he toggled its switch. "What is it?"

Mas Amedda's hologram bowed. "My lord, word has reached me that Obi-Wan Kenobi was injured in one of the terrorist attacks."

Obi-Wan? *Really?* "Don't say *terrorists*, Mas Amedda. It's such a partisan, emotional word. Leave words like that to our redoubtable friends in the HoloNet news service."

Mas Amedda nodded. "My lord."

Darth Sidious looked down, his thoughts seething. The gesture was a dismissal, and Mas Amedda knew it. The hololink disconnected. Unobserved once more, he looked up, knowing a red light gleamed in his eyes. Obi-Wan injured? That upright, sanctimonious, inconvenient Jedi injured?

Good.

He slid himself beneath the surface of the everyday, submerging his mind in the peerless currents of the dark side. Where was Anakin? What was he *feeling*?

Grief . . . fear . . . anger . . . guilt.

Excellent.

Would Kenobi die? No . . . no, which was sad. But this turn of events was certainly serendipitous . . . something could be made of it, surely . . . something useful. Something . . . permanent. For it was time, and more than time, that Anakin was weaned from Kenobi and his milkish light-side pap.

Time he truly began to sup upon the dark.

Sitting back, fingers steepled, Darth Sidious began to explore the possibilities.

Anakin wanted to go straight to the Temple's Halls of Healing and wait there for Obi-Wan to arrive. He'd given Yoda Obi-Wan's message. What further use could the Council have for Anakin Skywalker? None. But Obi-Wan needed him. Even unconscious he'd know his former Padawan was with him. Just as *he'd* known, stupefied after his disastrous duel with Dooku, that Obi-Wan and Padmé had him safe between them.

But Yoda wouldn't hear of it.

"A healer you are not, young Skywalker. Report to the Council you must," he decreed in that overbearing, irritating, pompous way of his. Making pronouncements that everyone was supposed to accept without question, just because he'd lived a long time.

A full Council session was convened, every Master in attendance—although three-quarters of their complement appeared as holograms. Ki-Adi-Mundi was so far away, almost to the very edge of the civilized galaxy near Barab I, investigating some rumor of trouble, that his hologram was little more than a shadow, his voice a whisper.

"Tell the Council, Anakin, what Master Kenobi told you," said Yoda, eyes half lidded and deceptively mild.

Anakin was able to control his anger, just. This was *pointless.* A *waste* of his time. "Yes, Master Yoda." He swept the Council with an impatient look. "Obi-Wan told me that Grievous plans to attack Bothawui."

"Grievous?" said Adi Gallia, as beautiful in a hologram as she was in the flesh. "You're certain?"

"What, you think I'm making this up?" he demanded. "*Yes.* Grievous. That's what he said." Again, he swept the Council with a look, harsher this time. "And I don't care how crazy it sounds, you have to believe him. He was in *agony,* and all he cared about was making sure Master Yoda got the message. The message came from Dex. That means it's the truth. Grievous is planning to invade Bothawui."

"It means," said Eeth Koth, his hologram wavering, "that Obi-Wan *thinks* it is the truth, young Skywalker. Your former Master could be mistaken . . . or misled."

Anakin could never look at the Zabrak Master without a shiver of distaste. Without seeing superimposed over him the menacing red-and-black Sith who'd murdered Qui-Gon. Even though he'd only glimpsed that dreadful face once, in the hangar on Naboo, he'd never forgotten it.

"Mistaken?" he echoed, not caring anymore if his anger showed. "I don't think so. As for Dex, he'd never lie to Obi-Wan."

A glum silence told him he'd scored a point. At last.

"Thank you, Anakin," said Master Windu heavily. "The Council will deliberate in private now. You're excused."

Anakin looked at Yoda. "I have your permission to—"

"Yes," said Yoda. "Returned to the Temple Obi-Wan should now be. Tell Master Vokara Che that to see her I will come, when I am able."

Anakin nodded. "Yes, Master Yoda." Added, grudgingly, "Thank you."

As he reached the Council chamber door, Mace Windu's voice made him pause. "The Force is with him, Anakin. You are wrong to be afraid."

Yeah, yeah. Wrong to be afraid, wrong to be worried, wrong to care two bantha pats what happened to Obi-Wan.

Everything I do is wrong. But you still expect me to save you, don't you?

"Yes, Master Windu," he said over his shoulder, and kept on walking.

"Skyguy! Skyguy, hold up! Wait for me!"

He spun on his heel to see Ahsoka racing across the meditation-level concourse toward him. *"Don't call me that!"* he snapped when she was only a handful of paces distant. "I'm Master Skywalker to you, or just plain Master."

As though he'd physically slapped her, she skidded to a halt. Slight, wiry, such a little thing, she stared up at him in shocked silence.

"I'm sorry," she said at last, in a small wounded voice. "I only meant—" She dropped her gaze. "I'm sorry."

Unfortunately they weren't alone on the concourse. The Jedi and Padawans entering and exiting the nearby swift-tubes did not stop or stare, but Anakin could feel their curiosity. Ten years in this place, and still he was an object of interest. Of speculation. All their hopes and dreams hanging on him like decorations on a bantha skeleton at Boonta Eve.

He hated it.

"What do you want, Ahsoka?" he said roughly. "I don't have time to look at yesterday's training session."

"I heard Master Obi-Wan was hurt in one of the explosions," she whispered. "I thought—I felt—"

"*What?*"

She was trembling. "You're frightened for him. And I wanted to—I thought you might like—" She turned away, defeated. "It doesn't matter."

Her pain knifed through him. He felt stupid, and cruel. "Ahsoka, wait."

Reluctantly, she turned back.

"You're right," he said. "I am frightened for Obi-Wan. I shouldn't be, but I am. And I would like some company while I wait to see him."

Not her company; he was desperate for Padmé. But that was impossible. Ahsoka would do, in a pinch.

"Yes?" Ahsoka's face lit up with joy. "You mean it?"

He wasn't sure how he felt about that, having so much easy power over one young girl. Why did she care so much? Why should what he said matter?

Qui-Gon mattered to me. I suppose it's the same.

He jerked his head toward the swift-tubes. "Come on. We can work through your training session while we wait. Don't suppose you thought to bring that droidcam?"

She smiled, a sharp flash of feral teeth. "Of course I did, Sky— Master. I know I'm thick sometimes, but—"

He sighed. "You're not thick, Ahsoka. And I guess you can call me Skyguy. But *only* when we're alone."

Her face lit up again, so much unbridled joy. "Thank you!"

He didn't want her gratitude. He didn't want her as his Padawan, though he liked her well enough. He didn't want *any* Padawan. But thanks to the Council they were stuck with each other. All they could do was make the most of the fact.

"Come on," he said again, and walked away.

With a gasp and a skip, she hurried after him.

SEVEN

"Senator Amidala!"

Padmé turned at the sound of Bail Organa's voice. He was pushing his way toward her through the crowded corridor, collecting stares and rude comments, which he ignored. They'd been called to an emergency session of the Security Committee. The terrorist attacks. The Senate complex was like a poked beehive, frantic with activity.

"Padmé," he said as he reached her, then pulled her aside into a convenient alcove. His dark eyes were anxious. "I don't know if you've heard, but Obi-Wan Kenobi is one of the bombings' casualties."

The lies came so easily now. "No! I didn't—oh, that's awful, Bail. How badly is he hurt?"

"He's not dead. But I'm told it's serious. I'm sorry. I know you're friends."

Well, she wouldn't precisely call them *that*. Not since she'd ignored his plea and promptly married the man he'd begged her to renounce. "Friends. Yes. Bail, how did you find out? There's been no announcement."

"The Jedi shuttle taking him back to the Temple got caught at an emergency checkpoint. The sister of one my Senate staffers is a security officer. She flew escort for it once the problem was resolved." He shrugged. "And sisters gossip."

They certainly did. "I want to know everything you know, but it'll have to wait till after the briefing. Which we should get to before we're late."

Bail nodded. "Of course."

When they reached their allotted chamber, though, they found it empty . . . save for Supreme Chancellor Palpatine.

"Don't be alarmed, my friends," he said as they slowed uncertainly on the chamber's threshold. "You're in the right place. But I took the liberty of canceling your briefing."

Padmé exchanged a cautious glance with Bail, who stepped forward. "Chancellor?"

"I wish to personally inspect the damage inflicted upon us by the Separatists," said Palpatine. "And I'd like both of you to accompany me. No fanfare, no elaborate escort. Just three concerned public servants united in a common cause."

Padmé frowned. "I'll come, of course, but—"

"Why you?" Palpatine smiled, gravely. "Because I value your advice, milady. Your experiences as a target of Trade Federation terrorism, first on Naboo and then more recently here and on Geonosis, afford you valuable insight. You've looked firsthand into that dreadful abyss, Padmé. It has tried to devour you and failed every time. I want to see these attacks through your eyes. You will see things I never would, or could. And if I'm to protect our great Republic, I must know what they are. No matter how alarming or upsetting that may be."

Taken aback, she nodded. "Anything I can do to help."

"And as for you, Senator Organa," Palpatine continued. "If you'll forgive my blunt speaking, I have felt of late that you're coming to regret the unconditional support you've shown my office."

"*Regret?*" Bail shook his head, vehement. "No, Supreme Chancellor. I support you without reservation, as always."

"Do you?" said Palpatine, gently. "I must say that's not the impression I've received."

"With respect, sir, you're mistaken. If I have regrets, it's that we've been forced into this war. That in creating our Grand Army of the Republic we've turned our backs on a thousand years of peace. On all the Senators who came before us and preserved that peace by steadfastly refusing to give in to their fears."

"Are you saying my negotiations for an equitable settlement with the Separatists were not genuine?"

"No, of course I'm not." Bail ran a hand over his close-clipped goatee. "Nobody could've tried harder than you did to give Dooku and his cronies what they wanted while still preserving the integrity of the Republic. It's just—"

"That now you've seen soldiers killing, and dying," said Palpatine. "Clones, to be sure, but even so. Am I correct?"

Bail nodded. "Yes."

"And you wonder if you did the right thing, agreeing to support a Republic army. Especially since your dear friend here, Senator Amidala, opposed the Military Creation Act at the risk of her own life."

"It was never that I disagreed with your stand, Padmé," said Bail, looking at her. "Not in principle. It was only that I feared—"

"I was being naïve?" She shrugged. "I know that. And perhaps I was. Certainly I'd be a hypocrite now, wouldn't I, to complain about the army when it saved my life."

"As well as lives on every planet the Separatists now wish to rip from the Republic by force," Palpatine added. "Including, it would seem, Coruscant itself. This is why I want you with me, Bail. So you can see what we're fighting for. Your scruples are worthy . . . but are they worth innocent lives? Come. I have an airspeeder waiting for us."

There was no question of declining Palpatine's invitation. Padmé nodded at Bail, then fell into step beside him to follow Palpatine out of the committee chamber's rarely used executive exit.

As they made their way through a labyrinth of corridors to his private shuttle bay, the Supreme Chancellor beckoned her to his side. "I wonder if you've heard about our good friend Master Kenobi."

"Yes, Chancellor. Do you know how he is?"

"Alas, no," said Palpatine. "I spoke briefly with Master Yoda a short time ago, and all he could tell me was that the Temple's healers were doing their best."

She nodded. "I see." *Oh, Anakin.* "But did Master Yoda at least sound . . . hopeful?"

"Hopeful?" said Palpatine. "I'm afraid I can't say, my dear. Mostly he sounded like Master Yoda. Convoluted and inscrutable. Still—" He patted her shoulder. "The Temple's healers did a splendid job with young Anakin. We must have faith they can do the same for Master Kenobi."

Padmé nodded again, feeling numb. "Yes. We must."

Palpatine sighed. "I can only imagine how poor Anakin is feeling," he said, his voice catching. "He's terribly fond of Master Kenobi, you know, even though our esteemed Jedi friend is so frequently disapproving. I do wish there was something I could do for him. Find a way to ease his pain. For you know, as much as I respect and admire the Jedi, Padmé, at times their insistence on emotional detachment almost seems . . . well . . . unkind. And Anakin—my goodness—he's not like other Jedi, is he? He's far more sensitive. More easily hurt. He needs people who love him, people whom he knows care for him, not *despite* his passionate nature but *because* of it." He sighed again. "At least, knowing him as I do, from such a young age, that's what I believe. But then *I'm* not a Jedi."

It was a moment before she could trust herself to speak. "However strange and difficult their ways seem to us, Chancellor, I'm sure the Jedi believe that what they're doing is right."

"Oh, I'm sure, too," said Palpatine. "But I wonder how many ill things are done by those who believe that what they're doing is right? Ah—here we are."

They'd reached their destination at last: Palpatine's discreet and private shuttle bay. Padmé breathed a sigh of relief, grateful for the distraction.

But at least I'm not the only one who realizes Anakin will be upset. At least Palpatine is allowed to be his friend. Perhaps he can help Anakin until we see each other again.

The Supreme Chancellor led the way onto the shuttle platform, dismissing the waiting guard with a nod. The first thing she noticed was the lack of crisscrossing traffic. Startled, she halted. She'd never seen Coruscant's skies *empty* before.

"Yes," said Palpatine softly. "A sobering sight, isn't it?"

It certainly was. Almost . . . *unnatural.* "And you're quite sure we don't need to extend the no-fly zone past the Senatorial and administration sectors?"

"As sure as I can be," said Palpatine. "What do you think, Senator Organa?"

Bail was frowning at the lonely buildings before them. "I think the disruption we have is more than enough victory granted to the terrorists, Supreme Chancellor. And the faster we can get the traffic moving again, the greater damage we do to *their* confidence."

Palpatine patted him on the shoulder. "My sentiments exactly."

Docked in front of them was a sleek, dark crimson open airspeeder, a four-seater, understated but with a whisper of power about it. Nimbly for a man of his age, Palpatine slid into the driver's seat and looked at his guests expectantly.

"*You're* going to fly us?" said Bail, comically surprised. "Sir, I can—"

"No, no, that won't be necessary," said Palpatine, waving aside his concern. "Actually, I'm quite an accomplished pilot. And every so often I enjoy carting myself about the place. Not that this is a pleasure trip, obviously. But I'd like you both to concentrate on the results of the Separatists' attack." Taking in their continued hesitation, he added, "Did you want to see my license? It is current, I promise. You'll be perfectly safe."

Padmé grinned. She couldn't help it. Here was the Palpatine she remembered of old. Energetic, unexpected, with a sly sense of the ridiculous. She turned to Bail. "The Chancellor's right, Senator. We'll be quite safe. He won several cups for airspeeder racing back on Naboo."

"He did?" said Bail, relaxing. "I don't recall that being mentioned in the Senate."

"Oh yes," said Palpatine drily. "What a useful recommendation for my candidacy. *Likes to drive dangerous machines very fast.*"

"Well, if you do, Supreme Chancellor, you're not alone," said Bail. "I've been known to break a speed limit myself, once or twice."

Palpatine's smile was conspiratorial. "And it shall remain our secret, my friend. Now, Senators, if you'd care to join me?"

Gravely courteous, Bail let Padmé go first. She settled herself in the rear of the speeder and he settled in beside her, maintaining as polite a distance as possible given the snugness of the backseat. Palpatine touched a button on the console, and the airspeeder was immediately enveloped in a high-security trans-shield. Then he took hold of the control yoke and swooped them away from the shuttle port, away from the Senate Building, and into the eerily subdued Coruscant sky.

The airspeeder's transponder, identifying its pilot as the Republic's Supreme Chancellor, kept them comfortably free of interfering security personnel. With only a fraction of his attention needed for piloting, Palpatine let his senses weave around his passengers as they stared down at the city, nervously anticipating the destruction to come. Since surprising them in deep conversation the other day, after the Senate sitting, he'd begun to wonder if a problem wasn't developing. What he learned now was . . . illuminating. And alarming.

She loves Anakin, there's no question of it. She stinks of love for him. It's nauseating. Useful, but nauseating. But does she realize she's attracted to Organa? No. I don't think so. He's a friend. She admires him. Her heart belongs to Anakin. But Anakin will soon be torn from her. War will keep them apart. And male friends can sometimes become far more.

It was the merest danger, not even the hint of a hint, hardly worth his consideration. But he hadn't achieved what he'd achieved by leaving anything to chance. The smallest suggestion of an impediment to his plans could not be ignored.

And what of this lump of a Senator, this dull, worthy Bail? He's married, but his barren wife remains distant on Alderaan. He's an honorable dolt; he would never betray her. Yet he has feelings for Naboo's brave little former Queen. Respect and admiration are a dangerous mix. These Senators work closely together, and that can make for fertile ground.

An interesting conundrum, then. On the one hand there was Anakin, influenced by Kenobi who stubbornly, inconveniently, refused to die. And on the other hand his Padmé, slavishly devoted, but at the same time vulnerable to the constant presence of Bail Organa.

Though she remain faithful, discontent and distance might start a rot. And Anakin is faithful, too. He rails against Kenobi but would die for him in a blink.

The time had come to kill two birds with one stone.

"Oh no," said Anakin's wife, almost weeping. "Oh, Bail. *Look.* It's the Central Court complex. What's left of it."

Obligingly, Palpatine swooped the airspeeder groundward, affording them a closer view of the terrorist bombs' most satisfying results. Not even transparisteel windows and duranium-reinforced outer walls had been able to withstand the powerful blasts. The judicial buildings were ruined, peeled apart like ripe tilly-fruit.

And the destruction didn't end there. Littered across the wide, spacious concourse was the twisted wreckage of airspeeders, gondolas, shuttles, and citibikes, blown out of the sky and fallen groundward again in a bitter, bloody rain. Over there, in the main fountain—how *delightful*—an entire broken maxibus. Not even smoke damage and charring could disguise the spilled, splashed gore. The falling vehicles had further damaged the surrounding court buildings. Coruscant's judicial processes would be crippled for weeks, if not months. Tensions would rise. Dissatisfaction would spread, cancerous, through the city's fragile fabric.

The more entrenched is a society in its comforts, its safe routines, the more easily is it disrupted. The more swiftly does it fall. Soft fools. They have no idea. The corruption of affluence has rotted them from the inside out.

Overwhelmed by the carnage, security had yet to take away all the bodies. They lay on the sidewalk, their horrors decently shrouded.

"How many dead, Supreme Chancellor?" Organa asked, pathetically moved. "How many injured? Do we have any idea of the final casualty tally?"

"Alas," Palpatine said, his voice mimicking sadness. "That information is incomplete. But I think it's safe to say that we have lost more brothers and sisters today than our hearts can easily bear."

He engaged the airspeeder's hovermode, and they lingered above the destruction. Shifting in his seat, he watched Padmé's tears brim and fall, silvering her cheeks. Watched Bail Organa take her hand, comforting, his own eyes slicked with angry grief.

"Never again," said Organa, jaw clenched. "We cannot allow this to happen again. We have to find out how it happened at *all.*"

"That won't be easy, I'm afraid," Palpatine said, shaking his head. "Coruscant is such an open, unsuspecting society. We have always trusted one another. I fear we won't want to question that trust. I fear that in fearing to lose what makes us great, we'll leave ourselves open to more attacks like this one."

"How were the Separatists able to bypass the security measures?" Padmé whispered. "There are procedures in place, methods of detecting explosives and tracking questionable characters. We know we have enemies out there. How did they get so *close* to us?"

"Because, my dear Senator, we trusted too much," he replied. "We made assumptions. We did not ask the right questions, at the right time, of the right people."

Organa dragged his bleak stare away from the destruction. "You're saying we've been betrayed from within."

"No!" said Padmé. "No, I don't believe that. I *won't* believe it."

Palpatine released a heavy sigh. "I think we must consider it, milady. Painful as it may be, we must look at one another. Quietly. Discreetly. We don't wish to start a panic. We certainly don't wish for the innocent to suffer. But under the circumstances a little inconvenience, a little discomfort, cannot be considered an onerous sacrifice."

"Spy on our own people? We can't," said Padmé, revolted. "Supreme Chancellor, what you're suggesting is the very antithesis of democratic rule."

He gestured down at the bodies, the ruin, the toiling personnel tasked with clearing up the mess. "Tell that to the widows and orphans created today, Padmé," he said softly. "Tell that to the husbands who must soon bury their wives. The parents who must say farewell to their precious children. Tell *them* justice is not as important as protecting our feelings."

Even distressed, she was beautiful. "We didn't resort to this on Naboo, after the Trade Federation. We turned *toward* each other, not *on* each other."

He shrugged. "Coruscant is not Naboo, my dear. Find me another way, and I shall pursue it with alacrity. Until then, my only duty is assuring that attacks like this *never* happen again." He waited a moment for reality to sink in. "As the leading lights of the Security Committee, can I count on your support, Senators? Will you help me unmask the vile criminals responsible for such pain and ruin?"

"We don't have a choice, Padmé," said Organa. He was still holding her hand.

Realizing that, she pulled herself free. "You *like* this idea? You're *comfortable* with it?"

"Of course not. I *hate* it," he said fiercely. And then he pointed through the trans-shield. "But I hate that more. It's the lesser of two evils, Senator. Just like the formation of the Republic's Grand Army, or making deals with the Hutts. It's the lesser of two evils . . . and to save lives, we'll have to live with it."

And thus do the honorable weak cut their own throats.

Outwardly solemn, inwardly laughing, Palpatine disengaged the airspeeder's hovermode and proceeded to the next bomb site . . . just in case their resolve should falter.

"So," said Yoda, regarding Mace Windu with half-shuttered eyes. "Believe this Dexter Jettster, do you?"

Cross-legged on the chamber's other meditation pad, Mace shook his head and sighed. "Obi-Wan believes him."

"And in Obi-Wan you believe."

Mace frowned. "Don't you?"

It was Yoda's turn to sigh. "Yes."

"Then what do you propose we do?"

What, indeed? That was the question.

The deliberations following Anakin's angry departure from the Council Chamber had been brief. Those absent Masters caught up in desperate missions of their own had declared their faith in Yoda's judgment and swiftly withdrawn from the holoconference. The others present in the Council Chamber had echoed their support and also retired, leaving just himself and Mace Windu to make the final decision. Of them all, they were the most experienced in war, the best strategic thinkers. Of them all, they were closest to Palpatine. And guiding Palpatine during this crisis was one of the Jedi's greatest tasks.

"Blunder blindly toward Grievous we must not," he said at last. "A wily adversary he is. A creature steeped in malice and hatred. Stop at nothing he will to see us defeated. Slaughter tens of thousands to distract us from our goal he would."

Glumly, they considered that. Already Grievous had proven himself capable of such a barbaric tactic. On a smaller scale, so far, but its success had promised greater destruction to come. His battle droids had razed an entire township on Ord Mantell in order to divert Republic troops so he could effect an escape.

Stoic Ki-Adi-Mundi had wept, reporting it. Wept for the fathers, cut down without a chance. Wept for the murdered mothers with their babies in their arms.

The problem with Grievous—the greatest challenge they faced—was that his army was devoid of emotion. Machines felt nothing. They could kill, and kill, and keep on killing, and never sicken of the blood.

"It seems he has an endless supply of ships and battle droids," said Mace, grimacing. "Clearly he and Dooku have been planning this war for months. Who knows, perhaps *years*. We're desperately playing catch-up while this self-styled general and his army stay three easy steps ahead of us at every turn."

"Be careful," Yoda warned him sharply. "Despair a Jedi should not feel."

Mace stared, startled. Then he nodded. "Forgive me, Master. You're right. With everything that's happened I was allowing myself to feel . . . overwhelmed."

Yoda considered him. Mace was courageous often to the point of madness. Fierce, dedicated, disciplined, and obstinate in the face of defeat. To see him despondent was chilling.

"Recover Obi-Wan will, Master Windu," he said. "Dwell on his hurts you must not. Distractions we cannot afford. Not when Grievous we must defeat."

For a moment Mace said nothing. Then he lifted his gaze. "Don't you find it alarming that Obi-Wan wasn't able to sense trouble before the explosions? When was the last time you can remember a Jedi blindly walking into something like that? You *can't*. It doesn't happen, Yoda. Not without interference. Whoever this Darth Sidious is, whatever mask he wears to walk among us, his influence is growing. The confusion of the dark side is growing. It's spreading like poison. Obi-Wan Kenobi is one of our best. If *he* can't see clearly . . ."

Yoda said nothing. Students had to find their own way.

"I'm sorry, Yoda," Mace said, at last. "It's just . . . to the Jedi Knights and Padawans, even to the other Masters and Council members, I am the solemn and wise Mace Windu. Nothing disrupts my calm. No danger disturbs me. But I am a man, as well as a Jedi. Here, alone with you, I can admit the truth. I *must* admit it. *I am afraid.*"

"Then release your fears, Mace Windu," Yoda retorted. "You know the mantra. You know the truth. Fear leads to anger."

"To hate, then to suffering," said Mace, nodding. "It leaves us vulnerable to the dark side. Yes. I know. And I know I have to control my emotions. Especially now, with the dark side surrounding us. I am trying, Yoda, I am—"

"Ha!" said Yoda, and slapped his meditation pad. *"Do or do not!"*

"There is no try," Mace finished, with a wry smile. "You're right." He rubbed a hand over his face. "I'm weary. It's no excuse, but I am."

He looked it. Ever since Geonosis he had pushed himself to his limits. Left those limits behind and kept on brutally pushing. He felt the pain of every lost and wounded Jedi. Every Republic defeat was a stab wound through his heart. Despite his own severe self-discipline, Yoda worried for him.

If rest he does not, kill him this war will without spilling a single drop of his blood.

"Your mentor I have been, Mace," he said gently. "Your friend I am now. To your fears you must not surrender. The dark side this is, attacking you. Fight it you must, for need you we do. Need you *I* do. Defeat the dark side alone I cannot."

Mace breathed in deeply, then let out the breath in a slow, shuddering sigh. "You're not alone, Yoda, and you never will be. I will *never* let the dark side win." He sat up straight, fresh purpose in his face. "Grievous is a slippery customer. If we chase him, we're more likely to lose him. We're going to have to get him to come to us. If we blockade the Bothan system . . . broadcast our presence there . . ."

Yoda pursed his lips, considering that. "A lure, you would make of our people?"

"It's risky, I know," said Mace. "But Grievous is arrogant. If we dare him to come after us . . ."

"Resist temptation he might not. A bold plan this is, Master Windu."

"Bold and risky. But we've been on the defensive long enough. It's time we took the fight to him." More wry amusement lit Mace's strained face. "Even if it's in a sneaky, backhanded way."

"Made his move upon Bothawui, Grievous has not," Yoda murmured. "Ready to attack it he might not yet be. Your plan could force his hand to our advantage."

Mace shook his head, his momentary enthusiasm dimming. "The only problem is, we're already fighting Separatist fires on too many fronts. Our resources are at their limits."

Yoda stroked his chin. "Three new cruisers at the shipyards of Allanteen Six, there are."

"Earmarked to patrol the Mid Rim, yes," said Mace. "Once Ki-Adi-Mundi comes home."

"No. Deploy them instead to protect Bothawui, we must."

"Under whose command?" said Mace, frowning. "Neither of us can go, we're needed here, and we can't spare anyone from their current campaigns. As for Obi-Wan, even with our best healers working on him he won't be fit enough for at least—" Sudden understanding dawned, and his spine snapped even straighter. "*Ana-*

kin? Yoda, I don't think so. He may be the Chosen One, but that doesn't make him ready to command a battle group."

Yoda swallowed a sigh. Mace might be right, but this was war. There was no such thing as the ideal time for a promotion. "Acquit himself well on Christophsis and Teth, young Skywalker did. Allow his past on Tatooine to interfere with his mission there he did not. Matured he has."

Mace snorted. "I noticed precious little maturity in him when he spoke to the Council earlier."

"Worry for Obi-Wan that was. Disappoint us Anakin Sky-walker will not."

Mace unfolded from his meditation pad and restlessly paced the small chamber. "Yoda, are you sure?"

"Sure?" Half closing his eyes, Yoda sought in the Force for some sense of rightness about this decision. Fought his way past the pall of the dark side to the still-light place wherein he'd dwelled most of his long, eventful life. "Sure of anything can anyone be in these troubled times?" He shook his head. "Right, I think I am. But before a final decision I make, speak to his former Master I will."

Swinging around from the shaded window, Mace stared at him. "Now? Yoda, he's not strong enough. You heard what Vokara Che said. He nearly died."

"Nearly is nearly, Mace," said Yoda, and with a grunt got to his feet. "Strong enough he will be. Know, does Obi-Wan Kenobi, that desperate times these are."

Mace nodded slowly. It was almost a bow. "Whatever you think is best, Master."

There was no *best* about any of this. There was only what they could do at any given moment.

Yoda summoned his hoverchair and went to see Obi-Wan.

EIGHT

THE AFTERMATH OF DEEP HEALING WAS AN ODD SENSATION.
Floaty. Disconnected. An almost unpleasant feeling of being adrift.
There was pain, or an echo of pain, somewhere nearby. Hazy memories shifted behind his closed eyes, like cloud-shadows dancing
over an empty meadow.

*Explosions. Flames leaping. Shock. An impact. Falling . . .
falling . . . in slow motion. Watching the rooftop coming closer and
closer, no hope of avoiding it. Oh dear, this is going to hurt rather
a lot, isn't it? And then darkness, reaching for him. Sucking him
down. Swallowing him alive. Death, beckoning. No . . . no . . . not
yet. Not now. I'm too busy. Another time.*

Despite the pain, despite the drifting, he thrashed feebly on his
rooftop. It felt soft now, which was wrong. And there was silence.
That was wrong. Where were the sirens? Where was the screaming?
Hadn't it been noisy?

Where am I?

"Be still you must, Obi-Wan," said an imperious, familiar
voice. "Or scolded by Master Vokara Che will you be."

His eyelids were dreadfully heavy. Someone had turned them to lead. But he found the strength to drag them open, because Yoda was here. Wherever *here* was.

"Master," he whispered, and was shocked to hear his voice so thin, so insubstantial. Squinting against the mellow light, he let his gaze roam around him. Saw pale walls. A high ceiling. Smelled sweet incense in the warm air. Nonsense resolved itself into sense.

Oh. That's right. I'm in the Halls of Healing. I was only here a few weeks ago . . . and now I'm back? How very inefficient of me.

"Speak do not, Obi-Wan," said Yoda firmly, in his hoverchair by the bed. "Listen instead."

Obi-Wan nodded, cautiously. Something was niggling at him, something important. "Yes, Master. But Master—"

"Fret you must not," said Yoda. "Dexter Jettster's message we have heard."

Message? There was a message? His memory was fragmented, splinters scattered here and there. A single word. *Bothawui.* Fear. Urgency. Dex's tense, unhappy face. *Grievous. Grievous. Grievous is coming.*

Horrified, he tried to sit up. Cried out instead as his mended body protested. The healing chamber disappeared in waves of bright and blinding pain.

"*Be still,* Obi-Wan!" Yoda commanded. "A relapse do you desire?"

There was no time to be still. Bothawui's time was running out. "Master, we must defend the Bothans," he said, his teeth gritted as he struggled to banish weakness. "Assign me a battle group. Let me take it to the Bothan system, let me—"

"*No*," said Yoda, leaning close, one small hard hand pushing him flat to the mattress. His face was stern, his gaze piercing. Centuries of authority blazed in his eyes. "Finished healing you have not. Young Skywalker a battle group will lead to Bothawui."

Anakin? In charge of a *battle group*? No—no—it was too soon, it was too much to ask of him, too great a burden to place on such young shoulders. The danger was too great. *They can't choose Anakin.*

"Obi-Wan," said Yoda, and poked his healed shoulder with a finger. "Remember our talk of attachment, hmmm? Let go of your fears for Anakin you must. Look at him as a Jedi Knight you must. Not your Padawan. Not the boy you knew, and trained, and protected. A man he is now. *Look at the man.*"

The man who had overcome his crippling injury. Put aside love for the sake of duty. Triumphed on Christophsis and Tatooine. The man who was born to bring balance to the Force. The man whose potential was unmatched in Temple history. The man whose sheer brilliance was growing daily.

"Mistaken am I, Obi-Wan?" Yoda asked softly. "The wrong man is Anakin Skywalker, to battle General Grievous?"

Wrong? No. No. Not wrong. But—

You always knew this day would come. All this means is that it's come a little sooner.

"No, Master Yoda," he said. "You're not mistaken. He's grown since Geonosis. Since his mistake in rushing to face Dooku. He's more settled. More self-controlled. His focus is where it belongs now. He's learned to let go of his attachments. If anyone can take down that monster Grievous, it's Anakin."

Yoda's eyes closed. His head dipped. He sighed.

"Then lead a battle group to Bothawui, young Skywalker will." He produced a datapad from a pocket in his hoverchair and tossed it onto the bed. "The mission details, these are. Tell him you can, when allowed to visit you he is."

"Yes, Master," Obi-Wan whispered. His eyes closed, against his will. And then he felt the gentle touch of a small, ancient hand, lightly skimming over his head as he slid toward sleep.

"Rest, Obi-Wan," said Yoda. "For need you at full strength our suffering Republic does."

"A battle group?" said Palpatine, hands neatly folded on his desk. "To the Bothan system? Why? Has something happened, Master Yoda, of which I haven't been made aware?"

He watched closely as Yoda considered his reply, the garish night-lights of Coruscant flickering over his wrinkled face. The stench of the light side in him was enough to make a man vomit.

How I long for the day when I can squash this disgusting little creature. The dark side willing it will be soon, now. Very soon.

"Intelligence have we received," said Yoda. "A whisper of trouble. Against Bothawui a threat is made . . . by General Grievous."

Palpatine permitted himself to reveal horror. Inside he felt a nasty sting. How had the Jedi learned of this? Someone, somewhere, would have to be punished. "And you'd deploy a whole battle group on the strength of a whisper?"

"Yes, Chancellor. A chance to vanquish Grievous this is."

Well, that was hardly what he wanted to hear. Grievous was proving more useful with each passing day. Slaughtering Jedi and clones with gleeful abandon. Obliterating whole townships. Sowing misery and discord wherever he went.

If Dooku hadn't found him, I'd have been forced to invent him.

"I see," he said gravely. "Then it's no wonder you wanted a private meeting, Master Yoda. With terrorists in the administration precincts, we must not risk this news leaking. I congratulate the Jedi on their efficient intelligence network. But do we have ships to spare for this mission? I rather thought we were pressed."

"We do," said Yoda. "From Allanteen Six they will arrive tomorrow."

Then he would have to arrange some kind of unfortunate accident. A tiny spot of sabotage that would destroy the cruisers on their way to Bothawui, and subsequently be traced back to the shipyards. The resulting recriminations and investigations, not to mention the loss of morale, would slow cruiser production significantly, thus hampering the Republic's efforts to bring the Separatists to their knees.

For the war must continue. The Republic's not nearly weak enough yet. And as for Grievous . . . he's not done serving me.

It amused him to think such things with Yoda standing mere feet away. Standing there sublimely oblivious to the enemy under his nose. The Jedi were so arrogant, so self-important, so drunk on the sense of their own superiority—none more so than their beloved Yoda.

But your domination of the galaxy is in its dying days, my puny friend. In time . . . in so little time . . . I will snuff out the light.

"Supreme Chancellor?" said Yoda.

"Forgive me," he said wearily. "It's been a hectic day. Another full session of the Senate, and it's not long ended." He frowned. "I'm afraid there's been some agitation. Questions raised as to how much longer the fighting will continue."

"Doing everything within our power we are, Chancellor, to end this destructive conflict," said Yoda, pricked—as intended—by the gentle complaint. The subtly implied criticism.

It's the slow drip of water that wears away the stone. Thus are the foundations of any edifice undermined. Sudden onslaughts inspire heroic defenses . . . but nobody notices a constant, whispering trickle. Not until the house falls down.

"Oh, I know, Master Yoda," he said, exquisitely sympathetic. "I completely understand. And I did explain to the Senators just how hard the Jedi are trying to achieve victory." He smiled. "We must hope that this time, at Bothawui, you succeed in defeating that dreadful Grievous and end his rampage of terror. Tell me, who have you chosen to lead the charge against him? Not Master Kenobi, by any chance?"

Say yes. Say yes, little toad. That would be such an elegant solution. And I could eliminate Organa at some other time.

"No. Lead the battle group Anakin Skywalker will."

Anakin? Staring, Palpatine felt an unpleasant, unaccustomed emotion. *Surprise.* "Well. What a singular honor."

And I did not see it coming.

How . . . disconcerting. And how unwelcome the news. Anakin pitted against Grievous? What were the Jedi thinking? Yes, he'd acquitted himself well in his last mission, but even so. To give him command of a battle group was folly.

He's not ripe yet. He's not ready to be plucked. These Jedi fools will waste him. They will waste him, and he's mine.

"Master Yoda . . ." He steepled his fingers. "Are you quite certain young Anakin is ready for such a task?"

"Yes," said Yoda flatly.

And that was a lie. Yoda was a master at masking his emotions, but not even he could hide them from the greatest Sith Lord ever known. He was worried . . . and backed into a corner.

"I see," Palpatine said. "Well, I only hope, for all our sakes, you're not asking too much of Anakin too soon."

From the look on his face, Yoda didn't relish his decision being questioned. Nobody crossed him these days, that was his trouble. The Jedi bowed and scraped before him, choking on their flattery.

Not that I'm complaining. It makes him so much easier to deceive.

"Ready for the challenge young Skywalker is," pronounced Yoda. "Have faith in him the Jedi Council does."

"As do I, Master Yoda. Thank you for keeping me apprised of this crucial development. Naturally, given the extremely sensitive nature of the mission, I shall keep its details to myself. And I would count it as a personal favor if you made sure to tell me how Anakin is faring."

"Apprised we will keep you, Supreme Chancellor," said Yoda, taking his leave. At last.

Once he was alone, Palpatine activated his holointercom. "See that I'm not disturbed again for *any* reason," he told Mas Amedda. "I shall tell you when I am available again."

"Of course, Supreme Chancellor," Mas Amedda said, bowing. Then his image winked out.

Palpatine swiveled his chair until he faced his office's transparisteel wall. Normal traffic flow had not yet been restored to the administration sector. That strange gap in the sky continued, exaggerated now that night was fallen, further unsettling the people of Coruscant. He could feel their dismay seething, their fears building, their confidence eroding: a bouquet like fine wine upon his palate.

Then the bouquet soured slightly. Destroying the battle group was obviously out of the question now. Ah well. Never mind. As Yoda was so tediously fond of saying: *Always in motion the future is.* He'd have to adjust his plans, that was all. It wouldn't be the first time, nor would it be the last. In the larger scheme of things it made no difference. Now or later, Kenobi *would* die. And the Republic would fall. He had foreseen it.

On the *other* hand . . .

Perhaps I should merely cripple the cruisers. Scuttle the Bothawui mission entirely. For if there's even the slightest chance of losing Anakin to Grievous . . . or Grievous to him . . .

Guaranteed his privacy, he plunged his consciousness into the dark side. Searched the shifting matrix of the future . . . sifted possible from probable . . . likely outcomes from unlikely . . . seeking, seeking, always seeking . . .

When at length he emerged from his trance, he was smiling. Anakin would not destroy Grievous at Bothawui. Neither would he perish by the creature's hand. No, thanks to this new assignment his secret apprentice would merely grow in stature, in speed, and in breathtaking skill, never once suspecting whom and what he truly served. As for Grievous, he—it—would continue on its bloodthirsty way, cutting a swath through the ranks of the Jedi. The war would continue, slowly but surely unraveling the Republic. Laying it to waste, for his delectation.

Equally important, the dark side had shown him how to rid himself of Kenobi and that stalwart fool, Organa. A nudge here. A string pulled there. Pathetic friendships, so easily exploited. Trust and loyalty, the currency of weaklings. And best of all, the instrument of their destruction already existed. He hardly needed to lift a finger. An ancient planet, hidden and safeguarded by the Sith for centuries. A sarlacc of space, hungry for Jedi prey.

Retrieving his Sith robe and holotransmitter, he transformed into Darth Sidious and contacted Dooku.

"Darth Tyranus, the opportunity to eliminate two important enemies has arisen."

Dooku bowed. *"That is good news, Master. How can I serve?"*

"The infiltration of Bail Organa's private intelligence network. It holds?"

"Yes, Master. Of course."

"Then contact your agent. I have information for our dupe of Alderaan. Information that will lead him and Obi-Wan Kenobi to their doom."

Dooku's hologram chuckled. *"What a tragedy, Master."*

The fool was overconfident. He imagined himself an equal. "The tragedy will be yours, Tyranus, if you should fail," Sidious snapped, with a sting of the dark side, and smiled to see how Dooku cringed. "Now, my apprentice, pay very close attention . . ."

"Anakin . . . ," said a soft female voice. A gentle hand touched his shoulder. "Anakin, wake up."

He opened his eyes, leapt from slumber to wakefulness within a heartbeat. Not his mother. Vokara Che. "Yes, Master."

The Temple's leading healer was smiling. "Master Kenobi is awake, Anakin. It's very late, but you may visit with him briefly."

Beside him, Ahsoka stirred, then uncurled in her chair. Like him, she had the knack of instant alertness. It was a Jedi thing, but also owed something to their particular backgrounds: his as a slave, hers as a Togruta. Whatever the reason, it came in handy.

He glanced at her, a warning to keep quiet, no comments about how long they'd been waiting. Then he nodded at Vokara Che. "Yes, Master. Thank you. Before I see him, is there anything I should know? Anything I should prepare for?"

"A perceptive question, Anakin," said Vokara Che, warm with approval. "He is mended well enough . . . but as you know, the body has its own wisdom. Recovery cannot be rushed."

As if he needed the reminder. Even now, after time and so much healing, he sometimes felt pain in the arm Dooku had taken. And there was pain of a different kind, too. Touch, the simple sensation of flesh to flesh, was so important. Yes, delicate sensors in the prosthetic limb fed pseudo-sensations to his brain, but it wasn't the same. *He* wasn't the same. And a part of him would always know that . . . and grieve for what he'd lost. Even though they all told him, those superior Jedi on the Council, that he was wrong for feeling cheated and deprived.

Oh, how he resented their smug assurance. The Supreme Chancellor was right: sometimes the Jedi were so stupid. Not that Palpatine had ever come right out and said as much. But he'd come close once or twice, exclaiming over some slight or criticism shared with him out of lonely desperation.

When you lose the ability to touch the woman you love with both hands, Masters, then you can advise me on how I should feel. But since that'll never happen, I wish you'd keep your ignorant opinions to yourselves.

"Anakin?" said Vokara Che. Her head-tails were twitching. Dedicated healers were the most sensitive Jedi of all. She could feel his disquiet, the fear and resentment that too often simmered so close to his surface. "You must not concern yourself. Obi-Wan will recover fully in time. Come with me now, so he can tell you for himself."

With a deep-breathing effort he banished every emotion but relief. "Yes, Master." Turning, he nodded at his Padawan. "Wait here for me, Ahsoka. I won't be long."

Ahsoka nodded, sitting bolt-upright and alert. "Yes, Master Skywalker," she said. She sounded positively chirpy.

She thinks I don't realize when she's twisting my tail. Ah well, she'll learn soon enough. I wonder if two hundred repetitions of Niman form level one will give her the hint?

Ahsoka's bright expression dimmed, just a little bit. "Master? What's so funny?"

"Nothing," he said. "Mind your manners. I'll be back soon."

He followed Vokara Che out of the peaceful waiting chamber, with its soft blue lighting, its calm pink walls and deep blue carpets, to the place where they were keeping Obi-Wan.

It wasn't the same room he'd been made to call home.

Standing before its closed door, Vokara Che raised a warning finger. "No excitement, Anakin. Don't let him become agitated. Satisfy yourself that he is indeed recovered and come away. Since you're the one who found him, you must know he has had a lucky escape."

Oh yes. He knew. "I will, Master Vokara Che," he promised. "Thank you."

With a searching look and a sharp nod, she departed. He tugged his tunic straight, pressed the door release, and entered the room. It was discreetly lit, so as not to distress its occupant. There was a window looking out to the city, but its blind was drawn. No bustling nightlife for the convalescent.

Obi-Wan was in bed, propped up by a mountain of pillows. His hair and beard were neatly ordered and blood-free. That made a nice change. The wicked gash on his cheek had vanished, leaving behind it a thin pink line. The rest of his face was untroubled, but too pale. From the chest down his body was smothered in blankets, but to all outward appearances he was most definitely whole again. There was a datapad on the nightstand beside him. If he was reading, he really must be better.

Obi-Wan smiled. "Anakin."

"Master," he replied, then walked softly to the chair beside the bed and sat down. "You know, we really have to stop meeting like this."

"I couldn't agree more," said Obi-Wan with a breath of laughter.

"So. What was the damage?"

"Various bumps and bruises," Obi-Wan replied evasively. "A bit of scorching. A cut here and there."

Anakin sat back, arms folded, one eyebrow skeptically raised. *"And?"*

"And really, there is no need to make a fuss," said Obi-Wan, shifting uncomfortably. "I hardly think I look at death's door. Do you?"

"Not now you don't," Anakin agreed. "But then, everyone knows Master Vokara Che is a genius. So—what else?"

It was almost comical to see the vaunted Master Kenobi wriggling like a tiska-worm on a hook. "Concussion," he mumbled. "Broken hand. Broken leg. Broken shoulder. Cracked pelvis. Four broken ribs and a punctured lung. One or two internal organs jostled a bit."

"Is *that* all?" Anakin snorted. "And to think I thought it was actually *serious*. That should teach me to overreact."

Obi-Wan gave him a fulminating look.

"Sorry," Anakin said, grinning. "That doesn't work on me anymore."

"Did it ever?" Obi-Wan retorted. Then he sighed. "I'm fine, Anakin. Truly. Thanks to you."

Suddenly it wasn't something he could joke about anymore. "You're welcome, Obi-Wan. Please . . . just . . . don't do anything like that again."

"You mean ride a citibike at speed headfirst into an exploding terrorist bomb?" said Obi-Wan. "Well, I'll certainly do my best. Repeating oneself becomes tedious, after all."

"That's one word for it."

Silence, as they shared a wry grin.

"I made sure Master Yoda got your message," Anakin said at last. "I don't know if they believed it, but—"

"Oh yes," said Obi-Wan, sobering. "They believed it, Anakin. They're sending a battle group to intercept Grievous at Bothawui. Admiral Yularen has been appointed the ranking Republic military official, transferring from the *Spirit of the Republic*. Your flagship will be the *Resolute*. It's one of three newly commissioned cruisers."

What? His what? "I'm sorry. Did you say *my flagship*?"

There was no trace of amusement in Obi-Wan now. His expression was watchful; his eyes were guarded. "Yes."

Anakin stared at him. *If I didn't know better, I'd say he was afraid.* "That can't be right. I've only just been made a Jedi Knight. I'm not ready to—"

"Then get ready," said Obi-Wan. "You're leaving as soon as those ships arrive. You, and your Padawan, and as many clone pilots and troops as we can spare. Given its sensitivity, the mission's been classified at the highest level of security. The Supreme Chancellor's being privately briefed by Master Yoda. No one else in the government will be told. Not until it's over, one way or another." He frowned, his tension humming through the Force. "I can't possibly overemphasize the importance of this mission, Anakin. For the first time since the war started, we have the element of surprise. We may never get it again. This could be our only chance to take down Grievous once and for all."

Anakin's heart was pounding so hard he thought *he* might end up with broken ribs. "Yularen. He's a good man. Who'll command the other two cruisers?"

"The Council hasn't decided yet."

Hopefully no one likely to get bent out of shape because wet-behind-the-ears Anakin Skywalker was the Jedi in charge. "And Rex? Do I get Captain Rex?"

"If you want him."

Oh, I want him all right. Rex and the 501st are mine. "Yes. Please."

"Then you'll be happy to know he's on standby," said Obi-Wan. "Captain Rex and his men will be ready to ship out when you are."

"So you knew I'd want him?"

A brief smile. A shrug. "Of course. Don't tell me you're surprised. I know *you,* remember?"

Yes. Yes, Obi-Wan did. Not as well as he thought, but well enough. Still shocked by this unexpected news, Anakin sat back in his chair and stared at the black glove covering his prosthetic hand.

Why me? Master Yoda and the others don't really trust me. They never have. Since Qui-Gon, Obi-Wan's the only Jedi who's stood up for me against the Council.

He looked up again. "This command should be yours, Master. You've got the experience, you've got the—"

"Concussion, broken hand, broken leg, and so on," said Obi-Wan, impatient. "Or I did have a few hours ago. I'm not fit, Anakin. I won't *be* fit for days. At least not fit enough to safely endure battle stress. And there's a good chance Bothawui doesn't have days. For all we know Grievous is bearing down on the Both system as we speak."

"We still don't have a fix on his location?"

"No," said Obi-Wan. "And we don't dare ask the Bothans in case they've been compromised. That means we're flying blind on this one, Anakin."

Anakin grinned. He couldn't help it. Exultation was swiftly overtaking doubt. *A battle group of my very own. Yes!* "That's fine by me. Flying blind is what I do best."

Obi-Wan didn't return the grin. Instead he sat forward, his eyes anxious. "This isn't a joking matter, Anakin! The fate of the Republic could rest on this mission. We *can't* lose Bothawui to Grievous and Dooku. Countless lives in the Bothan system are depending on you. Was the battle at the Teth monastery amusing? All the clone troops who died there, all of Rex's men—was losing them funny?"

Stung, Anakin pushed to his feet. "No! Of course it wasn't."

"Then take this seriously!"

"I am taking it seriously," he retorted, indignant. "I know exactly how important this mission is, Master."

The room's soft lighting showed a fresh sheen of sweat on Obi-Wan's pale face. "Do you, Anakin? Do you really? I hope so, for all our sakes. I hope—"

Frustrated, Anakin swung about, feeling the servos in his prosthetic hand pulse as its fingers clenched. "You don't think I can do this, do you? Despite Christophsis you still see me as a kid, your apprentice. Snot-nosed Anakin who can't be trusted to get the job done."

"Oh, don't be ridiculous," snapped Obi-Wan, breathing heavily. "That's your own fear talking, Anakin. You'd best defeat it before it defeats you."

"I'm *not* afraid!" Anakin snapped back. "I know I can do this. I know I'm ready. I've changed. I'm not that greenie anymore, the Padawan who let himself get caught out twice on Geonosis." He held up his gloved hand, clenched to a fist. "*Trust* me, Obi-Wan, I learned my lesson!"

"You learned *that* lesson, yes!" said Obi-Wan, blankets twisted in his fingers. "But it doesn't mean you know everything yet, Anakin. You're still young, there are still many things you must—"

The rest of his lecture was lost in a gasp. Appalled, Anakin saw his former Master's face drain dead-white. Saw the sheen of sweat on him transform to a drenching. Felt pain explode through Obi-Wan like random, vicious Sith lightning.

"Master!" he exclaimed, and leapt for the bed.

Obi-Wan curled onto his side, knees snapped to his chest, teeth sunk into his lower lip. Anakin took hold of his shoulders and held him against the cruel, racking shudders.

"I'm sorry," he muttered, as Obi-Wan shook. "I shouldn't have shouted. I didn't mean what I said. You're right, I've still got a lot to learn—from *you*, Obi-Wan. Nobody else has the patience to teach me. No other Jedi understands the way you do. Hang on . . . hang on . . ."

The chamber's door slid open and Vokara Che entered like a whirlwind. "*What is going on here?* Anakin Skywalker, I told you not to agitate him! What did you say to him? *What have you done?*"

"Nothing," said Obi-Wan, through chattering teeth. "He's done nothing. It's not his fault. Anakin—"

"I'm here, I'm sorry, I—"

"Stand back, you wretch!" snapped Vokara Che, ruthlessly shoving him aside, as fierce as he had ever seen her. Fiercer than he would have thought possible for such a gentle being. "Get out of my way!"

Stunned to silent obedience Anakin retreated, watching as Vokara Che pressed a dull green healing crystal to Obi-Wan's chest. Then he felt a massive surge in the Force, heat and light and Vokara Che's will combined. The crystal pulsed, bright as an emerald sun. Slowly, resentfully, Obi-Wan's pain surrendered.

"There," said Vokara Che, gentle again, her face and voice soothing. As familiar now as she'd been a stranger moments before. "There, you foolish Jedi. Be at peace, Master Kenobi. Be still. Sleep."

Obi-Wan sighed, the sound almost a groan. "Anakin."

"He's gone," she said firmly, darting a glare in Anakin's direction. "You can rest."

Frowning, Obi-Wan rolled his head on the pillows. "No—no—"

Ignoring Vokara Che's reawakened anger, Anakin slipped around to the other side of the bed and took Obi-Wan's hand in a firm clasp. "I'm not gone, Master. I'm here."

Obi-Wan dragged open his eyes. They were dull, improperly focused. "You're to meet with the Council first thing in the morning." His voice was a grating whisper. "Final instructions. Be polite. Don't gloat."

Anakin nodded. "Yes, Master."

Obi-Wan was fighting to remain conscious. "You can defeat Grievous, Anakin. I know it. *Never* doubt my faith in you."

Frightened, he stared into Obi-Wan's bloodless face. *Echoes of his mother . . . her final, pain-racked words . . .* "I won't. I don't. Master—"

He nearly leapt out of his skin when Vokara Che touched his shoulder across the narrow bed. "He's not dying, Anakin," the healer said with rough sympathy. "He's exhausted. You've exhausted him. Now *leave*."

There was nothing he could say to that. No protest he could make that wouldn't be wrong, or selfish. He let go of Obi-Wan and turned for the door . . .

. . . where Ahsoka was standing, her thin, childish face shocked.

"Time to go," he told her. "Come on."

NINE

He left the Healing Halls without once looking back, Ahsoka trotting silent and uncertain by his side.

"Master Skywalker . . . Skyguy," she ventured at last, in a whisper, as they took a swift-tube to the Temple's Archives. "What's going on?"

He glanced down at her. "We've got a mission."

"I . . . kind of worked that out already. We're going after Grievous, right?"

He nodded. "Right."

She swallowed. "Alone? I mean, just you and me?"

"You, me, Captain Rex, a bunch of clone pilots and troopers and three Jedi cruisers." Another glance down. "Ours is called the *Resolute*."

"A battle group?" gasped Ahsoka. "We've got a battle group of our very own?"

He rapped his knuckles on top of her head. "*I've* got a battle group. You get to tag along, if you behave yourself."

As the swift-tube thundered its way up Tranquillity Spire, Ahsoka jittered on her feet, a kind of nervous little dance. "Is Master Obi-Wan coming with us?"

Obi-Wan. His dreadful pain. *Never doubt my faith in you.* "No."

"He looked bad. Will he be all right?"

"Of course," he said, with quick confidence. "No Separatist terrorist can kill Obi-Wan."

"Do you believe that, Skyguy?" she said, her voice small. "Or are you just saying it because you're scared, and you want to feel better?"

Jaw dropped, he stared at her. *Where does she come up with this stuff?* "I believe it, Padawan," he said repressively. "I never say anything I don't believe."

The swift-tube slid to a smooth stop, and its doors opened. The Jedi Archives occupied almost a third of Tranquillity Spire. He'd directed their swift-tube to the main entrance and reference carrels, where the data crystal catalogs were kept. Their arrival was noted by various Jedi who were diligently working on projects of their own, but nobody interrupted their tasks to speak with them.

"Here," said Anakin, guiding Ahsoka to an empty desk. "I'll get you started, and then I'm going to leave you for a while."

Sliding into the seat, she pulled a face. "You're always going off somewhere, Skyguy. When do I get to come?"

"You don't," he said curtly. "Now pay attention."

She heaved a resigned sigh and watched as he accessed the primary Archive database, then engaged the privacy mode with his personal key. This way only the Council would see which archives had been accessed . . . and that was all right. They were in on the secret.

After what happened with the records on Kamino, and today's terrorist attack, I'm not taking any chances.

"Master!" Ahsoka squeaked, as the primary directory guide to Bothawui came on screen. She straightened out of her morose slump. "Is that where Gr—"

"Not a word," he told her, and tightened warning fingers on her shoulder. "Now, I want everything on our destination that you can dredge up, ready for me to look at when I get back. Okay?"

She was hyperalert again, all her instincts firing. One of these millennia she'd make a pretty good Jedi, probably. Provided he could smooth the rough edges off her.

"Yes, Master," she said. "You can trust me."

He frowned down at her. *Was I ever this young? Was this how I used to look to Obi-Wan?* He doubted it. Slaves lost their innocence while they were still in the cradle. "Good girl," he said, and patted her on the back. "I won't be gone long." *More's the pity.* "If anyone asks what you're doing, tell them to see me."

She nodded. "Yes, Master."

Satisfied she couldn't go too far wrong here in the Archives, he took an airspeeder from the Temple docking complex and flirted with disaster all the way to Padmé's apartment.

"Oh, Master Anakin! How wonderful to see you!" C-3PO said, tottering out on to the apartment's veranda. "Look, Artoo-Detoo! Master Anakin's here!"

Behind him, at the apartment's open sliding transparisteel doors, the stubby blue astromech droid tooted and spun his dome.

Anakin stared at them. Threepio could be effusive, and usually was, he knew that, but—"Okay. What's wrong?"

But before the droid could answer, Padmé emerged from her bedroom. When she saw him on the platform, her strained face crumpled and she held out her arms. *"Anakin!"*

Cursing, he shoved past 3PO and nearly sent R2-D2 tumbling in his desperation to reach her. "What is it? What's happened?"

She didn't answer, just tightened her arms around him as though one of them were dying. Her breathing was ragged, her pulse erratic. He could feel her heart pounding against his chest. And now that she was in his arms, now that he was breathing in her subtle perfume, he could feel, too, the depths of her distress.

"I'm sorry," he murmured. He'd been so worried about Obi-Wan, angered by the Council, overwhelmed by the news of Bothawui, the battle group. An emotional cacophony had deafened him to the voice inside that whispered of Padmé whenever she was near. "I'm sorry, my love. I should've known you were upset."

She shook her head, then leaned back to look up at him. "No. No. I'm all right. How's Obi-Wan?"

"Recovering," he said. "Padmé, you're not all right. What's happened? Tell me. Whatever it is, I'll fix it."

"Oh, Anakin . . ." She pressed her smooth palm against his cheek, then stood on tiptoe to kiss him. "I love you so much."

"And I love you. But you're making me cross. *What's happened?*"

Taking his hand, she led him over to the sofa and pulled him down beside her. "Nothing's happened. Not exactly. It's just . . . Palpatine took me and Bail Organa on a tour of the bomb sites." She shuddered. "They were awful. And after that, Bail and I visited some of the injured in the medcenters. That was even worse. Men, women, and children—humans and Twi'leks and Chalactans and Sullustans and, oh, a dozen other species. All maimed and disfigured, in so much pain . . . and for *what*? For *nothing*! For going about their lives harming *no one*, Anakin. Not a one of them could ever threaten a Separatist, but the Separatists hurt them anyway. It was Naboo all over again." Her voice broke, and she hid her face against his shoulder. "I can't bear it. And I can't see the end of it. Sometimes I think this war will go on until every last one of us has drowned in blood."

"No, it won't," he said, holding her. "The Jedi won't let it. *I* won't let it. We'll stop the killing, Padmé. I promise you. We'll stop it." His arms tightened. "What was Palpatine thinking? Those bomb sites weren't safe. There could've been more explosions. He never should have taken you to them. You shouldn't have had to see any of it, you shouldn't have—"

She pulled away. *"Don't."*

"What?" Puzzled, he stared at her. "Don't what? What do you mean?"

"Don't diminish me, Anakin," she said, and smeared her

cheeks dry with one unsteady hand. "Don't think that because I'm upset, because I turn to you for comfort, that it means I'm weak or incapable of carrying out my duties."

"I'm not! I don't think that!"

"No?" Now her eyes were challenging. "Are you sure?"

He had no hope of hiding anything from her. "Okay, so I want to protect you. What's wrong with that? You're my *wife*, Padmé. I love you and I'll do anything to keep you safe. Is that a crime?"

She kissed him, a swift sweet pressure of her lips on his. "No. Of course not. But I'm not just your wife, Anakin. I'm a Republic Senator. I don't have the right to hide from the truth, no matter how brutal and ugly it is."

He frowned. "And what is the truth?"

"That our only hope of winning this war was not letting it start in the first place." She punched him gently on the chest. "Anakin, I hated every second of that tour this morning, and I hated seeing what those bomb blasts did to their victims. But I'm not sorry I saw it. I don't wish I hadn't gone. I'm heartbroken by the suffering and the waste. There's a difference. Do you understand that?"

Slowly, he nodded. "Yes. But do *you* understand what it does to me, seeing you cry over it? Don't you know that your pain is my pain? That it kills me, knowing you might've been in danger? Padmé, if anything happened to you I'd lose my mind!"

She took his flesh-and-blood hand and held it. "Oh, Anakin. Don't be silly. We are going to grow old together, my love. Well . . ." She pulled a comical face. "Almost. Since I'm five years your senior, I'm actually going to grow old first. But the *point* is that we—"

He pressed his black-gloved fingers to her mouth. "No," he whispered. "The point is that without you, Padmé, I'm *nothing*. Without you, Anakin Skywalker doesn't exist."

He watched her eyes widen and fill with tears. Watched those tears tremble on her lashes then fall to wet her pale cheeks. "Don't say that, Anakin. Don't ever say that."

"Why not? It's the truth."

She bit her lip as she struggled for composure. "Are you staying tonight?" Leaning forward, she rested her forehead against his. "Stay tonight," she whispered. "We'll exist in each other."

"I can't," he said, hating himself. "I can't even stay five more minutes. I have to get back to the Temple."

She drew away, her eyes abruptly bleak. "You're leaving."

"Yes. Bothawui's under threat from Grievous. I'm going to stop him. The mission's top secret—you can't let on you know." Despite his pain, he smiled. "Padmé, they've given me a battle group. My own cruiser. The *Resolute*."

"I see." She stood and wandered a few paces, to stare across the glittering cityscape. The droids had discreetly withdrawn. They were alone. "And Obi-Wan?"

"He's staying here. He was hurt pretty bad."

"Oh."

"But I will need Artoo."

"Yes," she said. "Of course."

He joined her. Slid his arms around her from behind. She didn't melt against him as she usually did. Instead she felt brittle. "My own command, Padmé. A chance, at last, to show the Council what I can do." She didn't answer. He tightened his embrace. "Aren't you pleased for me? Be pleased for me, my love."

"I want to," she said, her voice low. "But I'm too frightened."

"Don't be," he said, cajoling, and turned her to face him. "I'll be fine, I'll be—"

"*Anakin.*"

She was right. He was patronizing her. Humoring her, as though she were a child. "I'm sorry."

"Oh, my darling," she whispered. "Don't be sorry. Be careful. Come back."

He framed her face with his hands. "Always. I will *never* abandon you, Padmé."

They kissed, then, desperately . . . and held each other hard until he had to go.

The *Resolute* was a beautiful ship.

Standing with Master Yoda, Admiral Yularen, and battle-scarred Captain Rex, Ahsoka watched Anakin inspect the vessel's pristine bridge. No blaster burns. No scorch marks from shorted wiring. No war wounds at all . . . but of course, that would soon change. Soon they'd be crossing paths with General Grievous and his merciless army of battle droids.

She felt a tiny prickle of fright. *No, no, no. Don't think about that. We haven't even left orbit yet. There's plenty of time to think about that.*

She was excited . . . sort of . . . to be going into combat again. War was bad, of course. No sane sentient wanted it. But if there had to be fighting, at least she was fighting on the right side. Fighting against the forces of darkness. Fighting to protect everything the Jedi held dear—most especially the Republic.

If we're not prepared to fight for it, then we deserve to lose it.

So yes, their cause was just . . . but that didn't mean she couldn't die defending it. It didn't mean Anakin couldn't die. Lots of Jedi had died already. Again she felt that prickle of fright. Sent a desperate plea out to the Force.

Don't let him be one of them. Don't let me be the Padawan who gets the Chosen One killed.

Her Master's unguarded expression was tender as his gloved fingers trailed along every shiny, flat surface of his flagship's bridge: the long-range scanning station, comms, helm, tactical, atmospherics. A tall, athletic figure in unrelieved black, the faintest of smiles curving his lips. Oblivious to his audience, to the urgency of their mission, he communed in leisurely silence with the newly commissioned cruiser. As though they shared a telepathic conversation. As though the ship were whispering secrets in his ear.

Baffled, she marveled at him. *I'll never understand Skyguy. He loves machines like they're living, breathing creatures. I just don't get it. A ship is a tool, that's all it is. How can anyone love a tool? It's like saying you feel affection for a—a hydrospanner.*

Beside her, Master Yoda tapped his gimer stick to the deck. She didn't think he was annoyed with her Master, but it was hard to tell. Yoda was the biggest mystery she'd ever met. All she knew for certain was that though he was the most accomplished living Jedi, he wasn't so grand he couldn't feel tense, too.

"Anakin," he said.

Her Master turned, still smiling. "Master Yoda?"

"Satisfied are you that in order everything is?"

"Everything's perfect, Master," said Anakin, his smile widening to an unrestrained grin. "My compliments to the shipwrights. They've done a wonderful job."

"Then if satisfied you are, leave you I must," said Yoda. "And for the Bothan system you should depart."

Sobering quickly, Anakin clasped his hands behind his back and nodded. "Yes, Master."

"In constant communication with us you will remain, Anakin," said Yoda. "Your best judgment you must use, but take unnecessary risks you will not. Wily, Grievous is. Seek to distract you he will. Prepared you must be for his deceptions and feints. More than one battle you might have to fight."

Another respectful nod. "Yes, Master."

Yoda looked up at Admiral Yularen. "The importance of this mission you know, Admiral. Nothing else there is that I or the Council can tell you. May the Force be with you."

Yularen bowed. A soft-spoken and self-contained veteran who wasn't afraid to bite when he had to, he was the perfect counterweight to Anakin's fierce eagerness. "And with you, Master Yoda."

"Master . . ."

Yoda looked back at Anakin. "A final question you have?"

"A request," said Anakin. "When you next see Obi-Wan, please tell him I said thank you and—I won't let him down."

Ahsoka felt some of Yoda's tension ease. "Know that he does, Master Skywalker," he said, almost gently. "Know it as well does the Jedi Council."

She hadn't been Skyguy's apprentice for long, but it had taken very little time to figure out he and the Council bumped heads a *lot*. In fact, Padawan rumor had it he had stood up to them the very first time they met. Nine years old, and he was challenging the Jedi Council. Unbelievable. Did it matter to him now, to hear their endorsement of him? Did he care what they thought? Or was it only Obi-Wan's opinion that counted?

I don't know. I can't work it out. Sometimes he's as big a mystery as Yoda.

"Thank you, Master," said Anakin. Giving nothing away. "May the Force be with you."

Yoda nodded. "And with you. Farewell . . . and good hunting."

The ancient Jedi Master departed then, and the *Resolute*'s crew leapt to obey Admiral Yularen's clipped, succinct orders, preparing to break orbit. Anakin turned to Rex.

"Your troops are settled, Captain? And ready for the fray?"

Calm as always, his newly grown fuzz of blond hair bright under the bridge lights and his dented armor spotless, Rex nodded. "Yes, sir. They've adjusted well, and will do you proud."

Ahsoka felt a shiver of sorrow. They'd lost so many of the 501st at the Teth monastery. Replacement clones had been quickly assigned to the unit, but cohesion took time.

I hope these new men stay around longer. Losing people is too hard.

Anakin's solemn expression had eased. "I'm sure, Captain. Rex . . ."

"Sir?"

"I'm glad you're here. I wouldn't want to take on Grievous without you."

Rex didn't smile, because that wouldn't be proper. But his jet-black eyes warmed, and he nodded. "It's an honor to have your back, General. Now, with your permission, if there's nothing more I can do for you here I'll return to my men. They may be ready, but there's no such thing as too much preparation."

"Of course," said Anakin. "Captain, you're dismissed."

Ahsoka smothered a grin as Rex, in passing, spared her a slow wink.

The bridge was alive now, its crew staffing every station, the comm channels lively with chatter between Anakin's flagship and her subordinate sisters, the *Dauntless* and the *Pioneer*.

"Master Skywalker," said Yularen, turning. Though he was admiral of the battle group, protocol dictated he defer to the Jedi Council's representative. Unless, of course, said representative did something foolish—like forget to disengage an enemy transponder. Then he got barked at like any rank and file pilot. "All stations report ready. Commanders Vontifor and Isibray report ready."

"Very good, Admiral," said Anakin. He sounded serene. Looked almost disinterested. As though he'd stood on this bridge a hundred times already; as though he'd been a battle group commander for years. All his life. "In your own time, break orbit and proceed as plotted to the Bothan system."

"Understood," said Yularen. "Helm—"

"And Admiral?"

Surprised, Yularen raised a hand to the helmsman. "Master Skywalker?"

"As soon as we're clear of Coruscant, set the deep-space comsats to maximum gain and monitor all bandwidth chatter, no matter how obscure, until further notice. Advise the *Dauntless* and the *Pioneer* to do likewise."

Yularen hesitated, then cleared his throat. "That'll prove a significant drain on power."

Anakin nodded. "I know. Do it anyway. I have a funny feeling our friend Grievous is in a playful mood."

Yularen had been around long enough to know that a smart man didn't argue with a Jedi's *funny feeling*. Especially not this Jedi. "Of course," he said, and nodded to the officer at comms.

Under cover of bridge business, Ahsoka gave Anakin's sleeve a quick tug. "What does that mean, a funny feeling?" she asked, almost under her breath. "Do you know something I don't, Sky— Master?"

His glance down at her was severe. "The things I know that you don't, Padawan, would fill a Corellian spice freighter. Twice."

Fine, all right, there was no need to get *nasty*. "Yes, Master," she muttered.

He relented. "You heard what Master Yoda said. Grievous is wily. We already know the Separatists have infiltrated Coruscant security. And this mission may be top secret, but it's not like we can hide three brand-new Republic Cruisers. On top of that, a lot of the crew at the shipyard are civilians. Civilians go to cantinas and sometimes drink too much. And when they drink too much, they talk."

"About us?"

He shrugged. "Maybe. Or maybe I'm just being overcautious. But I'd rather be overcautious than caught by surprise."

That made two of them. "Yes, Master."

The *Resolute*'s bridge was graced with an encompassing transparisteel viewport. Apparently content to let Yularen run the show, at least for the time being, Anakin withdrew to stand before it. Ahsoka hesitated, then joined him in staring down at glorious, gleaming, glittering Coruscant.

She felt a pang. *Is this the last time I'll see it? I don't want this to be the last time. I want to see it again, and again. I don't want to die.*

Furtive, ashamed, she stole a sideways look at Anakin, expecting him to know what she was thinking, expecting a reprimand, a lecture. Instead she saw in his face something that shocked her, something she'd never expected: a dreadful, painful, frozen grief. So haunting, so piercing, it was like a spear of ice run through her. It seemed he had forgotten her completely, that in this moment only Coruscant existed.

Does he see something I can't? Does he know we won't be back? Is he saying good-bye? Should I say good-bye, too?

She couldn't ask him. His sudden, unexpected misery had infected her, had choked her throat with scorching tears. She watched, her vision blurred, as he stretched out his naked human hand and pressed its palm to the viewport. Coruscant fractured beneath his wide-spread fingers.

And then the planet fell away beneath them as his battle group broke orbit.

Weary beyond even groaning aloud, Bail Organa returned from the Senate to the empty solace of his apartment. Voiceprint and a retinal scan verified his identity: the outer door slid open, and as he stepped across the threshold into the apartment's foyer the lighting came on.

"Reduce by a quarter," he said, wincing.

The illumination moderated. Sighing his relief, he unpinned and removed his dark green cloak and slung it across the back of a chair. Then, as he kicked off his boots and stripped off his socks, he called for a playback of any received messages.

Just one. His wife. *Breha.*

Bail felt his heart thud, looking at her beautiful hologram face. *"Don't worry, B, nothing's wrong,"* she said, her image flickering, losing its cohesion. Ion storms somewhere between Alderaan and Coruscant; they always played havoc with galactic communications. *"I just wanted you to know I'm thinking of you. I was watch-*

ing the HoloNet feed from the Senate. You look tired. Are you get-
ting enough sleep? I'll bet you're not. Go to bed, hotshot. I'll try to
catch you tomorrow."

She flickered out entirely. Aching for her, unsettled, he wandered barefoot across the deep-pile carpet to brood on the extravagant light show that was Coruscant at night. No—the early
morning. A time when sane people were in their beds, asleep.

Three days had passed since the Separatist terror attacks and
the city, it seemed, was itself again. More or less. Of course there'd
been some adjustments. The damaged court buildings were still off-
limits, under assessment for reconstruction, with current cases on
suspension and new cases backing up until replacement judiciary
officials were found and sworn in, as well as temporary premises
arranged. Which wasn't proving a simple task . . . Coruscant was
such a crowded city. The same problem faced the various government officials who'd survived the attacks but lost their offices.
There was an unseemly scramble for desks and holovids and every
other kind of equipment.

And of course extra multisector security measures had been put
in place, devised largely by himself and Padmé. Why was it they
were the only two members of the Security Committee who seemed
capable of reaching a decision quickly? The rest of the committee
appeared paralyzed. The whole kriffing Senate was paralyzed, as
though the Separatists' success had infected the entire government
with inertia. Most of it, anyway. The Senators from worlds on the
front lines of the fighting were energetic enough. They railed
against Dooku and his allies, railed against the Jedi for failing to
rescue them, and looked to the Supreme Chancellor for an instant,
bloodless solution. And when Palpatine explained that wars took
time to win, and the Jedi were fighting their hardest, when he did
what had to be done—impose emergency levies on those worlds to
help finance the blightingly expensive counteroffensive against the
Separatists—they immediately railed against him.

The rest of the Senators, from those worlds as yet unaffected,

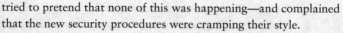

tried to pretend that none of this was happening—and complained that the new security procedures were cramping their style.

I've a good mind to leave them to their whining and fly home to Breha.

But of course he couldn't do that. What would become of the Republic if every Senator gave up when the going got tough? Padmé wasn't giving up. She railed right back at them, waved her fist in their faces, scolded them for laziness, called them to account. And they listened. How could they ignore her? She was the child-Queen who'd faced down the Trade Federation and won. She was the Senator who'd defied assassins to speak out for peace. She'd fought on Geonosis alongside the Jedi.

And she was a close personal friend of Supreme Chancellor Palpatine.

So, however reluctantly, they listened to Padmé . . . and, however imperfectly, some things got done.

Morose, disconsolate, he turned away from the window and crossed to the wine cabinet. Peace, and a generous helping of fiery Corellian brandy. Then, perhaps, he could start to relax.

Glass in hand, brandy-warmth lingering, he set the bottle on a side table and sank into his favorite chair. He wanted to call Breha, to lose himself in her soft voice and heal his hurts with her smile. But it was midmorning on Alderaan and she'd be in the Legislate, taking care of their people. Without her, he could never have remained on Coruscant. The welfare of Alderaan was cradled in her hands.

And the welfare of the Republic is cradled in mine.

Well. Not only his . . . although on days like this one it seemed like it. How did Palpatine stand it? How could he bear the desperate hunger of all those planets looking to him for their salvation? A lesser man would have broken long before now. But Palpatine withstood the pressure. In a strange way he seemed almost to thrive on it, as though being needed gave him the strength to go on. The man was remarkable.

I don't know where we'd be without him.

He poured himself more brandy. Sipping slowly, he stared again at the unsleeping city. He should eat something. He hadn't eaten for hours, and brandy on an empty stomach was a recipe for disaster. But he was too tired to move. He let his eyes drift closed . . . he fell gently into sleep . . .

. . . and then startled awake, heart pounding, as the comlink in his tunic's inner pocket, the comlink not even Breha knew about, erupted into insistent beeping.

TEN

———◉———

THE ROOM SMELLED OF BRANDY: THE GLASS HAD SLIPPED FROM his oblivious fingers and spilled its contents on the carpet. Beyond the apartment window, the sky's darkness had given way to first light; the impudent splendor of Coruscant's brash night fading to its discreet daytime face.

With a shaking hand he retrieved the beeping comlink and acknowledged receipt of the communication. The beeping stopped. His apartment fell silent. So silent he could hear his hard-beating heart. Sweat prickled his skin. His breathing felt ragged. A spike of pain between his eyes woke to stabbing life.

He took the comlink into his bedroom and connected it to the small datareader he kept in his bedside odds-and-ends drawer. It was an old Alderaanian unit, battered and outmoded. Not worth a second look. At least, that was how it appeared on the outside. Inside it had been remade. Upgraded to an unmatched sophistication. A series of apparently random characters came up on the datareader's screen. Decoding them was a manual task. He'd committed the decryption algorithm to memory years ago.

It was part of the arrangement.

The process of downloading a message from the comlink to the datareader triggered an automatic comwipe. No record of the incoming message remained. The same protection was built into the datareader. He had precisely five minutes to decode the downloaded transmission. After that it also was wiped.

That was part of the arrangement, too.

Because this was too important to get wrong, he jotted down the message's random symbols onto old-fashioned flimsiplast with an old-fashioned pen. Probably his contact would be horrified to learn that, but he or she never would, and it couldn't be helped. He wasn't prepared to make a mistake. Besides, flimsi could be burned, his scribbling lost forever to prying eyes.

Once the message was decoded, he stared at it. Was this right? *Could* it be right? Secrecy was his mysterious benefactor's watchword. Paranoia their religion. They could be wrong, couldn't they? And surely the Jedi would know of this, surely—

Don't try second-guessing them now. Either you trust them or you don't.

He activated his house droid. "There's brandy spilled in the living room. Clean it up, and then I want breakfast."

"Yes, sir," said the droid, and withdrew.

Next he placed a call to Padmé's apartment.

"I'm sorry, sir," said her officious protocol droid. It actually sounded *offended.* It even *looked* offended. How was that possible? *"I'm afraid my mistress has not yet arisen. Perhaps you'd care to call back at a more reasonable—"*

The kriffing thing was *arguing* with him? "Perhaps you didn't quite catch my name," he said, letting his temper loose, just a little. "This is *Senator Bail Organa* and my business can't wait."

As the protocol droid dithered, a familiar voice spoke in the background. *"Threepio? What's going on?"*

The droid turned. *"Oh, Mistress Padmé, I am so sorry. I was just trying to explain to Senator Organa that you were—"*

"Bail?" said Padmé, appearing on the viewscreen, pushing the droid aside. *"What is it? What's happened?"*

She'd had as little sleep as he, probably, but it was impossible to tell. Padmé's stamina appeared to be inexhaustible. "Sorry to call so early, Senator, but I've got a full day of meetings lined up and I needed to run some of my tactical analyses past you. Can we meet in, say, half an hour? I'll come to you."

She didn't answer immediately. Questions burned in her eyes . . . but she didn't ask them. Amazing woman. "To me? Yes," she said at last. "Of course." She sounded quite relaxed, but he could see the tension in her. He had no doubt she saw it in him, too. "Half an hour."

Relief flooded through him as the vidlink disconnected. He re-read the decoded message three more times, made certain it was accurately committed to memory, then burned it and washed the ashes down the kitchen sink. After that he showered, changed, bolted down his breakfast, and departed for Padmé's residence.

Half an hour didn't leave much time for eating or dressing, but Bail wouldn't have called so early if the matter weren't urgent. Ignoring fussing and fidgeting 3PO, Padmé rushed through her morning toilette, hastily swallowed the scrambled eggs the droid handed her, then stood on her apartment's docking platform and waited for her unexpected visitor.

Something's scared him. Something big.

Which hardly left her feeling sanguine. Bail Organa was a courageous, capable man. If he was unsettled—and he was unsettled, she'd seen the turmoil in his eyes—then it could only mean more trouble for Coruscant. Or for somewhere else in the Republic.

As if we don't have trouble enough.

Still. The call hadn't been about Anakin. Nothing terrible had happened to her husband, and that meant she could face with equanimity any news Bail brought, no matter how dire. There could be no greater disaster than disaster befalling Anakin.

She hadn't heard from him, of course. And there'd been nothing, not even a whisper of a suggestion of a rumor, on either the HoloNet or from any Senatorial staffer, about conflict in or near the Bothan system. If there had been, she would have heard it.

They say no news is good news. I say no news is agony, but surely Obi-Wan would tell me if something had gone wrong.

She thought he would, even though they didn't move in the same circles. Even though they were to all intents and purposes estranged—while being at the same time inextricably tied.

"Forgive me," Bail said upon his arrival. "I didn't know where else to turn."

As always, he presented an immaculate face to the world. Perfectly groomed, conservatively attired, elegance personified. But they'd worked together for a good while now, and she could see beneath his polished surface. She hadn't been mistaken about him during their brief vidcom conversation: he was alarmed.

She tried to reassure him with a smile. "There's nothing to forgive, Bail. And whatever's wrong, we'll fix it."

Leaving his airspeeder safely docked, they went into her living room, where C-3PO served tea and then made himself scarce. Covertly considering her colleague, Padmé activated the apartment's privacy seals, which automatically engaged her listening devices and denied access to all visitors and incoming communications, save for Anakin, Palpatine, and a Senate alert.

"There you are," she said, choosing her favorite chair. "We won't be disturbed. Please, Bail, tell me what's happened."

Bail hesitated, then sat on a sofa. But he was clearly ill at ease, perching on its very edge, fingers close to gripping his knees. "I'm in possession of some information. From a source that's reliable, but . . . let's say *unconventional*. It has serious implications for the Republic. And for the Jedi. I've been asked to tell them what I've been told."

She reached for her mug of tea and sipped, frowning. "If it's Jedi business, why come to me? You should be speaking with them."

Ignoring his own tea, he shook his head. "I don't know them,

Padmé. At least, not well. Not the way you do. And they don't know me. There's no reason to think they'd believe what I have to say. Especially given the circumstances."

"Your—unconventional—source?"

"Exactly." As though sitting was intolerable, he pushed to his feet and began to roam between the sofa and the window. "Of course, it's possible the Jedi already know about this. But if they don't—if they are in danger and don't realize it—" He pressed a fist against his lips, as though fighting to hold back an intemperate outburst. It was so unlike him, such an outward expression of an inner agitation. "Padmé," he said, and swung about to face her. "Have you ever heard of the Sith?"

Sith. The name alone was enough to raise her hackles. Twice their machinations had nearly killed her. And because of the hurt inflicted upon Anakin, and the murder of Qui-Gon Jinn, and the sufferings of Naboo under Trade Federation occupation, the Sith had earned her undying hatred.

But she couldn't tell Bail that. As Naboo's child-Queen, she'd promised Master Yoda she would never reveal what she'd learned of them. She'd renewed that promise to Obi-Wan on the desperate flight from Geonosis to Coruscant, when she'd overheard things not meant for her ears. *Sith lightning. Dooku. A dreadful betrayal.*

So with only the smallest twinge of conscience, she looked at Bail Organa and lied to him a second time. "Sith? No. Why? Who—what—are they?"

"I don't know," he said, frustrated. "Until this morning I'd never heard of them, either."

She sipped more tea. "Well, what did your contact tell you?"

"That they're plotting an attack that will devastate the Jedi."

She felt herself go cold, then hot. "You're sure of this?"

Bail dropped to the sofa again. "I didn't misunderstand the message, if that's what you mean. Padmé, please. I can't do this without you. You're the Jedi's friend, a trusted ally. If you speak up for me, if you vouch for me to them, then—"

"They'll trust you?" Though she was deeply disturbed by his news, she had to smile. "The friend of my friend is my friend?"

His own smile was as brief. "Something like that."

The Sith. Anakin had told her what little he knew of them. He never admitted it, but she knew they scared him. Knew he still mourned the loss of Qui-Gon Jinn. And she knew that the scars from his loss to Dooku were more than physical. But he didn't only fear them for himself. He feared for the Republic, for the galaxy, should their darkness win, should they prove victorious in their clandestine war against the Jedi.

Sworn to secrecy or not, he'd want me to help.

She nodded at Bail. "All right."

As Bail watched, chewing the edge of his thumb, she retrieved her private comlink from a nearby display shelf and opened a channel to the Jedi Temple. "This is Senator Amidala. I need to speak with Obi-Wan Kenobi."

Bail was right about one thing: the Jedi counted her an ally. There was no objection to her request.

"Senator Amidala? This is Obi-Wan Kenobi. How can I assist you?"

He sounded surprised. Cagily cautious. "Master Kenobi, I wonder if you could spare me a little of your time. Something's come up, and I'd appreciate your advice."

"Of course," he replied, after a moment. *"Did you wish to come to the Temple, or—"*

"If you could come to me at home I'd be most grateful," she said quickly. "Now would be convenient, if that's convenient for you."

"Certainly, Senator. I'll be with you shortly."

"Thank you, Master Kenobi," she said, disconnecting the link.

Bail was staring at her, almost bemused. "Just like that? You snap your fingers and the Jedi jump?"

She raised an eyebrow at him. "Isn't that why you came to me, Bail?"

"Well . . . yes, I suppose, but I didn't think—I wasn't aware—"
He shook his head. "I'm impressed."

"Don't be," she told him. "I might be able to get Obi-Wan to
come here, but I can't make him believe you, or your story."

"Do you believe me?" he asked, considering her closely.

"I believe you think there's a genuine threat." She shrugged.
"That's more than enough for me. Will you be all right for a moment? I want to go outside and wait for Obi-Wan."

"Of course."

"Good." She smiled. "I suggest you take a moment to order
your thoughts before he gets here. Marshal your arguments. It's
true you have an excellent reputation, but I have it on good authority that this particular Jedi's not overly fond of politicians."

"Yet he makes an exception for you?"

"Sometimes," she replied, and left Bail to think about that
while she waited outside for Anakin's former Master.

He came in an unremarkable Temple airspeeder, swinging the
vehicle to a halt beside Bail's sleek, expensive model with a casual
expertise that echoed Anakin's, and with enough speed to betray
impatience—or anxiety. She hurried to meet him as he leapt to the
veranda.

"What is it?" he demanded. "Have you heard from Anakin?"

From Anakin? She stared at him. "No. Why would I have
heard from Anakin? He and I—you made it quite clear—I don't
even know where Anakin is, Obi-Wan."

A muddle of emotions touched his face: chagrin, relief, annoyance, uncertainty. Then his familiar self-control returned. "I'm
sorry. A misunderstanding, Senator. I thought that—you sounded
concerned over the comlink and I—" He looked down at her hand
on his arm.

"You're worried for him," she said, leaving her hand where it
was. "Is he in trouble?"

Faint color touched Obi-Wan's pale face. "Padmé, I can't—it's
not appropriate that I—" He shook his head. "I can't."

"Can't what?" she said softly, and withdrew her hand. "Admit you're worried? Of course you can. You can to me. I'm not Yoda. I'm not Mace Windu. I don't think caring for someone is a crime. *Is Anakin in trouble?*"

She didn't think he'd answer. Thought instead he'd put her in her Senatorial place with a few chilly, well-chosen words. He was good at that. But he didn't. Instead she saw his Jedi mask slip again, just for a heartbeat. Saw that beneath his stoic exterior he was as conflicted as Anakin so often was. In his eyes, the need to talk. To share. To know he wasn't alone in being afraid.

"He's . . . on a mission," he said at last. "I can't tell you where, or what it is. But it's not proving as straightforward as we'd hoped. We'd thought to have heard from him by this morning . . . but we haven't."

She felt her heart thud. "Is he hurt?"

"No," he said quickly, vehemently. "Just . . . challenged. This mission is important, a great deal depends on its success. I should be there with him, he shouldn't be facing it alone, but my injuries— I was prevented—"

It was so unlike Obi-Wan to be incoherent. It was his articulate self-possession in the face of danger that so impressed her. Even though she hadn't entirely forgiven him for his interference in her life, she felt a surge of pity.

For all our differences we have this one thing in common. We both love Anakin, and we always will.

"It's not your fault, Obi-Wan. You didn't abandon him. You nearly died. Although . . ." She looked him up and down. "It seems you've made a remarkable recovery."

He shrugged that away. "The Temple healers are very skilled. Padmé, why am I here?"

She glanced over her shoulder. "I have a visitor, Obi-Wan. Senator Bail Organa of Alderaan. He claims to have received word of a planned attack against you . . . by the Sith."

Between breaths he changed. She felt it. Felt the warmth of his humanity flash-freeze to ice. Felt the air surrounding them crackle with power. In the hangar on Naboo, facing the red-and-black Sith assassin—in her apartment bedroom, having narrowly escaped being murdered by the bounty hunter Zam Wessell—in the arena on Geonosis, staring at monstrous, mechanical death—she'd felt it then, too: *Jedi*.

She stepped back, her skin prickling. "I've told him nothing. Whatever he knows, his contact told him."

"*What contact?*" Obi-Wan asked. "What precisely does Senator Organa know?"

"You'll have to ask him that," she said. "He came to me because the Jedi don't know him very well. Because he trusts me, and he knows you trust me, too."

Outwardly Obi-Wan seemed to do nothing, but his terrible aspect eased. Her skin stopped prickling. "And do you trust him?" he asked, mildly enough.

"I do. He's a good man, Obi-Wan. He loves the Republic. He works as hard as any Jedi to see it kept safe."

There was the faintest derision in Obi-Wan's clear blue eyes. "He's a politician, Padmé."

She raised an eyebrow. "So am I. Isn't that your biggest problem with me?"

My biggest problem? No. The answer flashed across his face, as easy to read as any holo-billboard, but he didn't say the words out loud. "You're a lot more than a mere politician," he said instead, and now his eyes warmed with a faint, reluctant smile. "As we both know."

"A compliment?" she said, pretending shock. "You should warn me next time, Obi-Wan. Give me a chance to sit down first."

He didn't rise to the bait. "It's odd, but now that I think of it, Padmé, you've encountered the Sith as often as I have," he murmured, frowning. "Almost as if they're as interested in you as they are in us."

She shivered. *Oh please, let him be wrong.* "Don't say things like that."

"This threat," he continued, his eyes hinting at apology. "Do you find it plausible?"

"I don't know the details," she said, wrenching her thoughts from that dark place. "I don't know Bail's contact. But for what little it's worth, Obi-Wan . . . I do know him well enough to promise he doesn't scare easily. And he's not a gullible fool, either, to fall for any old story."

"I see," said Obi-Wan, and sighed. "Very well, then, Padmé. Let us hear what Senator Organa has to say."

"They call themselves the Friends of the Republic," said the Senator from Alderaan. "They first contacted me a little over four years ago. At the time, the Alderaan government was in negotiations with Chandrila for a joint mining venture on Aridus. My wife's family has connections to the Corporate Sector, and some of those connections were involved with the project. The information provided by this group helped avert a diplomatic and humanitarian disaster that would have engulfed not only Alderaan and Chandrila, but several other key Republic systems as well."

Obi-Wan considered him, frowning. "And they did so because they are friends of the Republic?"

A flicker in Organa's eyes showed he heard the skepticism, but he didn't respond to it. "And because they would have been directly impacted by the resulting scandal if the mining venture had been allowed to continue as planned."

Ah. Of course. "In other words they were motivated by personal gain."

"I don't deny enlightened self-interest was a factor," Organa said, mildly enough. "But it's also true that many lives and livelihoods were saved by their intervention." He shrugged. "After all, self-preservation isn't a crime."

Perhaps not, but as a motive it did tarnish the altruistic halo.

"And they assumed you would also act out of enlightened self-interest?"

"They gambled that even if I wasn't motivated by doing the right thing, I'd use all my political power to avoid a scandal that would damage my House. But I can assure you, Master Kenobi, that if doing the right thing had meant exposing my family and connections to censure, then I would not have hesitated. There were many lives on the line."

An interesting admission. *Is this man a typical politician, or isn't he? The Jedi Council thinks of him as a friend, but these are proving to be deceptive times. Trust is a more expensive commodity now.* "I don't recall hearing anything of this narrowly averted mining disaster."

Organa's brief smile was grim. "It was handled at the highest diplomatic levels, with the utmost discretion. If the details had leaked, we'd still be mopping up the political fallout today."

Really? Well, that certainly confirmed what the Jedi knew of Organa's credentials and influence. "So, Senator, you handled a difficult situation neatly. Congratulations. But forgive me if I point out that one mynock does not an infestation make."

Organa leaned forward, fingers fisted so tight his knuckles whitened. "Master Kenobi, please. Give me some credit. These Friends of the Republic proved themselves five more times after our initial encounter. They were . . . matters of internal Alderaan security. I don't propose to divulge the details, but I can assure you they have done me and my House great service. By extension, they have served the Republic. And for all I know, I'm not the only one they've helped. I'm sorry I can't be more specific about them, but what I've told you is the truth. Are you prepared to take my word on that?"

"Of course he is, Bail," said Padmé, breaking her silence at last. Her pleasant tone was deceptive: beneath its sweetness a sharp blade lurked. "Obi-Wan knows the Jedi have no better friend than you. I'm sure he hasn't forgotten how you defended the Order in the Senate against the Quarren's unjust accusations of child-theft."

No, he had not, but that incident had no bearing on the current situation. He shot her a quelling look. *Do not push me, Padmé.* Then he nodded at Organa.

"Your support of the Jedi is well-known in the Order, Senator," he said, at his most reserved. "Please do not misinterpret my concerns as suspicion."

"I don't," said Organa. "It's in all our best interests to be cautious these days, Master Kenobi."

"Obi-Wan," said Padmé. Her tone was softer, more cajoling than commanding. "These are dark times, it's true, but some friends remain friends until the end. I believe Bail is one of them."

So she understood, did she, the wariness that now pervaded the Jedi Council? Interesting . . .

He turned again to Organa. "Senator, I accept your assertion that these people—whoever they are—have proven themselves to be friends of Alderaan, and their information in that regard is reliable. But what makes you believe they're reliable beyond that?"

Organa flicked an apologetic glance at Padmé. Then he braced his shoulders. "You're not going to like this, either of you."

Obi-Wan swallowed a sigh. *Probably not, no. I already don't like it and I hardly know anything yet.* "Let me be the judge of that, Senator."

Slowly, choosing his words with care, Organa detailed the other information that had been passed to him by his mysterious contact. Information concerning certain wartime engagements that was rigorously restricted, such as the fact that the clone army had been ordered by an unknown Jedi, and that Anakin Skywalker had nearly been killed by the fallen Jedi Count Dooku. That a traitor in the Bakuran government was responsible for Grievous's annihilation of the entire Ruling Synod, and that during the Christophsis mission Dooku's pet assassin Asajj Ventress had only just failed to murder two Jedi Knights.

Padmé was staring at Organa. "But Bail—why did you never mention this? Surely the Security Committee should know—Chancellor Palpatine should know—that there's been a breach of—"

"I couldn't tell you. Or anyone. I'm sorry, Padmé," said Organa. He sounded defensive. "I gave these people my word *years* ago that I would never reveal their existence. How could I repay all the good they've done with treachery? They told me these things as a show of good faith, as a way to demonstrate that their wartime intelligence network is extensive and accurate. That if they give me information about the Separatists, I can trust it's correct."

"Yes, well, that sounds good in theory," she retorted. "But Bail—"

"Have they told anyone else? Have they undermined the war effort by making any of the information public?" Organa demanded. "No. They haven't. Instead they're trying to help me. Help us. Again. And we have to let them. Because if they're right—and they've *never* been wrong—the stakes are higher than ever before."

And that was true, if the Sith were involved. Obi-Wan frowned at his interlaced fingers, inwardly shaken. Then he looked up. "How does your arrangement with these people work, Senator? Do you meet with them?"

Organa shook his head. "No. I've never seen or even spoken with them. Their communications are text-based and encrypted. Coded messages sent in shortburst over a secure link they gave me at the time of the Aridus situation. And I can't contact them. They don't work for me, Master Kenobi. If they learn something they think I should know, they tell me. That's it."

Extraordinary. "You are taking an amazing leap of faith, Senator. And now you're asking me to leap with you."

"Don't you think I *know* that?" Organa demanded. "But given what they know, what they've managed to learn, is it any wonder they guard their identities so jealously? Is it fair to blame them for protecting themselves the only way they know how?"

No, it wasn't fair. And there was nothing but truth in Bail Organa's passionate defense of them. Alderaan's Senator believed every word he said. But was that enough? Profoundly unsettled, Obi-Wan let his gaze shift from Organa to Padmé.

She trusts him. Just as she trusted Qui-Gon and Boss Nass. As she trusted herself when she felt Dooku was behind the Separatists, even when Mace and Ki-Adi-Mundi spoke against her. She wasn't wrong then—I just have to trust she's not wrong now.

He looked back at Organa. "And now these unidentified, secretive *friends* of yours have warned you about an attack on the Jedi by the Sith. Yes, Senator," he added, as Organa stared at Padmé. "Your colleague told me that much. She wanted to be certain you had my full attention. You do."

Organa stood and paced to the apartment's panoramic window. Rigid with tension, he stared out across the city, toward the Jedi Temple. Then he turned, his face pinched. "So you're telling me they exist, these Sith? They're real?"

Obi-Wan hesitated. *If I tell him the truth . . . if I reveal to this man one of our greatest secrets and he proves false . . .*

The problem was, Organa already knew the truth. He'd learned the secret. Well. Part of the secret.

And a little knowledge is a dangerous thing. If I try to put him off, dismiss what he's been told as rumor or hearsay, will he believe me? I don't think so. I think he'll try to discover more on his own. And that would be far more dangerous, for all of us. I have no choice but to tell him the truth.

He could only hope that Yoda and the Council agreed with him.

ELEVEN

"Yes, Senator," he said quietly. "The Sith are real."

Organa stared, almost as though he'd been expecting a denial. Then he nodded. "All right. So at least we know my contact's not been misled about that. How many are there? Who are their leaders? I presume they have names."

Obi-Wan didn't dare look at Padmé. "We don't know their leaders' true identities. We know only that they exist."

"And do they present a danger to the Jedi?"

It was too late to turn back now. "They threaten not only the Jedi, but the entire galaxy. Every life now breathing, sentient and nonsentient, and every life that is yet to be born."

It was Organa's turn to be shaken. "Are you serious?"

"Yes. I am not at liberty to divulge more details," Obi-Wan said, briefly enjoying the irony. "I simply ask you to accept my word on the matter."

The irony wasn't lost on Organa, either. But his thin smile faded quickly. "If the Sith are such a threat, Master Kenobi, why have I never heard of them? I'm head of the Republic's Security Committee. I should have heard of them."

Now there was an edge of temper in his mellow voice. A hint of an anger that masked a deeper fear. Accepting it, Obi-Wan maintained his own composure. "The Sith live in the shadows of the dark side, Senator. The Jedi believed they were long dead. Vanquished a thousand years ago."

"Really?" Organa snorted, derisive. "Then it would appear the Jedi were mistaken."

"Bail," said Padmé. "That's not fair."

"Not *fair*?" said Organa. His dark eyes were glinting. "I'll tell you what's not fair, Padmé. It's not fair the Jedi know of a threat that make the Separatists look like playground bullies and they haven't seen fit to inform the Senate! It's high-handed, autocratic decisions like this that fuel mistrust and resentment of them in the Outer Rim! And sometimes even closer to home. It's not *good* enough. We *must* work together, as equals, or we'll *fail*."

Padmé slid out of her chair and took a step toward him. "Bail, please. Calm down and—"

"Calm down?" he echoed. "No. I'm *angry,* Padmé. Why aren't you? What else is going on that they haven't told us? What do they know that you and I should know, as representatives of the people and members of the Security Committee? That *Palpatine* should know, as the Republic's duly elected Supreme Chancellor? Don't you see what's happening here? As hard as it may be to believe, the Jedi have placed themselves above the rule of law."

"No, Bail, they haven't," Padmé said hotly. "They're *dying* to uphold the rule of law."

"Well, at least they're dying with their eyes open!" snapped Organa, unappeased. "How many innocents are going to die—*are* dying—in ignorance because the Jedi aren't being open and honest?"

Obi-Wan pushed to his feet. *I've been a fool. Supportive or not, this man is a politician, an outsider, and he will never understand. I should heed my own advice: it's never wise to trust them.* "Senators, this matter cannot be resolved here and now. Therefore I shall return to the Temple and refer it to the Jedi Council. Until such time as a decision is made on how best to proceed, I'd ask that you both—"

"No. Wait," said Padmé, and caught hold of his arm. "Master Kenobi, please wait." She turned. "Bail, I'm sorry. I do know about the Sith. I've known for ten years."

Obi-Wan stared at her, taken by surprise. *Though really, after Geonosis, I shouldn't be.* But she had no business telling Organa anything. She'd given the Jedi her solemn word that her knowledge of the Sith would remain secret. *"Padmé—"*

"It's all right, Obi-Wan," she said quickly. "I promise."

Which was easy for her to say, but from the look on Organa's face things were far from *all right.*

"Ten years?" the Senator said blankly. "How do you—"

"They were behind the invasion of Naboo," she said. "And they're behind this war with the Separatists. Bail, you *must* listen to Obi-Wan. He knows what he's talking about. He's the only Jedi in a thousand years to have faced a Sith in mortal combat and lived."

"You *know,*" said Organa, still sounding dazed. "And you stayed silent? Padmé—"

"Trust me, Bail," she said, her voice unsteady. "There are worse things than silence."

"You mean like not bothering to mention an enemy like the Sith?"

Her chin came up. "I see. So you're turning hypocrite on me, is that it?"

"I'm not a hypocrite!"

"Oh? So you're *not* withholding intelligence from the Security Committee? From the Senate? From Palpatine? I *imagined* what you just said you were told about Bakura and Christophsis and the clones?"

Organa's face tightened. "That's different."

"Yes, yes, that's what *all* the hypocrites say!" she retorted, close to snarling. "There's always a reason why the rules don't apply to *them*!"

There was molten silence as they stared at each other, breathing hard, like two lightsaber opponents fought to a momentary standstill. Obi-Wan sighed. *This really was a mistake. Yoda is going to peel my hide.* "Senators—"

Padmé stopped him with an imperious, upraised hand. "Bail," she said, more calmly. "You have your reasons for not telling anyone about your Friends of the Republic. As far as you're concerned they're good reasons, and you expect me to respect them. So why can't *you* respect the Jedi's decision—*my* decision—not to reveal the existence of the Sith?"

Scowling, Organa folded his arms. "You think I don't see the parallels here? I do. But Padmé, there is the very real question of degree. We are talking about the safety of our entire *galaxy*, not just—"

"I know that," she said, and moved closer to rest a hesitant hand on his forearm. He was so tall, so imposing, and she was so small in contrast. But only physically. There was nothing small about her spirit. "It's because the galaxy stands at risk from the Sith that I agree with how the Jedi are handling this. Bail, I've seen what they can do. Believe me, *only* the Jedi can handle this. Are you going to tell me *you* know how to defeat an enemy who lives and breathes the dark side of the Force? That Palpatine does?"

"Of course not. But at the very least, Palpatine should be told that—"

"He was told, Bail," said Padmé, reluctantly. "When he came to Naboo for Qui-Gon's funeral and the formal reconciliation and treaty between our people and the Gungans. And he agreed that the Sith should be kept a secret."

Organa's eyes widened in shock, but he recovered himself quickly. "That was then. But things are different now, Padmé. And if we're at war with these Sith, then—"

"Then how is our cause helped by spreading *more* fear, *more* confusion, when so far very little is known about them?" Padmé argued. "When we're already struggling against the Separatists? Or are you saying this news wouldn't provoke panic?"

Organa hesitated, then shook his head. "No, I'm not saying that."

"*Well* then?"

He looked down at her, clearly torn between resentment and contrition. "How is it you contrive to put me in the wrong when I know I have a legitimate grievance?"

She smiled at him, fleeting mischief banishing the last of her temper. "It's a gift."

"Ha," he said, his anger evaporating. "One woman's gift is another man's curse." He shrugged. "What can I say, Padmé? I'm afraid."

"If it helps," she said, her eyes full of sympathy, "you're not the only one."

Obi-Wan looked at her. *She's afraid for Anakin. Because, like a fool, I allowed my concerns for him to loosen my tongue. I should peel my own hide.* He cleared his throat. "Senators . . ."

Organa turned. "Master Kenobi." His expression shifted from warm apology to a cooler, more distant regret. "Forgive me. I was intemperate. And I should heed my own advice. Only by working together—trusting each other—can we hope to win this war. The Jedi may have their own way of doing things, often difficult to fathom by outsiders, but nobody is making a greater sacrifice for the Republic. I know that."

Obi-Wan nodded, acknowledging the sentiment. *But he's still a politician. Trust extends only so far.* "Thank you, Senator. Your support is appreciated."

Organa wasn't a stupid man. He knew unenthusiastic when he heard it. And so did Padmé.

"Look," she said firmly, "I think we can agree, can't we, that our dedication to the preservation of the Republic is a given? In which case, let's finish what we've started here. Because surely the *only* thing that matters is preventing the Sith from hurting the Jedi and, through them, the Republic."

Despite his concerns, Obi-Wan had to smile. She was indeed an impressive young woman: wise beyond her years, her diplomatic skills honed to a lethal edge.

"Yes," he said quietly. "It is the only thing that matters."

She nodded, pleased. "Then I suggest we sit down again and continue this discussion bearing that in mind."

They resumed their seats, a trifle awkward, somewhat off-balance. The aftermath of anger was always uncomfortable.

"Senator Organa," said Obi-Wan, "can you tell me, precisely, what your contact told you?"

Organa's fingers drummed the arm of his chair. "It wasn't much, I'm afraid. A warning of a Sith plot to destroy the Jedi. Mention of a planet called Zigoola. And an *express* request that I inform you of your danger. Which tells me the situation's desperate. They would *never* chance discovery if it weren't."

"Zigoola?" said Padmé, frowning. "I've never heard of it. Have you, Obi-Wan?"

"No," he replied. But then he'd never heard of Kamino, either. It was a large galaxy, after all. With luck there'd be a reference to it in the Temple Archives.

Unless, like Kamino, someone's deleted the files.

His gut tightened, the merest thought of more Archive meddling enough to make him ill. *Stop it. You've enough trouble in front of you without borrowing more.*

"If the Sith managed to hide their existence from the Jedi for a thousand years," said Organa, "that implies they are masters of deception. Is it within their power to hide a whole planet?"

"I'm afraid I'm not at liberty to discuss that," Obi-Wan said, standing. "Senator, as I said, this matter must be referred to Master Yoda and the Council. I will be as discreet as I can. I know you're anxious to protect your source's anonymity."

"Very anxious, Master Kenobi."

"In the meantime, if you hear from your contact again, I'd ask that you bring me any new information without delay."

Organa's lips tightened, but he nodded. "All right."

"Thank you. And Senator, should Master Yoda wish to speak with you about this, would you be willing to do so?"

"Yes . . . ," Organa said slowly. "But you must understand, Master Kenobi, I won't compromise my relationship with these people by telling him any more about them than I've told you. What *they* tell you is up to them. But I gave them my word."

Wonderful. First Dex, now Bail Organa. *It seems I'm making a habit of collecting uncooperative informants.* "Of course, Senator. We would never ask you to violate a confidence."

"That's good to know," Organa said drily. "You'll keep me informed, Master Kenobi, of what you learn?"

"If I can," Obi-Wan replied. "Though I can make you no promises. I do, however, thank you, Senator Organa. I know telling me this can't have been easy."

Organa shrugged. "I was honoring my contact's wishes. That's all."

"Of course." Obi-Wan hesitated. *He won't like this, but I'm bound to say it.* "Senator, you'd do well to forget everything you've heard today. Let the Jedi handle this. And never speak of the Sith to anyone, *ever.* It's quite impossible to overestimate the danger they pose."

Organa half smiled. "It's good of you to think of me, Master Kenobi, but . . . I'm quite adept at protecting myself."

Obi-Wan let the bleakness touch his face, unrestrained. "So was my former Master, Qui-Gon Jinn. He was a great man, a great Jedi, yet the Sith still murdered him."

"I see," said Organa, after a moment. "I . . . wasn't aware of that."

"Few people are. Your discretion would be appreciated."

Organa nodded. "Of course."

"If you'll excuse me for a moment, Bail, I'll walk Master Kenobi to his speeder," said Padmé. "I won't be long."

Outside, Coruscant's air traffic had increased to its midmorning height. With it the sky's ambient noise had increased, and the gentle buffeting of the slipstreams. Halting by his plain, serviceable vehicle, his cloak tugging in the breeze, Obi-Wan turned to Padmé. "I didn't realize you and the Senator from Alderaan were such good friends."

A hint of censure touched her eyes. "We've been working together on Senate committees for almost two years now. We share the same goals for the Republic, and have the same impatience with indecision and inefficiency. I'm friends with his wife, Breha, too."

Which neatly put *him* in his place. But he was sorry for it. He'd rather see Padmé conducting an ill-advised romantic affair than pining after an unattainable Anakin. And he had no doubt that she was pining: she possessed remarkable self-control, but he was a Jedi . . . and he did know her quite well.

"Of course," he said. "Padmé, I do wish you hadn't told him of the Sith."

"You can trust him."

I hope so. "Most likely his information will prove to be a false alarm, but I am pleased you felt able to call on me," he said, letting the matter go, for now. "I know we haven't always . . . seen eye-to-eye . . . but I do hold you in the highest regard, Padmé. I hope you know that. I hope nothing happens to make you feel you can't call on me, if ever you find yourself in trouble."

Instead of answering, she stared across the cityscape, letting her gaze rest upon the distant Temple, so beautiful in the sun. "Yes," she said at last. "I hope so, too."

"By the way," he added, climbing into his airspeeder. "I never thanked you for your assistance in the recent Hutt kidnapping matter. Your intervention proved crucial."

I didn't do it for you. I did it for Anakin.

She didn't say the words aloud, but he heard them anyway. Saw the stark sentiment in her face. "It doesn't matter who you did it for, Padmé," he said softly. "You did it, and you made a difference. Every day, you make a difference. Anakin is the man he is now because he knew you. For that alone I shall always be grateful."

She blinked, a little too rapidly. "Thank you."

He shouldn't ask . . . he should leave . . . but there was something in her eyes, and he felt responsible. "You still miss him, don't you?"

"Oh, Obi-Wan," she sighed, "What do you want me to tell you?"

"The truth."

Her eyes chilled. "Then yes. *I still miss him.*"

"You did the right thing, Padmé," he said gently, regretting the question. "And in time the pain will fade. In time, you'll forget."

"Like he forgot his mother?"

If she'd stabbed him with a Talasean stiletto, she couldn't have pierced him more sharply. More deeply. "Padmé—"

She looked away. "I'm sorry. That wasn't fair."

"It's nothing. I know I hurt you, asking you to walk away. *I'm* sorry."

Looking back again, she managed a smile. "Well, I won't say *that* was nothing but . . . it's in the past. We need to worry about the future." She shivered. "If these Friends of the Republic are right, and the Sith are planning something . . ."

"Then we shall deal with them," he said. "If the Sith think to destroy the Jedi, then I promise you, Padmé: they'll learn their mistake."

She stared at him. "You sound so fierce. You hardly ever sound fierce, Obi-Wan. Confident. Determined. Cross, even, sometimes. But not fierce. Not . . . *frightening.*"

Firing up the speeder's engine, he shook his head. "You've nothing to fear, Padmé. You're not a Sith."

And with a sharp nod, he peeled the airspeeder away from the veranda and plunged into the traffic stream heading for the Temple.

He entered the Council Chamber to find Yoda and Mace Windu in conversation with a hologram Anakin.

"—cut us out of our hyperlanes three times, if you can believe it!" his former Padawan was saying. He sounded exhilarated, and furious, and exhausted. "I don't know how Grievous knew where we'd be. He's got some good intelligence, I'll give him that much. Or a new kind of tracking system. Something. But even so we've singed his feathers pretty neatly, Masters. I don't know what we paid for these new cruisers, but I can tell you they're worth every last credit. I'll transmit a full performance report as soon as I get a moment to think straight."

Yoda and Mace Windu exchanged guarded glances. Then Yoda turned to the door and beckoned. "Join us, Obi-Wan. Informing us of his progress, young Skywalker is."

Almost dizzy with relief, and working hard not to show it, he crossed the chamber floor. "Obi-Wan," said Anakin, as Obi-Wan entered the Council's holocam transmitter field. "Hey. You look much better than the last time I saw you."

"Thank you," he said, repressively. Would the boy never remember his protocols?

Hologram Anakin frowned. "Except—is something wrong?"

He knew. He always knew. Acutely aware of Yoda and Mace Windu staring, he shook his head. "Nothing you need concern yourself about, Anakin. Have you not yet reached the Bothan system?"

"No. Unfortunately. Like I was telling Masters Yoda and Windu, every time we turn around Grievous is on our tail."

"So he still eludes you?"

"I think what you meant to say is Grievous has failed three times to blow us to smithereens," retorted Anakin. "Even though he's got four cruisers to our three."

"What about casualties?" Mace Windu asked. "Have you lost any fighters, Anakin?"

Some of the ebullience died out of Anakin's face. *"Five destroyed, Master. Six damaged. We're working on them now."*

"So, not a victory," said Mace. "More like a stalemate."

"Which is better than an outright loss, Master Windu," Anakin said edgily.

"True," said Yoda. "But engaging Grievous in open space your mission is not. To the Bothan system at once you should proceed, young Skywalker. Protecting Bothawui is your task."

"Yes, Master Yoda," said Anakin, still curt. *"We have been trying to get there. We're on a direct course now."*

Obi-Wan cleared his throat. "But will you get there before Grievous, Anakin?"

"I think so. I'm pretty sure. We left him licking a few good wounds after our last engagement, and that's given us a head start. It'll be tight—I expect he'll chase us all the way there—but we'll be ready for him. He's not going to get his stinking metal hands on Bothawui, Masters. You've got my word on that."

"Keep us apprised of your situation, Anakin," said Mace Windu sternly. "If you're in any doubt as to how you should proceed, seek our advice. This mission is too important for heroics. Is that clear?"

"Yes, Master," said Anakin. *"I'll contact you again when we reach Bothawui."*

The hololink disconnected. Obi-Wan watched Yoda and Mace Windu exchange another guarded look. He wanted to say, *Anakin will do fine.* He wanted to say, *You can trust him not to let you down.* But he held his tongue. Not only because to say those things when his opinion was not invited would be a gross breach of protocol, but also because a part of him echoed Mace Windu's concerns.

Keep your head, Anakin. Don't let overconfidence creep up on you. You're good . . . you're exceptional . . . but you're not perfect. Not yet.

Yoda was considering him, his head tipped to one side. "Perceptive young Skywalker is," he said. "Troubled you are, Obi-Wan. What strife brings you here?"

Strife. Now there was a good word. "Masters, I am in receipt of some disturbing information. There is a chance we will soon face direct attack by the Sith."

Yoda and Mace Windu stared at each other, then back at him. *"Tell us,"* said Yoda.

Bail sat in silence with Padmé for a long time after Obi-Wan Kenobi's departure. Even though he had no time to waste. Even though his day was crammed from top to bottom and side to side with commitments. The enormity of the situation, its implications, had left him enervated. Oddly lost. And beneath that . . . afraid.

An ancient enemy that frightens the Jedi. Wonderful. Just when I thought things couldn't get any worse . . .

Seated across from him, Padmé stirred. "I'm sorry I shouted at you. I'm sorry I called you a hypocrite."

He smiled ruefully. "I'm sorry I've been keeping secrets like this. It hasn't been easy . . . but I didn't have a choice."

"I know," she said. "I understand. Sometimes secrets are necessary."

"Doesn't make keeping them any easier."

"No. I suppose not," she said, sounding almost sad. "Bail, you don't have to worry. I'll keep this one with you."

He felt a rush of surprised relief, and was ashamed. "Are you sure? I know I've put you in a difficult position. I never wanted to. I just—" He shrugged and sighed. He'd run out of words.

Her eyes warmed briefly. "You needed to trust someone. I'm glad you chose me."

He dredged up another smile. "So am I."

"And you can trust Obi-Wan, too. You really can."

Master Kenobi. "He's quite intimidating, isn't he? Even for a Jedi."

"Just a little bit," she agreed, and pulled a face.

"You two seem . . . close."

Startled, she stared at him. Then she shook her head. "No. Not really. At least—sort of—" She tugged at her loosely bound hair. "It's complicated."

Was she in love with Kenobi? he wondered. If so, *complicated* didn't begin to describe the situation. She trusted the man, that much was obvious. Kenobi trusted her, too, and that was interesting. It might not be love, but there was definitely something between them, something beyond a polite acquaintanceship or the mere political give-and-take between the Senate and the Jedi.

But it's none of my business. Her life is her own.

"I really need to go," he said, standing. "Thank you. Again. If I hear anything else from my contact, I promise I'll tell you."

She stood, too, her expression somber. "Only if you want to. Only if I can help in some way. Not because you feel guilty, Bail. Decisions made because of guilt usually turn out badly for everyone."

"True," he admitted, and withdrew.

The day dragged on, interminable. Bail found himself short-tempered, easily distracted, easily startled. He kept holding his breath, expecting a summons to the Jedi Temple at any moment. None came.

Perhaps this whole thing is a false alarm. Perhaps this is one time when my contact got it wrong.

Or perhaps the Jedi had decided he'd played his part and wanted nothing more to do with him. Padmé had been right about one thing: Master Kenobi wasn't fond of politicians. Not even his legendary Jedi courtesy and self-control had quite masked the undercurrent of disdain.

His path crossed with Padmé's twice, once in their daily security briefing, and again in a short Senate recall when the house was required to vote on increasing the Munitions Levy on the Core Worlds consortium.

His meeting with the other consortium representatives, shortly thereafter, left him with a truly monumental headache.

After that he was swallowed alive by domestic concerns: appointments with Alderaanian citizens registering complaints, making representations, begging favors.

Tell me again why I wanted to be a Senator?

It was approaching midnight before he finally escaped. Exhausted, punch-drunk, he almost staggered through his front door. Too tired even for the restorative consolation of Corellian brandy, he bumped his way to the bedroom and fell face-first across the bed.

Even his capillaries were aching.

Sleep descended with blunt force, bludgeoning him into oblivion. But oblivion didn't last till sunrise. In his hidden tunic pocket, the secret comlink began to buzz . . .

Nauseated from lack of rest, he stared at the decoded message. Decoded it again, just in case his fragile state had led him to making a disastrous mistake. It hadn't.

Well . . . stang. This is not what I had in mind.

Heedless of the unsociable hour, he commed the Jedi Temple. "I need to speak with Master Obi-Wan Kenobi. It's a matter of urgency."

"Master Kenobi is not available at this time, Senator. Perhaps you would care to leave a message?"

A message. His life had just turned inside out, and he was supposed to leave a message? "Yes. All right. Tell him I must see him as soon as possible." He hesitated, then added, "He'll know why."

The Jedi on the other side of this insane conversation was silent for a moment. "Yes, Senator," he said. He sounded disapproving. *Too bad.* "I will relay your request at the first opportunity."

In other words, *Don't think you can throw your weight around, you're just a politician.* Clearly he lacked Padmé's magic snap of the fingers. "Thank you," he said, and terminated the link.

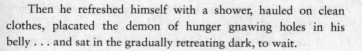

Then he refreshed himself with a shower, hauled on clean clothes, placated the demon of hunger gnawing holes in his belly . . . and sat in the gradually retreating dark, to wait.

The disastrous news had come through to the Temple at six minutes past two in the morning, local Coruscant time. By two twenty Yoda and Master Windu were on their way to the Supreme Chancellor's office for an emergency conference. At two thirty-one Anakin Skywalker made contact via hololink.

"*Obi-Wan!*" he said, startled. "*I asked to speak to Master Yoda, or Master Windu.*"

Eyes gritty from lack of sleep, nerves jangling, fighting fresh grief, Obi-Wan shook his head. Alone in one of the Temple comm center's booths, he was able to answer bluntly, without circumspection. "They're with Palpatine. What do you need?"

"*An explanation,*" said Anakin, sounding baffled and irritated. He stood at the *Resolute*'s tactical holotable, flanked by his Padawan and silent, self-assured Clone Captain Rex. "*We've reached Bothawui, but there's no sign of Grievous. It's like he's just—changed his mind. Or given up.*"

Obi-Wan's throat closed, and he had to wait a moment before replying. Given up? If only they could be so fortunate. "No, Anakin. He hasn't."

Hologram Anakin stiffened. By his side, his Padawan looked up at him, reacting instantly to his shift in mood. One hand touched her lightsaber.

"*Something's wrong,*" said Anakin harshly. "*What's happened?*"

There was no easy way to say it. No kind way to break the news. "Grievous has only delayed his pursuit of you. A few hours ago he picked up two more cruisers and coordinated attacks on three separate fronts. It's bad, Anakin. We've lost the battle group at Falleen." Eight more Jedi dead. Eight more friends to mourn.

"The Separatist fleet commanded by General Grievous is now headed your way."

Anakin's face tightened with anger. *"Seems like that coward always knows where and when to attack us."*

Yes. He did. Which was something else they'd have to address, and fast. Because if their losses continued at this pace, there'd soon be no Jedi left. No planet in the galaxy safe from Grievous's predations.

But for the moment, his concerns were far more immediate. "You're heavily outnumbered, Anakin. I advise retreat."

"If we run, the Separatists will take control of this sector." Anakin's anger hardened into stubborn resolve. *"I can't let them do that."*

Of course he couldn't. Retreat wasn't in his nature. *But it's something he's going to have to learn, if he wants to survive this war.* "You might have to."

Anakin's outspoken Padawan lifted her chin. *"Master Kenobi is right. We should regroup; we don't stand a chance against—"*

"Ahsoka," said Anakin. Curt. Repressive.

But she didn't back down. Yoda had been right, as usual. The young Togruta was more than a match for headstrong Anakin. In fact, she was exactly the Padawan he required.

"Suicide is not the Jedi way, Master."

Obi-Wan considered her approvingly, then shifted his gaze. "You should listen to your Padawan, Anakin."

A sly smile curved Anakin's lips. *"As you listened to yours?"* He shook his head. *"No, we are going to stay and fight."* Bending, he considered the tactical display on his holotable. *"And I think I know how to beat Grievous at his own game."*

Was there any point in arguing? No. None at all. If for no other reason than Anakin was there, on the spot, in command, and it was his call.

He mustn't see I'm afraid. He can't for a moment think I don't have faith in him. "Anakin, you'll do what you think is right. As always. Just—and I realize I'm wasting my breath, but I'll say it anyway—*don't take any unnecessary chances.*"

Anakin grinned. *"You know me, Obi-Wan."*

Obi-Wan couldn't quite manage a smile in return. "Which would be why I said it. May the Force be with you."

"And with you, Master."

The hololink dropped out. Obi-Wan stared at the deactivated holocam, feeling his heart thud against his ribs. A throb of pain echoed the beat, thrumming his bones in unpleasant counterpoint. A reminder that not enough time had passed since his recent brush with death. Vokara Che's instructions had been clear and pointed: under no circumstances was he to overexert himself. He pulled a face.

Tell that to Grievous, and to Bail Organa's mysterious friends. Tell that to Anakin, who's determined to make me old before my time.

As he stepped out of the comm booth, one of the Temple's newest Jedi Knights approached. What was his name? Oh, yes. T'Seely. "Master Kenobi. I have a message for you, from Senator Bail Organa."

Boom went his heart. "Yes?"

"He wants to see you, Master. Now." T'Seely frowned. "He said you'd know why."

Boom boom. "Thank you."

Outwardly serene, inwardly disconcerted, Obi-Wan accessed the relevant datafile, noted Organa's private address, and took his leave of the Temple.

TWELVE

"Master Kenobi," said Bail Organa, standing in his apartment's open doorway. He looked exhausted. "You came."

Obi-Wan nodded. "Your message sounded urgent, Senator."

"Yes. Yes, I suppose it did." Organa blinked, then shook his head and stepped back. "It was. I'm sorry. Please. Come in."

Obi-Wan entered the apartment and followed Organa through to the sitting area. The place was spacious. Immaculate. Possessed of a typically restrained Alderaanian elegance. Beauty mattered, but it was never ostentatious.

Organa indicated a long, low couch. "Have a seat. Can I offer you something? I have Corellian brandy, or a fine white wine from my family's vineyard. Tea."

First an urgent, peremptory summons, and now the man was playing the gracious host? *I am too tired for this.* "Thank you, no."

"No," said Organa, and dropped into a chair. "Did I drag you from your bed, Master Kenobi? If so, I apologize."

"No, Senator," Obi-Wan said, taking a seat on the couch. "I was awake."

Organa straightened, alarm burning away the tiredness. "Something's happened."

Given his position on the Security Committee, the senator would find out soon enough. No harm in telling the truth. "We lost the Falleen battle group. Senator, was there a particular reason you needed to see me or—"

Organa wasn't listening. "The whole group?" he asked. "Every cruiser?"

Every cruiser. Every Jedi. Every Republic officer. Every clone. "Yes. Senator Organa, you—"

Organa pinched the bridge of his nose, hard. "The *Bespin Dancer*. Is—was—she still part of the Falleen group?"

"I believe so. *Senator*—"

Organa's eyes were blanked with shock. "My wife's cousin is a tac officer on the *Dancer*."

Ah. Unfortunate. "Then, Senator, I am sorry for your loss. But if we could perhaps—"

Some dark feeling—almost revulsion—touched Organa's face. "Some people say the Jedi are cold. Unfeeling. Are you trying to prove them right, Master Kenobi?"

There was no answer for that. Obi-Wan stood. "Senator, I think—"

"You lost Jedi in the battle group," said Organa. He sounded accusing. "Were they your friends? Aren't you grieving for them?"

Lobis Lobin. Kydra. Tafasheel Arkan. "Senator, you said you needed to see me urgently. If that is not the case, I shall return to the Temple."

"*Sit down.*"

Obi-Wan stared at him. *The man is distraught, exhausted, and a senior government official. Master Yoda needs no more trouble tonight.* He sat, very slowly. "Senator."

Organa pressed his palms flat to his face. Took a deep, shuddering breath. Exhaled it sharply. "I'm sorry, Master Kenobi," he said, his voice muffled, then lowered his hands. "That was uncalled for. Tell me, what were you able to find out about Zigoola?"

"Nothing, I'm afraid," said Obi-Wan, grimacing. "Master Yoda and Master Windu have never heard of it, and there is no record of a planet by that name, or any name close to it, in the Temple Archives." Dex hadn't heard of it, either. Neither had any of his contacts . . . and Dex could cast a wide net. If it weren't for the first message's mention of the Sith, he'd be convinced the whole thing was a mistake. Or a hoax. "Senator, why did you ask me here? Have you been contacted by your source again?"

"Yes," said Organa, fingers drumming his knee. A new tension deepened the lines in his face. "They say they know where Zigoola is. They want to meet us there. Show us something to do with the Sith that they can't—won't—discuss via coded shortbursts. They've sent the first set of coordinates for the journey."

"Meet *us*?" Obi-Wan shook his head. "Absolutely not, Senator. If this Zigoola exists, and if it does have a link with the Sith, it's far too dangerous a place for you. I'll go alone."

Organa's eyebrows shot up. "I don't think so. We go together. Or *I'll* go alone. I'm more than happy to leave you behind."

"I'm afraid I can't agree to that. Or to you accompanying me."

"Well, if you want anything to do with this, Master Kenobi, I'm afraid you'll have to," Organa retorted. "Because if you think I'm going to hand over my comlink, my datareader, and my decryption codes and wave good-bye as you fly off to meet my contact without me, you're a much stupider man than I thought."

Obi-Wan bit back an impolite epithet. *Politicians.* "Senator, we have been through this already. The Sith are Jedi business. Not yours."

"*Wrong,*" Organa snapped. "Given my security duties they are very much my business. And they're going to stay my business for as long as I'm the one receiving the coded information about them. Now it seems to me we have a choice, Master Kenobi. Either we can sit here till sunrise arguing, or we can agree that like it or not, you and I are about to become much better acquainted."

He stared. "Meaning?"

"Meaning I have a fully provisioned ship standing by. It's nothing fancy or particularly fast, and it's a bit on the small side, but it's spaceworthy and civilian-registered. No Senatorial or Alderaanian connections. It'll get us to Zigoola without drawing undue attention or breaking down, you have my word. Especially since—at the risk of sounding immodest—I happen to be an accomplished pilot."

The man was so ridiculously cocksure. *How very like a politician, to believe his limited power to control events is in fact unlimited.* "Senator, I don't wish to be rude, but I must point out to you that there is a great deal of difference between comfortable Core-World-hopping and deep-space expeditions."

Organa's eyebrows pinched in a frown. "No. Really?"

"Really," Obi-Wan said, letting a little of his impatience show. "In the event that I become incapacitated, are you saying you can strip down a malfunctioning hyperdrive unit, correctly identify the problem, replace its faulty components, or improvise new ones, and reassemble it to full performance capacity?"

Organa grinned. "A standard LT-five unit? Yes. Did it last week, as a matter of fact. It's good relaxation, and I like to keep my hand in. Timed myself, just for the fun of it. Thirty-eight minutes. How about you?"

Thirty-eight minutes? That was three minutes faster than his own best time. *How aggravating.* "I am mechanically proficient."

"So that makes two of us. Any more questions?"

Yes, there was one. Something Organa had said earlier . . . "What did you mean when you said *first coordinates*?"

Organa's grin vanished. "I told you, these are very cautious people we're dealing with. They'll guide us to Zigoola in several stages."

Us. Obi-Wan shook his head. *Letting him accompany me is a very bad idea.* "Senator, you must reconsider. Your place is here, in the Senate. Be guided by me and remain on Coruscant."

"The last time I looked, Master Kenobi, I wasn't your Padawan," said Organa, shrugging. "I don't need to be guided by you. And who knows? I might even come in handy."

Come in handy? This man was *insufferable*. A typical politician after all, obsessed with power, control, and turning a situation to his personal advantage. *Oh yes, I'm Senator Bail Organa, the man who saved the Jedi when they couldn't save themselves!*

For the second time, Obi-Wan stood. "I very much doubt that. And if anything untoward should happen to you, it would be most unfortunate. So on behalf of the Jedi Council, I thank you for your information, Senator, and request that you take no further action in this matter."

He was halfway across the apartment's spacious entry hall when Organa came after him. "Master Kenobi. *Wait.*"

At the touch of Organa's fingers on his shoulder he spun around, a heartbeat from reaching for his lightsaber. Organa stepped back, hands raised, eyes suddenly wide and watchful.

"Sorry. No disrespect intended," he said. "I only want you to hear me out."

Heart thudding, Obi-Wan took a step back himself and slowly, deliberately, clasped his hands before him. *I'm too tired to be here. My judgment is clouded. I should not have come.*

"Senator."

"Look," said Organa, and he put his hands down. "We both want the same thing, right? The Republic safe. The Sith stopped. And like it or not, without my contact you've got nothing. Are you really going to let Jedi pride get in the way?"

"Pride has nothing to do with this, Senator," he said, uncomfortably close to losing his temper. "The Sith are *dangerous.* How many more times must I tell you before you believe me?"

Organa folded his arms, his expression settling into stubborn lines. "I already believe you. But my life is sworn to the safeguarding of this Republic, just like yours. I've got as much right to risk myself as you do. If anything, it's my duty to pursue this matter."

Frustrated, Obi-Wan stared at Padmé's aggravating friend. *She trusts him, remember? And you trust her . . .*

"I must confer with the Council," he said curtly. "Wait there.

Don't move." A presumption on his part, given that this was Organa's home, but he was past caring.

"Yes, Master," said Organa, one eyebrow lifted.

Obi-Wan returned to the Senator's living area, pulled out his comlink, and contacted Yoda with an update.

"A disturbing development this is, Obi-Wan," Yoda said. "Convinced, you remain, that this danger is real?"

Obi-Wan sighed. "I'm convinced Organa's convinced, Master Yoda," he said, keeping his voice low. "I sense no deception in him."

"Perhaps. But a Sith trap this still could be."

"Yes, Master. The thought has crossed my mind. Do we know where Dooku is?"

Yoda snorted. "A Separatist convention on Chanosant he prepares to attend, Obi-Wan. Support for his disloyalty he seeks to expand. Reports there are on the holonews."

Which still left the mysterious Darth Sidious. But if Dooku had told the truth, and Sidious was influencing the Senate, chances were he wouldn't abandon Coruscant. Not for long. "Master, I know it's risky, but I think we must pursue this matter."

"Hmmm," said Yoda, his grumbling tone so reassuringly familiar. "Correct you are, Obi-Wan. But comfortable I am not with further involving Senator Organa in Jedi business."

Obi-Wan glanced behind him, but there was no sign of Organa. "Nor am I, Master, but do we have a choice? His contacts won't talk to anyone else. If I'm going to question them about this possible Sith threat, it will only be through him."

"True," said Yoda. "But an important man he has become, Obi-Wan. Regarded highly by the Supreme Chancellor. To Bail Organa must no harm come."

"I understand, Master Yoda. Although he'll not appreciate a Jedi nursemaid. In that respect he's very like Senator Amidala."

Yoda snorted again. "And like Senator Amidala, accept our protection he will. But strong enough are you, Obi-Wan, to undertake this task?" Now Yoda sounded . . . doubtful. "The truth I need *to know. Depend on it your life might, and the life of Senator Organa."*

In other words, *Obi-Wan, don't be a hero.* Precisely the advice he kept on giving Anakin. *Like Master, like Padawan? Is that what Yoda means?* "Vokara Che has said I am healed. I feel fine, Master Yoda. Besides, this isn't all-out battle, it's a recon mission. More than likely a false alarm. But if it's not, you have my word I won't do anything foolish. At the first sign of trouble I will call for reinforcements."

If there were any to be had, of course. With the loss of the Falleen battle group, their situation had gone from *spread thin* to *close to breaking.*

With an effort Obi-Wan wrenched his thoughts away from that disaster. It was done; it could not be undone. The Jedi who had perished were returned to the Force. They would be remembered in ritual, and life would go on.

Yoda sighed again, breaking the heavy silence. *"A dangerous undertaking this is. Perhaps another Jedi I should send with you."*

It was a comforting, but impractical, thought. "You can't, Master Yoda. The Senator's instructions were quite specific: one Jedi to accompany him, and no more."

"Then follow you someone could. Disappear without a trace you might, Master Kenobi."

He had to smile. "Who would you send? There's no one, and we both know it. I will be all right, Master Yoda."

"Thought that we did when to Kamino we sent you."

A decision that had sparked a train of events ending under a hot sun on the bloody sand of cruel Geonosis. *So many dead Jedi, who came to rescue me.*

With a small effort, he pushed the thought away.

"History will not repeat itself, Master Yoda," he said harshly. "On that you have my word."

Another long silence. And then another heavy sigh. *"Very well,*

Obi-Wan. Permission you have to follow this lead with Senator Organa, for unravel this new Sith mystery we must. Your ship's transponder frequency give to the Temple comm center. Out of contact you must not be."

"Of course." He was ready to end the call, but then memory prodded him. "Master! I'm so sorry. Anakin has—"

"Yes, I know. The transmission recording I have seen," said Yoda. Now he sounded stern. *"Monitored young Skywalker's progress will be."*

The warning was unstated but abundantly clear: *Focus on your own mission. He is not your concern.*

It wasn't true. It would never be true. But he could pretend it was true, at least for now. "Yes, Master."

And that was that.

"Well?" said Organa, strolling into the living area. "Do I pack myself a spare shirt, or don't I?" His tone was amused, his manner unconcerned—at least on the surface. Beneath it, however, trepidation and doubt churned.

Obi-Wan turned away from the window and met Organa's tired gaze without hesitation, knowing his own thoughts and feelings were nowhere to be seen.

"Yes, Senator. You do."

As promised, Organa's ship was entirely unremarkable. An early-model *D*-class Starfarer, designed for economic utility, not luxury, it was one of the Corellian Engineering Corporation's most popular small civilian craft. Sturdy, reliable, shaped like an elongated lozenge, it plowed through the layers of Coruscant's atmosphere without incident.

They'd filed a false flight plan with Coruscant Space Central. Once they were clear of its autotracking sensors and well into free space, Organa programmed the nav computer with the coordinates provided by his contact, then turned in the pilot's seat to look at Obi-Wan, neatly tucked in behind and to his right at the comsat console.

"Before we jump to hyperspace I'd like to tell Breha—my wife—about the *Bespin Dancer*," he said quietly. "Do you have a problem with that?"

Obi-Wan finished coding the ship's transponder beacon frequency for transmission to the Jedi Temple. "It might be better if you didn't, Senator," he replied, hitting the console's transmit toggle. "It's sensitive information, and there is the question of security."

"You think you need to lecture *me* about security?" Organa snapped. "Why do you think I didn't call her from my residence?"

Obi-Wan had wondered, in passing, why Organa would log his emergency absence from the Senate and leave a voice message for Padmé but not contact his wife. "Your domestic arrangements are none of my affair, Senator."

"Not domestic arrangements," Organa said impatiently. "Security measures. Because of the terror attacks that nearly killed you we were forced to implement some extra precautions. Communications safety checks. Monitoring. They don't apply to offworld transmissions not destined for Coruscant. I can talk to Breha from here without creating a problem for anyone."

Extra precautions? Monitoring? That sounded ominous. "I see."

Organa wasn't an imperceptive man. He heard the note of reserve. Of doubt. "The measures are temporary," he said. "They'll last as long as the current security climate dictates, and no longer."

Obi-Wan nodded. "Of course. But I still don't advise that you discuss the *Bespin Dancer*'s fate with your wife. I don't know what Palpatine has authorized, in terms of information being made available to the public."

"Breha is not *the public*," said Organa, his voice chilling.

"She's the head of the Alderaan government. And it's her cousin who's died. They grew up together. They're more like brother and sister. I don't want her finding out from a HoloNet news bulletin or in some impersonal Senate communiqué. I want her to hear it from me."

Obi-Wan looked at Organa, torn between bemusement and irritation. "Since you're clearly determined to tell her, Senator, I don't see why you're bothering to ask my opinion."

"Neither do I," said Organa, and linked through to his wife.

Eyes closed, unhappily aware that when he'd told Yoda he was fine he'd perhaps exaggerated a trifle, Obi-Wan let Organa's quiet sorrow wash through him. Denied himself any response to Breha Organa's muted cry of grief. Allowed the physical pain in his weary, too recently insulted body to drown the emotional pain of remembering his own friends lost at Falleen. Physical pain was more acceptable than the suffering brought on by misplaced attachment.

As Organa warned his wife he'd be out of contact for a little while, some unexpected offworld business, no need to be concerned, Obi-Wan slipped into a light trance that he hoped would in some small way replenish his diminishing reserves of strength. Reality faded. At some point he was dimly aware that they jumped to lightspeed.

Organa startled him to wakefulness by tapping him on the shoulder.

"Here," said the Senator, and he held out a medi-cup. "Painkillers. You're not looking too good. And then you should go lie down. Get some sleep."

Obi-Wan looked out of the cockpit viewport at the lazy swirlings of hyperspace, then at the drugs—and didn't bother to hide his lack of enthusiasm. "No. Thank you."

"Take them," Organa insisted. "You got blown up a few days ago, in case it slipped your mind."

"Oddly enough, I do remember the incident," Obi-Wan said.

"Senator, your concern is appreciated, but I am a Jedi. I do not require chemical assistance."

Organa frowned. "Okay. So is this how it's going to be? Me making sensible suggestions, and you kicking against them just because you can? Master Kenobi, I'm bored already. Take the kriffing drugs."

It was childishly tempting to pluck the medi-cup from Organa's fingers using the Force. But that would be beneath him. So he took the wretched painkillers like any non-Jedi and swallowed them dry.

"There. See?" Organa said, ridiculously pleased. "That wasn't so hard, was it?" He dropped back into the pilot's seat. "You really should go lie down. I've seen white sheets with more color than you."

"I feel bound to point out that you are looking equally beleaguered, Senator. When was the last time you enjoyed adequate rest?"

"I'm fine," said Organa. "I took a stim."

"A *stim*?" Wonderful. "And when your metabolism crashes after its effects wear off, then what?"

Organa shrugged. "Then you can sit in the pilot's seat and I'll put my head down. Assuming, of course, you know how to fly this thing?"

Obi-Wan stood. "Now you're just being deliberately provocative. Very well. I shall retire."

"Good idea," said Organa. "Wish I'd thought of it. I calculate it's a little over three hours' flying time to reach the first coordinates. I'll wake you when we drop out of lightspeed."

"That won't be necessary, Senator," Obi-Wan replied over his shoulder. "I'll know when we shift back to normal space."

Organa muttered something uncomplimentary under his breath. He sounded irritated.

Declining to acknowledge either the comment or the tone, Obi-Wan retreated to the compact—some might have said claustrophobically small—passenger compartment at the rear of the ship. Four economical sleep-bunks were built into the gently curving walls, each one concealed behind a self-sealing curtain. He selected the nearest cubicle, unstrapped his boots, and placed them neatly to one side. Then he unclipped his lightsaber and tossed it beside the single pillow, unbuckled his belt and put it with his boots, and rolled onto the mattress, which obligingly gave to his weight and immediately began warming to provide optimum comfort. One swift tug pulled the curtain closed. A single flick of his fingers activated its malleable nanopolymers.

He closed his eyes, breathed out, and was immediately asleep.

Drifting in the Force, he sees a great space battle. Three Jedi cruisers, valiant and overmatched, hold their own against the might of a merciless enemy. Hold the line to protect an innocent planet, its innocent citizens, from slavery and worse. To protect an ancient Republic from falling into chaos. The distant sun turns an asteroid belt to fire, splinters of a dead moon reflecting the light. A swarm of starfighters, angry metal hornets, burst from their safe nest into the rocky night. The enemy flogs them with fire, lashes them with laser whips. Brief life. Bright death. It looks hopeless. A rout. A pointless wasteful slaughter. Mired in horror, he says no and no. He cannot help them. He is only a witness. And then lumbering out of hiding come the ponderous AT-TEs, belching plasma. Thundering death. Like prehistoric predators they come, delivering harsh justice. The merciless foe founders, choking on defeat. A stricken enemy starship burns. It burns. One small ship escapes it. One hornet pursues. Closer. Closer. Coming closer. And then a plume of flame. A wave of disbelieving fear. The enemy, triumphant, smears against the stars. Escapes to kill another day. And the hornet dies in a shower of exploding shards . . .

"Anakin!" said Obi-Wan, and sat up on his narrow bunk, his heart pounding erratically.

On the other side of the sealed curtain, Organa cleared his throat. "Master Kenobi? Are you awake?"

Obi-Wan unsealed the curtain. "What is it?"

Organa's eyes were red-rimmed from his ill-advised stim intake. "Your Padawan is asking to speak with you."

Not dead, then? Not lost? For a moment the relief felt like fresh pain. Then Obi-Wan nodded, groggy, his mind sluggish. A vicious headache pounded through his temples. He felt like a dishcloth, wrung dry by careless hands.

Blinking, he cleared his blurred vision. "Not my Padawan. Not anymore." He swung his feet to the deck and stood. "Please tell him I shall be there momentarily."

As Organa nodded and withdrew, Obi-Wan put his boots back on, and his belt, hooked his lightsaber where it belonged, then went forward to the cockpit where realspace glimmered through the viewport and a small hologram Anakin shimmered and shivered on the comsat console's holoreceiver pad.

"Master. Where are you? I transmitted through to the Temple but the signal was rerouted."

"I'm running an errand," Obi-Wan replied. "So. You're in one piece after all. How did you manage that?"

"In one piece?" said Anakin, surprised. *"You mean you know—"*

"Of course." He managed a smile. Managed to sound calm. Even bored. "But why are you reporting to me and not the Council?"

Anakin shrugged. Was it a trick of holography, or did he look . . . evasive? *"Old habits die hard, I guess. What kind of errand?"*

"The irrelevant kind," Obi-Wan said repressively. "It's a shame about your starfighter, Anakin. It's not like they grow on trees, you know."

Anakin sighed. *"Sorry."*

It wasn't fair to scold. Not after his brilliant achievement.

"Don't apologize. You saved Bothawui. With boldness and daring, against significant odds. Congratulations, Anakin. Your resource-fulness always amazes me."

He expected a grin. Some kind of cocky, inappropriate re-joinder. Instead Anakin seemed suddenly downcast. *"Thank you, Master."*

A tickle of unease. *What's happened now?* "You look troubled."

"I lost Artoo in the field."

Machines. Again. His ridiculous affection for nuts and bolts and circuitry. *It's time he grew out of this.* "Artoo units are easily replaced."

Anakin wasn't listening. *"I could take a squad out there, track him down."*

What? "Anakin, it's only a droid," he said, letting his voice snap a little. "You know attachment is not acceptable for a Jedi."

Anakin seemed to brace himself then. Seemed to lose his newly acquired confidence and polish. *"It's not just that. Um . . . how do I put this?"*

Oh no. Put what? *Anakin, what have you done?*

Anakin's expression was a muddle of defiance and contrition. *"I didn't wipe Artoo's memory."*

Obi-Wan stared as the words sank in. *"What?"* The enormity of the confession almost stole his breath. "He's still programmed with our tactics and base locations?" *No, no, no. This was impossible. Surely I trained him better than this!* "If the Separatists get hold of him . . ." A dozen nightmare scenarios ignited his imagination. Scenarios that made the Falleen battle group's loss seem insignificant. He didn't even try to moderate his anger. "What possessed you not to erase that droid's memory?"

As Anakin stared at him, miserably silent, Ahsoka stepped into holotransmitter range. *"Master Obi-Wan, sometimes Artoo having that extra information has come in handy."*

So the Padawan was defending her Master, was she? *She cer-*

tainly doesn't lack courage, I'll give her that. But her defense, her justification, meant nothing. Changed nothing. He wanted to shout at Anakin. Reach through the holotransmitter, grab his shoulders, and *shake* him. *Stupid, stupid, stupid . . .*

But that was physically impossible. And shouting was ill advised, with Organa listening to every word. With a wrenching effort he banished profitless temper.

"Find that droid, Anakin," he said flatly. "Our necks might very well depend on it."

Anakin brightened, doubtless surprised to escape so lightly. Doubtless pleased that he got to save the machine. *"Right away, Master."*

No wonder he hadn't wanted to contact the Council. "I'll inform Master Yoda you're . . . engaged in mopping-up operations. But handle this quickly, Anakin. Time is not on our side."

Determined now, Anakin nodded. *"I will. I promise. Thank you, Obi-Wan."*

"You're welcome," he growled, and severed the hololink.

THIRTEEN

"TROUBLE?" SAID ORGANA, SHAMELESSLY EAVESDROPPING.

"No," he said. He coded an update for the Council for transmission as text, then sent it. With luck they'd take the report at face value and not attempt a holographic follow-up.

He still couldn't believe Anakin had been so reckless. Or was he just being willfully blind? Anakin had always pushed far beyond what sensible people considered the bounds of safety. Of sanity. It was a kind of untamed genius. Qui-Gon had seen it. Had gambled on it, all those years ago on Tatooine. Had chanced many lives on the outcome of a Podrace, risking their futures on the untrained, untested skills of a slave boy.

And he'd been right.

Ten years of rigorous training later, it seemed the genius still wasn't completely tamed. Would never be tamed. Anakin continued to defy logic, ignore protocol, trample underfoot the rules he was meant to follow. Confident, always, that he would prevail. Confident his former Master would have his back.

And I did. I still do. But one of these days he's going to do something I can't justify. And what will become of him then I don't dare to contemplate.

"So," said Organa, intruding on his thoughts—or possibly rescuing him from them. "Everything's all right?"

"Of course," he said, shifting in his seat to stare through the viewport at the scattering of distant stars beyond. "We're at the first coordinates?"

"Got here nearly an hour ago."

So much for knowing when they dropped out of lightspeed. "What's our location?"

"About three parsecs trailing of Kuat."

"So we're still within the Core Worlds."

Organa shrugged. "Just."

"And we've yet to hear from your contact?"

"Oh no," said Organa, leaning back in his seat. "I received the next coordinates ten minutes after we got here. We're just sitting around because I like the view. You hungry?"

Obi-Wan looked at him. *This is going to be a long, long journey.* "Yes."

"We've got mealpacks in the galley." Organa pulled a face. "Well. The closet that's masquerading as a galley. Help yourself. Bring me one, too, could you?"

"Certainly, Senator," he said with exquisite courtesy. "It would be my pleasure."

He made his way to the ship's compact kitchen, extracted two mealpacks from the well-stocked conservator, and took them back to the cockpit.

"Thanks," said Organa, taking his and twisting the heat seal. "That Padawan of yours seems quite the handful," he added as he waited for the meal to warm up. "I'll bet he keeps you on your toes."

Obi-Wan returned to his seat at the comsat console. "I told you," he said, activating his own mealpack's heating mechanism. "Anakin is no longer my Padawan."

"You remember to tell him that?" said Organa, amused. "Because he sure called you fast enough when things went wrong."

Obi-Wan stared at him. *Whatever happened to reserved, for-*

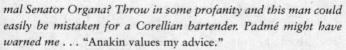

mal Senator Organa? Throw in some profanity and this man could easily be mistaken for a Corellian bartender. Padmé might have warned me . . . "Anakin values my advice."

"Uh-huh," said Organa. He peeled back his mealpack's lid and immediately the cockpit filled with the rich scent of spicy-sauced Fondor fowl. "And you value his safety."

There it was again: that sly, prodding, poking undertone. "Meaning what, Senator?"

Organa shrugged. "Meaning nothing. It's just an observation."

He wanted to say, *Keep your observations to yourself.* But he didn't. Replies merely encouraged more comments. Prolonged a conversation for which he had no desire. He turned his attention to his own meal, which had also reached its optimum temperature. Peeled back the lid, snapped free the attached spoon, and began to eat his fish hotpot.

"Do you ever wish you weren't a Jedi?" said Organa around a mouthful of food.

So much for enjoying the peace and quiet. "No."

"Not ever? Not even once? You've never considered what it might be like to have a different life?"

"No."

Frowning, Organa sat back, another spoonful of fowl paused partway to his mouth. "It's never bothered you that you didn't have a choice about being a Jedi? That you were given to the Temple as a baby?"

Clearly, short of gagging the man—now, there was a tempting thought—conversation was going to take place. Obi-Wan repressed a sigh. It wasn't the first time he'd heard such a sentiment expressed, and it wouldn't be the last. It was only to be expected: outsiders did not understand.

"You sound as though you're regretting your defense of us against the Quarren's allegations, Senator."

"Not at all," said Organa. "Only a fool or a troublemaker believes the Jedi are baby thieves."

Obi-Wan considered him. "But?"

"But . . ." Organa shrugged. "I have wondered, from time to time, about the way Jedi are raised. You must admit, Master Kenobi, it's not exactly a . . . normal . . . life."

"That would depend on how you define *normal,* Senator." He shook his head. "While it's true that many children are given to the Temple as infants, no child is kept with us against his or her will. The Temple is not a *prison.* It is a home. A school. A world within a world. A safe haven for those born with peculiar sensitivity to the Force. Believe me, Senator, there is more suffering experienced by those Force-sensitives denied Jedi training than any Padawan you might meet."

"So there is suffering?" said Organa, discarding his emptied mealpack. "You don't deny it?"

"Nobody's life is devoid of suffering, Senator."

"That's not what I mean, and you know it." Organa's gaze narrowed. "Come on, Master Jedi. Don't dance with me."

"If you are asking me whether it is sometimes difficult being a Jedi, the answer is yes," he replied calmly. "Is it your assertion that being a Senator is a bed of haffa-blossoms?"

Organa snorted. "One full of thorns, maybe. But at least I'm not forbidden—what did you call it? *Attachment.* At least I don't have to pretend I don't care about things. About people."

"There are many different ways of caring, Senator. Surely you're not so arrogant as to claim your way is superior to everyone else's?"

"Huh," said Organa, amused and irritated in equal measure. "You know, Master Kenobi, for a Jedi you're a pretty good debater. You should think about a career in the Senate yourself."

He shuddered. "Perish the thought."

"You really don't like us, do you?" said Organa, half smiling. Intrigued, and a little piqued. "Politicians, I mean. As a breed. What did we ever do to you, that you'd be so—"

"What?" said Obi-Wan, putting aside his meal.

Organa slid his hand inside his plain blue tunic and pulled out a small, innocuous-looking comlink. "Contact," he said quietly. "Excuse me."

He left the cockpit, heading for the passenger compartment. Obi-Wan watched the separating curtain pull shut, shrugged, and returned to his meal. Three more mouthfuls finished it, so he collected Organa's empty container, slotted it into his own, then used the Force to crush both into a small, neat cube ready for disposal in the waste chute.

Organa returned a few minutes later. Slid into the pilot's seat and began programming new coordinates into the nav comp.

"Where to now?" he asked. "If you don't mind my asking."

"Don't know yet," said Organa, punching the CALCULATE key. The nav comp hummed, then flashed a green light. "Ah. Atzerri." He flicked a sideways glance. "More or less. Assuming nothing goes wrong, nearly seventeen hours' flight time."

So. With each jump they were getting closer to the Inner Rim. Did that mean Zigoola—if indeed the planet existed—lay somewhere in the less rigorously charted regions? Was it located in the Outer Rim? . . . or even beyond? It seemed a reasonable hypothesis. Surely not even the Sith could hide a whole planet if it lay close to the heart of the Republic. Or close, at least, to any systems already familiar and regularly visited.

There is no point speculating. I'll find out soon enough if we are destined for the Outer Rim . . . or farther.

"Something wrong?" Organa said, frowning at him.

"Not at all. Tell me, Senator, how is it your contact knows when it's time to transmit the next coordinates?"

"They have my private link ID," said Organa. "The message I left on it, saying I was taking care of some family business, was our prearranged starter's flag. After that, I suppose it's a simple case of chrono-watching and mathematics."

"I see. And—given Coruscant's recently adopted security measures—how is it you've managed to keep the communications from your contact secret? I am assuming that all incoming transmissions are monitored, as well as outgoing?"

Organa looked down. For the briefest moment his expression twisted with discomfort. Uncertainty. Then he sighed, his olive skin tinting from a rush of blood. "You need me to spell it out for you, Master Kenobi?"

Not even the first word. "You want to know why I distrust politicians, Senator? *This* is why. You have a disconcerting habit of making up rules that don't then apply to you. It's a common hobby for those in power, I've found."

"I didn't hear you complain when I filed that bogus flight plan," Organa retorted, stung to self-defense.

"Senator, you know perfectly well that such an action falls under the purview of the Clandestine Operative Act. As a Jedi I have often filed a false flight plan. You are being—disingenuous. I doubt the same legislation covers your activities."

"No. It doesn't," Organa said, his voice low. "And if you think I'm happy about it, you're wrong. But I can live with it. Because I know I'm not acting against the Republic's interests. I'm acting *in* its interests. Right now I'm probably risking my life for its interests. So I'd be careful, if I were you, about accusing me of disloyalty."

"I would never do that, Senator. I don't question your motives, or your commitment to the Republic. But it's so easy to justify and rationalize one's actions. To find an excuse for doing what we want to do even though we know it's wrong. Yes, your motives are pure. But will that be true of the next politician who ignores the rule of law? Who says, *Trust me. What I'm doing is illegal but it's for such a good reason.*"

Organa shook his head. "I had no idea the Jedi were so cynical."

"Not cynical," Obi-Wan said gently. "Realistic. We do get to see rather a lot of the galaxy, Senator. And we're called in so often to clean up the messes politicians have made."

"Politicians don't just make messes, Master Kenobi," said Organa, his eyes troubled. "Good things are achieved, too. I think the scales are more evenly balanced than you'll admit."

"Perhaps. It's an interesting hypothesis, at any rate. But rather than debate it now, I suggest we continue our mission. I fear our window of opportunity might be closing as we speak."

"True," said Organa, but he didn't initiate the jump to light-speed. Instead he leaned forward, his expression taking on an intent, hunting-bird aspect. "But I want to get one thing straight before we make another jump. You Jedi see things, right? Feel things? Other places, other times. I mean, you knew something had happened to your Padawan. You woke up, and you *knew*."

"I fail to see what—"

"Don't interrupt me, and I'll explain," said Organa. "I know you think you're humoring me right now. Letting me tag along with you like a—a pesky kid. And maybe you think I need protecting like a kid. But I don't. In fact, I won't stand for it. So if your Jedi powers show you something about us—about this mission—you tell me. If we're flying into danger, you tell me. You don't keep it to yourself because you think I'm a soft politician who can't deal with harsh realities."

This man. He thought he knew about the Jedi, but he was ignorant. He knew *nothing*. "Do you think I would lie to you, Senator?"

"In a heartbeat," Organa said promptly. "If you thought it was for my own good. But *my own good* is what *I* determine it to be. Not you. So I want your word that what you know, you tell me. The moment you know it. Or I swear I will turn this ship around right now and take you back to Coruscant."

"And continue on your own?"

"Yes."

"That would be a grave mistake, Senator."

Organa shrugged, smiling thinly. "Maybe. But I'll make it without thinking twice. If you Jedi really can read people, you know I mean it."

Oh yes. He meant it. "Very well, Senator. You have my word." He offered a thin smile of his own. "And just for the record: beyond a general, and not unreasonable, unease, I do not feel we are in danger."

"Now," said Organa. "But how long will that be true?"

"I cannot say, Senator."

"Because the dark side clouds everything?"

And he hadn't been expecting *that*.

"It's something Padmé said once," Organa explained. "I've never forgotten it."

And how would she know? Was that Anakin, speaking out of turn? *Wonderful*. The last thing he needed was Organa worrying about the dark side, especially when there was nothing he could do about it. "It was a figure of speech, Senator. The Jedi are hardly crippled. If there is danger, I will sense it. *And* I will tell you."

"Okay," said Organa, nodding. "I can live with that." His lips quirking in a brief smile, he threw the ship into hyperspace. "But you know," he added, standing, "you really need a better reason for disliking me than the fact that I'm a politician. Disliking me just for that makes you shallow. And you're a lot of things, Master Kenobi, but shallow isn't one of them. Maybe you can think up a few more reasons while I'm getting some sleep."

He raised an eyebrow. "I'll do my best, Senator."

"I'll bet you will," Organa said, with another brief, twisted smile. Then he left the cockpit, whistling a jaunty tune under his breath.

Obi-Wan stared after him. *This is a test. The Force is testing me. Twelve years of Qui-Gon, ten years of Anakin, and now I get him.*

Exhaling sharply, banishing dismay, he slid into the pilot's seat, checked the flight console to make certain every system was running smoothly, then folded himself deep within the Force to rest.

And hopefully pierce the dark side's cloying veil, to search for dangers as yet unannounced.

Ten hours later Organa returned to the cockpit, bringing a datapad and a preoccupied expression with him. Relieved that the man appeared to have lost interest in conversation, at least for the moment, Obi-Wan left him to his work and withdrew to the passenger compartment. Not needing more sleep, he gave himself over to a deeper Force meditation than he'd been willing to undertake while on duty at the helm.

Still no hint of danger could he sense. Zigoola . . . the Sith . . . remained elusive. He searched for Anakin, but beyond a vague impression of urgency could not bring him into focus. And really, there was no point in trying. Anakin had his mission . . .

. . . and I have mine.

As Qui-Gon had told him, so many times, he had to keep his concentration on the here and now.

After an hour he stirred and checked the cabin's chrono. Six more hours before they reached their destination. He wasn't a Senator with committee work to ponder, new rules to dream up that he could ignore or circumvent when it suited him, but still—a Jedi did not lack for tasks. The passenger compartment was too small for lightsaber drills, but there was enough room—just—for him to work through his *alchaka* meditations. Stripped down to his leggings, barefoot, he drove himself through the meticulous repetitions, striving for perfection of form and execution. Failing, as always, but never forgetting that the striving was all.

Time slid by, sleek as cool water. Strengthened by the Force, buoyed by its constant presence, he lost himself in familiar motion. Invigorated himself with physical toil.

After two hours he felt his edge begin to dull. Felt the loss of concentration that heralded the end of effectiveness. Slick with sweat, breathing hard, he eased himself out of the Force and back to the paucity of an exterior life.

As always, it took him a little time to reacquaint himself with mundane reality, where the light seemed thinner, colors dimmer, scents and sounds less vivid. Less true. As always he felt a dreadful tug of loss, leaving behind the Force-fed richness of his inner life.

He availed himself of the ship's extremely small refresher then dressed again, noting that his tunic and leggings were looking a little the worse for wear. There was a compact laundry unit, however, which was fortunate since he hadn't brought a change of clothing with him. Presentable again, he went forward to the cockpit, where Organa was scowling at his datapad.

"So here's the thing," said the Senator, not looking around. "The argument goes—according to Ralltiir, anyway—that because they're on the very edge of what's designated as the Core Worlds region they shouldn't be expected to carry the same burden of Core Worlds Consortium levies because they are, in effect, the first line of defense for planets like Alderaan and Coruscant, which are closer to the center. To be precise, they think Alderaan and Coruscant—oh, and Chandrila—should subsidize their Munitions Levy." Now Organa spun his chair around, datapad in one hand. "What do you think?"

Obi-Wan smiled. "I think I'm glad it's not my problem."

"And I think *I'm* starting to think you've got the right idea about politicians," Organa muttered, rubbing his eyes. "Shoot me now."

"Before or after you've eaten?" he replied. "I was about to heat another mealpack. Can I do the same for you?"

"Thanks, but I ate earlier." Organa tapped a key on the datapad and tossed it onto the console. "I'll have a drink though. A Blackmoon ale, in a glass. No ice. Just a twist of sarsata peel. You'll find that in the conservator," he added helpfully. "In the jar beside the pickled rata-bulbs."

Treating me like a waiter, Senator? Ah well. It was his own fault for offering. Organa's eyes were glinting. He was waiting—hoping—for an offended refusal. *Not a chance, Bail Organa. As you say, I'm not that stupid*. He offered the man an ironical bow. "Certainly, sir."

Organa laughed, suspecting mockery. "Okay."

He chose a mealpack without bothering to read its contents. Poured Organa's ale into a glass and added a twist of blue sarsata peel. The astringent fumes made his eyes water. Then he returned to the cockpit.

"Sir," he said, handing the glass to the Senator with another bow.

Organa considered him, uncertain. "I was only joking, you know. I didn't actually intend for you to—"

"I know," he said, resuming his seat at the comsat console. "But I'm sure you'd do the same for me."

Organa swallowed a generous mouthful of the ale. "What was that you were doing before?"

"Before?"

"Yeah." Organa jerked his chin. "In the passenger compartment. I saw you when I was getting dinner. Lunch. Breakfast. Food, anyway. I lose track of which meal is which. What was it, some kind of Jedi training program?"

The mealpack finished heating, but he ignored it, disconcerted. Organa had watched him? But the *alchaka* meditations were deeply personal. "Some kind. Yes."

"It looked like hard work," Organa said, swallowing more ale. "But you were breezing through it. And I couldn't help but notice there's hardly a mark on you. A man gets himself blown up, you'd think he'd have a few scars."

Obi-Wan opened his mealpack to find some kind of curd-and-vegetable stew. It smelled pleasant enough, but his appetite was abruptly dulled. "Jedi healing is most effective."

"Yeah. So I saw. One scar only, on your arm."

There was an undercurrent of disapproval in his tone. Obi-Wan looked up, frustrated. "From a lightsaber. If I'd realized it would distress you, Senator, I'd have worn my tunic during my private meditation."

"I'm not distressed. Just curious."

He put down his mealpack. "You are not curious, you're critical. Are you suggesting I should have refused healing? Had I done so, I most certainly would have died."

"No," said Organa. "No, of course I'm not suggesting that."

"Then what? Senator, if you have an observation to make about the Jedi, you should feel free to make it. We are not some secret society, immune from public commentary."

Organa swallowed the rest of his ale in one gulp. "No. But you are pretty mysterious."

"Mysterious? I hardly think so."

"Ha," said Organa. "Now who's being disingenuous? Sure, you've got a public face. Guardians of the peace. Upholders of the law. Protectors of the weak and helpless. Wherever there's trouble, there's a Jedi trying to put out the fire. Everyone knows that. But you're a bit spooky, too. You've got this mystique. This—this *aura*. You're not like the rest of us, Master Kenobi. You're beings apart, with powers and abilities ordinary folk can't understand. *You* get blown up and hey presto! You're healed. Not a mark to show for it. Not a limp. Not *anything*. When normal people get hurt, there's a consequence. But not for you Jedi."

Obi-Wan felt his jaw clench. "Really? You should advance that theory to my former Padawan sometime, Senator. He'd be most interested to hear it. And when you've done pontificating, he can show you his prosthetic arm."

Organa blinked. Then he dropped his gaze to the empty glass he nursed in both hands, and stared at the bedraggled blue twist of sarsata peel at its bottom.

"All I meant," he said at last, his voice tight, "is that it's a shame the other people hurt in the terrorist attacks can't experience the same benefits of Jedi healing that you did." He looked up, then, and his eyes were haunted. "I saw some of them, you know. After.

And even with intensive bacta treatment there are now children who'll have to go through life hideously maimed and disfigured. It's . . . sad. It's cruel. That's all I meant."

The man's compassion was laudable, but his inferences were insulting. "I think what you meant, Senator, is that it's somehow unfair that I'm not sharing their fate," Obi-Wan snapped. And then he caught hold of his temper. Crushed it before he said something truly unfortunate. "It's not because we don't care," he continued, far more moderately. "We do, I assure you. However, healing is one of our rarest gifts. We help as many as we can, wherever we can, and keenly regret that we cannot help more. But are you saying that because we can't help everyone, we shouldn't help *anyone*?"

"No. I'm sorry," said Organa, shaking his head. "This isn't coming out right. I really am on your side, you know. I admire the Jedi enormously. I am in awe of what you do. But in case you hadn't noticed it, this war has thrust you onto center stage. You're in the news every day. Everything you do is being *examined. Magnified.* And when the novelty's worn off, it's going to be second-guessed, and maybe even held up for censure. *Especially* if the war drags on, or doesn't go our way. Because you have been placed on a pedestal as tall as any Coruscant skyscraper."

"That was never our intention, Senator, I assure you."

"I know," said Organa. "But you're up there regardless. You're the *Jedi,* Master Kenobi. Larger than life and twice as hard to kill. Still, the more systems the Separatists entice or strong-arm to their side, the more suffering and fear the Republic experiences, the closer the Separatists creep to the Core, and the longer it takes the Jedi to end this conflict—the harder your pedestal is going to rock. Especially if it's perceived that you're not suffering like everyone else."

"Not *suffering*, Senator?" he said, incredulous. "After Geonosis? After the engagements we've fought already? And losing the Falleen battle group? Must the Jedi Temple itself fall before it can be agreed that the Jedi are also paying a price for this war we did not start?"

"Of course not," said Organa. "I'm talking about perception, not reality. The bedrock of politics. I think you'll grant it's one of my areas of expertise."

The least honorable of them all. Obi-Wan nodded. "I concede your point."

"And I wish you didn't have to," Organa replied. "Master Kenobi, the Jedi have been the Republic's peacekeepers for generations. Citizens are used to you solving their local problems. Their community disputes. But we both know that what we're facing is far more complicated. And I promise you, I *promise*—when things get really bad you *will* be blamed."

Curd-and-vegetable stew forgotten, Obi-Wan stared in silence at the Senator from Alderaan.

"I'm sorry," said Organa, turning away. "You don't have to say it. I'm just a politician. It's none of my business."

Just a politician? No. Far from it. Now it was clear why Padmé liked and trusted this princeling from Alderaan. He was . . . unexpected.

"The Jedi aren't blind, Senator," he said, at last. "We're perfectly aware that our elevation in the public eye is problematic. We opposed it vigorously. We continue to oppose it. We are, as you say, peacekeepers. Not celebrities. The Supreme Chancellor should reconsider his tactics. We feel very strongly there is a chance they could end up doing us more harm than good."

Surprised, Organa turned back. Then he pulled a face. "Palpatine means well. His problem is he's not *enough* of a politician. He never has been. He's just a kindly provincial Senator who blundered into high office by chance. If the Trade Federation hadn't invaded Naboo—if Valorum hadn't lost his grip—someone else would be Supreme Chancellor now. He doesn't see the pitfalls of what he's doing. He genuinely believes it's all for the best."

Obi-Wan reached for his mealpack and took refuge from troubling thought in food. "Perhaps it will be," he said, forking up his first mouthful. The stew had cooled almost completely, but his empty belly didn't care. "Though I do not think so."

"Neither do I," said Organa. He looked again into his glass. "Think I'll help myself to another ale. Can I get you one?"

He shook his head. "Alcohol is not recommended for Jedi. Water will suffice. Thank you."

"We've still got a few hours' flying time," Organa said casually, returning to the cockpit with their drinks. "And I've had as much as I can stand of Ralltiir's whining, at least for now. Fancy a game of sabacc? There's a pack of cards around here somewhere, and a few tins of pocho-nuts we can use for credits. Unless Jedi don't gamble?"

"On the contrary," said Obi-Wan. "We gamble all the time. Just not on games of chance. Besides, for some strange reason we tend to make our fellow gamblers uneasy."

"Can't imagine why," said Organa, grinning. "So, sabacc it is. Do you promise not to use any Jedi sleight of hand?"

"Only if you promise to spare me your wily politician's ways," he replied, deliberately placid.

Organa nodded, still amused. "Deal. We can play in the passenger compartment. The nav comp alarm will let us know when we're approaching Atzerri."

"What?" said Obi-Wan as the Senator considered him, his gaze narrow and speculative.

"I didn't think you'd say yes."

"Why wouldn't I?" he said, pretending surprise. "Sabacc is a perfectly respectable way to pass the time."

"I guess," said Organa, gesturing. "After you."

Hiding a smile in his beard, Obi-Wan pushed past the curtain into the adjoining passenger compartment.

Yes indeed. It's perfectly respectable, and a keen diagnostic tool for those who know how to use it. And I intend to use it, Senator. There is far more to you than meets the eye, it would seem.

FOURTEEN

OBI-WAN WON THE FIRST GAME, WHICH TAUGHT HIM THAT BAIL Organa was a bold thinker, an innovative strategist, a man not afraid to take risks for the chance of a reward—but one also inclined to act on faith rather than a surety of good cards. The second game he lost, which taught him that Padmé's friend was a very fast learner who could sum up an opponent quickly and didn't make the same mistake twice. Armed with these useful nuggets of information, he immediately abandoned his previous tactics and began to play the next hand like Qui-Gon used to. But just as it seemed that he might, possibly, win the third game, the nav comp started beeping again.

They'd reached Atzerri.

"You know much about this region of the Republic?" Organa asked as they sat a safe distance off the busy planet's single, craggy moon.

He nodded, dark memories stirring. "I know a little. I was involved in settling a dispute on Antar Four—nearly sixteen years ago now."

"Sixteen years . . ." Organa chewed his lip. "The colfillini plantation dispute? You were involved in that debacle?"

He cocked an eyebrow. "Well, I didn't cause it, if that's what you're suggesting."

"I know what caused it," said Organa, his eyes hot with memory. "Local organized crime. My uncle was murdered by those scum. Killed in cold blood, just for standing up to thugs who thought working people to death was acceptable economic practice."

Stinking smoke in the morning. The stench of burned flesh. A scarecrow figure nailed to a stake, charred to friable ash. But not even fire could hide the brutal fingerprints of torture.

Obi-Wan swallowed. "The agricultural expert? Tayvor Mandirly? He was your uncle?"

"My mother's youngest brother." Organa grimaced. "She never got over what they did to him. In the end his death killed her. So you could say they murdered *two* members of my family."

"I'm sorry."

Organa shrugged the condolence aside. "Raxis and Nolid should have paid for what they did."

"They did pay, Senator."

"*Fines*," spat Organa. "*Money*. They should have paid more. They shouldn't have been allowed to buy their way to absolution. You Jedi should've made them pay a *real* price."

He sighed. "We are not executioners, Senator. Nor are we instruments of vengeance. The government of Antar Four asked us to assist them in apprehending those responsible for outrages committed on the planet's largest colfillini plantation, and we did. What happened after that was an internal matter. We are limited by our mandate."

"That's easy for you to say!" retorted Organa. "Did you *see* what those animals did to Tayvor? Did you *see* how he—"

"Senator, I found him."

Found him. And for many nights afterward screamed for him in my sleep. Because you were right, Senator. The Force shows us the past, as well as the future.

Silenced, Organa stared at him. "I didn't know that," he said at last, subdued. "I never knew the names of the Jedi who went to Antar Four."

"Yes. Well," he said drily. "Those were the days when the Jedi weren't HoloNet news stars."

"So. It was you." Organa shook his head. "Now, there's a co-incidence. Small galaxy, isn't it?"

"Sometimes it feels that way." Except there were no coinci-dences in the Force . . . and everything happened for a reason. This was meant. It was meant. The question was, why?

"I suppose now you think I'm uncivilized," said Organa, taking Obi-Wan's silence for disapproval. "After all, no proper peaceful Alderaanian would bay for the blood of those murdering beasts."

Such pain in him. Such grief and loss. Sixteen years and the an-guish hadn't dulled. Was this Anakin's fate, now that Shmi was dead?

And is it mine, also? Qui-Gon was father and brother to me. Family, as the world outside the Temple counts such things. Is it the relationship that won't let the wound heal, or the way that they died? Stolen. Murdered. Ripped from life before their time.

Perhaps. It was a troubling thought. As a Jedi he wasn't sup-posed to care so much. Attachment, again. His perennial stumbling block. *Let go,* said Yoda. So much easier said than done. Perhaps if he lived a few hundred more years . . .

"No, Senator, I don't think that," he said gently. "I think you're a son who loved his mother, and her brother. I think you're a man who despises greed and cruelty. Who burns for justice." He hesi-tated, then added, "Qui-Gon and I also wished they had paid a steeper price."

Organa was frowning. "Qui-Gon, who was killed by the Sith?"

"That's right."

"Just as a matter of interest, Master Kenobi . . . what happened to the Sith who murdered your Master?"

Obi-Wan took a deep breath. Let it out, very slowly. "I believe you know perfectly well, Senator."

Organa pretended to think. Pretended amazement. "Oh yes! That's right, Padmé said. You killed him." A thin, knife-edged smile. "But you're not an agent of vengeance, or anything."

He said nothing to that. There were no words.

"The thing is, Master Kenobi," said Organa, still smiling that thin, dangerous smile, "you're not the only one who can learn things playing sabacc."

He took another deep breath. Let it fill his lungs completely; no more twinges from his healed broken ribs. Eased it out again, and with it all emotion. "Apparently not, Senator."

And then Organa's comlink buzzed, and it was time to receive their new instructions.

"Munto Codru," said Organa, reading off the nav comp. "That's . . . a long way from the Core Worlds."

It was indeed. Munto Codru lay in the distant reaches of the Outer Rim Territories. Perturbed, Obi-Wan considered his inconvenient companion. "Senator, I think we need to reconsider our situation."

"Why?" said Organa. "We've got plenty of supplies. The ship's still sound. What is there to reconsider?"

"Your participation in this mission," he said bluntly. "We have no idea how much farther from home your contact will send us. We might well end up deep within the Unknown Regions."

"So far?" said Organa, skeptical. "Surely not. Why would the Sith be all the way out there?"

He shrugged. "I don't know. But with the Sith, anything is possible. My point, Senator, is that it's not *safe* out here."

Organa pretended shock. "Not safe? Master Kenobi, I had no idea! Why didn't you warn me? Quick! Let's go home!"

"Mock me if you must, Senator," he said, resisting the urge to grit his teeth. "But I would be remiss if I did not point out that while we have traveled without incident until now, our circumstances might easily and swiftly alter. There is still time to change your mind."

Organa looked at him steadily. "Do you want to turn back?"

"No. But this isn't about me. I am a Jedi, and this is what we do. You are a married Republic Senator."

"I don't want to turn back," Organa said flatly. "I don't want to give up. I want to stop the Sith, and put a face to the faceless people who've been helping me all these years. And to be perfectly frank, Master Kenobi, I'm getting pretty tired of your attitude. Would you be asking Padmé if she wanted to turn back?"

No. But Padmé had long since proven herself. This man was an unknown quantity. "Padmé isn't here, Senator. I am merely concerned for your safety."

"Let me say this for the last time, Master Kenobi: you let me worry about that."

The problem with being stuck in a very small spaceship, in what amounted to the middle of nowhere, was that one couldn't simply . . . walk away. *I swear, he's as bad as Anakin. But at least I could tell Anakin to be quiet and do as he was told, and he had to obey me.*

"Very well, Senator," he said. "It's your decision. I can only hope you don't come to regret it."

And with that trenchant observation, turning his back on Organa, he tried to contact Yoda. But distance and the vagaries of interstellar galactic phenomena combined to degrade his comm signal to fragments. He did, however, manage to raise Adi Gallia, who was battling a Separatist detachment on the comparatively close Outer Rim planet of Agomar. She promised to relay his message back to the Temple as soon as possible, and bade him be careful, whatever else he did. She didn't ask what he was doing so far from

Coruscant; not from lack of concern, but because the days where they could talk freely were behind them.

Even knowing that, it was on the tip of his tongue to ask her about Anakin, if she'd heard any news, if he was returned safely from his droid hunt. But he couldn't. He didn't want to betray Anakin's miscalculation to a member of the Council. Not before it was absolutely necessary, at least.

"May the Force be with you, Adi," he said, and terminated their comlink. Then he turned to Organa, who was running a check on the nav comp calculations. "When you're ready, Senator."

"I'm ready," Organa muttered, clearly still rankled. "Munto Codru coming up." He fired up the stardrive and nudged the ship away from Atzerri into open space. When the nav comp beeped the all-clear, he kicked them over into lightspeed.

Beyond the viewport the stars swirled and streaked. Realspace vanished, and they were at the mercy of otherness.

Obi-Wan stood. "If you'll excuse me, Senator, I have meditations to perform."

"Sure," said Organa, reaching for his datapad. "Knock yourself out. Don't let me hold you up."

The words were colloquial, conversational; the tone was curt. The lofty galactic representative dismissing an underling. The hired help.

I am a Jedi. We do not take such things personally.

They didn't attempt to slam curtains, either. But it took a lifetime of training to resist the urge.

Three more days in hyperspace, claustrophobically cocooned. Such a pity it wasn't a faster ship. Organa buried himself in the work he'd brought with him, a virtual mountain of domestic and inter-system legislative business. Obi-Wan, observing this, found himself reluctantly admiring. Just like Padmé—and unlike so many other

Senators the Jedi had observed—Organa was no pretender. He took his duties seriously. It was a curiously comforting discovery.

For his own part, he turned captivity to his advantage, surrendering himself to the kind of deep meditations usually practiced by Jedi on retreat or committed to the contemplative life. To his relief, he could sense no lowering danger. No threat from Grievous to these distant hyperlanes. Which wasn't surprising. There was little out here for the Republic to want. And if the Republic didn't want it, neither did Dooku and his Separatists.

What he did perceive, in glimpses, were some of the Jedi's Outer Rim campaigns. Adi Gallia triumphant on Agomar. Ki-Adi-Mundi defeated almost to death on Barab I. Eeth Koth defending the besieged people of Korriban, surrounded by drifts of dead and dying clone troopers. Saesee Tiin in desperate straits closer to the Core, on Bimmisaari—but no. No, that was not now, that was then. A trade dispute of the past, long since peacefully settled.

He caught a single impression of Anakin, more feeling than vision. Sorrow. Frustration. A crushing fear of failure. He couldn't find that wretched droid.

Well, try harder, Anakin. Did you think I was joking? R2 in the wrong hands could spell defeat for us all.

Irritation battled with a razor-sharp concern. His greatest fear was that they kept asking too much of the Order's vaunted *Chosen One*. That, dazzled by his potential, they blinded themselves to his youth. And now that he'd scored such a decisive victory at Bothawui, with the crisis of war deepening the trend would surely continue.

But not to his detriment. No matter what it takes, or what it costs, I must continue to protect him.

It was hard, being out here, so far from the Temple, from the war, suspended in this bubble of waiting. Unable to help Anakin, to help Ki-Adi-Mundi or Eeth Koth. Help any of his fellow Jedi fighting on too many desperate fronts. He'd never been like Qui-Gon, able to stop in the midst of action and simply suspend thought and feeling. Accept the moment as it was, without question, until the moment transformed into a new reality. No. He'd always needed to be *doing* something. Making things happen. Seizing the moment by the throat.

"You're a restless spirit, Obi-Wan," Qui-Gon used to say, rueful and resigned. And as usual, he was right.

The life of a contemplative is most certainly not for me.

But he could endure it for a short while, if it meant thwarting the Sith. And when he wasn't sleeping, or meditating, and Organa was safely out of the way in the cockpit cursing Ralltiir, or whoever, he performed his *alchaka* forms, disciplining his body as rigorously as his mind, banishing the faint lingering traces of recent injury. Becoming himself again not a moment too soon.

And so the time passed . . . and they came at last to Munto Codru.

"Nearly seven hours and not a whisper," said Organa, his fingers drumming a staccato tattoo on the console. "They've never made us wait this long before."

Obi-Wan slid his gaze away from the looming bulk of the planet, a cloud-banded sleeping jewel surrounded by twelve spinning moons. Their ship sat high above the planet's night side, deep within the twelfth moon's shadow, unobserved. Below them Munto Codru's surface was spackled with lights from its cities. Brighter lights flitted like firedrakes, ships arriving and departing at irregular intervals.

"Be patient, Senator," he said. "If your contact is as reliable as you claim, we will hear from them."

Frustrated, Organa glared at him. Then he punched the helm console. "Patience is all well and good, but we can't sit here forever."

"No, we can't," he agreed mildly. "It's only a matter of time before we attract the attention of the Codru-Ji. Which is not advisable."

Another glare. "Then what do you suggest?"

Obi-Wan reached into the Force with his newly honed senses. "An hour," he murmured, drifting in the light. "Let's give your contact one more hour."

But in the end they waited less than half that. And when Organa's comlink buzzed this time, and he answered it, there came no coded shortburst—but instead the sound of a living human voice. Mature. Female. Confident.

"Senator Organa. Do you copy?"

Organa snatched up the comlink from the console. "Yes! Yes, I copy. I hear you. Who is this? Who am I speaking to?"

"A friend."

"Yes, I know that. But—"

"Names can wait, Senator. I'll introduce myself properly when we meet."

Organa was gripping the comlink so tightly he was in danger of breaking it. "I've been looking forward to that. Where are you, somewhere close?"

"Close enough," said the woman. *"I'll shortburst you the nav comp coordinates in a moment."*

"We thought something had gone wrong," said Organa. "You took so long to—"

"A precaution," said the woman. *"We wanted to be certain you were truly alone before allowing you to see us face-to-face."*

Organa frowned. "Of course I'm alone. Well, aside from—from the Jedi who's accompanied me. Surely you know by now that I honor our arrangement to the letter."

Through the slight background slush came soft, not entirely amused laughter. *"These are dangerous times, Senator. It doesn't pay to take anything or anyone for granted. Not even you. Not even the Jedi."*

"I appreciate that," Organa said, after a moment. "And I hope you know I don't take you for granted. What you've done—what you're doing now—"

"Thanks can wait too, Senator," said the woman. *"Let's focus on defeating the Sith. Stand by for our coordinates and transponder beacon frequency. It'll guide you right to the front door."*

"Understood," said Organa. "We'll see you soon."

"These friends of yours are indeed cautious," said Obi-Wan as they waited for the coded shortburst to come through.

"I told you," said Organa. "So it's a good thing you—" He broke off as the comlink buzzed, then received their next location. When the data was downloaded, he stood. "As I was saying. It's a good thing you and Master Yoda didn't try anything tricky—like have another Jedi trail us."

Obi-Wan kept his face blank. "Senator?"

"Don't tell me you and Master Yoda didn't discuss it," said Organa, deceptively reasonable. There was a cold glitter in his eyes. "Back on Coruscant. In my apartment."

He sighed. *A timely reminder, this, not to underestimate our friend from Alderaan.* "What Master Yoda and I discussed then is hardly relevant now, Senator. You and I are here, and about to meet your contact. I suggest you decode that shortburst so we don't keep these Friends of the Republic waiting. After all, that would be impolite."

Organa gave him a look but didn't pursue the matter, just withdrew to the passenger compartment. On returning to the cockpit he programmed the nav comp, then the transponder beacon.

"Well?" Obi-Wan asked, as the Senator stared at the readout. "Where to this time?"

"I don't know," Organa said slowly. "The nav comp's accepted the coordinates, but the destination's coming up as unknown."

For the first time since his vision of Anakin's battle against Grievous at Bothawui, he felt a prickle of definite, specific unease. "Interesting. What's the distance between here and there?"

"Nine parsecs. Which definitely takes us beyond the Outer Rim."

"Beyond the Outer Rim and into Wild Space." Obi-Wan stroked his beard. "A leap of faith indeed, Senator."

"Yes," said Organa, very quietly, the merest shadow of uncertainty ghosting across his face. As though at long last the implications of his actions were beginning to sink in.

Now do you understand, Senator? Now do you grasp what I've been trying to tell you? We are standing on the edge of the unknown, and if we fall . . . there is no one to catch us.

"So let's leap," said Organa. He engaged the ship's thrusters. Pushed them away from Munto Codru's twelfth moon—and jumped them into hyperspace.

Leaving Organa to distract himself with more legislative brouhaha, Obi-Wan withdrew to the passenger compartment and sank himself into a light trance. That prickle of unease had unsettled him. There was something *not right.* He could feel it. A potential of trouble approaching. A possibility of strife.

But what was its source? Was the woman on the comlink in danger? Or did she pose a threat to himself and the Senator? Was this meeting a trap? Was he about to fly into another unanticipated explosion? Would this leap of faith prove fatal? He couldn't tell. Couldn't see ahead clearly. It only made him more unsettled.

He pushed himself deeper, seeking answers . . . but none came. All he found was a headache, punishment for trying to bully information from the Force. Abandoning his fruitless search at last, he broke free of his trance and went forward to the cockpit, where Organa was muttering under his breath as he made copious notes on a datapad.

"How far out from our destination are we, Senator?"

Organa took one look at him and stopped muttering. Tossing

the datapad aside, he straightened out of his slouch. "What's wrong?"

He shook his head. "I don't know. Something—a feeling—I can't pin it down."

"What do you mean, you can't pin it down?" said Organa, not quite hiding his alarm. "You're a Jedi."

He dropped into the comsat seat. "Which has never equated to being infallible—breathlessly gushing HoloNet news reports notwithstanding."

"But there's trouble?" Organa persisted. "You're sure of that much?"

"I'm sure I have a bad feeling," he replied. "Which I'd be foolish to ignore. How far out are we?"

"Oh." Organa checked the nav comp. "Not far. We're practically there. What do you want to do?"

Turn back time so this mission never happened. Or, failing that, tie you hand and foot and stuff you in a cupboard.

"Proceed," he said. "I don't see that we have any choice."

"No," said Organa, a new tension in his voice. "We don't." He slid out of the pilot's seat, collected his various datapads, and carried them back to the passenger compartment. When at length he returned to the cockpit he had a small, lethal-looking personal blaster belted at his hip.

Obi-Wan bit back a colorful curse. *Wonderful. Bail Organa in a shooting match. And if anything happens to him . . .* "Senator—"

Organa flicked him a forbidding look. "I don't want to hear it, Master Kenobi."

Of course you don't. Nevertheless, he was duty-bound to say it. "I am expressly mandated to keep you safe, Senator. Therefore I cannot permit you to—"

"Okay," said Organa, ignoring him. "Dropping out of hyperspace in three—two—one—"

As the elongated stars contracted, returning to their usual configurations, Obi-Wan felt a wave of foreboding surge through him, thick and cloying, coating him with dread. Negligently dangling beyond the cockpit viewport was a short squat spindle of tarnished metal, burnished with low lighting. A space station, many decades old, chosen from the economy catalog. Corellian in design, he was almost sure. It had that particular raffishness about it. A reckless disregard for convention and neatness. There was no planetary body in sight; the space station hung lonely against a backdrop of unrelieved black.

"Well," said Organa on a long, slow exhalation. "That would explain why the nav comp didn't recognize the coordinates." He flicked a glance sideways. "Still got your bad feeling?"

He nodded. "Oh yes."

"So—maybe it's not such a good idea to activate their homing beacon."

"Maybe not," he agreed. "I suggest we glide in, Senator. No bells and whistles. No signature at all. A nice, inconspicuous, *silent* approach."

"Uh-huh." Organa pulled a face. "All right. It'll be like trying to glide a brick, but I'll do my best. And have you got a nice big blanket we can hide under while we're at it? They're going to have external security cams, you can bet on it."

Obi-Wan closed his eyes, feeling his Force awareness hum and thrum with alarm. "If they do, I have a nasty suspicion they're no longer functioning," he murmured. "Senator, I strongly suspect we're flying into mayhem."

"Not flying," said Organa, rolling his eyes. "*Gliding*. Like a brick. Hold on. Here we go."

He powered down all superfluous ship functions, fingers dancing over the helm console, then cut the dull, serviceable Starfarer's sublight drive. The engine's subliminal rumbling fell silent, leaving an odd kind of emptiness in its wake. The cockpit lights dimmed almost to darkness. Feeling the ship's immediate intertial drag, its sluggish wallowing through the void toward the battered space station, Obi-Wan shifted sideways a little and braced himself against the nearest bit of wall.

Like a brick indeed. May the Force be with us.

In the fuzzily greenish glow from the helm console, Organa's face was grim and set, jaw clenched against the effort of wrestling with the deliberately crippled ship. His fingers were bloodless on the helm controls, fighting to keep their course true, fighting to prevent them from crashing into the space station. Obi-Wan, watching him, was prepared to concede his skill. The Senator wasn't an idle boaster after all; he was in fact an excellent pilot.

But even the best pilots can sometimes use a helping hand.

Sinking into the Force, he gathered its measureless power to him. Felt the light fill him, sparkling in his blood. Once he was supremely centered, aware of himself and his place in the universe, aware of Organa's place, the duet they sang within the Force's living glory, he extended his senses and control. Wrapped them around the struggling starship, the gliding brick, and cradled it in a cocoon of pure light-side energy. Immediately the ship's sluggish inertia smoothed. Became malleable. Frictionless now, and rendered opaque to any prying eyes that might be watching, it floated toward their target, the space station.

"What the kriff?" Startled, Organa almost let go of the helm controls.

He felt himself smile. "Relax, Senator. There's no need to worry."

"Easy for you to say," Organa muttered. "What are you doing?"

"Think of me as your copilot," he replied. "And be calm."

Floating within himself, suffused with the Force, the source of every comfort and joy, he poured more control through the skin and bones of the ship, exerting his will on the lumpen machine. It answered him, a part of his body now, as responsive as his arm or his hand, and through the Force became as his own flesh and blood. His eyes showed him the space station, swiftly filling the viewport.

Like a shark beneath deep water, unease flicked its tail.

Soaked in serenity, his focus absolute, he let the darkness flow through him like water through a sieve. Yes, there was danger. He would meet it in due course. But he was in the light of the Force now, and would remain there until his task was complete.

"Nudge port," said Organa, shifting the helm control. "We've got a clear docking ring."

He nodded, dreamily. "I see it, Senator."

"We're still coming in too fast."

"I know." He breathed in deeply, feeling the power surge in his blood. Breathed out, hard, impressing his will upon the stolid Starfarer, tightening the Force around its sturdy frame. The ship lost more momentum. Glided slower. And slower. Slowed further. Was barely moving. And as he slowed the ship, Organa played its helm controls like a master musician, coaxing it to pirouette like a dancer on an opera stage.

The Starfarer docked with the space station, sweet as a summer kiss.

Organa released a noisy sigh and sat back. "Now, that was something. That was—that was—"

"That was the Force, Senator," Obi-Wan said, and breathed himself free of its sublime embrace. Felt the dreadful wrenching as they were gently sundered. Was overwhelmed, just for a heartbeat, by a dreadful sense of loss.

And even as the bright light drained from his blood, he felt that cold lash of foreboding, redoubled.

Organa had powered up the sensor array and was running a scanner over the space station. "Vape it," he said, looking around. "It's got some kind of shielding. I can't read through it."

Obi-Wan touched fingertips to his lightsaber, holding his shouting instincts at bay. "I can," he said grimly. "Senator, are you sure you want to do this? Are you *competent* to do this? Answer me honestly. We're on the brink of an abyss."

Instead of uttering some bravado reply, Organa looked at him. Even after nearly five days in this cramped starship the man was neat and tidy, impeccably presented, a self-aware politician from groomed head to polished boots. But his eyes were uncertain. In their shadows, lurking fear.

And then he nodded. "Yes, Master Kenobi. I'm sure, and I'm competent. I must do this. I know it probably sounds crazy, but those are my people in there."

Obi-Wan shifted his gaze, letting it rest on the space station. *I could drop him in his tracks without laying a finger on him. I should. This man is a civilian. It's my business to protect him and the people we came to meet.*

Organa unclipped his holster guard. Eased the blaster on his hip. "Master Kenobi, we're burning daylight."

Yes. Yes, they were. Burning daylight, and burning bridges. *Those are my people in there.* "Then come, Senator," he said, and snapped his lightsaber free. "Let's go and save your people, if we can."

FIFTEEN

THERE WERE THREE BODIES ON THE OTHER SIDE OF THE DOCKING ring door. All male; Bail swallowed a nauseating mix of relief and rage seeing them. His contact might still be alive then, even if three of her colleagues were slaughtered. If these men were her colleagues, of course. They could be intruders, cut down by defenders of the space station.

A buzz hummed beside him. Blaster in hand he turned, his nerves jumping, to see that Kenobi had ignited his lightsaber. The Jedi held it before him, angled slightly across his body, its electric blue light clean and lethal in the sputtering illumination of the small docking bay interchange, with its riveted metal walls and discolored metal ceiling. The door into the space station proper was partially open, the corridor beyond it tinged a dirty reddish orange. Emergency lighting? Possibly. This was certainly an emergency.

Kenobi dropped to a crouch and checked the pulses of the fallen men. "They're gone," he said, rising smoothly again to his feet.

It would've been shocking if they weren't; each man had an ugly, blood-wet hole burned through his chest. Three blaster pistols were discarded around them on the buckled metal floor. Kenobi stabbed his lightsaber through them in three swift, methodical moves. Melted blaster metal puddled and ran; the air thickened with a scorching stink.

Bail frowned. "Ah—couldn't we have used those, maybe?"

"Perhaps," Kenobi said, shrugging. "But so could whoever killed these men—and we don't know yet whose side they're on."

True. Acutely aware of sweat trickling down his spine, down his face, into his eyes, aware of his heart drumming hard against his ribs, Bail nodded. "Fair enough."

Soft-footed in his supple leather boots, Kenobi crossed to the half-open door and bent his head, listening. Or maybe feeling. Something Jedi, anyway. He looked unnervingly remote, the light-saber casting odd blue highlights over his face. Bail was abruptly aware of his own lingering awe.

He floated a starship with the Force. A whole starship. And he didn't even break a sweat. I wasn't expecting that. It's just not something you see every day.

"Senator," said Kenobi, glancing up. "The corridor is clear. Are you ready?"

Was he ready? Well, he could handle a blaster, he knew that much. Regular practice on a Coruscant firing range ensured that he was—as the experts said—a crack shot. And of course, being the scion of his House, as a much younger man he'd been taught certain self-defense techniques and tactics. But the galaxy was a different place now. So because he believed in being prepared, no matter how remote the chance of danger seemed; because he'd seen how narrowly Padmé had escaped death on Coruscant; and because he knew that the coming of war changed everything, whether he wanted change or not—he had made it his mission to be further trained by experts in the messy business of a more aggressive self-defense. They'd trained him well. He was indeed . . . competent.

But he'd never fired at a sentient being in his life. Never tried to kill anyone. Never had anyone try to kill him. And now he was staring at the likelihood of both experiences—maybe within the next few minutes. There were three men dead on the floor behind him as proof. Men who had shot at other men before. Men who most likely had killed, many times.

I thought I was ready. I might be wrong about that.

But he couldn't afford doubts and second thoughts now. Somewhere in this rickety old space station was a woman who'd risked her life to help him. He wasn't about to let her down when she needed *his* help. When her life might depend on that crack shot, Senator Organa.

Kenobi was waiting for his answer.

He nodded, his mouth dry. "Lead the way, Master Jedi."

"Stay close behind me," Kenobi said. His forehead was creased, and his eyes were dark with furious thought. "If I tell you to do something you must do it, without hesitation. This is no time for self-importance or pride."

Bail opened his mouth to say something cutting—then swallowed the hasty words. *Don't be a fool, Organa. He's a general in the Grand Army of the Republic. He's seen more life-and-death warfare in three months than you likely will your whole life. Right here, right now, he outranks you in every way.*

"Understood, Master Kenobi. I will follow your lead."

Kenobi nodded, a little of the tension easing from his face. "Good."

And they entered the silent and dingily lit access corridor, treading lightly, breathing softly. Bail felt the hairs stand up on the back of his neck. There was a scarlet trail on the metal floor leading them to the corridor's far end, where another door, closed this time, blocked their progress.

Blood. He was walking through *blood.* As he followed Kenobi, who seemed oblivious to those red splatters and smears, Bail felt his fingers tighten on his blaster.

I could be dead soon. This could be the last thing I ever do . . .

"Control your thoughts, control your feelings, Senator," said

Kenobi, not turning, a bite in his voice. "Focus on the moment. Don't let your mind stray."

Thus spake the Jedi Master to his sweating, heart-hammering, unlikely apprentice. Bail blinked hard, to clear his vision, and did as he was so curtly told.

They reached the end of the corridor. The door sealing them off from the space station's interior was solid metal, no handy porthole so they could see what they were getting into. But apparently Kenobi didn't need a porthole; pressing his left palm flat to the door, he closed his eyes and . . . disappeared. Not physically, of course, but mentally. Just as it had in the starship's cockpit, his face softened into the most extraordinary expression of serenity . . . with hints of an iron will beneath it.

The access corridor continued eerily silent. The door had to be soundproofed. Anything could be happening beyond it. It was so hard to wait for Kenobi to speak, to share what he was learning through his mysterious Force. To be patient, like a Padawan, and do as he was told.

Kenobi exhaled and returned to the moment. His fingers curled around the door's handle. It was sticky with blood. Then he turned, all serenity burned from him now, nothing but implacable determination in his eyes.

"We'll be going in hot, Senator. Prepare yourself. *Now.*"

Kenobi flung the door open, and they leapt into bloody mayhem and violent death.

No time to think, to feel, to be afraid. Time only to react, as the experts had trained him. His wide gaze swept the room in front of him, seeking hostiles, seeking cover, seeking to tell friend from foe. Blaster bolts screamed through the chaos, seeming to fire from every direction. This was some kind of command center, consoles and desks and chairs and equipment, comsat-panels, a weapons station, four banks of monitors, racks of shelving, spare parts scattered across the floor. The air stank of energy weapon discharge, was hazed with acrid smoke from burning wiring and equipment. Here and there small, greedy flames flickered. He saw three attack droids protected by heavy shields, squat and deadly, relentless fire pouring from their extended weapon arms. Three male humans, apparently their allies, crouched behind cover and shot their ostentatious blasters without stopping. It was impossible to tell who they were, what societies had spawned them. Two more men slumped in death on the floor. No way of telling their origins, either, or whose side they'd been fighting on.

As Bail threw himself obliquely toward a tipped-over desk, good enough cover, his blaster extended, finger taut on its trigger, shooting at the attack droids, he saw a woman returning fire from behind one of the four banks of monitors, darting out of cover to increase her chances of a strike. She had an athlete's physique, clothed in a sleek dark gray bodysuit, blond hair pulled back tightly into a long braid. Everything about her suggested determination and courage.

Her head turned and she saw him. A crooked smile, furious and relieved and feral, flashed across her strong, hawkish face, and she said his name, *"Organa,"* her voice lost in the cacophony. Then, staying behind her cover, she tugged a comlink from one pocket and waggled it at him. A signal. A gesture to tell him that she was indeed his mysterious benefactor. But before he could shout to her, ask for her name, the comlink was discarded and she was ducking behind the monitors as a fresh barrage of blasterfire tried to annihilate her.

Eyes burning, ears ringing—the noise in the confined space was excruciating, shuddering through his bones—Bail choked on the stinking smoke and looked for Kenobi. Found him immediately, and nearly choked on a shout instead. *You fool, you mad fool, what the vape are you doing?*

Kenobi had made of himself a deliberate target, was standing in the open between the door and the nearest wing of the command console array, willfully drawing fire from two of the droids and all

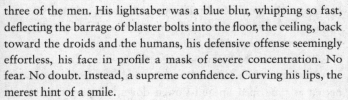

three of the men. His lightsaber was a blue blur, whipping so fast, deflecting the barrage of blaster bolts into the floor, the ceiling, back toward the droids and the humans, his defensive offense seemingly effortless, his face in profile a mask of severe concentration. No fear. No doubt. Instead, a supreme confidence. Curving his lips, the merest hint of a smile.

Dazed, Bail shook his head. *He's enjoying this. He's enjoying this? He really is mad.*

But mad or not, Kenobi was also brilliant. The men had dived for deeper cover, and the attack droids were starting to give ground before him. The one on the left moved slowly, unevenly, its shield apparently failing. Kenobi's lips parted in a fierce grin and he focused his deflections on the weaker machine. Risking himself further, but not seeming to notice, or care.

Unsure if Kenobi needed help, incapable of doing *nothing*, Bail sighted his blaster on the same vulnerable droid and let loose. The droid's shield flared scarlet, then collapsed in a dying screech of failed power. Half a heartbeat later the droid blew apart in a white-hot flurry of metal fragments and flame. He saw Kenobi leap vertically, his lightsaber still whirling, escaping the explosion even as the other droid increased the ferocity of its attack against him, and two of the men joined it in a fresh assault.

"Organa, behind you!"

It was the blond woman, his contact, who'd refused to tell him her name. Abandoning Kenobi to his amazing Jedi devices, Bail swung about—to see one more droid and another two men blasting their way into the space station's control center from a door he hadn't noticed in the most distant, partly obscured wall.

Fierfek. Whoever these attackers were, they'd come as a small army.

Instinct and training and a desperate determination to survive swallowed him alive then. Scrambling for fresh cover, skin-crawlingly aware that now he had armed enemies behind him *and* in front of him and maybe even on both sides as well, he remembered something one of his military trainers had told him: *"We can and we do make these scenarios authentic, Senator, but nothing can take the place of a real live firefight."*

Captain Varo had in no way been exaggerating.

Panting, feeling battered and bruised and bizarrely disconnected as time sped up and slowed down, warping fantastically around him, Bail drained his blaster's power pack against the enemy, replaced it with a new one from his holster belt, his fingers shaking but sure, and continued to defend his own life, and the life of his anonymous benefactor. He couldn't see anyone else fighting with her, which meant either she was alone on this station . . . or any colleagues she'd had were dead.

The air was so thick with smoke now it was hard to see, even harder to breathe. He could feel his lungs tightening, his stomach churning, taste something foul and bitter on his tongue, feel it coating the mucous membranes of his mouth. Probably it was toxic, probably every gasp of air, every swallow, was poisoning him. But he didn't have time to worry about that. He couldn't worry about the stinging burns on his hands and face, either, or the razor-thin cuts through his shirt and trousers and into his flesh, from the metal slivers peeled off the space station's consoles and floor and walls by the endless barrage of blaster bolts. Couldn't think about the three men who'd fallen to his weapon. To his honed expertise. Senator Organa was a crack shot indeed.

Through the wreathing smoke he caught sight of Kenobi, a blur of motion and a dazzle of lightsaber, as he leapt and spun around the cramped, crowded command center. So many hazards in this place, so many chances to miscalculate . . . and die. But the Jedi didn't put a foot wrong. If something was in his way he Force-pushed it clear or leapt it in a blur of motion, unnervingly aware of every potential obstacle. He'd taken out two more of the attack droids. At least one man. How many did that leave? He didn't know, couldn't count, he was punch-drunk from adrenaline, numbed by all the noise. His head was ringing. How long had they been here? It felt like days. Like moments. Like all his life had been lived in war.

He aimed his blaster at another of those vaping attack droids, pulled its trigger—and the weapon droned, its charge empty. Vape it, *vape it*. The droid's shield was damaged, sputtering as it lurched toward him, toward the blond woman, and he only had one power pack left. She was still firing, she still had a working weapon. Exhausted, half blinded by sweat and by smoke, he fumbled out the dead power pack, struggled to shove the new one in. The vaping thing jammed, it *jammed*, this wasn't happening, *no no no no no*. Come on, come *on*—

He rammed the pack home, felt the charge run through his blaster, turned and raised it to fire . . . as one of the remaining attack droids unleashed a fresh volley of fury. He saw the edge of a console blow apart. Heard a terrible scream. Saw Kenobi flip up and over the right-handed console array, deflecting the droid's blaster bolts back on itself and toward an enemy human beside it, keeping the man pinned down and harmless. Smart move. And then came a high-pitched scream as the last deflected energy bolt found its target. Even better. Best news of all, the functioning attack droid stopped firing. At least one of the deflected blaster bolts had scored a hit.

Landing lightly behind the droid with the weakened shield, Kenobi speared his lightsaber through its defenses, piercing its central control node. Killing it . . . if a machine could be killed.

An odd silence fell then, broken only by the sound of a woman in agony, made all the more terrible by her struggle to stay silent.

Kenobi, looking tired now—and who would have thought that was possible?—spun around again, his lightsaber raised. "It's over," he said, staring through the drifting smoke. "Whoever you are. You're the last man standing, and you can't defeat me. Nor can that attack droid beside you. We both know it's done for. Surrender your weapons and I promise you won't be harmed. You don't have to die here. There's been enough death."

The last man standing said nothing. Bail lifted his head cautiously and caught a glimpse of their surviving enemy, on the far side of the charred and ruined comm console. Wounded and furious, he clutched his burned shoulder with a bloody hand. For himself, he was desperate to get to his injured contact but didn't dare move. Wounded or not, the enemy was still armed and likely to shoot.

"Don't be a fool, man," said Kenobi. In his voice, a hairline fracture of stress. He was brilliant, but he was human, and he'd borne the brunt of this battle. *Stand down.*"

Bail saw the man shift. Saw his blaster slowly lower. Heard him say, "All right. All right. I surr—"

The droid beside him opened fire—clearly not as done for as they'd hoped. Three quick bursts and the surrendering man was dead. And then, as Obi-Wan leapt for it, the droid exploded in a plume of flame. His leap carried him over the burning shrapnel, left him singed and smoking and for the first time thrown off-balance. He landed awkwardly, lightsaber disengaging as he stumbled against a partly destroyed bank of monitors.

Bail lurched to his feet, coughing. "Master Kenobi, are you all right?"

The Jedi straightened and swung around. His face was streaked with sweat and smoke. "Yes. Are you unharmed?"

He nodded, even though a hundred small and not-so-small pains were clamoring for his undivided attention. "I'm fine. But my contact—"

"Do what you can for her," said Kenobi, reigniting his lightsaber. "While I make sure there are no more surprises waiting for us elsewhere on this station."

As Kenobi left the station's command center, Bail shoved his way through smoldering debris to the woman he'd come so far to meet. She lay on her back, her cut face slowly bleeding, her shallow breathing labored, an ominous glaze creeping over her eyes. Her relief when she saw him was palpable, and closed his throat. *She* was worried about *him*? Oh mercy.

"Organa," she whispered, her voice bubbling in her throat. It was the sound of drowning, when all around was dry land. Her dark gray bodysuit was shredded and soaked in blood, dreadful wounds in her chest, her belly, her right arm stripped of flesh almost to the bone.

Kneeling, putting his blaster to one side, he took her unhurt hand in his and held her, lightly. "Yes. Will you tell me your name now?"

"Alinta," she said, then closed her teeth on her lower lip as a spasm of pain racked her head-to-toe.

"What happened here, Alinta?" he said, leaning a little closer. "Who attacked you? And why? Is it to do with the Sith?"

"No," she said, the word almost a groan. "Another . . . mission. A double cross. Kalarba pirates. They came in . . . so fast. Jamming equipment, took us . . . by surprise. No time . . . to warn you." Tears filled her glazed eyes. "Sorry. So sorry."

He pressed her hand to his lips. "Don't say that, Alinta. Don't you dare. After all that I owe you? After everything you've done for Alderaan? For the Republic?"

She rolled her head on the scarred metal floor beneath her. "Not enough," she said, her voice fading. "So much . . . still to do. And now . . . and now . . ."

"Alinta," he said, and tightened his fingers around hers. "Don't you think that way. You have to hold on."

Her lips twisted in a grimacing smile. "I can't, Organa. I'm dying."

"No," he said, though in his heart he knew denial was futile. "Please. Hold on a little longer, try to, you can't give up, you can't—" A sound behind them had him turning. It was Kenobi, his lightsaber disengaged and clipped again to his belt. "Well?"

"No other survivors," Kenobi said quietly as he dropped to one knee.

Alinta shifted, a small sound of distress escaping her lips. "None? They're all dead? My people?"

"I'm afraid so," Kenobi said, his voice gentle. "I'm very sorry."

Bail tightened his hold on her hand, feeling the tremors of grief now as well as pain. "Master Kenobi, this is Alinta," he said, his voice not quite steady. "A friend of the Republic. *My* friend. A dear friend. Can you help her?"

Kenobi touched the back of his hand to Alinta's forehead. His gaze turned inward for a moment, then he shook his head. "I'm sorry," he said again. "Whatever talent I have for healing is insufficient to tend her injuries."

"You're not even going to *try*?" His eyes were stinging . . . and not just from the smoke. "How can you not *try*, how can you just—"

"Organa," Alinta whispered. "It's all right." Her unfocused gaze shifted to Kenobi. "Left bodysuit pocket. Data crystal. Nav comp coordinates for Zigoola."

Kenobi retrieved the data crystal and slipped it into an inside pocket of his tunic. "Thank you, Alinta. What can you tell me about the planet?"

Bail stared at him. *What?* What was *wrong* with the man? The woman was dying, and he was *interrogating* her? He felt a rush of anger, so hot that it cleansed his body of its insignificant discomforts. "Master Kenobi—"

The Jedi seared him with a look. "There are questions I must ask, Senator. If Zigoola is truly a Sith planet, I need all the information I can get. We can't afford to fly in blind."

"Wild Space," said Alinta, her voice almost too faint to hear. Underneath it, that awful bubbling. "Zigoola . . . in Wild Space."

"What else?" said Kenobi, and pressed his hand to her shoulder. Dangerously, wickedly, close to shaking her. "Alinta—*what else?* How do you know it's a Sith planet? How do you know they're planning to attack the Jedi? What sort of attack are they planning? What should I look for when I get there?" He leaned closer again. "Alinta, are the Sith on Zigoola?"

Sickened, Bail watched Alinta raise her heavy eyelids. "No. No Sith," she said, her voice ghostly. "A temple. Artifacts. Plans. Location . . . on data crystal."

"Plans? Sith plans?" Kenobi demanded. "Do you mean their plans to attack the Jedi?"

Alinta's face was drained of all its color now. Beneath the drying blood, her lips were turned blue. "Yes."

Kenobi pressed the back of his hand against his mouth, fingers clenched, brows pulled low and tight. "And how do you know all this? Have you been there, to this Zigoola? Have you seen these things with your own eyes, Alinta?"

"Organa . . . *Bail* . . ." Alinta's pallid skin looked waxen. In the strangest way, as death crept closer, she somehow looked younger. "I've . . . never lied . . . to you. Trust me. Please."

"I do, Alinta," he said, chafing her cold hand. "I trust you. It's all right."

She looked up at him, and as he stared desperately into her face he saw the lines of pain slowly smooth from around her eyes and mouth. "Space station," she breathed. "Self-destruct. Protect . . . secrets. Promise?"

Again, he pressed her hands to his lips. "Yes. How?"

Her eyelids drifted closed. "Right . . . pocket. Data crystal. Center comm console. Insert—and run."

"I will," he said. "I'll do it. Alinta. *Alinta?*"

But Alinta was gone.

Not looking at Kenobi, not trusting what he might say or do, he retrieved the data crystal from her bodysuit's other pocket, pushed himself unsteadily to his feet, and picked his way over to the battered, blaster-scarred center comm console.

"Senator, I'm not sure you should—"

"I didn't ask for your opinion, Master Kenobi," he said coldly. "I just made a promise to a dying woman, and I intend to keep it."

"By all means," said Kenobi, behind him. "But first we should see if it's possible to contact the Jedi Temple from here."

Fierfek. He was right. So they checked all the consoles until they found the comsat array . . . which was now a melted slag of wiring and metal, victim of multiple direct blaster hits.

Bail glanced at Kenobi. "That would be no, then." Turning back to the center console, which luckily hadn't sustained fatal damage, he located its data crystal slot and slid the self-destruct key halfway in. "On three, and then we run. One—two—*three*."

He thrust the crystal home then waited, just to make sure the console accepted the instruction to destroy Alinta's station. The comm console lit up, the data crystal pulsed red, and urgent fingers closed hard around his arm.

"Run or die, Senator," said Kenobi, his eyes glinting. "It's your choice—but choose now."

He ran.

With his starship disengaged from the docking ring and standing off at a safe distance, he sat in the pilot's seat and watched Alinta's space station blow itself apart, taking the pirate's vessel with it. There was something unbearably melancholy about the silent explosions, so brief and bright against the midnight velvet of space. A funeral pyre should last longer, so the dead could be honored properly.

"I am sorry," said Kenobi, behind him. "But she was hurt beyond saving."

He nodded. "I know."

"And I'm sorry I had to—"

"You didn't have to," he said flatly. "You chose to. I don't wish to discuss it."

Silence. Then Kenobi sighed. "Was that the first time you ever fought for your life, Senator? The first time you killed?"

It was a moment before he could trust himself to answer. "Yes."

"I see."

And Kenobi probably did. He'd had a first time, too, doubtless years before today. But he didn't want to discuss that, either. The only person he wanted to bare his soul to about what he'd done—what he'd had to do—on Alinta's space station was Breha. And he would, eventually. For now, he wasn't even going to think about it. What was the point? The past could not be unwritten.

"There is one thing we must discuss, Senator," Kenobi said, so politely. "And that is whether or not we will proceed to Zigoola."

He swung the pilot's chair around. "Why wouldn't we? Alinta's death changes nothing, Master Kenobi. We have the information she procured for us. And while she didn't die for it, she did die because of her work. Work from which I have derived great benefit. I want to see this through. Are you saying you don't?"

Kenobi shook his head. Gone was the smiling warrior who'd stood his ground against terrifying attack droids and pirate assassins. Gone, too, the ruthless interrogator who had closed his heart to the suffering of a dying woman. This man looked almost ordinary . . . and weary to the bone.

"You disapprove of the way I spoke to Alinta," he said, hands clasped neatly before him. "I accept that, Senator. But disapproving or not, you must see how many unanswered questions her death leaves in its wake. All we have to guide us is a set of nav comp coordinates and her dying assertion that this Sith threat is genuine. I find that . . . problematic. Zigoola could still be a trap. And leading you into a trap is *not* part of my mandate."

Bail shook his head, feeling as weary as Kenobi looked. "And so we've come full circle, have we? Arguing again about whether my contact can be trusted? Whether *I* can be trusted not to get you or myself killed? Master Kenobi, I thought I'd at least proven myself competent on that score." Even though, distracted, he'd left his blaster behind, to be blown into random, scattered atoms.

Not my finest moment. I guess it's a case of live and learn.

"Senator, you acquitted yourself well," Kenobi said, with care. "But you could just as easily have been killed."

"So could you. So could any of us in this time of war." He leaned back in the pilot's seat, frowning. "Shall I make this easy for you, Master Kenobi? Shall I, in my capacity as a Senator of the Galactic Republic, *order* you to accompany me to Zigoola?"

Kenobi's lips tightened, and he folded his arms. "I wouldn't advise it."

They stared at each other, both hurting and tired. And then Bail sighed. "We have to go, Master Kenobi. You know we do. Neither of us will sleep another night through if we don't uncover the truth about the Sith."

After a long silence, Kenobi nodded. So reluctant. "Very well, Senator. We'll go."

"Good," he said. "Then give me that data crystal, and let us be on our way."

SIXTEEN

WILD SPACE.

The fanciful expression alone was enough to give a man pause. Redolent of mystery, of adventure, the great untamed unknown, it was a term to ignite the dullest imagination. It meant space beyond the limits of the safe, the predictable. Where dangers never before glimpsed by human eyes lurked, stalking the foolish and unwary. The great emptiness. The horror of nothing. Where a Sith planet named Zigoola had hidden for centuries.

As he stared through the viewport at the otherness of hyperspace, Bail found himself wondering, despite his bold protestations of commitment to the mission: *Am I doing the right thing?* Because if this crazy enterprise failed—if he died—he'd be leaving one kriffing mess for Breha to clean up.

But his wife would say he had no choice. That helping the Jedi was worth every risk.

Even when the Jedi are convinced they don't need help?

Yes, she'd say. Because a friend doesn't let another friend push him away.

Which sounded fine in theory. The only fly in Breha's ointment was the fact that he and Obi-Wan Kenobi weren't friends—a state of affairs that didn't seem likely to change anytime soon. Which, to his surprise, he found himself regretting. Because for all his irritating Jedi hauteur and that startling streak of ruthlessness, so unexpected and confronting, Kenobi was an admirable man. And remarkably good company, too, when he wasn't laying down the law . . . or displaying his startling array of Jedi skills. When he was relaxed, not being a Jedi, Kenobi was intelligent, insightful, and possessed of a sneakily dry wit.

And best of all, I don't have a single thing he wants. How often do I meet someone who wants nothing from me?

Rarely. Senator Organa's days were filled with people who cared only for his position, his influence. They flattered, they bowed, they scraped, they begged. The ones who didn't know him well or hadn't paid sufficient attention to the news even tried to bribe—much to their eventual regret. But Kenobi was the opposite. The man was indifferent to family background, political power, social influence.

It was proving to be a . . . salutary . . . experience.

As the scion of an ancient, noble House, privilege had been his from the moment he drew breath. And though he'd never been spoiled, he wasn't so self-deluded he couldn't recognize his advantages. Magnificent home. Doting parents. Slavishly devoted personal attendants. Human, not droid. Yes, he'd been schooled from the cradle that such advantages required service in return, but that didn't change the fact he'd never gone hungry a day in his life. He was a *Prince*. The Prince of Alderaan. A blue-blooded member of that most exclusive club: the ruling class.

If he hadn't been handsome, he never would have known it. Everyone would have told him he was.

Everyone except for Obi-Wan Kenobi. I doubt he's told a single flattering lie his whole life.

All right, Kenobi's unflattering opinion of politicians was irritating. But given the acerbic observations about other Senators that

he often exchanged with Padmé, he couldn't say the man was entirely wrong.

He's just wrong about me.

The console chrono ticked over, its display bright in the soft
lighting. Nine hours completed of an eleven-hour trip. Two more
hours before they reached Zigoola. Before he could prove to
Kenobi once and for all that Alinta had been everything she'd
claimed. Before he could put her final offering of intelligence to
good use, so she might truly rest in peace.

*I promise you, Alinta. We will defeat the Sith. That will be your
greatest legacy.*

In the passenger compartment behind him, Obi-Wan Kenobi
screamed.

Shocked, Bail practically fell out of the pilot's seat and stumbled to the rear of the ship. Sealed into his bunk space Kenobi
screamed again, flailing, his fists and feet thudding against the
bunk's rigid curtain.

Bail unsealed it using his pilot master's override. Kenobi half
fell, half thrashed himself off the bunk and landed face-first on the
deck. Then he flipped himself over and began clawing at his face,
his chest, his legs.

"Get them off me!" he choked out. *"Get them off me!"*

Bail dropped to his knees, not quite certain what to do. After
the space station, seeing what Kenobi was capable of, he was reluctant to lay so much as a finger on him. Far safer to take a *softly,
softly* approach.

"There's nothing on you, Master Kenobi. There's nothing
there."

Kenobi ignored him, or couldn't hear him, tearing at himself
like a man in the throes of Sullustan plague-delirium. His cheeks
and forehead were scored with red marks. Any moment now he
was going to draw blood.

Vape caution. Bail seized the Jedi's wrists and held on tight.

"Master Kenobi, *listen*! There's nothing there! I swear it!" Still no response. Kenobi twisted and fought. "*Stop* it, you fool, you're going to hurt yourself!"

Shocked, Kenobi stared up at him. "Senator?" His gaze flickered around the passenger compartment, as though he couldn't quite remember where they were. "What happened?"

Bail let go of him and eased back, giving him some space. "You tell me. One minute you were meditating and the next you were yelling fit to wake the dead."

"It was a dream," Kenobi muttered. "A memory." Wincing, he sat up and shifted to brace his back against the bunk space behind him. Then he pulled his knees to his chest and wrapped his arms around them.

Bail stared; it was a disconcertingly vulnerable gesture. Jarringly at odds with the vivid memory of a Jedi who could carry a starship with the power of his mind . . . and emerge unscathed from a hail of blasterfire that would have slaughtered any ordinary man.

And yet here that same Jedi sat now, lost and uncertain. As far from laying down the law as it was possible to get.

He stood, brushed carpet lint from his trousers, then retreated to the galley and poured Kenobi two fingers of Corellian brandy. He returned to the passenger compartment and held out the glass.

"Drink," he said sternly. "And if you think you don't need it, go look in a mirror."

Kenobi took the brandy without argument and tossed its contents down his throat. And if that wasn't a clue that he'd been shaken to his bootstraps, well . . .

"Thank you," he said hoarsely, handing back the glass.

Bail waggled it. "More?"

"No."

He put the glass in the galley's minuscule sink, then headed for the nearest empty chair and sat. "Should I be concerned? For the mission, I mean."

"No," said Kenobi. Despite the brandy he was still ashen, the livid finger marks on his skin unfaded. "I'm sorry if I disturbed you, Senator."

"So . . ." He leaned his elbows on the table. "We're heading toward a planet with a Sith temple on it, which apparently contains Sith artifacts, their purpose unknown, you're having bad dreams . . . and this is just a coincidence?"

"Correct."

Vape that. "Master Kenobi, we had an agreement," he said coldly. "What you know, I know. Remember?"

Kenobi glared. "I remember."

"Then what was the dream about? What did you remember?"

"Nothing of relevance. It was personal, Senator. Unrelated to Zigoola."

"How can you be sure?"

"Because I'm sure!" Kenobi clambered to his feet, awkward, with none of his usual oiled ease. "It was my dream, I think I know what it meant."

"And that would be my point," said Bail. "Now I want to know, too. Because we both know you're perfectly capable of massaging the truth when it suits you."

Kenobi's chin came up, his eyes glittering with temper. There was angry color in his face. "It concerned an incident from my childhood."

"Your childhood," he repeated, and heard the skepticism. "Really?"

"Yes, really," said Kenobi. "I did have one."

He should let it go at that. In truth, what Kenobi had dreamed was none of his business. And if the Jedi said it wasn't connected to this mission, he should accept that assertion. It was, after all, a matter of trust. And in order to get it, one had to show it. But he *really* wanted to know what could so rattle someone like Obi-Wan Kenobi. Curiosity: his besetting sin.

"So . . . what happened?" he said, giving in to temptation. "In your unlikely childhood?"

For a long, silent moment, Kenobi just stared. Then he folded his arms and frowned at the deck. "I was thirteen. Nearly fourteen. On a field trip to Taanab. Part of my Padawan training with Qui-Gon. I was doing a blindfolded Force-seeking exercise. Being young, and inexperienced, I underestimated its complexity. As a result I tumbled into a firebeetle pit."

"*Firebeetles?*" Bail shuddered. "I thought those things were eradicated thirty years ago."

Kenobi looked up. "They were, from populated areas. We were in a wasteland on the Ba-Taanab Peninsula." The faintest of wry smiles. He had himself well in hand again. "There's no point to a field trip if you don't encounter obstacles."

Obstacles? The Jedi considered carnivorous beetles obstacles? *The more I learn of them, the less I understand. What would they consider a nest of gundarks, I wonder? An amusing diversion?*

"It must have been . . . terrible."

"Not at all," Kenobi said politely. "It was hilarious."

No, you nearly got eaten alive. But he didn't say it. He wished now he'd kept his mouth shut. No wonder Kenobi had come out of his trance screaming. "Look—"

"Fortunately there was no harm done," Kenobi continued briskly. "And in the end, the incident was a useful lesson about the folly of overconfidence."

A useful lesson. Bail swallowed bemused disbelief. "Well, so long as the trip wasn't a *complete* waste."

Ignoring that, Kenobi frowned again. "Overconfidence," he murmured. Then his expression sharpened. "I was mistaken. The memory *is* relevant. In short, it's a warning. One I would be criminally remiss not to heed. By not curbing your overconfidence, Senator, by allowing you to override my better judgment, I am putting you in danger."

Bail straightened. "What? How the kriff am I overconfident?"

"You insist on going to Zigoola when you are ill equipped for such a mission."

"I thought we'd agreed that I'm more than able to handle myself."

"Against droids and pirates, yes," said Kenobi, dismissive. "But now we are talking about the Sith."

"Alinta said the Sith weren't on Zigoola."

"I know what she said, Senator. She could have been wrong." Kenobi shook his head as though confronted by a particularly slow-learning Padawan. "Have you for one moment stopped to *think* about this? Before today you had never fought for your life. You'd never even been in danger of losing it. The worst defeat you've ever suffered is in the Senate, failing to pass a legislative amendment. And yet you think you're qualified to accompany me to a Sith planet. *You.* A politician born into privilege and luxury. What is that, if not overconfidence?"

Oh. Bail cleared his throat. "I had no idea you despised me so much."

Kenobi seemed genuinely surprised. "I don't despise you. Unlike many of your colleagues you have never exploited your inherited advantages. As far as you've been able, you've used your political power to better the lives of millions. That is admirable, Senator."

He couldn't decide whether to feel insulted or praised. "I see."

"No, I'm afraid you don't," said Kenobi, not able—or not wanting—to hide his frustration. "Because outside of the Senate, political power is *meaningless.* This far from the Republic's influence your only value lies in what Alderaan would pay to ransom you home!"

"Then I have no value at all, Master Kenobi. My government has strict instructions not to part with a single credit in exchange for my life."

Again, Kenobi was surprised. "Really?"

He laughed, though he was far from amused. "What, you think the possibility of kidnap never crossed my mind?"

The Jedi's silence answered him, eloquently.

"Really, Master Kenobi," he said. "You must temper this extravagant flattery." He stood. "I don't deny that my chosen battlefield has been the Senate and not somewhere like Geonosis or Christophsis. But the choice doesn't make me inferior to you. And you seem to have forgotten that we're out here *because* I'm a politician. I'm the one who learned of this Sith plot. Not you."

"Yes. But our circumstances have changed significantly since then," Kenobi retorted. "We have the information we sought from your contact. To be blunt, Senator Organa, I no longer need you. And while your political achievements might be admirable, this stubborn insistence on childish heroics is *not*!"

Silence. Bail stared at him, stunned. Nobody spoke to him like that. *Nobody.* And then, as the tide of his own anger rose, he saw something flicker deep in Kenobi's eyes. Understanding dawned.

"You're afraid."

Now it was Kenobi's turn to be stunned.

"Politician, not moron," he explained, very dry. "Also not blind. What aren't you telling me, Master Kenobi? Did you dream about Zigoola as well as those firebeetles? What has the Force shown you that has you so concerned?"

Kenobi began pacing, one hand rubbing the back of his neck, fingers kneading at the muscles. It was another reminder that while the man might be a Jedi, he was also human.

"Nothing."

Because the dark side clouds everything.

"And that's why you're afraid."

Kenobi shot him a sharp look. "We may well only encounter Sith artifacts on Zigoola, but they could be as dangerous as the Sith who made them." His lips twisted in a thin, unamused smile. "If I am . . . cautious . . . it is with good reason. So I urge you—*again*—to reconsider your position. Now that we have Zigoola's location I can return you to the safety of Coruscant and—"

Bail shook his head. "We don't have that kind of time to waste.

For all we know, this attack on the Jedi is imminent. Besides, if the Sith are as dangerous as you claim, you'd be crazy not to have someone with you. Even someone as limited as me. Now I'm going back to the cockpit to get some more work done. We're about an hour and a half away from Zigoola. I'll let you know when we're ready to drop out of hyperspace."

"Senator," said Kenobi, halting. There was a nasty bite to the word, but as well as infuriated frustration his eyes also showed reluctant respect.

Well. That's something, I suppose.

As he reached the compartment doorway he hesitated, then turned back. "Oh—yes. Just one last thing. I want your word you won't try any of your Jedi mind tricks on me."

Kenobi's eyes chilled. "I beg your pardon?"

"Please. Don't insult my meager, privileged intelligence. I have access to certain . . . classified material. When it's convenient, or expedient, you Jedi . . . influence . . . people." Bail let his urbane, polished mask slip then. Let Kenobi catch the merest glimpse of what he kept hidden. "But I give you fair warning: attempt to influence me against my will and I'll show you what exploiting privilege looks like."

Kenobi nodded. "Senator." No reluctant respect now. They were back to hauteur.

Arrogant man. Insufferable Jedi.

"So do I have your word?" he persisted. "No funny business?"

Kenobi nodded. "You have it."

"Thank you," he said and, leaving Kenobi to his own devices, to meditate or dream or nightmare himself into unreason, who cared, he returned to the cockpit. Picked up his datapad, accessed his files on the latest Mimban dispute, and buried himself and his riled temper in work.

Obi-Wan watched Organa stamp out of the passenger compartment and swish the dividing curtain closed behind him. Then he closed his eyes and released a long, slow breath.

Politicians.

Practically always far more trouble than they were worth. And *this* one—this one was proving inconveniently stubborn. Uncomfortably astute. Because he *was* . . . afraid.

No matter how hard he tried, how deeply he meditated, he could sense nothing about Zigoola. And he should be able to. It was one of his particular talents, the ability to sense the shape of things to come. It wasn't an infallible gift—the droids on Geonosis had taken him completely by surprise—but it didn't fail him often. It certainly hadn't failed him at the space station. This close to Zigoola he should be able to feel *something.* But all he'd achieved with his meditation was that one annihilating dream.

His skin crawled, remembering: *the excitement of a field trip. His eagerness to impress Qui-Gon. His blithe self-belief, that this exercise would be so easy. He was a Padawan at last: no Agricultural Corps for him. Nothing was beyond him now. The dry Taanab wasteland beneath his running feet. The cool wind in his blindfolded face. How he'd let his attention drift, imagining Qui-Gon's admiring praise. So stupid. And then the dirt beneath him crumbling. His body falling, striking the ground. A hot rush of embarrassment that he hadn't saved himself with the Force. Followed swiftly by terror as the firebeetles attacked . . .*

Breathing deeply, he wrenched his mind from the past. An hour and a half until they reached Zigoola. Hardly any time at all to unravel its mystery. To arm himself with something, anything, that could help him win this latest battle with the Sith.

He felt his belly tighten and his skin crawl again, this time with apprehension. Seeking comfort, he turned to the mantra he'd learned as a small boy, long before he became Qui-Gon's Padawan.

Fear leads to anger. Anger leads to hate. Hate leads to suffering. Beware the dark side, Jedi.

Returning to his bunk space, he sealed himself behind the curtain and reached for the clarity recent meditations had granted him.

If I only try harder, I will see Zigoola. I will see what's waiting for us there. I must see what's waiting. We can't fly in there blind.

But as he slipped once more into the first level of meditative trance, a whisper of pain began to throb in his temples . . .

The nav comp's beeping roused Bail from the light doze that had claimed him. Still angry—although Breha would probably call it sulking—he looked around and shouted. Not in the mood to play humble messenger boy to a Jedi.

"We're here! Zigoola!"

He double-checked the nav comp's readings—good, definitely clear space—then disengaged the hyperdrive, easing them back to sublight speed. His heart was pounding. His palms were damp. As hyperspace began to warp and twist, stars emerging from its unreality, he heard Kenobi's footsteps behind him and turned. Swore.

"What in—Kenobi, are you *sick*?"

The Jedi's face was bloodless again, tightness pinched around his eyes and mouth. "No," he said shortly. "A headache. It's nothing."

He was tempted to grab the man by his shoulders and *shake* some sense into him. "It's not nothing. You look like you're about to retch. Have you taken a painkiller?"

"I have not. Drugs, like alcohol, blur the Force."

"And I suppose a megrim *enhances* it?"

Kenobi raised an eyebrow. "Keep shouting at me, Senator, and I will retch. All over your clean cockpit. Is that what you want?"

What I want is for you to stop being a Jedi, just for one lousy minute. Admit you're human and accept some help. But that didn't seem likely this side of a galactic miracle. Defeated, Bail turned around again. And sucked in a sharp breath.

Zigoola.

An ocher globe suspended against the dark. Bathed in the light of a mild yellow sun. Courted by three dignified small moons. Beautiful. Unknown. Full of secrets to be carefully unhidden. In the distance behind it, like a backdrop on a stage, a baleful, raging scarlet nebula. The intensity of its color took his breath away. *Wild Space.* He felt his heart thump his ribs, hard.

"Look at that, Master Kenobi. Isn't that a sight?"

"Yes."

Bail felt himself scowl. *Well excuse me for being excited. I'm not a galaxy-trotting Jedi. I've never been this far from home. It's a sight for me. Do you mind?*

He snatched up the datapad into which he'd coded the coordinates from Alinta's data crystal and punched their new destination into the nav comp. The machine hummed, then flashed green.

"Okay," he said. "Local planetary destination is coded and locked. We'll be guided directly to the Sith temple." He glanced over his shoulder. "So. Do we go in?"

Kenobi nodded, then winced. "Yes. But with great care. And don't forget to sweep for life-forms. We don't want any unpleasant surprises."

The man looked dreadful. Bail almost told Kenobi to sit in the comsat seat, but held his tongue at the last moment. They'd only have another argument. "You're not picking up any Sith presence?"

"No."

"And you've been trying?"

Kenobi gave him a lethal look. "Of course."

Which would account for the megrim. Unless . . . "I don't begin to know how this Jedi and Sith business works—and I know this sounds far-fetched—but is there any chance the planet's making you sick?"

Kenobi blotted his face on his smoke-stained sleeve. "It's a Sith haven, Senator. Anything is possible."

That sat him up. "Really? Then maybe we should rethink this, Master Kenobi. I don't want to—"

"I'm sorry?" said Kenobi, incredulous. "After demanding to

accompany me on this mission then steadfastly refusing to turn back at every opportunity, *now* you're having second thoughts? *Now* you want to give up and go home?"

Well . . . yes. Maybe. Because you look like death and I'm not a Jedi and you were right about one thing: we have no idea what's waiting for us down there. But he couldn't say that out loud. It was hard enough admitting it to himself. *So does this mean I am what he thinks I am? Nothing but a pampered politician?*

No. He wasn't. "This isn't about me wanting to go home," he retorted. "I'm just not sure how wise it is to continue if you're not well."

"I have a headache, Senator. I am not at death's door," Kenobi said grimly. "But were I blind, deaf, and lame I would still need to know if there's a Sith threat to the Jedi down there. So let us proceed as planned. Agreed?"

Bail stared at the planet, so tauntingly within their grasp. Stared again at Kenobi. Felt his skin crawl with unease. *How does the saying go? When in doubt, don't?* "You're sure?"

Kenobi lowered his head for a moment, as though gathering his strength. Then he looked up and nodded. "Quite sure."

"All right," he said, feeling his heart thud. "But if the pain gets worse—if you feel anything else, *anything*—then we turn back. We think of another way to do this. Deal?"

"Deal," said Kenobi tightly, taking hold of the comsat chair. Didn't sit, though, no, he was too kriffing stubborn for that.

Bail shook his head. *Jedi.* "All right," he said. "Here we go."

Here I go, Breha. Wish me luck, my love.

He pushed them out of cruising speed, and the ship hurtled toward Zigoola. Moment by moment the planet seemed to expand until it filled the viewport. They flashed past its moons. Hurtled closer, closer. Breathing deeply, he eased back the ship's speed, preparing to enter the planet's exosphere.

"How's the headache, Master Kenobi?" he asked, tossing the question behind him. "Are you all right?"

Kenobi grunted.

The ship's bones vibrated, gently, as Zigoola's highest atmospheric layer claimed them. His heart was beating so hard it felt like his veins would explode. He couldn't drag his eyes away from the planetary surface so far below them, the cloud-swirls and the continents, the dearth of open water.

The nav comp beeped again, a minor course correction. Atmospheric conditions were knocking them around. He eased back the speed a little farther, mindful of making a smooth reentry, mindful that Kenobi was a pilot, and watching. Then he engaged the ship's sensors and swept Zigoola for life-forms.

"Nothing human or humanoid registering," he said. "Low-level animal and plant signatures. At least the life-support readings confirm the planet won't kill us."

Another grunt from Kenobi.

They slid through the ionosphere, gliding lower and lower toward the surface. Bail wanted to press his nose to the viewport, be the first to see their destination. The Sith temple. But Zigoola seemed abandoned: no civilization, no infrastructure.

No Sith.

So that was something, at least. He was worrying for nothing. They were going to be fine.

He slowed their rate of descent again, just to be on the safe side. Now he could make out tracts of scraggled woodland. Cliffs and valleys. Stretches of open, barren plain. Boulders scattered like marbles. Everything looked sere and lifeless. Inhospitable. Formidable. He glanced at the nav comp. According to the readout they were only minutes from the temple.

Behind him, Kenobi muttered something. "I'm sorry," Bail said, reluctantly turning. "I didn't quite catch—"

His heart punched so hard it nearly broke his ribs.

Kenobi was on his knees, his face gray, the whites of his eyes turned a gaudy blood red. Sweat poured off him, soaking his battle-

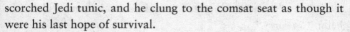

scorched Jedi tunic, and he clung to the comsat seat as though it were his last hope of survival.

"What is it?" he demanded. "Master Kenobi—"

"*Sith,*" Kenobi groaned, his throat working, the long muscles in his neck standing out like metal hawsers. "*Getusoutofherenow!*"

Bail felt his mouth suck dry and his heartbeat stutter.

Sith? But Alinta said—she wouldn't lie—I don't understand, how could we get so close without you feeling their presence?

He reached for the helm, ready to pull the ship up. Felt his fingers close around the controls—and then cried out as an invisible hand caught him by the back of the neck, dragged him out of the pilot's seat and threw him like a child's rag doll down the length of the cockpit and into the corridor beyond. He struck the wall then fell to the deck, his head hitting the plating with a sickening crack. Bright lights burst before his eyes and reality spun on its crazy axis. Breathless, all he could do was sprawl on his back and stare at the green ceiling above him.

Kenobi? Was that Kenobi? What the kriff is going on?

Reality kept on spinning—he was falling—he was falling—

No. The *ship* was falling, it was diving without restraint or sanity toward Zigoola's unkind surface.

Where's Kenobi? Why doesn't he do something?

Sweet-sour saliva flooded his mouth as he rolled first on his side and then to his knees and finally as he found his feet. Heaving, spitting, bile burning his throat, he staggered into the cockpit—and saw Master Kenobi at the helm, both hands on the controls, aiming their starship toward the unforgiving ground.

"Hey! What the *stang* are you—"

Kenobi's fist came up, clenched to white knuckles. "*I'm sorry.*"

Bail cried out as that terrible power closed around his throat. He was a statue of flesh, a living man turned to stone. But he could still see. They were crashing into daylight. Into wilderness desolation. Death was rushing up to meet them.

"Sorry," Kenobi whispered, anguished, one hand still on the helm. *"So sorry."*

Bail's ears were ringing. His vision blurred and darkened. *Breha. Breha.* "Don't be sorry," he croaked. "*Do* something. *I don't want to die.*"

No response from the Jedi. Then Kenobi's face twisted, and he began to shake, bone-deep tremors that chattered his teeth and shivered his hair.

Bail heard the man's harsh breath, rasping. *Come on, Kenobi, come on. You've beaten the Sith before. You can beat them again.*

He stared out of the viewport, starving for air. He could count the trees now, they were so close to the ground. Count the trees, count the rocks, imagine the pain as they punched Zigoola's grim surface. They flashed over something—an elaborate black structure—the Sith temple? Too late, they were gone, he'd most likely imagined it. Closer to the ground now—nearly there—nearly there—

Kenobi howled, a shocking sound of rage and pain. His hand on the helm controls wrenched their small ship's nose up, dropped its tail, dropped speed, tried to undo what he had done. And then, still howling, he let go of the helm completely. Unfisted his other hand, finger by finger, and turned away from the sight of oncoming death. Blood was pouring from his eyes, his nose, his mouth. He looked like a bleeding ghost, blood jeweled in his beard.

Released from that pitiless fist, gasping, Bail flinched as the Jedi's arms closed hard about him, smothered him like a desperate parent trying to protect his child. He felt a rush of heat. Felt the cockpit warp. Marveled at the way the air seemed to turn gold. Fear ceased. Anguish ceased. He felt safe and calm. Serene.

Breha.

And then the ship's belly struck the first of the trees with a shriek like a cat's claws along the metal hull. It ripped through their foliage, splintering their branches, shredding their leaves. The ship slewed wildly, like a maddened harpooned whale. As the strident crash alarms blared, the emergency impact bags deployed—but imperfectly. One ballooned out, one didn't, and the ship began to roll. Bail felt the cockpit tip, slowly, felt himself and Kenobi obediently follow. Time slowed down, stretching like warm caramel taffy. With a sound as loud as the universe's creation the ship struck the hard ground. Metal groaned and buckled. Transparisteel shattered. Flesh tore.

The golden light vanished . . . and reality disappeared.

SEVENTEEN

CONSCIOUSNESS, GRUDGINGLY RETURNING, TOLD OBI-WAN HE wasn't dead quite yet. Nobody who'd died could hurt this much. Piecemeal memory replayed the recent past in fits and starts; the sourness of defeat stung his eyes and churned his belly.

I should have fought harder. I should not have succumbed.

The voice had struck out of nowhere, a deafening shout rank with malice and hate. Battering his spirit. Annihilating his will. Ink pouring into a glass of clear water. Ink with blood in it. Ink full of rage. It was the voice of the Sith, smashing through his defenses as though they weren't there.

Submit. Submit. Jedi, submit.

Only once before had he felt a darkness like it. Felt the dark side trying to turn his blood to sludge, trying to disrupt his light and brilliant connection with the Force. On Naboo, in Theed, fighting the red-and-black Sith assassin. But then he'd been able to resist that dark slurry. He'd been able to purge himself of its taint, and win.

But not this time. This time it was as though an army of Sith had bent their malevolent minds upon him. And though he'd fought against them, battled the shattering compulsion to fly the ship to its

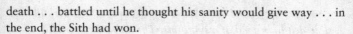

death . . . battled until he thought his sanity would give way . . . in the end, the Sith had won.

Jedi, submit.

The voice no longer shouted its hate and rage. But even in the silence, something bubbled in his blood. Something rotten. Something insidious. A creeping sense of dark decay. A lingering malaise, smoldering, patient, promising a later conflagration. With every breath he took, he could smell the stench of Sith. Zigoola was steeped in it. No wonder the place was barren. *And I didn't feel it. I was blind and deaf to it.* A harsh truth to ponder, when he was able to think straight.

Memory stirred.

Organa.

Where was the Senator? Had he survived? He remembered Force-flinging Organa out of the cockpit. Remembered closing the Force around the man's throat. After that—after that—

Did I kill him? Is he dead?

"Senator Organa. Senator, can you hear me?"

His voice sounded ridiculous, slushy and uncertain, as though he were drunk. Or at least how he imagined it would sound if he were drunk. He'd never been drunk, so it was only a guess.

Organa didn't answer. *Don't let him be dead.* "Senator Organa. Answer me, if you can."

Nothing.

With a grunting effort he opened his eyes . . . and was dazzled by weak sunlight, pale yellow washed with red. An overcast from the nebula, that baleful scarlet curtain. Blinking slowly, he let his gaze track from side to side and waited for his battered mind to make sense of what he saw and felt.

He was still in the ship. Lying neatly on his back in the corridor running between the cockpit and the passenger compartment. The deck was buckled beneath him, digging into his midspine and lifting his knees. The hull overhead was torn wide from nose to tail. This was a starship that would never fly again.

So I'm imprisoned here. We're imprisoned, if Organa still lives. A slow death, instead of a swift one. The Sith win after all.

No. That was defeatist. A Jedi did not think such things.

He closed his eyes and took closer stock of his condition. Everything hurt, yes, but it wasn't the same kind of pain he'd felt after flying into the Coruscant terrorist attack. Then he'd been broken, and the pain had been diamond and scarlet and bright. This pain was a sluggish sullen crimson. An echo of his previous hurts only, which were healed but not forgotten.

With difficulty he lifted his head and stared into the cockpit itself. The helm had been crushed, as though a giant had hammered it with one angry fist. The transparisteel viewport was a mass of jagged splinters. Charred wiring, some of it intermittently sparking, dangled from the ceiling and lay on the deck in colorful intestinal tangles.

As though sight had spurred his other senses into action, now he could hear and smell his surroundings. The flat tang of that burned wiring, the acrid sizzle of spilled hydraulic fluids. In the cool outside air drifting through the breached hull, metallic smoke and floating ash, coating his tongue with a patina of soot. It mixed with his saliva, a horrible taste. And crackling through the silence, what sounded like flames. Not huge flames, not devouring flames, just cheerful campfire flickers. What did that mean? Was the ship on fire? If it was on fire, was he about to burn to death?

A hideous thought. *Tayvor Mandirly. Get up. Get up. Don't just lie here.* But his bones seemed disjointed, his muscles lax, without tone. His disobedient body ignored the command. Deep in his veins, the black sludge weighed him down. And deeper still, faint but insistent, he heard a gleeful, spiteful Sith whisper.

Die Jedi, die Jedi, die Jedi, die.

A fresh surge of adrenaline drowned the command. His mind cleared again, and he realized the flames were burning outside the ship. Its superheated hull must have ignited dry grass or deadwood around the crash site. There was no strong wind blowing, that would help to keep the fire contained. How much available fuel was there to feed the flames? There were trees . . . he thought he remembered trees in those last desperate moments before they struck the ground . . . but since he didn't appear to be in the midst of a raging forest inferno . . .

Perhaps I won't be burned alive after all.

But he could still starve. Or bleed to death from an untreated wound. Or freeze, if Zigoola's night temperatures plunged. The ship could be perched on the edge of a cliff. One earth tremor or a strong wind could send it hurtling into a ravine and he'd be crushed to a paste.

In other words, Kenobi, don't just lie here. Get up. Get out. Take control, and find a way out of this mess.

Still his recalcitrant body refused to listen.

Die Jedi, die Jedi, die Jedi, die.

Without warning, with a swiftness that stole his laboring breath, the ship vanished around him and he was back on Taanab. Thirteen years old again, skinny and scared, screaming in horror as the firebeetles feasted.

Qui-Gon! Qui-Gon, help me!

But Qui-Gon couldn't hear him. Qui-Gon was dead.

Suddenly he was twenty-five, still a Padawan, fighting the Sith. Trapped between force fields he saw the Zabrak assassin strike. Saw the shock and pain in his Master's face as the Sith's scarlet lightsaber thrust home. Felt the Sith's vicious triumph, felt his own grief and rage.

And on the floor of the cavern on brutal Geonosis, rendered helpless by two lightsaber cuts, he watched Dooku toy with bold, rash Anakin. Silver hair gleaming, teeth bared in a smile, the ageless Sith, the treacherous Jedi, prowled around Anakin with insolent ease. Deflected each blinding attack with casual, consummate skill. Forced the error—and took Anakin's arm.

He came back to himself shouting. "Anakin! *Anakin!*"

"Sorry," said a tired, familiar voice. "I'm afraid you're stuck with me."

Organa.

The Senator knelt beside him, a steadying hand on his shoulder. Confusion and horror surrendered to a deluge of relief. He let his head fall back. "You're not dead."

"Not quite," said Organa. "Believe me, I'm as surprised as you are."

His olive skin had a greenish cast to it. He had a black eye and a split lip. His left arm was supported by a makeshift sling: the sleeve of a sacrificed shirt. His usually immaculate clothing was dirt-smudged and wrinkled, his trousers torn at both knees.

Obi-Wan's heart eased its racing. "Senator."

"Master Kenobi." Because of the split lip, Organa spoke slowly and with great care. "So . . . do you want to say it first, or will I?"

He frowned. "Say what? *I told you so?* And how would that help?" His head was pounding. "Where have you been?"

"Outside," said Organa. "Exploring."

Exploring. "Wonderful."

The Senator raised an eyebrow. "It's been nearly an hour since we crashed. You were unconscious. I got bored."

"So you played tourist. And what did you find?"

"Not a lot."

"There's a fire."

Organa shrugged, one-shouldered. "I started that. Thought we might need it come nightfall. Given what's happened, I'm not prepared to accept the sensor readings at face value. If this place does have predators, fire should make them think twice about attacking us."

"Very enterprising."

"Thank you." Organa sat back on his heels. "Our bad luck with communications equipment continues, by the way. The ship's comsat array is completely destroyed, and the emergency transpon-

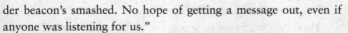

der beacon's smashed. No hope of getting a message out, even if anyone was listening for us."

Which was unlikely. The chances of his last message reaching the Temple were slim to none. "I see."

"Look, you're banged around," said Organa, "but I don't think anything's broken." He grimaced. "At least not . . . physically."

Their predicament wasn't the least bit amusing . . . it was light-years from amusing . . . but still he felt his lips twist in a smile. "Is that your diplomatic way of asking if I've gone insane?"

"The thought did cross my mind."

Die Jedi, die Jedi, die Jedi, die.

He closed his eyes. Felt his blood-caked eyelashes scratching his skin. "And mine."

"But . . . you're all right now?"

Firebeetles. Qui-Gon. Anakin's severed arm. *I have no idea, Senator.* "Yes," he said. "I'm fine." He opened his eyes. "Are you?"

Organa's expression was a muddle of bewilderment and anger. "I'll mend. What the hell *happened*?"

"What do you think? We sprang a trap."

He tried to sit up. Flopped like a landed fish. Organa helped him, one-handed. Dizzy, heart pounding, he leaned against the damaged corridor wall. Organa propped himself up opposite, and they stared at each other in silence.

The Senator spoke first. "Alinta wouldn't betray me. She was used. Manipulated, somehow."

Loyalty was an admirable trait. "Perhaps. But it's a sad fact, Senator, that most people have a price."

"You don't."

The crackling of little flames, the sighing of a rising breeze. A metal screech as branches scraped their starship's twisted hull.

"No," he said at last. "And neither do you."

Organa sat a little straighter, wincing as the movement jarred his hurt arm. "So who was the trap for, do you think? You, or me?"

Die Jedi, die Jedi, die Jedi, die.

He shrugged, trying to ignore the gibbering whisper. The pain behind his eyes drummed, relentless. "We each have enemies. But I suspect the Sith want both of us dead."

"*Both* of us? You I understand . . . but me?"

"Come, Senator," he said. "Don't be so modest. Like the Jedi, you are becoming a familiar public person."

"Yes, but that doesn't explain why the Sith would want to kill me."

"Put at its simplest, they are a corruption of the Jedi," he said. "Like us, they can . . . see things. Perhaps you're destined to become an obstacle to their ambitions."

"So they used Alinta to get to me. And they used me to get to you." Another silence, as Organa made his fretful peace with the truth. Then his face twisted. "Obi-Wan, I am sorry."

"I know. So am I."

"I wonder how they—" Organa shook his head. "Oh well. I don't suppose it matters now. Alinta and her people are dead."

It mattered. And if they survived this, he'd make it his business to learn the truth. But first, of course, they had to survive . . .

Another silence. Then Organa cleared his throat. "I need to know, Obi-Wan. Before. When you—"

"When I lost control of myself and tried to kill us?"

"Yeah," said Organa, uncomfortable. "Then. You said it was the Sith, but—how is that possible? We were still a long way from Zigoola's surface. And you're saying they still were able to—to reach out and control you? Are they truly that powerful?"

Obi-Wan let his gaze drop. Stared at his filthy, bloodstained leggings. "It would seem so, Bail."

"And you weren't expecting that."

So hard to admit it . . . "No."

Organa picked at a rip in his trousers. "That's . . . a worry. I find that worrying. How much, exactly, do you know about these Sith?"

"Not enough, apparently."

"You think this is *funny*?"

He looked up. "I'm not laughing."

But Organa wasn't mollified. And beneath his anger was turbulent fear. "So was Alinta wrong? Are there Sith on this planet, Master Kenobi? Are they coming for us now? Should we—I don't know—*run*?"

So much for first-name pleasantries. "Run?" he echoed. "Run where, do you suggest?"

"I don't know! *Away*?"

"Senator, I was not attacked by an individual Sith," he said carefully. "I suspect the source of the onslaught was some kind of Sith technology. A modified holocron, perhaps."

"Whatever that is," Organa said, impatient. "But if you're not sure, you could be wrong. You said it yourself, you know hardly anything about them. There could be a whole *tribe* of Sith somewhere out there and here we are *waiting* for them to come and kill us."

Die Jedi, die Jedi, die Jedi, die.

"Calm yourself, Senator," he snapped, then took a deep breath. Eased it out with care. *Fear leads to anger, anger leads to hate, hate leads to suffering. Beware the dark side, Jedi . . .* "There is no tribe. There are only two."

"*Two?*" said Organa, taken aback. "That's all? Are you sure about that?"

"Quite sure." He was equally certain he shouldn't have mentioned it, but under the circumstances . . .

"All right," said Organa warily. "If you say so. But they could still be here."

"They're not."

Baffled, the Senator stared at him. "You say that like it's a foregone conclusion, but how do you *know*?"

Time to end this unfortunate conversation. "Because I am a Jedi. Accept it."

"Oh, *enough* with the lofty Jedi pronouncements!" said Organa, pushing untidily to his feet. "You flattened your moral high ground when you crashed my ship. What *proof* do you have that the Sith aren't here? How can you state with *any* degree of certainty we won't face them? Unless—"

Obi-Wan saw the realization dawn. Watched Organa make that inconvenient, intuitive leap. Felt the man's jolt of disbelief . . . of incredulous anger . . .

"You know where they are," Organa breathed. "Don't you? *Where are they,* Master Kenobi?"

He held Organa's hot stare steadily. "Not here."

"What else do you know? What else did you lie about? Do you know *who* they are, too?"

"Even if I did, and I told you, what purpose would that serve?"

"You—you—*Jedi*!" said Organa, then pressed the back of his hand to his lips, heedless of his hurt, as though struggling to contain a torrent of foul abuse. "I want to know *everything.* And I want to know now. *Tell* me, Master Kenobi, or I'll—"

"You'll what?" he said, suddenly so tired. "Send me to bed without my supper? Must I remind you again, Senator? I am not— I have never been—answerable to you."

"Oh yes, that's right," Organa retorted, seething. "You're answerable to Master Yoda and the Jedi Council. And who are *they* answerable to? *Themselves.* How *convenient*!"

"Your insinuation is insulting," he said coldly. "Master Yoda is the most honorable—"

"I don't care! I'm not interested! I want the Sith's names, Kenobi. You might as well tell me because I'm not going to stop asking. I'm going to drive you mad with questions until you tell me—or kill me."

"I don't need to kill you, Bail," he said gently. "There's every chance Zigoola will do that—sooner, rather than later."

Organa spat out an incoherent curse in some angry alien

tongue, then stamped out of the corridor. Then came a groaning sound of metal as the ship's damaged hatch was shoved aside.

Obi-Wan let his head fall back against the uneven wall behind him. His headache was ferocious now, and the black sludge in his veins was bubbling. It clogged his heart. Darkened his vision. The only thing he could see was death.

Die Jedi, die Je—

No. He scrambled upright, then fell against the wall, panting. Fought against the words. Fought against corrosive despair, against capitulation, fought to feel the light side in this place of utter dark. Threw his nearly thirty-five years of Jedi training and discipline at the gibbering Sith voice that was bent upon his obliteration.

The dark retreated. Not far, but far enough. Barely.

Nauseous, dizzy again, he staggered along the corridor, found the half-crushed hatchway and pushed himself outside. Looked for Organa, worried the Senator had stormed off in his fury and even now was breaking his leg . . . or his neck . . .

But no. Organa was standing a stone's throw away, by the fire he'd made, feeding it some of the dead branches he'd collected. If he knew he was being watched, he gave no sign. Anger billowed off him like the heat from his flames.

More than happy to leave him alone, now that he was assured the man hadn't let temper lead him into disaster, Obi-Wan stared at their surroundings. They'd crashed onto a plateau. Stunted trees, their foliage drab-brown and scanty. Scattered red rocks. Yellowish brown soil. A ragged, jagged ravine. No sight or sound of water: the river that had formed it must be long dead. Or this was the dry season. If Zigoola had seasons. Beneath the acrid stink of smoke and crashed starship the air smelled cold. And old. No birdsong. No beast sounds. No paw prints in the dirt.

And everywhere the dark side, a slurry in his blood.

The pale blue sky, washed with hot red behind it, wheeled high overhead. The fire roared. Tayvor Mandirly screamed as his fingers splintered, one defenseless bone at a time. A tall man, a thin man, dying for principle. Dying with courage. Murdered by greed. His eyes were gouged from their sockets so he couldn't see his own blood. His tongue was cut out so there were no cries for help. No pitiful pleas for mercy. When they set him on fire, he wasn't yet dead.

Obi-Wan, on his hands and knees, retched and retched. Nineteen years old he'd been when Mandirly died. Barely younger than Anakin. He'd wept like a youngling, and Qui-Gon did not reprove him.

Exhausted, he collapsed onto the cold dirt of Zigoola, the memory so raw, like the firebeetles, like Qui-Gon and Anakin. The worst of his past dredged into the daylight, as fresh and as frightful as when it first happened.

"Kenobi."

He dragged open his eyes and rolled his head to the side.

"What was that?" said Bail Organa, standing a few paces distant. His face was stricken. "What the hell is going on?"

He tried to speak. Had to cough and spit again. Used the time to consider how best to reply. Did Organa need the details? No. He didn't. "It's still the Sith, I think," he croaked. "The dark side. Using difficult memories against me. Bail, you must be careful. Beware negative emotions. This place will feed on them. It will glut itself and gorge on you until you die."

"Obi-Wan, I'm fine. You're the one in trouble. Whatever this is, it's affecting your mind!"

His mind. His body. His bones were scouring thin. His blood was getting thicker, turgid with the dark. Aching, he sat up. "I'm fighting it."

Instead of answering, Organa went back into the crashed ship. Obi-Wan braced his elbows on his knees and rested his head in his hands. On a deep breath he reached within for the Force, reached for the light side . . .

. . . and instead drowned in the dark.

A warm hand touched his back. "Hey. *Hey*. It's all right. We'll figure this out."

Obi-Wan gathered the shreds and tatters of his self-control. Stared at the cloth and bottle of water Organa held out to him.

"Your face is covered in dry blood," said the Senator. "If you don't clean up I'll be the one having nightmares."

He touched his cheeks. His chin. Felt the truth of Organa's words. Took the cloth and bottle and washed his face, his beard. Tried to wash the foul taste from his mouth, and couldn't. The dark side was a poison, permeating his flesh.

Die Jedi, die Jedi, die Jedi, die.

Dropping cloth and bottle, he clapped his hands to his ears. As if that could make a difference. As though the voice were not inside him. Its spiteful whispering continued. He let his hands fall away.

Organa stepped back. "Are you—you're not . . . really going crazy, are you?"

"Not if I can help it, believe me."

"And can you?" said Organa. "Help it, I mean."

It was a fair question, and deserved a fair answer. "What attacked me on the ship has fallen silent. This isn't so bad as that. It's . . . not pleasant, but I can deal with it." *I hope.*

"Well, with luck you won't have to deal with it for long," said Organa, pulling mini electrobinoculars from his pocket. "Look." He gestured, then held them out. "Back there."

Obi-Wan found his feet, awkwardly, bereft of his customary Jedi ease. Then he took the binocs and stared behind them, across open rock and shadowed forest to another, distant plateau. Through the screening of trees he caught a hint of weak sunlight reflecting off a flat black surface. A shape that was not natural, but had been crafted by design.

He lowered the binocs. "The Sith temple?"

Organa nodded. "I think so. When the ship was going down I thought I saw something. Thought I'd imagined it. But I didn't." His voice caught. "Not everything Alinta told us was a lie." Where there had been fear, now there was a thread of hope. "We could find another ship there, Obi-Wan. Or communications equipment. We could still get out of this. You just have to hold on."

Hold on? Hold on to what? The light side was his bedrock, and his bedrock had crumbled. He felt the dark side's triumph. Felt its gluttony. Its glee. With a wrenching effort he reestablished self-control.

No. I will not feed my fears. Let the dark side starve without me.

"There's enough bottled water," said Organa. "And most of the mealpacks survived the crash. We can reach the temple on foot. It won't be easy but we have to try. We can't stay here and just give up. If we're going to die, Obi-Wan, at least we can die *doing* something."

The Senator sounded like Qui-Gon. It should have been comforting . . . but it only made him sad. He handed back the electrobinoculars.

"I agree we must do something, but I'm not sure your plan is the best idea. If that structure is a Sith temple, it's almost certain that the cause—the source—of what's attacking me is in there."

Organa shoved the binocs back in his pocket and folded his arms. "All the more reason to go, then. We find what that is—a holocron, did you call it? We destroy it, and you'll be fine. And after that, we find a way home."

The Senator didn't understand. How could he? A life in politics could not prepare Bail Organa for this. "I fear it won't be quite so straightforward. The closer we get to the temple, the more severely I'm likely to be affected. Which means the more you could be in danger. The Sith are ruthless in their use of dark power, Bail."

"I understand that," Organa said calmly. "And I agree, it's a risk. But you've already proven you can beat them. I believe you can beat them again."

Obi-Wan stared, puzzled. "What are you talking about?"

"You don't remember? On the ship, before we crashed."

"No. It's all a blur."

"Whatever hold the Sith had on you? You broke it. Just before we hit the ground. It nearly killed you, but you broke it. You pulled us out of our nose dive and you—did something with the Force. I don't know what, but it's the reason we're not in the same shape as the ship." Organa shook his head, rueful. "Why do you think I can't stay mad at you?"

He pulled a face. "I thought it was my boyish charm."

"Ah—*no*."

Turning, he stared again at the hinted Sith structure. Assessed the distance between the plateau it stood on and where they stood now. "That's easily three days' travel, you know. Sunup to sundown over unknown terrain. At the mercy of the elements." If he was himself he wouldn't blink at it. But he wasn't himself. And Organa deserved to know that. "I might become a liability to you."

"I think you underestimate yourself, Obi-Wan."

He felt a flash of temper. Felt the dark side's delight, and stamped out his annoyance before it caught fire in his blood. "And you underestimate the power of the Sith. Any man who does that, does so at his peril."

"I don't deny it'll be a challenge," said Organa. "I'm banged up, and you're . . . under siege. But I know what I'm capable of. And what you're capable of, too. Padmé was right when she told me to trust you."

He managed a small smile. "Why, Senator, are you by any chance attempting *politics* on me?"

"That depends. Is it working?"

He tipped back his head and stared at the fading sky. *This is a desperate plan. It's also our only plan. And he's right about one thing: we must do something. We can't just sit here waiting to die.*

"It would appear we're beginning to lose the light," he said. "I suggest we retire, replenish our energy reserves with food and rest . . . and set off at dawn."

"So," said Organa. "That would be yes."

"Hmmm," he said, his best Yoda-impersonation, then swung around to return to the ship.

The sight of it struck him to a standstill. Just a bargain-model Corellian Starfarer. Nothing fancy. No luxury about it. A sturdy starship beast of burden that had kept them safe as they crossed the airless void. And now it was a twisted pile of scrap metal. A dead ship, beached on Zigoola like a Roonish ice-whale on a glacier.

For once, just once, he understood how Anakin felt.

I hope you're all right, my friend, wherever you are. I hope you find your silly little droid.

After sharing a mealpack and drinking five capfuls of water each, they crawled into their twisted, tilted bunks and tried to sleep as daylight slowly drained into night. But sleep was elusive, for so many reasons.

"I've been thinking," said Organa, breaking the brooding silence.

Obi-Wan sighed. "In my experience, no conversation that starts with those three words ever ends well."

"Ha. I've been thinking about something Padmé said. About the Sith. In her apartment. She said: *They're behind this war with the Separatists.*"

He knew what was coming. Bail Organa was too intelligent for anyone's good. "Don't," he said, staring into the darkness. "What does it matter now?"

"Count Dooku's one of the Sith, isn't he?" said Organa, relentless. "I just realized it. He has to be. He's the Separatists' leader."

I knew it. "No."

"Sorry. I don't believe you."

"Senator—Bail—" He sighed again. "You're wasting time that would be better spent sleeping. I will not confirm or deny any name you suggest."

"I know," said Organa, after a moment. "You're answerable to the Jedi Council. But I give you fair warning, once we get home I'll be taking this up with them."

Good luck. "You must do what you feel is right, of course."

A shifting creak of metal as Organa turned in his bunk. "Just—tell me this, Obi-Wan. If you know who they are, and where they are, why haven't you taken them?"

He smiled. Deep in his mind the dark whispered its desire. In his slow blood, it festered and burned. "If it were that simple, Bail, don't you think we would have? We are doing our best to apprehend them."

"I know. But—do better. Please? They have to be caught. Justice must be done."

Justice? "Are you saying we should put the Sith on trial?"

"I don't know," said Organa. Now he sounded uncertain. "I never thought about it. Before now I never had to. But—yes. There should be a trial. The Republic is founded upon principles of law. If the Sith are in violation of those principles, they must answer for it. Publicly."

He doesn't understand. It's not his fault, but still. "No Sith can be tried in a court of law, Bail. For one thing they'd never recognize its authority. And for another, you'd never get them there."

"So what's your solution? Kill them out of hand?"

"It's the only solution. The Sith are irredeemably evil."

"What? There's no such thing as irredeemable," said Organa. He sounded almost . . . shocked. "Every sentient being is capable of change."

It was hard not to be impatient with his naïveté. "I know you believe that, but where the Sith are concerned you could not be more mistaken. You must realize: *they do not want to change.* They *live* for death and domination. Every dark emotion feeds them: fear, anger, jealousy, hate. The things we find abhorrent are meat and drink to them. After what's happened, I would have thought you'd at least *begin* to comprehend that."

"Obi-Wan . . ." Now Organa sounded deeply troubled. "You're talking about murder."

The accusation was unfair. To his surprise, it rankled. "Really?

And was it murder on Geonosis, when I killed the acklay that was trying to kill me?"

"The acklay was an animal," Organa protested. "A brute beast. It knew no better!"

"Believe me, Bail," he said quietly. "A Sith is just another brute beast. Those who turn to the dark side are lost. They think they control it, but they're tragically mistaken. The dark side of the Force controls and consumes them, consumes all trace of goodness and light. Whatever—whoever—they were, is utterly destroyed. You must accept this hard truth: if we don't put the Sith down when we have the chance, then trust me. *Trust me*. We will live to regret it."

"You may be right," Organa said at last, reluctantly. "But you'll forgive me if I prefer to hope that you're wrong."

And so did he hope . . . but instinct told him that in this instance, hope was misplaced.

Organa slid into sleep after that. The silence and the darkness deepened, broken only by his steady breathing. Obi-Wan, envying him, lay wide awake, knowing he needed rest yet fearing what the dark side would send him if he slept. In the end exhaustion defeated fear—and fear proved well founded. With his mental defenses lowered, the dark side launched a fresh attack. Plundered his memories and plagued him with dreams. Grimly, doggedly, he endured the onslaught.

His war with the Sith had truly begun.

EIGHTEEN

"*MASTER YODA,*" SAID ANAKIN, VIA HOLOGRAM. "*I REGRET TO IN-form you, and the Jedi Council, that during the Bothawui engage-ment with Grievous I lost my Artoo unit. And that, despite an extensive and exhaustive search, I have been unable to locate him. Therefore I must declare Artoo-Detoo officially lost in action.*"

Yoda exchanged a look with Mace Windu, then tapped a bent forefinger against his lips. Even through a hologram, Anakin's angry chagrin was evident. There seemed little point in a severe scolding; he doubted either he or Mace could be more unforgiving of Anakin than Anakin was of himself.

"Unfortunate this news is, young Skywalker. A valuable asset your droid was."

Anakin's shoulders tensed. "*Yes, Master Yoda. I know that. I am deeply sorry I've failed to find him.*"

Mace leaned forward into holotransmitter range. "Anakin, what's done is done," he said briskly. He had little patience for ex-cessive self-recriminations. "You'll be assigned a new droid as soon as possible. In the meantime we have a war to conduct."

"*Yes, Master Windu. Do you have a new assignment for me?*"

"Nothing on the front lines. This recruitment party Dooku's

been holding on Chanosant means he's eased back on the obvious aggression. At least for the moment."

"*Dooku's put Grievous on a leash? Master Windu, that's hard to believe. Especially—especially after him taking out the Falleen battle group.*"

Mace permitted himself a small, grim smile. "He took out the Falleen group, and then lost Bothawui to you. I'd say there are some tactical readjustments going on behind the scenes. In the meantime the current front is a public relations battle between Dooku and Palpatine. They're fighting it out on the HoloNet news service."

"*My money's on the Supreme Chancellor,*" said Anakin, swiftly amused. "*Master, Dooku can't actually believe this—this redroot-and-stick approach is going to work, can he? Not when he's got droid detachments occupying Lanos?*"

"Not occupying. Liberating," said Mace, dust-dry. "From its crushing servitude to the corrupt and decayed Republic. Or haven't you been paying attention to the HoloNet?"

"*No, Master. The HoloNet puts me in a bad mood, and I know how much you and Master Yoda disapprove of Jedi in bad moods.*"

Yoda felt his lips twitch, and exchanged another glance with Mace. Stepping forward, he said, "Pleasing it is to know, young Skywalker, that remembered your Temple lessons are."

"*Always, Master Yoda,*" said Anakin, with a slight bow. "*Masters, if I'm not heading back to the front lines, may I ask what it is you want of me now?*"

"We've received your final report on the new cruisers' battle performance," said Mace. "And I'll admit, I'm surprised. If I recall correctly, Anakin, your previous comments were glowing."

"*Yes, they were, Master Windu. I'm sorry, I didn't mean my report to be critical, exactly,*" said Anakin. He was cautious now. A little on the defensive. "*The cruisers are fine. It's just—you see— look, the truth is, I think they could be better.*"

Frowning, Yoda started pacing the edge of the Council circle. What was this now?

"Better?" Mace said, steepling his fingers. Letting his voice chill. "It's your considered opinion that *you*, Anakin Skywalker, can improve upon the work of a highly qualified and experienced team of professional shipwrights? A team whose members' combined experience in the design of heavy cruisers totals, I believe, some eighty-four years?"

Anakin's hologram nodded. *"Yes, Master Windu. That is my considered opinion."*

Mace sat back out of holotransmitter range. "Call me crazy," he murmured, "but it's precisely *because* he makes claims like this that I'm inclined to believe him. No Jedi would say such a thing if it wasn't true."

Halting beyond the holotransmitter, Yoda planted his gimer stick before him and rested his chin on his hands. "An affinity with machines has young Skywalker always possessed. And while prideful he can be, dishonest he is not."

Mace leaned forward again. "Anakin, take the battle group back to the Allanteen Six shipyards for maintenance, repairs, and upgrades. Consult with the experts there, and give them your findings. At this stage I don't know how long you'll have. You could receive a new assignment at any moment. If you do, and the *Resolute*'s not available, you'll be given another ship. Probably the *Twilight* again. Any questions?"

"No, Master Windu," said Anakin. *"Thank you."* Then he hesitated. *"At least, no questions about that. But . . . may I ask whether Master Kenobi has returned from his mission?"*

Interesting. Yoda stepped to the holotransmitter. "Returned he has not, young Skywalker. Why do you ask?"

Anakin's hologram flickered, but not even a degraded holosignal could mask his worried expression. *"I don't know what to tell you, Master Yoda. I have a bad feeling."*

"Concerned for Obi-Wan you need not be, Anakin," he said, very careful this time not to look at Mace. "Word from him we received a short time ago. Continuing his investigation he is."

"Investigation into what, Master? Can you tell me?"

"No," said Mace flatly. "Anakin, you have your orders. Follow them without delay."

"Yes, Master Windu," said Anakin after a moment.

"You did good work at Bothawui," Mace added, more gently. "The Council's pleased with you, Anakin. And with your apprentice. Keep it up. A few more victories like that, and perhaps we can begin to hope this war will end soon."

"Yes, Master Windu."

Anakin's hologram bowed, and then his image flicked off.

Yoda shook his head, sighing. "A bad feeling he has. Like that, I do not."

"Which is more worrying?" said Mace, fingers drumming his knee. "The fact that he confirms your concerns . . . or that at his age, with his still-limited experience, he can sense something's wrong when thousands of light-years separate him and Obi-Wan?"

It was a good question. Yoda considered his answer, acutely aware of the disquiet simmering in the back of his mind. *A bad feeling, yes. About those I know.* "Powerful the Chosen One must be, if he is to bring balance to the Force."

"I'm aware of that," said Mace. "But there's so much power there, Yoda. And he's still so young."

"Which is why guide him we must," said Yoda. "Though resent it he does."

"Yes," Mace said, and then leaned forward, his own unease simmering to the surface. "Yoda, what are we going to do about Obi-Wan?"

Sighing, he restarted his wandering around the Council Chamber, the *tap-tap-tapping* of his gimer stick a counterpoint to his thoughts. The Chamber's polished wooden floor glowed warm and comforting in the transparisteel-filtered light. Beyond the panoramic windows the sky was wreathed in a pink-and-gold sunset. One by one the airspeeders and shuttles and maxitaxis and gondolas were switching on their running lights, gaudy as firedrakes and tamarizi beetles.

"We will wait, Master Windu," he said at length. "For his transponder signal we will continue to scan. And hope, we will, that the Force is with him."

"Waiting," said Mace, and grimaced. "Not my favorite occupation."

"Know that I do," said Yoda, teasingly grave. "Patience did I never manage to teach you."

"You taught me enough," said Mace. "You taught me everything important. Yoda . . ." He slid out of his chair to the floor and braced an arm on one raised knee. "I'll take care of everything out here. The Council, Palpatine—whatever comes up. You should do nothing but listen for Obi-Wan. You're the best we have at navigating the Force. If he's gone beyond Munto Codru—if he's in trouble . . . if he needs us, and can't reach us any other way—you're the only one who'll hear him."

Troubled, Yoda halted again. He wanted nothing more than to lock himself into his meditation chamber, but . . . "Much work that will make for you, Mace Windu. And greatly burdened you are already."

"I don't care about that! Yoda, how many times have you said it? Obi-Wan has a destiny as important as Anakin's. If something happens to him—if we should lose him—"

Yoda nodded, as the weight of the hazy future tried to crush him. "Even with the Chosen One, the Force may never be rebalanced," he finished heavily. "Remember what I have said I do, Master Windu. Very well. Your advice I will take. Seek for Obi-Wan in the Force, I will, and hope his way home to us he can safely find."

Standing in the *Resolute*'s hushed war room, Ahsoka considered Anakin as he stared at the deactivated holotransmitter, arms folded, chin tucked low.

Oooh, he's not happy. He's not happy at all.

"So, Skyguy. What are we going to do now?" she asked. When he shot her a sharp look she added, "We're alone! You said I can call you—"

"Be quiet. I'm thinking."

She chewed her lip while she waited. Tried to read the thoughts tumbling through his mind. But when he wanted to, Anakin could hide himself completely. For all the good his face did her right now he might as well be a protocol droid.

He's not going to disobey the Council, is he? I mean, there was no wiggle room in those orders. He can't disobey them. Not even for Master Kenobi. Can he?

Anakin looked at her again, more kindly this time. "What are we going to do, Ahsoka? What do *you* think we should do?"

She took a deep breath. Snapped her spine straight. She'd do him no favors by telling him what he wanted to hear instead of what he needed to hear. Master Kenobi had practically said as much when they were at Bothawui. And who was she, a lowly Padawan, to argue with the great Obi-Wan Kenobi?

"I think we have to do what Master Windu told us. I know you're upset about losing Artoo. I know you're worried about Master Kenobi. So am I. But we're at war, Skyguy, and that's bigger than both of us. How can we beat the Separatists if we don't work as a team?"

A muscle leapt along Anakin's tight jaw. "How can we beat the Separatists if we follow bad orders? The Jedi Council isn't always right, Ahsoka."

"Maybe not," she said, after a doubtful pause. "But they can't always be wrong."

He pulled a face. "Can't they?"

And what she was supposed to say to *that*? "Ummm . . ."

"Never mind," he said, glancing at her. "You're probably right. Besides, I might have a bad feeling about him, but I can't tell where Obi-Wan is or what he's doing. So even if I was prepared to disregard Master Windu and go after him, I wouldn't begin to know where to start looking."

Which was why he was so worried. "I don't think he'd want you to go after him, Master. Do you?"

"Maybe not," Anakin admitted with the faintest of smiles. "But Obi-Wan doesn't always know what's best for him."

Ahsoka felt her mouth drop open. "And you do?"

"Yes," he said simply, then headed for the door. "Come on. We need to get this battle group headed for Allanteen Six. Then you and I can put in some training time with Captain Rex."

Great. I wonder if Rex can teach me any tricks that'll help me keep you under control?

Bemused, resigned, she followed him from the room.

They abandoned the crashed starship soon after daybreak. Zigoola's early-morning air was cool and dry, the sky unclouded, a faint breeze stirring. Bail hitched up his makeshift backpack, trying to fit it more comfortably against his shoulder blades. Trying to ignore the ache in his wrenched, complaining shoulder.

As he and Obi-Wan headed across the sparse plateau, he slid a considering gaze sideways toward the Jedi. Had the man gotten any sleep? He suspected not. There was a heavy-eyed weariness about him this morning that spoke eloquently of a troubled night. And during their preparations for leaving, they'd exchanged only a handful of words.

So do I say something, or do I pretend nothing's wrong? If I pretend nothing's wrong, and then something happens, how will I know what to do? How to help?

Obi-Wan sighed. "I'm fine, Bail. You don't need to worry."

How profoundly unsettling to have one's thoughts read so precisely. "You're fine now, maybe," he conceded. "But what if that changes?"

"I'm doing my best to see that it doesn't."

Doing his best? What did that mean? More secret, unsettling Jedi business, probably. "Can you still feel the Sith?"

"Yes," said Obi-Wan after a moment. "Yes, I can feel them."

"And?"

Obi-Wan shifted his own roughly constructed backpack. "And what?"

"And so does that mean they're—they're attacking you? Right now? While we're walking?"

"Yes, Bail," said Obi-Wan. His voice sounded tight. "But you must not concern yourself. I am in control."

Bail slowed. Stopped. Obi-Wan kept walking for three strides, then he stopped, too. Turned around slowly, revealing a pale face grooved with lines of stress.

"What?"

Bail grimaced. "I want to help you. How can I help you?"

"You can be quiet," said Obi-Wan. "Talking is a distraction. And the Sith . . ."

"What about them?" he prompted when the Jedi didn't continue. "Obi-Wan, what are they doing?"

"Trying to find a way in," said Obi-Wan. "It would be best for both of us if they failed."

Well, yes. By all means state the obvious. "They're still . . . playing with your mind? Making you remember things?"

"Not at this moment."

"But they were? Last night?"

Obi-Wan looked away, then nodded. "Yes."

He wanted to ask, *What kind of things?* He wanted to know exactly what the Jedi was facing, because they were in this mess together, whether Obi-Wan liked it or not.

But he won't tell me, I know it. He'll say I'm distracting him.

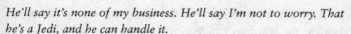

He'll say it's none of my business. He'll say I'm not to worry. That he's a Jedi, and he can handle it.

Frustrated, Bail chewed at his lip. "How bad is this going to get, Obi-Wan? Honestly."

"Honestly?" Obi-Wan shrugged. "Honestly, Senator, I have no idea. But I think it's safe to say things will get worse before they get better."

Wonderful. "Maybe this is a mistake. Maybe you should stay here, with the ship, and let me investigate the temple."

"A kind thought, but unfortunately impractical," Obi-Wan replied. "Even if you reached it safely, you'd have no idea of what was in there. No way of identifying the purpose of its artifacts. If there are artifacts. No. We continue as planned."

He nodded. "All right. But you have to tell me what's going on, Obi-Wan. No shutting me out. No treating me like an idiot. And if you need help, you have to ask for it. Agreed?"

Small dust devils danced across the landscape, whipped up by the rising breeze. Obi-Wan watched them, his face impossible to read. At last he sighed.

"Agreed," he said. He sounded profoundly unhappy. "Now please, Bail. No more talking. I need to concentrate."

So they kept on walking, in silence, and the Zigoola morning expanded around them.

Nearly two hours later, as they tramped steadily across the vast, uneven plateau, Obi-Wan abruptly halted. Stood completely still, his expression suspended, like someone trying to recall a name or some other elusive piece of information. And then, without warning, his face twisted and he dropped to his knees. Began clawing at his own body, his eyes wide open in horror.

Bail felt a sharp breath strangle in his throat. He knew what this was. The Sith had breached their enemy's defenses, and now Obi-Wan was once more reliving the firebeetles on Taanab.

So much for him being in control. What do I do? What do I do?

He had to stop it somehow, couldn't let the onslaught continue. Just like the last time, Obi-Wan was in danger of inflicting serious self-harm. Shrugging out of his backpack, he let it fall to the hard ground, crouched in front of the Jedi, and took hold of his upper arms.

"Obi-Wan! Snap out of it!"

But instead of waking up, Obi-Wan attacked. Not with the Force this time, but with clenched fists and desperate strength. He wasn't a particularly tall man, and his build was wiry, not bulked with muscle, but he could strike hard and strike fast.

The flurry of blows caught Bail in his face and his belly. Split open his scabbed-over lip and punched the air from his lungs. Toppling sideways, gasping, he felt himself hit the ground in an ungainly sprawl, skewered with pain. He tasted blood. Saw the brightening sky wheel uncontrollably overhead. Thought, *Maybe that wasn't such a good idea, Organa.*

Vision smearing, he urged his rudely woken hurts to subside. Tried to sit up, failed, tried again, and succeeded.

"You *fool*!" shouted Obi-Wan, looming over him. "What were you thinking? Don't you know I could have *killed* you?"

Bail squinted up at him. "Oh. So it did work. You're welcome, by the way."

Spitting a colorful Toydarian curse, Obi-Wan tugged off his own makeshift backpack and rummaged among the water bottles and mealpacks. "I can't heal you," he said, pulling out the starship's compact first-aid kit. "My control is compromised. You'll have to make do with this."

"Fine," he said, reaching for the kit, but Obi-Wan slapped his hand away. Beneath the temper, there was fear.

"I'll do it," the Jedi snapped. "Sit still and be quiet."

"Fine," he said again, and let the man minister to him.

Obi-Wan's doctoring was brusquely efficient. When he was finished he repacked the first-aid kit, shoved it into the backpack, then looked up. "Bail, you must *never* do that again."

"You should have more faith in yourself, Obi-Wan," he said quietly. "I don't for a minute believe you'd kill me."

"Then you *are* a fool," said Obi-Wan, sitting back on his heels. "Because I've already tried once."

True. But if they were going to survive this disaster, they couldn't afford to lose themselves in mistrust. "I can suffer a few bruises, Obi-Wan, if it means you don't have to relive what happened on Taanab—or anything else the Sith want to throw at you."

Obi-Wan stood. Ran a hand over his beard, clearly frustrated. "More misplaced heroics? Spare me, Senator—and do as you're told. If—when—I lose ground to the Sith the next time, *stay back.* Let the attack run its course."

"Let you hurt yourself, you mean?" he retorted, clambering to his feet. "I don't think so, Master Kenobi. If for no other reason than self-preservation. I won't get off this rock without you in one piece."

"And you won't get off it if you're dead!"

Stalemate.

They glared at each other as the dust devils danced. Then Obi-Wan's furious expression faded . . . and once again that unexpected vulnerability was revealed.

"Please, Bail," he said. "Don't make me worry about you. If you do, you'll weaken me. And this is hard enough as it is."

Bail folded his arms and stared at the ground. *Stang.* It wasn't fair, he wanted to fight. Didn't want to concede the argument. But he was beaten and he knew it, his stubborn resistance neatly punctured by Obi-Wan's simple, heartfelt plea.

He lifted his gaze. "So I'm supposed to . . . what? Just sit on my hands? No matter what happens? No matter what the Sith do? No matter what *you* do?"

"That's right."

"And then what . . . pick up the pieces afterward?"

A little of the strain in Obi-Wan's eyes eased. "Provided it's not too much trouble, yes."

Unfolding his arms, he shoved his hands in his pockets and stared around them at the plateau, and the dust devils, and lastly toward the first distant tree line. Three days of this? Three days, or maybe longer?

I should've stayed at home, in bed.

"Bail," said Obi-Wan. "You said I must ask for your help if I needed it. Well, I'm asking. *This* is how you can help me."

Kriff, their games of sabacc hadn't lied. This man certainly knew how to play dirty. "All right," he said reluctantly. "We'll do things your way. For now. But the discussion isn't over. It's merely suspended. If this gets out of hand, Obi-Wan, if it really does look like you're putting your own life at risk. Then we think again. We find a different way of doing things. Agreed?"

Obi-Wan picked up his makeshift backpack and shrugged into it. "We'll see."

Bail stared at him, dumbfounded. Kriff, *kriff* if Kenobi wasn't the most stubborn, the most infuriating, the most *impossible*—

"Come along, Senator," said the Jedi, and started walking. "As someone said recently, we're burning daylight."

And that had him hustling his own makeshift pack back on, cursing his aching shoulder, cursing Kenobi, and the Sith, and the galaxy at large. Cursing fate, for landing him in this predicament. With the backpack settled, he jogged to catch up.

What a tale I'll have to tell you, Breha, when I get home.

Because he was getting home. The Sith weren't winning this one. They weren't . . . they weren't . . . they kriffing well weren't.

A Jedi youngling in the Temple is taught many things. First among them is this: *Fear leads to anger, anger leads to hate, hate leads to suffering. Beware the dark side, Jedi.*

And the second lesson goes: *Mastery of self is the only mastery that matters.*

Obi-Wan feared greatly his self-mastery would fail.

The world outside, the world beyond his inner world, involved walking beneath an inimical sun, upon the skin of a planet that was trying to kill him, toward the stronghold of an enemy bent upon his destruction. It involved a good man, Bail Organa, who should not have been by his side. Involved insufficient nourishment, fractured sleep, and a litany of physical ills that made the physical world a trial.

But the discomforts of that world were nothing but an echo. Reality lay behind his eyes, in the realm of spirit . . . where he felt like a candle set to burn in a hurricane.

Since last night the wind of the dark side had blown upon him without cease, bludgeoning him with the cruelest of memories. Seeking to tear his battling spirit apart. The firebeetles . . . Tayvor Mandirly . . . Qui-Gon's death . . . and Geonosis. A pitiless procession of fear and death and loss, with barely enough time between each assault to properly recover. To catch his gasping breath. To rebuild his defenses, ready for the next attack.

Turned inward, turned upon himself, brutally cut off from the light side of the Force, he husbanded his flame. Drew upon the lessons of every Jedi who had taught him: Yoda and Mace Windu and most especially Qui-Gon Jinn. And Anakin had taught him; he leaned on that unlikely strength. The Sith in Theed had taught him, and Dooku in his cave. Those last lessons were the most bitter; they'd not go to waste.

He saw himself a candle. He saw himself behind a wall. Brick by brick he tried to raise it. Brick by brick, it was destroyed. Every death was a hammer blow. Every loss a chisel. The Sith were a wily foe, they knew where and when to strike. They were drawn to weak places, to old griefs and unhealed wounds. He built his barricade against them. They laughed and tore it down.

And as they laughed they whispered, like a lover in his ear: *Die, Jedi. Die, Jedi. Die, Jedi. Die.*

Dimly, he was aware of Bail Organa's concern. Could feel it like a warm hand, placed in comfort on his shoulder. But even as he drew strength from that he felt its burden. Felt the crushing weight of the man, who was his to protect . . . or fail.

I should have left him at the starship. I shouldn't have brought him at all. I should have found a way to keep him out of this. I'm going to get him killed.

In a strange way, Bail reminded him of Padmé: bold and brash and stubbornly brave. Willing to risk himself without a second thought, for another, for a cause, to uphold what was right. If the Sith were to be defeated, it would be by people like Bail and Padmé as much as by the Jedi.

So he can't die here, on Zigoola. The Republic needs him. I must protect him, no matter what it costs.

In the world beyond his spirit, precious time was passing. And in this place, time—like the Sith—was not his friend. Every faltering step took him closer to the hurricane's cold eye. Closer to the Sith temple, beating heart of the thing that burned and yearned for his death. He feared that when he reached it, he'd be burned out. Burned away. Nothing but a memory. Someone else's unhealed wound.

But fear leads to anger, and anger leads to hate, and hate leads to suffering. Which means the dark side wins. So he husbanded his flame. Brick by brick he built his wall. Because the alternative was surrender.

And no one had ever taught him that.

NINETEEN

THEY REACHED THE FIRST STRETCH OF TANGLED WOODLAND late in the afternoon. Gnarled branches latticed overhead, filtering the fading sunlight. Skeletal leaf litter covered the uneven ground, rustling beneath their feet. The air smelled old and dead. No birds in the twisted trees, no sign of life at all.

Sweaty and tired, Bail looked at Obi-Wan. "Are we stopping for a moment?"

They were the first words he'd spoken since their firebeetle argument. His voice sounded rusty. He wanted water, desperately, but they had to conserve their supply. Nothing about this place suggested they'd come across a river or creek or even a pond anytime soon. And if they ran out of water before they'd found a way home . . . well . . . it didn't bear thinking about. Dying of thirst was a wicked way to perish.

Slowing his pace a little, Obi-Wan glanced up through the brown, laceworked foliage. Haphazardly dappled with light and shade, he looked drained. Maintaining his own silence, he'd been fighting the Sith with every step he took. And this was only the first day . . .

"We should keep going," he said. His voice sounded hoarse, too. "At least until sunset."

"Why?" Bail demanded, abruptly rebellious. Resentful. *It's all right for you, Kenobi. But I'm not a Jedi. I'm a mere human.* "A few minutes rest. What can that hurt? There's no point killing ourselves to get there, Obi-Wan. We didn't even stop to eat." Instead they'd shared a mealpack while walking; he was still battling indigestion. "I say we take a moment to catch our breath."

Obi-Wan shot him an impatient glance. Then he nodded. "Very well."

The desiccated forest floor was crisscrossed with dead, fallen tree trunks. Swallowing a groan of relief, Bail dragged off his backpack and sat. He was a fit man, taking exercise daily, but walking for hour upon endless hour took its toll. His shoulders and neck ached, and his legs. His lower back felt unspeakably tight. His feet had blistered and were burning; his fashionable half boots hadn't been designed for wilderness hiking. All the shallow cuts and burns he'd sustained in the firefight on the space station were stinging. And his lip, where Obi-Wan had struck him, had swollen again and throbbed meanly, like a toothache. He hadn't taken a painkiller, wanting to save their first-aid kit's drugs for more serious mishaps.

Bending to the backpack, determined to discover the exact distribution of contents that would save him from a crippled spine, he looked again at Obi-Wan. The Jedi was still standing, still wearing his own backpack. As though the simple act of stopping had drained him of all momentum.

"Hey," he said. "Are you all right?"

Obi-Wan nodded.

"Then sit. Get that pack off for a while. You need to rest worse than I do."

Again, Obi-Wan nodded . . . but didn't move.

Uneasy now, Bail straightened. "Obi-Wan? What's wrong?"

Obi-Wan's answer was to shrug out of his backpack and let it fall roughly to the ground. He was frowning, his eyes not quite focused. Then he unclipped his lightsaber and ignited the blade.

"Hey!" Bail jumped back, heedless of his aches and pains. "What's going on? Do you sense someone? Are we alone or aren't we? *Obi-Wan!"*

The lightsaber's hum was loud in the tangled forest's eerie silence, its blue blade so vivid it looked alive in this dead, silent place. Obi-Wan raked his keen yet still oddly unfocused gaze around him, his body humming with tension like a Voolk-hound scenting prey. Then his eyes narrowed, his head lifted, and his lightsaber snapped up to guard position.

"Ventress."

Alarmed, Bail swung around, trying to follow where Obi-Wan was looking. His heart pounded, adrenaline drowning all pain. Asajj Ventress? Here? Where? The woman was lethal. Kriff, he'd been such a *fool,* leaving his blaster to be destroyed with Alinta's space station.

"Obi-Wan, I can't see her," he whispered, stepping sideways to take scant cover behind a stunted, twisted tree. "Where is she? What do I—"

Obi-Wan danced forward, his eyes alight with the same fierce fervor that had lit him in the battle on the space station. Lightsaber flashing, its buzz cleaving the silence, he launched a blistering attack—on nobody. Asajj Ventress wasn't there.

Realization punched Bail hard in the chest.

Oh mercy. He's hallucinating.

And suddenly he didn't feel safe at all.

Flattened against the tree trunk, heart pounding so hard he thought it might smash through his chest, he watched as Obi-Wan battled his phantom adversary . . . and though what was happening filled him with a kind of horrified pity, he couldn't help but feel with it an astonished admiration. What he'd witnessed in the fight on the space station had been nothing, *nothing,* compared with this.

Obi-Wan Kenobi wielded his lightsaber like some elemental force of nature. As though the blade were a living extension of himself, indivisible from his own flesh and blood. All trace of exhaustion was wiped clean from him; his energy seemed limitless as he leapt and twisted and somersaulted and spun, his lightsaber humming, flashing blue through the shadows. It was almost possible to believe he *was* fighting an actual, physical foe: every cut, every parry, every bind and counterbind with the blade seemed to encounter another slashing lightsaber. His body reacted as though to a series of jarring blows, every muscle in him tensed against the impact, his face set hard with a formidable determination to prevail . . . but still, with the wicked light in his eyes that said though in his tormented mind this was life and death, there was yet a kind of glory.

But how long can this last? Bail wondered, admiration giving way to a rising concern as Obi-Wan showed no sign of ending his battle. *He can't keep it up forever. He's already tired, and this is grueling. He's going to drop in his tracks, surely.* And then what? *I've got no hope of carrying him to the Sith temple.*

Should he ignore Obi-Wan's instruction and try to stop the fight? Try to break through the Sith-sent hallucination and bring the Jedi back to himself?

Ah . . . no. I don't think so. Not when he's got that lightsaber in his hand.

Breathing harshly now, no light in his eyes but a deadly, killing flame, Obi-Wan increased the ferocity of his attack. And now—what was happening? Something was—was different. Was Kenobi even fighting Asajj Ventress anymore? Staring, fresh dismay rising, Bail thought he could see a shift in Obi-Wan's focus. An odd, unpleasant twist in his face.

Something's wrong . . . well, more wrong. Somehow, something's changed.

And then the Jedi plunged his lightsaber through the heart of a tree.

Startled, Bail swallowed a shout as the cool dead air filled with the noxious stench of burned and burning sap. Stepped hurriedly away from his own sheltering tree trunk, because now Obi-Wan was slashing and stabbing the woodland's trees indiscriminately. Severed branches plummeted to the ground, twigs and leaves flying, a haze of stinking smoke rising.

Then it wasn't just branches falling victim to Obi-Wan's frenzy—entire trees were dying, cut in half with dreadful ease, with a single stroke of that vivid blue blade. Faster and faster and faster the Jedi whirled, slicing down trees as though they were his mortal enemy. As though each branch held a weapon that was trying to kill him. The frantic hum of his lightsaber was almost lost in the crashing of timber as it struck the ground, the old dead fallen tree trunks sagging into their neighbors like the staggering drunks in Coruscant's seedier districts. Leaves whirled and swirled in a blizzard and fresh sunlight poured through the widening gaps in the woodland's interlaced foliage.

Bail stared, transfixed, as Obi-Wan slaughtered a forest.

Oh no, oh no. This is out of control.

He couldn't stand still for long, though, because there was neither rhyme nor reason to Obi-Wan's pattern of attack. Like a man tap-dancing on the rim of a volcano he kept moving, kept moving, didn't dare stand still, as all around him Obi-Wan laid the Zigoolan woodland to waste. Twice a severed tree nearly crushed him, falling. Once he went sprawling across an old dead tree trunk as he leapt clear of a living tree's gnarly crown plunging to the ground. He escaped with bruises and scratches, dry-mouthed and starting to panic.

How do I stop this? I have to stop this. It's insane. Obi-Wan's gone mad.

And then he had to hurl himself sideways as the Jedi spun around from slashing three saplings with one blow, ready for a fresh attack. Spun toward *him*, his face almost unrecognizable. Twisted now with fury and a kind of blank and mindless hate.

Soundlessly snarling, Obi-Wan raised his lightsaber again . . . and advanced.

Sick to his stomach with fear, Bail threw up his hands. Backed up one step then stopped as he struck a felled tree trunk and nearly tumbled again.

"Obi-Wan! Obi-Wan, it's me. It's Bail Organa. Obi-Wan. Master Kenobi. *Stop*."

Unhearing, uncaring, Obi-Wan brought his lightsaber around and down.

Bail closed his eyes. *Breha*.

And then he didn't die.

"Bail?" said a small, uncertain voice. "Bail? What am I doing?"

Dizzy, he blinked . . . and Obi-Wan's stunned face swam into focus. He flicked his gaze sideways and down, to the thin humming bar of pulsing blue light that had stopped so close to his neck he could feel its searing heat.

"Right now, Obi-Wan?" he murmured. "Right now you're putting down your lightsaber."

With a soft hum the weapon's blade disengaged, and the black-and-silver lightsaber hilt slid from the Jedi's loosened fingers. Thudded to the ground.

"Ventress," said Obi-Wan, his voice still hushed with shock. "I saw Asajj Ventress. I fought her—on Teth. And the Separatist droid forces. I fought them on Christophsis. And I thought—I thought—" Slowly he looked around, at the felled trees and the freshly littered foliage, stark evidence of madness. Of a mind lost in a world of illusion. Without warning his knees buckled and he dropped. Collapsed onto his hands and vomited up the miserly half mealpack he'd consumed hours earlier.

Bail turned away, grimly, and removed his backpack from a tangle of severed branches. Retrieved one precious bottle of water, unscrewed the cap, and held it out to the Jedi.

"To the Hells with rationing it," he said. "Just drink."

Sitting back on his heels, Obi-Wan took the bottle, his hand shaking. But instead of drinking, he looked up. "Bail, I'm so sorry."

He shrugged. "It wasn't your fault."

"Yes, it was," Obi-Wan whispered. "I lost my focus. I let my guard down."

Stang. Bail crouched before him. "Obi-Wan, you're tired. You've been fighting the Sith for hours without respite. You may be a Jedi but you're not indestructible. And anyway, you beat them. You *didn't* kill me. Again. So they're not winning. *You* are. Now stop talking and drink."

Obi-Wan drained half the bottle, then handed it back. "We should keep going."

Keep going? After *this*? He shook his head. "No. You need to rest."

"Bail . . ." Obi-Wan's eyes were hollow with fatigue, and something worse. "I will never get a moment's rest while I am on this planet. If we are going to find a way off it, we must find it soon. Before . . ."

He didn't have to say any more. Bail could finish the sentence himself. *Before your mind is broken completely, and like Taanab's firebeetles the Sith eat you alive.*

He sighed. "All right. We'll keep going."

"My lightsaber," said Obi-Wan. He picked it up, held it out, his face set into difficult lines. "Take it. Keep it safe for me."

Bail stared at the elegant weapon in silence. Remembered the heat of it, its terrifying power. He knew enough about Jedi to know the lightsaber was their most personal, most important, most precious possession.

"Are you sure?"

Obi-Wan nodded. "I nearly killed you. I'm certain."

"All right," he said again, and took the proffered weapon. Closed his fingers around it, feeling its weight. Its significance. "I'll take good care of it, I promise."

"Thank you," said Obi-Wan. Then his gaze traveled around the ruin of the woodland, slowly absorbing the frenzied carnage. Shadows darkened in his eyes. "Now let's go."

As they trudged on, racing the setting sun, Obi-Wan took relieved refuge in silence. Struggled to rebuild his defenses against the dark, against the ceaseless, spiteful voice whispering in his ear.

Die Jedi, die Jedi, die Jedi, die.

Never in his life had he felt so unbalanced, so uncertain. He really had seen Ventress. And after her, the Separatist droids. Worse than that, when he'd fought them he'd used the dark side. Channeled it without thinking. That had been the most sickening realization of all. That thunderbolt of understanding was what had crashed him vomiting to his knees.

That, and the fact he had nearly decapitated Bail Organa.

It cannot happen again. I must not let that happen again. They can seal the light side away from me, but the Sith must never turn me to the dark. They must not make of me an instrument of murder.

Better that he did die than permit that to happen.

And so he and Alderaan's Senator picked their slow way through the remainder of the forest, the part of it he hadn't managed to fell, as daylight seeped from the sky and dusk lowered its mantle. Weighed down with their backpacks, and their memories, and their fears.

Painstakingly, laboriously, he rebuilt his shattered mental defenses. Shored up the bulwarks he'd hammered in place against the Sith, achingly aware that he was only half himself without the light side of the Force as his ally. Haunted by the fear that half a Jedi could not prevail.

The loss of his lightsaber was like an open wound in his side.

Night fell, and as though natural darkness were some kind of invitation the bludgeoning memories returned. He overrode Organa's demands to stop until dawn. Somehow it was easier to resist the Sith while he was moving. Let him slow, and they pressed him harder. So hard he thought he'd break.

"We have night-sticks," he told the Senator. "We'll go on a little longer."

Poor Bail. He'd been stubborn, and unreasonable, and ridiculously foolhardy, but he didn't deserve this. No one deserved this.

Eventually they did stop. But only because his legs gave way and wouldn't help him stand again. Since they were still in the straggled woodland, with plenty of easy fuel at hand, Bail started a careful, cautious fire. They shared another mealpack. Drank sparingly from their water supply. Wrapped their heat-seal blankets around them and sat before the flames in silence.

Sunrise was a long way away.

Eventually Bail slept, but he didn't. Every time he sank beneath the surface of waking, a memory tore at him with sharp, cruel teeth. His only hope of keeping the Sith at bay was to stay awake, so he could concentrate on the mental disciplines he'd spent his whole life perfecting.

But he was tired. He was so tired. And soon enough the memories savaged him even when he was awake, just as they'd attacked after he crashed the starship on the plateau. Standing naked in the hurricane, he fought his endless battle with the Sith. Relived Geonosis. Relived Taanab. Relived losing Qui-Gon. Again, and again, and again.

Bail slept through all of it. The sun returned, eventually. As soon as the sky lightened, he woke the man and bullied him onto his feet.

"You look like death," Bail told him bluntly. "You won't last until noon."

He shrugged into his backpack. "I'll last for as long as I need to, Senator. No more arguing. Let's go."

When Obi-Wan was felled by his third vision—memory—waking nightmare—whatever the kriff was happening to him—in less than two hours, Bail retreated to a safe distance, dropped to the rocky plain they struggled to cross, and despaired.

Never again. Never, never, never again will I say I wish I could be a Jedi. Not even for a week. Not even for a day.

Which vision was it this time? By all that was merciful, not Tayvor's death. If he had to relive by proxy his uncle's torture and burning yet again he thought *he'd* go mad. Or maybe just go mad faster. Because if this was tough on Obi-Wan—and of course it was, it was brutal—it was almost as difficult for him, having to sit on the outside looking in, knowing there was *nothing* he could do to stop the Sith's relentless assault. Having to relive that particular memory along with the Jedi.

But no, it wasn't Tayvor's death this time. He suspected—though he wasn't certain, because Obi-Wan steadfastly refused to discuss it—that the Jedi was dreaming of Geonosis. The memory always started off in silence and ended with him calling for his Padawan—sorry, his *former* Padawan—and mourning the loss of the young man's arm.

The look of horror on his face then was harrowing to see. But of course, it could always be worse. It could be another crazy hallucination. Mercifully, there'd been no repeat of that so far. Somehow the Jedi was managing to keep them at bay, at least.

This was their second day on the barren plain beyond the woodland that Obi-Wan had mistaken for a dark side assassin and a Separatist droid army. At his dogged insistence they kept up their punishing pace, walking steadily from first light and well into darkness, until even with their night-sticks it was too dangerous to continue. Then they made camp as best they could. Ate sparingly, drank less, and snatched what rest they could beneath Zigoola's nebula-stained dark sky and unfamiliar constellations. It wasn't much. Bare rock and hard-packed dirt made a miserably uncomfortable mattress. And Obi-Wan's capricious nightmares weren't conducive to sleep for either of them.

Bail rubbed his hands over his face, feeling how inelastic his skin had become, how his stubbled cheeks had fallen into hollows. If he looked in a mirror he knew he'd see a gaunt face looking back at him. His immaculately tailored clothes were baggy. He was losing muscle. Losing strength. His body was consuming itself, like a snake swallowing its tail.

They were still another day—maybe two—away from their intended destination. Not because of the terrain but because, just as Obi-Wan had predicted, the closer they got to the Sith temple the more vicious and more frequent his visions became. And no matter how many times he rebuilt his defenses, the Sith never gave up . . . and they were wearing him down.

Looking at him now, watching him shiver and sweat, Bail had to fight back a wave of crushing futility.

Jedi stamina is legendary, but even they have their limits. How soon before Obi-Wan reaches his? How much longer can he withstand these attacks? Can he hold out until we reach that temple? He says he can . . . but I'm not sure anymore.

Obi-Wan had said last night, in a rare exchange of words, that these assaults weren't personal. That he thought the Sith had set up safeguards, mental booby traps, this *holocron*, to protect Zigoola and its Sith treasures from any Jedi who might stumble across the planet. The compulsion to crash the ship hadn't been aimed at him specifically. And the Sith voice in his head, the voice imploring him to die, that wasn't personal, either. The Sith hated all Jedi equally. They wanted every Jedi to perish and would stop at nothing to achieve that goal. And this place was ancient; the trap ensnaring Obi-Wan had been set perhaps centuries ago.

Which I suppose is why it's not trying to kill me. Since I'm not a Jedi, I'm not a threat.

Well. At least not to Zigoola's Sith Holocron. But he was a

threat to someone. It was a sobering thought. Somewhere in the galaxy, a Sith knew his name and wanted him, Bail Organa, to die. When they got back to Coruscant he'd have to take some precautions. Assuming there were precautions he could take. The Jedi would have to help him with that.

Yeah. Right. When we get back.

Fear slithered in his belly like a worm. He suffocated it, as Obi-Wan had told him. Don't feed the dark side. Stay focused. Stay positive.

I'm not a Jedi, so this place can't see me, not like it sees him. And that's already working to our advantage. I'm helping Obi-Wan, so chalk one up for the puny human.

Lifting his head, Bail stared across the exposed, rocky plain. Took in the distance and terrain they still had to traverse. By nightfall, if they kept a steady pace, they'd reach the end of this unforgiving stretch of ground. Which would be a relief, because even though it wasn't unbearably hot beneath Zigoola's sun they were still expending more bodily moisture than they had water to replenish.

Dehydration is not our friend.

Beyond the plain there was another stretch of tangled forest, blanketing riotously uneven ground. He wasn't looking forward to tackling that. And just beyond those trees, he was almost sure, they'd finally reach the Sith temple. He could see the flat black top of it from here, squatting above the treetops like a malevolent stone cloud.

So we're almost there. This is almost over.

Except it was dangerous to think like that. Thinking like that made his throat close, and his eyes burn, and they *weren't* there yet. He was getting ahead of himself. He had to stay focused. Couldn't afford to think about anything except putting one blistered foot in front of the other.

Five paces away Obi-Wan coughed weakly and blinked at the sky.

"Hey," said Bail, cautiously. "Welcome back." He tugged a precious water bottle out of the single remaining backpack. Their supplies had dwindled alarmingly, but he refused to think about that. Instead he unscrewed the bottle's cap, filled it, and carried it to the Jedi. "Here."

Bone by bone, muscle by muscle, Obi-Wan levered himself upright. "Thank you," he croaked, taking the miserly offering. Nearly spilled it before drinking it, because his hand was shaking. Then he sat, just sat, breathing deeply. Unsteadily. "How long was I out for this time?"

"About as long as last time," he said. "That's good, isn't it?"

Obi-Wan handed back the empty cap, his face expressionless. All his secrets contained. "Yes. It's marvelous."

Bail winced and focused on screwing the cap tightly onto the water bottle. If his face was gaunt, Obi-Wan looked cadaverous. Chalk-white skin laid over jutting bone, eyes sunken like hot coals in shadowed snow.

"You should eat," he said. He took a step toward the backpack.

Obi-Wan shook his head. "No. I'm fine. We must press on."

"Obi-Wan . . ."

With difficulty, Obi-Wan stood. His belt sat too loosely, sagging toward his hips. *"Bail."*

Lips tight, he shoved the water bottle back in the pack.

This must be what it's like being a Padawan. Do as you're told. No arguments. I know what's best.

"Bail," Obi-Wan said again, gently this time. "The longer I stop, the harder it is to keep going. So let's be on our way, shall we?"

He was hungry. He was tired. His body ached without cease. He'd dearly love to rest awhile longer. But how could he insist on that, how could he complain, when he could see what Obi-Wan had to endure? So he picked up the makeshift backpack and shrugged it on, wincing again. It was heavy, and clumsy, and it hurt his wrenched shoulder, but that couldn't be helped. Ignoring the discomfort he settled the pack as best he could and followed Obi-Wan, who walked like a man whose bones might randomly fracture with any one step.

And so their unkind journey continued.

Four hours and no more visions later, a storm blew in from nowhere, black clouds edged lurid green boiling across the pale sky, blotting out sunlight, turning the air to ice. A thin wind, sharp as hunting knives, keened across the rock plain, slicing and sleeting and slapping them to their knees.

They were about an hour from the next tree line. There was nowhere to hide.

The rain came down like blaster bolts, soaking them within seconds. Exploding against the surrounding rock and their exposed skin, drumming them deaf, as though each drop was an iron ball and the rock was made of metal.

Bail looked at his hands and arms, expecting to see running blood. But it was water, only water, even though it felt like fire. So he tilted his head back and opened his mouth and let the deluge pour over his parched tongue and down his throat. Swallowing, he tasted metal. Tasted bitterness. Tasted life.

Obi-Wan grabbed him. Shook him, hurting his shoulder. "What are you doing?" the Jedi shouted, staccato, teeth chattering with the cold. "Not tested—could be dangerous—"

"If it's poison, then I'm poisoned," he shouted back while his own teeth rattled and clattered. "And you're as wet as I am, so that means so are you!"

Eyes slitted, Obi-Wan stared at him as the merciless rain hammered down. Eddies and rivulets were gushing past them, tiny rock pools overflowing, water rising all around. "Good point."

"And at least we won't die of thirst now."

"No, but we could drown!"

He laughed. He couldn't help it. *I'm on a Sith planet in Wild Space and my imminent cause of death has become a multiple-choice question.* "Or get struck by lightning!"

"Don't say it!" said Obi-Wan. "You fool, don't even—"

And the first blue spear of lightning stabbed toward the ground.

"You *idiot*! You had to say it!"

More lightning pierced the clouds, thunder roaring behind it. The freezing air crackled. The rain turned to ice. Little pellets, little splinters, little razors kissing flesh.

"Oh, this is not good," said Obi-Wan. "Not good at all!"

No. It wasn't. If the hailstones got any bigger, they could easily cave their skulls in. Break their bones.

Bail curled his arms over his head, tucked his chin to his chest, and made of himself the smallest possible target. It helped, but not enough. For all the good his clothes did him, he might as well be naked. The freezing rain flogged him. He could hear himself groan. Hear Obi-Wan beside him, lost in his own distress. More lightning. More thunder. He held his breath, waiting for death to strike him, to be seared flesh from bone. *Breha. Breha. Don't be angry. I didn't mean to.*

And then as suddenly as it started, the raging storm stopped.

They barely managed to fill their emptied bottles before the rainwater drained away down the rock plain's cracks and crevices. The sky was bare of clouds again, all that roiling green-edged blackness vanished as though it had never been. And Zigoola's sun shone once more, disconsolate, with a pale, halfhearted heat.

Cold to the bone, Bail thrust the last filled bottle into the backpack and hefted it into place. His spine cracked, protesting. Ignoring that, he looked at Obi-Wan.

"You ready?"

Obi-Wan nodded but made no attempt to stand. Instead he sat

slumped on the wet rock, shivering inside his soaked, filthy Jedi tunic.

"Come on. Walking will help dry us off," he added. "Help us get warm again."

Still Obi-Wan didn't move. His face was pocked with little red welts where the pellets of ice had left their mark. Doubtless he looked the same himself. He certainly felt it.

"I tried to shield us," Obi-Wan said, his voice low. "Using the Force. It's an early Padawan training exercise. You find a waterfall, you stand under it, and then . . ." He gestured lightly, gracefully, with his bruised, scraped hands. "You stay dry. And after that, you work your way up to rain. It's not that difficult. Just a question of degree. All in all . . . very *basic*. I had barely turned six the first time I did it."

Bail crouched before him, keeping balanced with his fingers just touching rock. "But you can't do it now?"

"No," said Obi-Wan, and his thin face twisted with revulsion. "For all that I can use the Force here I might as well be a *droid*. If you could feel what it's like—if you had *any* idea—my blood has turned *rancid*."

Was it wrong, to be so relieved he couldn't feel what Obi-Wan was feeling? *Probably. But I am.* "I'm sorry," he said. "I wish I could help."

"I was born feeling the Force," Obi-Wan whispered. "Every day of my life I've lived in its light, every minute, every *breath*, for thirty-five years. And now it's gone. All is darkness. And I don't know who or what I am without it."

Bail stared at him, lost for words. How could he answer such quiet misery? How could he counsel a man who had powers he couldn't begin to comprehend? But how could he say nothing in the face of such naked despair?

"The Force isn't gone, Obi-Wan," he said with all the conviction he could muster. "It's being smothered. It's this place. When we leave here, it'll come back. You'll be yourself again, you'll see. You are a Jedi. Nothing can change that."

Obi-Wan just shook his head. "I don't feel like a Jedi. I feel—I feel—"

And with no more warning than that, the Jedi fell into another vision. More than one. Memory after memory, the longest episode yet. Firebeetles to Tayvor to someone drowning in acid on Telos to Qui-Gon's death to Geonosis, the battle and then Anakin, losing his arm.

Bail sat safely apart from him, head propped in his hands, waiting . . . and waiting. Despair overwhelmed him, but—

Grown men do not weep.

TWENTY

"OBI-WAN. OBI-WAN. COME ON. COME BACK. WE CAN'T STAY OUT here. Please. Come back now."

He didn't want to. It was too hard. He was so tired. He needed rest. Needed peace. Needed a surcease of pain.

Die Jedi, die Jedi, die Jedi, die.

The voice never stopped whispering. Never left him alone. It was wearing him down. Like water on rock, it was wearing him away.

"Obi-Wan!"

He opened his eyes.

"Hey," said Bail, and cleared his throat. "There you are."

Yes. Here he was. Stranded like splintered driftwood on this rocky plain. *I'd rather be somewhere else, if it's all the same to you.*

"Drink this," said Bail, thrusting a bottle at him. "All of it. We've got plenty now. You'll feel better afterward. Drink."

The captured rainwater tasted foul. Tainted by the dark side, like everything on Zigoola. He drank it slowly, stomach rebellious, and took stock of his current condition. His clothes were dry again. His hair. He was almost warm. On the outside, anyway. On the inside he remained freezing cold. It was getting harder and harder to hold back the dark tide. To drown out that spiteful voice. All his years in the Temple, the rigorous study, the dedication . . . they weren't enough. He wasn't dead yet . . . but he was losing the fight.

He looked at Bail. At Senator Organa of Alderaan. Would his Coruscant colleagues recognize him in this moment? Filthy. Unkempt. His neat goatee bedraggled and his clothes cousin to rags. A lot thinner than he had been.

"I did tell you not to come."

Bail's face tightened. One hand came up. "Do not even start. Can you walk?"

Could he walk? It was a wonder he could breathe. The black slurry in his veins had turned to acid. Every muscle burned him. His bones were on fire. "No."

"Too bad," said Bail. "We can't stay out here tonight. We need to get to that tree line. Once we reach it I'll find some deadwood and start a fire. We need to get ourselves warm again, properly warm."

Die Jedi, die Jedi, die Jedi, die.

"You go on," he said. "Find that temple. See what's in there. I'll stay here. I'll wait for you."

"I don't think so," said Bail, and without ceremony, without permission, he roughly hauled him to his feet. Held him by the shoulders, glaring. The urbane, sophisticated Senator was nowhere to be seen. In his place this angry, ragged man, with bloodshot eyes and hollowed cheeks. "Look. Obi-Wan. I know this is difficult, but you have to keep going."

Die Jedi, die Jedi, die Jedi, die.

He grimaced, the voice echoing through his tired mind. "That's easy for you to say."

Bail let go of his shoulders and struck him open-handed across the face, hard. "Stop listening to it! It's just a *voice*, Obi-Wan! It's not even that, it's a *machine,* a stinking Sith machine, and it's trying to kill you. It's trying to get you to kill yourself. Don't give in to it. Remember who you are. You're Master Obi-Wan Kenobi, one of the greatest Jedi we have. You've beaten the Sith three times now. You can beat them again. You *can*."

His face was smarting where the Senator had struck him. Clean pain. Uncomplicated. Untainted. His heart thudded slothfully, struggling against the sludge. Standing straighter, he felt a flicker of light. His tiny, beleaguered candle, burning in the dark.

"You have to beat this, Obi-Wan," said Bail. "Because if you don't, *I die*."

Yes. That was true. Bail Organa would die. And that was unacceptable.

The sun was sinking to the horizon, its mean heat draining away like all that stormwater down the cracks and crevices of the plain. Night gathered around the edges, gibbering of darkness, like a Sith, and the cold was creeping in. The Senator was right. They shouldn't stay here in the open. Not for another night. Two nights were enough.

Bail had shrugged the makeshift backpack on again and was watching him closely. Wary. Exhausted. Ready to fight. "So, Obi-Wan. Your head's clear? We're going?"

Yes. They were going. For all the good it would do them. "My lightsaber," he said. "You still have it?"

Bail nodded, eyes narrowed. "Why? Do you want it back?"

Of course he wanted it. It was his *lightsaber.* He was incomplete without it. "No," he said. "Just keep it safe for me. And . . . keep it close at hand."

Bail hesitated, as though he wanted to say something difficult. Uncomfortable. Then he shook his head. "I will. Now come on. The day's not getting any younger—and neither am I."

A flash of humor. An indomitable spirit. Not your everyday, common-and-garden politician.

This is an uncommon man.

They fell into step, side by side. "You know, Bail," he said, striving for lightness, struggling to drown out that whispering voice, "it occurs to me you're wasted in the Senate. With a punch like that you'd make a killing in the ring."

Bail looked at him sideways. "Sorry. I needed to get your attention."

"No, no, don't apologize. You did what you—"

DIE JEDI, DIE JEDI, DIE JEDI, DIE.

His knees buckled. He would have fallen, but Bail Organa held him up. Held him hard and whispered in his ear, drowning out that other voice.

"Don't listen to it, Obi-Wan. Don't listen. It's a machine. Ignore the kriffing thing and keep on walking. Don't worry. I've got you. I won't let you fall."

He kept on walking, the dark side howling in his heart.

Sheltered by Zigoola's drought-stunted trees, they survived another night.

Waking first, just before dawn, cold despite his heat-seal blanket, Bail stirred up the almost extinct fire, coaxing it to flickering life and adding more fuel. The crackle of flames was almost . . . cheerful.

Cheerful. Now there's a laugh.

Curled up on the leaf-littered ground, Obi-Wan still slept. A true sleep, at last, after hour upon wearing hour of sliding in and out of wicked dreams. Wrenched with pity, Bail stared down at him. He didn't know for sure how old Obi-Wan was; he'd guessed that maybe ten years separated them. Now it looked more like twenty. As though the Jedi's desperate fight against the Sith's relentless onslaught was gradually stripping him of every adult defense. He was reminded of Alinta.

No. Don't think about her.

Obi-Wan was so pale now his face was nearly translucent, the bones of his body moving closer and closer to the surface. The only word Bail could think of, looking at him, was *fragile*.

Obi-Wan Kenobi, fragile. Not even a week ago he never would have believed it. He could hardly believe it now, though the proof lay before him.

But he's not going to die here. I won't let that happen. This man has given his life to the Republic. As the Republic's representative it's my duty to honor that gift. To not let these Sith destroy him.

He still found it hard to reconcile that there were only two of them. *Two.* How could two of *anything* wreak so much havoc?

And how is it the Jedi can't stop them? Can the dark side of the Force really be that powerful?

It must.

I never wanted to know this. I never wanted to know most of the dangerous things that I know now. Before the Separatists I used to be able to sleep at night. Now . . . with the things I know . . . I wonder if I'll ever sleep properly again.

Unsettled, he dumped the last of the gathered wood onto the fire, then stared at the sky as another Zigoola dawn broke, a sickly affair. Nothing like Alderaan's imperious grandeur or Coruscant's flamboyant transition. They'd have to break camp soon. But he'd let Obi-Wan sleep for as long as possible. He still needed to repack their ever-dwindling supplies and try to figure out the best way to get from here to the Sith temple.

With a last glance at the oblivious Jedi, confident the fire would keep burning, he left the small clearing they'd found just as night fell, and pushed his way through the twisted trees and creeping undergrowth, picking his way over and around gullies and rockfalls, looking for a break in the forest that would show him exactly how much farther they had to go. Every ten paces he gouged a mark in a tree trunk with the knife he'd brought with him from the ship, mindful of horror stories about lost tourists in Alderaan's wilder places. Of tearful relatives and blanched, bleached bones. Zigoola's trees where he cut them bled their inimical yellow sap.

There is nothing good here. Nothing beautiful. Nothing sweet, or kind. And that tells me all I need to know of the Sith.

After maybe half an hour of steady trudging he came at last to the end of the trees and found himself standing above a narrow-based ravine. Not a sheer drop—that was a mercy—but a dauntingly steep tumble of rock and weathered dirt and stunted saplings, nonetheless. A long way down to the bottom. A fall might not be fatal, but it would certainly do some damage. Negotiating it would be a challenge for two fit, healthy men. But when one was mentally bludgeoned almost to immobility . . . and both were battered and half starved and weary to the point of collapse, well . . . it was asking a lot.

But it's not impassable. Not impossible. Just difficult. And we have to do it.

Because on the other side of the ravine . . . so close if he were a bird, if he had wings, if he could fly . . . the Sith temple he'd first seen as they crashed onto Zigoola. Except to his eye, it looked more like a palace than a temple, a palace of black stone, shining dully in Zigoola's pale dawn. Blunt. Emphatic. A monument to hate.

Bail let out a sharp breath. "Hate us all you like," he murmured bleakly. "But we're still going to use your secrets against you. We're going to defeat you. Just you wait and see."

He turned his back on the building and returned to the clearing faster than was prudent, a new sense of purpose filling him with deceptive, fleeting strength. Obi-Wan was still sleeping, numbing exhaustion overriding his preternatural awareness of time and place. Leaving him undisturbed, Bail heated a mealpack and quickly ate his half. Then he emptied the backpack to check their supplies. Eight meals remaining, but for how much longer he wasn't sure. He had no idea how long they'd remain viable out of a conservator. He and Obi-Wan hadn't given themselves food poisoning yet, but likely it was just a matter of time. Anyway, there were eight. And since they were eating two a day between them . . .

But we'll be off this rock before we run out, or they go rotten. We have to be. That's all there is to it.

"Talking to oneself is counted a sign of instability, you know," said Obi-Wan, his voice so thin. So lackluster. "I don't suppose there's something you want to tell me, is there?"

Bail looked up. Found a smile from somewhere. "Yes, there is, as a matter of fact. This ends today, Obi-Wan."

Obi-Wan sat up, painfully, keeping his heat-seal blanket tugged close. "You've found the temple."

He jerked a thumb toward the forest behind them. "On the other side of the trees. There's this final belt of forest—it's rough going, but if we take it steady we'll be fine—then a ravine on the far side. The temple's at the top. On another plateau."

"A ravine," said Obi-Wan, thinking about that. "And then a Sith temple. I can't wait."

"Yeah," he said, pulling a face. "So. How are you feeling? Is the voice still—"

"Yes," said Obi-Wan curtly. "It's still shouting."

He rummaged in the pile of supplies from the backpack and pulled out the bottle of Corellian brandy, almost half full. "I know you don't drink, as a rule, but . . . is there any chance this could help?"

Obi-Wan blinked at him. "You brought brandy."

"I thought we might need it," he said, knowing he sounded defensive. "Alcohol's a disinfectant, I thought in case—" He stared, as Obi-Wan held out his hand. "Are you sure?"

"No," said the Jedi, shrugging. "But I've tried everything else I can think of and none of it's working."

He gave Obi-Wan the bottle. Watched him unscrew the cap and tip its contents down his throat. Cough. Splutter. Come close to throwing it straight back up.

"That—truly is—revolting," Obi-Wan croaked eventually. "You drink it—for pleasure? You must be—mad."

Bail retrieved the emptied bottle. "To each his own. But you should eat something now. That amount of brandy on an empty stomach is asking for trouble." He handed over the half-eaten mealpack. "Go on."

Obi-Wan eyed the nerf patties sourly. "I'm not hungry."

"I don't care."

Scowling, ungracious, Obi-Wan snatched the container. Poked the cold meat with one finger then ate it, morsel by morsel, gagging. When the container was empty he discarded it, then sat cross-legged with his head bowed and his hands on his knees.

"So?" Bail asked eventually. "What's the verdict?"

Obi-Wan pressed his fingers to his eyes. "It's a little better," he said at last. "The voice is . . . it's muffled now. A whisper again, instead of a shout." He sounded surprised. "It would appear alcohol helps."

He pulled a face. "In that case we should've brought the rest of the Blackmoon ale, too."

"No," said Obi-Wan, letting his hands drop. "Because if alcohol muffles the voice it might also interfere with my already limited ability to—"

His head jerked back and he toppled sideways, slowly. And so the first visions of the day began.

"Stang," said Bail, wearily, and began to repack their supplies.

This time he thought Obi-Wan might not come out of it. Memory after memory, a battering so prolonged and relentless that in the end he lost track of how many disasters the Jedi was reliving. But the visions ended at last. He had to help Obi-Wan sit up. After that, once he'd cajoled him into drinking a few mouthfuls of Zigoola's horrible water, then watched him compose himself into some semblance of calm, he folded his arms tight to his ribs and stared down at the man.

"So the brandy wasn't such a good idea, I'm thinking. Sorry."

"Not . . . your fault," said Obi-Wan, frowning muzzily. "You didn't make me drink it." He took another mouthful of water, rinsed his mouth, and spat it out.

"So we're good to go again? We should go," said Bail, hating the bullying tone of his voice. Hating that he had to be *this* man, poking and prodding and hustling to get his way. But Obi-Wan looked shattered. Looked ready to fall asleep again. And they were running out of time. "*Now,* Obi-Wan," he added. "And no matter what happens we have to *keep* going. We have to get inside that temple and find that Sith Holocron and break it into little pieces. And after that, we find a way back home. Because I'll be *kriffed* if I'm going to lie down and die on this rock. I am *not* giving these Sith the satisfaction."

"Bail . . ." Obi-Wan wrapped his arms around his shins, as though fighting to keep himself from falling apart. "I can't. I can't go any closer to that place. I'm not certain how much longer I'll be safe."

"Don't worry. I won't let you hurt yourself."

Obi-Wan smiled, very faintly. "Safe for you to be around, I mean. I fear I might soon become . . . dangerous."

Oh. "Well, you can't stay *here,*" he retorted. "I'm not leaving you behind. You're going to hear that voice and have these visions wherever you are, so you'll do it wherever *I* am. At least then I can keep an eye on you."

"*Bail.*" Obi-Wan dropped his forehead to his knees, hiding his face. Hiding his eyes. "Even I have my limits."

No. No. They were *not* giving up now. "Maybe," he said, keeping his voice tough. Unsympathetic. "But you haven't reached them yet. You haven't hurt me yet. And I don't believe you will. Besides, I've got your lightsaber. How much harm can you do? Now let's get a move on."

With an effort, Obi-Wan stood. "If that's your idea of diplomatic bargaining," he said, swaying on his feet, "then I must tell you your technique leaves a great deal to be desired."

Bail smiled, though he was closer to tears than laughter. "I'm borrowing a leaf out of Padmé's book."

Obi-Wan stared, puzzled, and then shook his head. "Oh yes. I remember. Anakin told me. *Aggressive negotiations.* Very droll."

"That's our Padmé," he agreed. "The queen of droll. Now come on. We're in the home stretch. We can do this. So let's go."

Closing his eyes, Obi-Wan tipped his colorless face to the empty sky. "Very well, Bail," he said at last. "We'll do it your way. On one condition."

"That sounds ominous," he said, trying for lightness. Failing, abysmally.

Obi-Wan opened his sunken eyes. Beneath the pain and exhaustion, something fierce and unflinching burned. "Make sure you keep that lightsaber close. And if you so much as *suspect* I'm about to turn on you . . ."

What? He had to be joking. "That won't happen."

"It might."

"It *won't*. You are Master Obi-Wan Kenobi."

"Yes. Well," said Obi-Wan wryly. So pale. So punished. "Master Kenobi has seen better days."

The pace was much slower the second time, heading for the ravine. Bail was shockingly tired, but Obi-Wan was almost spent. Struggled to keep his feet, to negotiate the uneven ground. Halfway to the ravine he collapsed, assaulted by more visions. Bail sat beside him, waiting, his spine braced against a gnarled, knotted tree trunk, shallowly breathing the stale mustiness of the forest. Remembering the sweetness of Alderaan's flowering tarla woods. The soft grass beneath the magnificent towering trees, the drifting birdsong, the deep blue sky, the warm shafting sunlight, Breha's hand in his. He closed his eyes and dreamed himself back there, dreamed his own memories so he wouldn't have to listen to Obi-Wan's anymore. It felt like a betrayal, but he couldn't help it. He had limits, too, and his had been reached.

At length Obi-Wan came to and they continued, following the yellow sap-scars he'd made at dawn. Bail found himself constantly tensing, waiting for the next round of visions to strike his companion. Worrying that Obi-Wan's worst fears would come to pass, and the Sith would break him. Shatter him with more hallucinations and turn him into a monster. Before they left the clearing, while Obi-Wan was buckling on his belt, Bail had pulled the lightsaber close to the top of the backpack. The thought of using the weapon made him feel sick.

It won't come to that. It won't. It won't.

But was that wishful thinking?

I don't care if it is. It won't.

They made it out of the woodland, to the ravine gashed so deep in the landscape. When Obi-Wan saw the Sith temple he staggered and nearly fell, his face draining to gray.

"Breathe!" said Bail, lowering him to the stony soil a safe distance from the ravine's edge. "Don't look at it. Just breathe."

"I don't need to look at it," said Obi-Wan, one clenched fist pressed against his heart. "I can feel it. I can hear it, shouting . . ."

Every muscle aching, Bail stared at the temple. Then he looked down at Obi-Wan. "Okay. I was wrong. You were right. You can't do this. Go back in the woods. I'll investigate the temple, destroy whatever I find. Then I'll—"

"What? No," said Obi-Wan. "You can't. You might destroy a way for us to call for help. You wouldn't recognize a Sith communications device if it bit you."

Grimacing, he dropped to one knee. *I should have thought of that.* "Good point. Okay. Then I'll bring whatever I find back here."

"*No.*" Obi-Wan grabbed his wrist, his face sheened with sweat. "There's no way of knowing if the artifacts are dangerous for you to touch. Besides, look at that ravine, Bail. You might make it down safely. You might make it up the other side safely. *Once.* You don't dare risk it twice. Not if you don't have to."

"Yeah, it's treacherous," he agreed, and eased his wrist free. "But *you* can't climb it. *Look* at you."

"I'm fine."

He almost laughed. "If *fine* was another word for 'on the brink of collapse,' I'd agree with you. But it isn't. *You're not fine.* You're *losing.*"

"From a certain point of view, possibly," said Obi-Wan. Then he smiled, a feral baring of teeth. "But I prefer to think of it as . . . not winning at the moment. So we go."

He was crazy. *They* were crazy, both of them. Starving, exhausted, pushed to the ends of their physical and mental limits. And now they were going to go rock climbing? And yet . . . what was the alternative? Curl up and wait for death? Bare their throats to the Sith and say: *All right. You win.*

He looked again at the temple. So close. So far away. Then he looked back at Obi-Wan. "You're sure?"

"Quite sure."

"Yeah, well, that's what you said when we were on approach to Zigoola," he muttered. Then he sighed, stood, and bent to help Obi-Wan to his feet. "All right. We'll risk it."

"Wait," said Obi-Wan, and unbuckled his belt. He fumbled the straps, his fingers clumsy. "Put this on. Clip my lightsaber to it."

Bail stepped back. "Why?"

This time Obi-Wan's smile was gentle. "It's called being on the safe side."

He shook his head. "I don't need it."

"You might."

"I won't."

"*You don't know that!*" said Obi-Wan, not smiling at all now. "You don't know what will happen when I'm in spitting distance of that Sith temple, and neither do I."

"I know you're not going to kill me."

"Bail," said Obi-Wan. His breathing was ragged. "Don't be a fool. You know nothing of the kind. And without that lightsaber you will never stop me. Take the belt and wear my weapon. *Please.*"

Ignoring Obi-Wan's desperation would be tantamount to cruelty, so he took the belt and buckled it around his waist. Pulled the lightsaber from his backpack and clipped it to the belt. It felt odd. Heavy. He couldn't bring himself to look at it. Glanced at Obi-Wan instead.

I'm sorry, I'm so sorry, that I got you into this.

They walked to the edge of the ravine, and looked over the side.

"Zigzag down there?" Bail suggested, pointing to a hint, a suggestion of a trail, running between the tumbled rocks and weathered gullies and twisted, half-grown saplings. "Go left, then track right?"

"That seems reasonable," said Obi-Wan, and he coughed. He sounded like Alinta, a ghastly dry-land bubbling.

"I'll go first," he said. "You stick close behind me. That way— if something happens—" *If you have more visions . . . if you fall . . .*

Obi-Wan slid a look sideways. "I don't think so. I'll go first. That way—if something happens—I won't take you with me."

Bail chewed his lip, but there was no time for more arguments. "All right," he said grudgingly.

They started down the ravine.

Sliding rock. Slipping dirt. Scrapes, cuts, and bruises. Step by uncertain, dangerous step, they navigated their way down the steep, jagged slope. More than once they overbalanced, or skidded down a rocky gully. Lost their footing as the dry yellow-brown dirt shifted beneath them. More than once they sat down, hard, clutching at sapling or rock to prevent disaster, their jarred spines screaming, their hearts hammering out of control. Sweat streaked their faces, stung their eyes, slicked their palms. Soaked their stinking, filthy clothes.

And brooding above them, a silent menace, a vulture of stone, the black Sith temple, the source of every ill.

With each jarring footfall Bail felt the lightsaber gently slap him. He resented its presence. Dreaded what it meant. Dreaded that

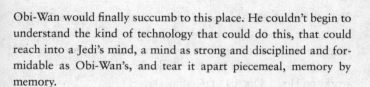

Obi-Wan would finally succumb to this place. He couldn't begin to understand the kind of technology that could do this, that could reach into a Jedi's mind, a mind as strong and disciplined and formidable as Obi-Wan's, and tear it apart piecemeal, memory by memory.

He couldn't understand a sentient being who'd want to.

The brutal descent continued, agonizingly slow. They reached the quarter mark. The one-third mark. They reached the halfway point, where a kink in the landscape led to one short, sharp drop, then unrolled more kindly to the ravine's uneven floor. Bail started to feel sick. His muscles shrieked, his tendons burned. His bones were throbbing. He wanted this to be over. He wanted to lay down and weep. Sleep. Wake up from this nightmare.

He looked at Obi-Wan, one tight pace ahead of him. *If I feel sick . . . if I feel like dying . . .* "Hey. You okay?"

"Yes," grunted Obi-Wan. He was breathing too hard. Too fast. His feet were faltering, his hands bloody, his balance uncertain. Surely, any moment now, the Jedi was going to fall . . .

"I need to stop," he said, and caught hold of a jutting tree root as a brake. "Obi-Wan."

Obi-Wan turned sideways, his boots skidding as he slid to a halt. "I said I—"

"I do, I need to stop!" he insisted as Obi-Wan glared. Tried not to betray shock, or dismay, or anything that would tell Obi-Wan just how bad he looked. "I'm not a Jedi, I don't have unlimited resources."

"Bail . . ." Obi-Wan blotted his ashen face on his sleeve. "Don't treat me like a fool. Don't—don't—"

His eyes rolled back. His rasping breath caught. He was going. Going under. The visions had returned.

"Obi-Wan!" Bail shouted and threw himself forward, his right hand still anchored to the sapling's jutting root. Rag-limp, Obi-Wan toppled. Bail flung out his left hand, caught hold of the Jedi's sleeve, his wrist, and was jerked groundward, hard. His face hit rough rock. Pain exploded through his nose and his partially healed split lip. He felt blood. Tasted blood. Bright lights burst behind his eyelids. The air left his lungs in a nauseating rush, and his wrenched shoulder—bearing Obi-Wan's full deadweight—lit up like fireworks on House Organa's Founding Day.

He let out the pain in one long, anguished cry. Heard its shivering echoes bounce through the ravine, and kept the next one trapped in his throat. Lifting his head he looked at Obi-Wan, but the Jedi was lost again in Hellish memories. He could scream until his skull cracked, Obi-Wan wouldn't hear him.

He put his head down. Locked the fingers of his right hand around that tree root and his left around Obi-Wan's narrow wrist. And then, on a deep breath, he closed his eyes to all sensation.

Don't let go . . . don't let go . . . don't let go . . . don't let go.

But of course, he did.

TWENTY-ONE

QUI-GON WAS DYING IN HIS ARMS, YET AGAIN, WHEN PAIN RIPPED him out of the memory. New pain. Physical pain. Sharp. Urgent. His forehead. His left knee. His left elbow. His right thigh.

The Sith voice silenced at last, incredibly, his mind startlingly clear, he opened his eyes and stared at the sky. Someone was shouting.

"Obi-Wan! *Obi-Wan!*"

A shower of dirt and small stones rained down on him. He spat gravel, tried to push to his elbows, and that hurt even more.

"No—no—don't move!" the voice shouted. "I'll be right there—don't move—don't even breathe—"

Well, that was silly. He had to *breathe*. He spat more gravel, trying to identify the voice. There'd been so many voices: Qui-Gon and Anakin and Dooku and Tayvor Mandirly and Xanatos. Even the firebeetles had voices, shrill ravenous squeakings as they chewed through his flesh.

Bail. Bail Organa. That's who had shouted. This was Zigoola. The absent Sith were trying to kill him. And—

Oh dear. I seem to have fallen down a ravine.

Breathing out hard he sat up, head swimming, pounding, and

found himself on the ravine's rocky floor. That wasn't good. He looked down at his left knee. His ripped leggings were soaked bright red. So was his left sleeve. And yes, that was more blood down his right thigh. Lifting his hand he touched fingertips to his forehead, above his right eye. The skin was split, he could feel it. His fingers came away wet and crimson, and the pain was like a vibrosaw. Bad. Very bad.

And yet there was relief, and something like laughter. Because his body's pain had stopped the endless recycling of memories . . . and silenced, however briefly, the Sith's relentless voice.

Well. That's wonderful. Let's hear it for pain.

A colder, saner part of himself knew only too well that this nonsensical giddiness was a reaction to the long days of unbearable strain and sorrow he'd endured since the crash. He knew that. He *knew* it. And yet he couldn't resist . . .

Bail skidded down beside him in a fresh shower of rocks and dirt. His lip was split open again, his nose scraped raw, and his hands, and his ruined shirt was shredded across the left shoulder. His left arm hung awkwardly, and his bloodied face was tight. But he still had the belt, with the lightsaber clipped to it.

"You fool, I said don't move!" Bail shouted. "Are you all right? I can't believe you're not *dead*."

How much longer would this respite from the Sith's assault last? *Not long, not long, surely. We are running out of time . . .*

"No, I'm not dead. Help me to stand."

"*Stand?* Obi-Wan—"

"Bail," he said sharply. "While I'm hurting I can think. Right now I'm hurting rather a lot so let's not waste it, shall we?"

Bail's bloodied lips thinned, which made him wince. "All right. I'll help you stand."

Which was an interesting exercise. It certainly got him thinking, as his left knee and right thigh shrieked a scarlet protest, and the vibrosaw cutting through his head shifted into top gear.

"Good thing you're wearing Jedi clothes," said Bail, inspecting the damage. "They protected you from the worst of it, but you're still pretty torn up."

"As long as there's no arterial bleeding I'll be fine," he said, letting his gaze track up the other side of the ravine, to the Sith temple squatting above it in the sun. In the depths of his mind, barely audible through the pain, a malicious voice started whispering . . .

"Come on," he said, and took a limping step toward the rising slope. Fresh pain flared and the voice fell silent. "Before it's too late."

"Wait a minute," said Bail. "You want to climb up there *now*?"

He stopped. Looked over his shoulder. "Certainly. Why? What do you suggest we do? Cultivate a suntan?"

"Obi-Wan!" said Bail, incredulous. "Have you lost your *mind*?"

He shuffled around to face Alderaan's Senator. "No, Bail. I have, against all expectation and most likely temporarily, regained it. Now, I realize you're malnourished, sleep-deprived, and quite possibly concussed, but I need you to *listen* to me, *very closely*. If I do not take advantage of this brief lucidity, the next time I lose awareness will likely be the last. I *must* get into that temple, I *must* find something that will help me help us leave this planet. I *must*—"

DIE JEDI, DIE JEDI, DIE JEDI, DIE.

"No!" he shouted, and struck his injured knee with a clenched fist. The pain was excruciating. He would have fallen again if Bail hadn't grabbed his arm. His injured arm. Which only made the flames roar higher.

Teeth gritted, eyes burning, he took Bail by the shoulder. "Stop arguing, Senator. We're not on Coruscant now and this is not a topic for endless Senate debate. I am trying to *save our lives*. Now are you going to help me or not?"

Bail stared at him, shocked silent, then nodded. The poor chap looked done in. *I'm so sorry, Bail, that I got you into this.*

"Okay, Master Kenobi," the Senator said shakily. "You're the Jedi. We'll do it your way."

They made it up the other side of the ravine.

Long since past caring if they swore or cursed or cried out, they dragged themselves over its crumbling edge and onto the parched, brittle grass of this new plateau. And when they'd crawled far enough to be certain there was no danger of falling, they collapsed facedown on the ground, sobbing for air. Sobbing with relief. Sobbing in the shadow of the brooding Sith temple.

Through the lava-hot pain, Obi-Wan felt the building's cold touch. Felt its menace freeze him and close its fist around his heart. His newly bright blood, which had begun to pump so freely, thickened and darkened and turned again to sludge. And the Sith's spiteful voice shouted, more gleeful than ever:

DIE JEDI, DIE JEDI, DIE JEDI, DIE.

No . . . no . . . not this quickly. It wasn't fair. The darkness was pouring back, the black wind was rising . . . and his tiny bright flame was guttering out . . .

"Obi-Wan! Don't listen to it. Stay with me!"

That was Bail Organa. The Senator from Alderaan. Far too good a man to be a politician. Echoing in his mind, all the failures of his past. A maelstrom of death and loss and misery, sucking him down. It had been bad in the crashed ship, in the first woodland, on the rock plain and within the second stretch of forest.

But those times were nothing compared to this.

"Obi-Wan!"

He rolled over. Opened his eyes. Stared at Bail.

DIE JEDI, DIE JEDI, DIE JEDI, DIE.

"I'm sorry," he whispered through the screaming in his head. "I can't hear you. It's too loud."

Bail's lips were moving. Dried blood flaked and fell. Was this important? It must be, the Senator was shouting, his wide eyes full of fear.

Should I be frightened? No. Fear is bad. Fear leads to anger, anger leads to hate, hate leads to suffering. Beware the dark side, Jedi.

Beware the dark side . . . for it's all around you now.

Bail fisted his stone-scraped fingers in Obi-Wan's dirty, blood-stained tunic and lifted him partway off the ground. The Jedi's head lolled as though he were a broken doll. There was nothing familiar in his eyes. His lips were moving, he was saying something, but no sound emerged to give the words life.

"*Obi-Wan!*" he shouted again, shaking him. "You have to *fight* it! We're so close. You can't give up now!"

Except Obi-Wan hadn't given up. He'd been defeated. The Sith had defeated him at last. He'd said it, he'd said he wouldn't stay lucid for long, and when he went away the next time, he'd go away for good.

And here he was. *Gone.*

When Obi-Wan slipped from his grasp in the ravine, he'd thought the Jedi was dead. He thought he'd killed him. Couldn't believe the man had survived. Then he'd thought Obi-Wan really had gone crazy, talking about suntans, punching himself in his injured knee. And then he'd climbed up that kriffing ravine. Bleeding. Hurting. Without his precious light side, finding strength from who knew where. It had nearly *killed* him, and still he climbed it.

He'd never met anyone like Obi-Wan Kenobi.

That kriffing climb nearly killed me too. But we did it. We made it. And was it all for nothing? Is this the part where we lie down and die?

Well, to the Hells with that. The crash didn't kill them. The lightning didn't kill them. The kriffing ravine didn't kill them. The Sith?

They can go to all Nine Hells, too.

Gently, he lowered Obi-Wan back to the plateau's stunted grass. Then he staggered to his feet, and it hurt, oh it hurt. How much pain could a body take before it said enough?

Guess I'm going to find out.

He didn't want to leave Obi-Wan lying there, exposed and defenseless, but he had to. He couldn't carry him into the Sith temple, even if he'd had the strength. The kriffing place would probably stop the Jedi's heart. He was starting to wonder if he had strength left to walk in there himself.

It doesn't matter. I have to. And if I can't walk, I'll crawl.

It occurred to him then, in a hazy, distant kind of way, that possibly he was no longer entirely sane himself. Certainly he'd never been in a situation like this before. Never been pushed beyond the bounds of physical endurance, never been so hungry and thirsty, never been so tired. Never been so angry, or afraid. Not even on Alinta's space station, with blaster bolts exploding at him from every conceivable direction.

Is this what being in battle is like? Is this what it was like for Padmé on Naboo? On Geonosis? For Obi-Wan on Christophsis? Is this what every Jedi is living through right now? Is this how the clones feel, fighting the Separatists? When I voted for the army, when I voted for war, is this the life I chose for them?

Because if it was . . . if it was . . .

But he couldn't afford to think of that now. Couldn't afford to dwell on buyer's remorse. Time enough to deal with his choices, with the consequences of his choices, when he was back on Coruscant, in the Senate, where a Senator belonged. Where he could really make a difference.

Though it hurt his twice-wrenched shoulder like fire, Bail shrugged out of the backpack and dropped it to the ground. Then he squatted and rested his right hand on Obi-Wan's shoulder. "Wait here, my friend. I'm not leaving. I'm doing what we came for. I'm finding a way to get us off this rock."

No answer. Empty-eyed, Obi-Wan stared at the sky.

Muscles burning, bones grinding, Bail pushed to his feet. Then he turned and faced the Sith temple, properly looking at it for the first time.

Darkness. That was the overwhelming impression. Darkness and—and *crimson*. A crimson sheen within the stone. The sheen of old blood, long since spilled and gloated over. Blood of the innocent. Blood of stolen lives.

Working past that first oppressive impression, he saw the temple wasn't all that big. It was tall, yes. Tall enough to be seen with inexpensive electrobinoculars, across a large distance, over rocky plain and straggled treetops. Large enough to be seen through the viewport of a crashing ship. Buttressed with stone wings to keep it tall and strong. But though he'd called it a palace, it wasn't precisely . . . *palatial*. It was oblong and windowless and peculiarly restrained. Almost self-effacing. Powerful, yet withdrawn.

As though it's hiding its true face. And if that's not Sith, then I don't know what is.

He couldn't feel a thing from it. Couldn't hear anything, either. Not a single sad memory stirred . . . and he had them. Oh, he had them. He remained deaf, dumb, and blind to this place. Its disinterest in him continued.

For which, given Obi-Wan, I must be profoundly grateful.

Besides the Sith temple, the plateau was empty. Even more barren than the plateau on which they'd crashed. No trees. No plants of any kind, save the shriveled brown grass. No sign, he realized, of a starship they could fly home. Disappointment shafted. Foolishly, he'd hoped . . .

If there was nothing of use to them inside the temple, he and Obi-Wan were about to die lonely, painful, lingering deaths.

Unless I kill him first, and then kill myself.

And on that cheerful thought he started walking toward the temple. It occurred to him, in a hazy, light-headed, beyond-the-end-of-his-endurance kind of way, that if the kriffing thing was locked he was going to look like a fool.

But it wasn't. The double doors swung open easily, at a touch. And when he crossed the threshold lights came on, dim and glowing and red like the distant nebula in Zigoola's night sky. As if to say, *Welcome, stranger. Enter and be amazed.* As if it knew he was nothing to fear.

These Sith. These kriffing Sith. Who—what—are they?

There were no stairs inside the temple. No second or third floor. It was one cavernous chamber, like a ballroom for giants. Or a church designed to make mortal men feel small. The air was cool and felt strangely expectant. Tasted slightly metallic. Not quite stale. The floor underfoot was tessellated black and crimson. The design was unsettling, crawling across the eyes. Slithering into the backbrain, invoking misery and loss.

Bail shivered, and lifted his gaze. The enormous room contained no furniture; no tables, or chairs. Not even a stool. And he couldn't see the source of the lighting, either; it seemed to ooze from the walls like a marshland miasma.

As his eyes adjusted to the low lighting he realized there were alcoves built into the walls. He headed left, his footsteps loud in the silence, the dirt and gravel ground into his boot soles sounding gritty and grating. He wondered if he was ruining the intricate mosaic-work and found he didn't much care.

The first alcove contained old books. Very old, and leatherbound. Thick, bulky tomes with raised lettering on the spines. Like the floor's tessellation, they made his skin crawl. He folded his arms, wincing at the burn in his shoulder, and quickly walked by.

The second alcove was empty, but from it emanated such a chill that he scuttled past like a child told that *this* house was haunted.

The third alcove contained chunks of geode, livid green and bile-yellow and dull purple crystals that glowed in the reddish light, unwholesome and diseased.

Feeling distinctly queasy, he moved to the next alcove. Now he was staring at flickering circuits contained in a large square transparisteel box. It looked vaguely promising, but he wasn't prepared to pick it up. Did that make him a coward? Maybe, but he was too tired to care.

The fifth alcove contained a single crystal. The size of a big man's loose fist, beautifully faceted, and utterly ruined. Before its destruction it had been the deep red of a sun's heart, but something had blasted it from the inside out, charring and cracking it.

It was Sith, and so must be evil, yet still he regretted the lost beauty.

He kept on walking, discovering more and more *things*. A hand-sized pyramid, not transparisteel but actual glass, dull black and traced with red. No hint of its purpose. More crystals, unshaped chunks of rock, some fist-sized, some as small as eggs, their edges sharp enough to draw blood, colored black and gray and murky dark blue. More books. Data crystals. Ribbon-tied scrolls. It was a Sith treasure trove, surely. If they escaped Zigoola they'd have to take it with them. The Jedi Council would want to study these artifacts. Perhaps they contained information that could bring about this unspeakable enemy's downfall. Which he would work toward in every way he could. For if he'd learned nothing else on Zigoola, he'd learned that he'd been wrong, and Obi-Wan coldly right. The Sith must be hunted down and destroyed without mercy.

And he was sure of another thing, too: he didn't begin to know what item or items among this collection of artifacts would help him and Obi-Wan get off Zigoola before they starved to death. Nor could he tell which one was affecting the Jedi. Probably Obi-Wan could. So he had to come in here. He had to see this for himself.

If I can reach him. If I can help him come back.

Abruptly aware he'd been in the temple for a long time, Bail turned away from inspecting the last alcoves and hurried outside to the real world, to make sure Obi-Wan was all right.

The Jedi hadn't moved. Hadn't died. He still lay on his back, eyes open but unresponsive. His torn flesh had stopped bleeding; all the blood on his tunic and leggings was dried stiff and dark red.

Grunting, aware of every muscle, every joint, Bail eased himself to kneel on one knee beside him, and again touched his shoulder. "Obi-Wan. *Obi-Wan.* I can't do this. I'm not a Jedi. You need to come back. You need to do your job."

Nothing. Was he even dreaming anymore? It didn't seem so. He seemed . . . *empty.* All his intelligence fled, and the oddly polite, unconscious arrogance with it. The wit, the dry humor. Just a shell left.

A drift of conversation . . . a memory to make him smile . . .

You know, Bail, it occurs to me you're wasted in the Senate. With a punch like that you'd make a killing in the ring.

Sorry. I needed to get your attention.

Sorry . . . sorry . . .

On a deep, indrawn breath, Bail backhanded Obi-Wan's face. Once. Twice. Loud, cracking blows that rolled the Jedi's head on the ground.

Nothing.

He couldn't keep on hitting the man. He might end up doing irreparable damage. Reluctantly, with a rising horror, Bail looked at Obi-Wan's damaged knee. It was swollen now, the torn flesh puffy and raw. He'd walked on it, climbed on it, but it was possible the patella had been cracked. If he punched it . . . if he punched it . . .

I can't do that. It's sick.

But Obi-Wan had done it, hadn't he? Used the pain to drown out the Sith's relentless voice? Used it to spur himself up the ravine?

He couldn't punch that injured leg. *Couldn't.* But he could lay his hand on it, gently, and maybe—possibly—squeeze . . .

Lost in the darkness, lost in despair, Obi-Wan feels his spirit wandering, adrift. Not sundered from his body quite yet, but soon. He has lost the light, and lost his purpose. Someone, somewhere, wants him to die. He wants to deny their desire. But he's cold. So cold. And then something changes. A point of heat. A point of pain. His body is hurting . . . and that means he's alive. Someone is shouting . . . and the darkness recedes . . .

"—wake up, vape you, I can't keep *doing* this! Wake up, Obi-Wan! Do you hear me? *Wake up!*"

His knee was on fire. Someone was punching it, pinching it, hurting him. With an effort he rolled over and said, "Leave me alone."

"Obi-Wan!"

He dragged his eyes open. Was this a rooftop? Where was Anakin? He'd crashed his citibike, hadn't he? The Temple transport droid would be displeased. And then he remembered. There was no Anakin. There was only the Sith. He was lying on the cold dirt of Zigoola, and that was Bail Organa's gaunt, bloodied, and bruised face above him.

What a sight.

On the far edge of hearing, a voice implored him to die. He closed his eyes again. "Senator."

"Come on," said Bail, sliding an arm beneath his shoulders. "Up. Now. We don't have much time."

Time? Time for what? *Please, leave me alone.*

Bail hauled him to his feet then swung him around. The damaged knee protested. And then gave way, both his knees gave way, as he stared at the Sith temple and felt its malevolence crash upon him.

"I know," said Bail, supporting him as he shivered. "I'm sorry. But we have to go in there. You have to find what we need. I can't tell."

The black wind was howling inside his skull, trying to batter him into submission. Dark side domination. The brutality of might. "There are artifacts?" he said, his tongue thick and clumsy.

"Lots of them. But I don't know what any of them do."

"Of course you don't." He dragged himself free of Bail's supporting arm. Struggled to hold on to the unraveling threads of his sanity. Made himself look at the temple, at the Sith's beating heart. "You shouldn't have gone in there, Bail. Nothing Sith is safe."

"I had to," said Bail. "I had to see—"

"Yes. All right. But now you have to stay here."

"No," said Bail, grabbing his arm again. "Wait. You can't go in there alone. We can—"

Again, he freed himself. *"I said stay here,"* he snarled, and turned his back on the man who'd helped him get this far, alive. Dimly he was aware of Bail behind him, struck silent. But he couldn't afford to worry about the man's feelings. Couldn't afford to think of anything but surviving for long enough to defeat the Sith.

Walking—limping—toward the temple's tall open doors sent his mind reeling. It was like trying to walk into an inferno, or swim through a tidal wave. He put his head down and pushed back, pushed through, feeling the drag against his bones and in his blood. Feeling the Sith's hatred corroding him like acid.

DIE JEDI, DIE JEDI, DIE JEDI, DIE.

The urge to surrender was almost overwhelming. Surrender. Succumb. Fall down and find peace. Let the darkness close over him. Let the pain finally end. But that would make him Xanatos. Qui-Gon Jinn deserved better. Bail Organa deserved better, because surrender would kill him, too, and make his wife a widow. And Anakin deserved better, much better, than a Master who would willingly give himself to the Sith.

It occurred to him then, with a clarity that was startling, given the dark side hurricane howling through him, that Yoda was wrong about the dangers of attachment. Or at least that he wasn't altogether right.

It was true that attachment could weaken a Jedi's resolve. But it could also strengthen it . . . as he was strengthened now by his love for Qui-Gon, and Anakin. Without them he would have failed long before this moment.

And so, leaning on them, he continued to fight.

Awkward, nearly crippled, nearly weeping because the light side had been so long denied him, because the shouting was so loud, because his body wanted to obey it, he pushed over the temple threshold and into a place that was anathema to him . . . that hated him as though it were sentient . . . that with every step and gasping breath tried to end him in the Force.

The moment he set foot beneath the temple roof the building's bones began to tremble, revolted by his presence. Rejecting him like poison. Deep beneath him a tremor ran through the Zigoolan ground. And the voice in his head began to scream . . . and scream . . . and scream . . .

Mind reeling anew, he staggered across the disturbing Sith floor toward the alcoves that were set into the temple's walls. The screaming in his head grew louder—wilder—

DIE JEDI, DIE JEDI, DIE JEDI, DIE.

Every step he took was torture. The inferno was inside him now, burning him alive. Almost sightless, hazily aware that the temple was shuddering—that he was shuddering—he fell against the wall and began blindly groping from alcove to alcove for the artifact responsible for his torment. For the hateful thing that wanted him to die. When his fingers closed around it at last he thought his bones had burst into flame.

Through a smearing crimson haze he stared at what he held: an ancient black glass pyramid, Sith sigils tracing its surface blood-red. *Holocron.* It felt alive in his fingers, vibrant with hate and rage and fear and loathing. Vibrant with raw power. Alive with the dark side as he had never felt it before, or ever thought to. Such a small thing to contain so great and malevolent a power.

His bones were crumbling now, they were turning to ash. He was dying . . . he was dying . . . the Sith had won.

With his last breath, he smashed the holocron. And the fires went out.

Lying on his back, on a mosaic floor that shivered and writhed beneath him, he listened to the silence in his mind and couldn't grasp what it meant. Looked up at the distant ceiling and watched it rock from side to side, uncomprehending. Watched the walls rock. Listened to the Sith temple's stony lament.

From somewhere outside, someone shouted his name. Shouted again.

"Get out of there, Obi-Wan, you mad fool, the building's going to come down!"

That was . . . Bail. Bail Organa. A good man, for a politician.

And suddenly he remembered why he'd come into this dreadful place. He was looking for a way home. Had to find the way home. Had to save Bail Organa, whose life was in his hands. Groaning, retching, he struggled to his fists and knees and then to his feet. So much pain in him now he almost couldn't see straight.

All around him the temple was shaking. He staggered from alcove to alcove, scrabbling through each collection of artifacts. Books, no. Scrolls, no. The geodes made him retch some more, but there was no sense they could help him. Hurry. Hurry. Every wall was swaying. Now the alcoves were vomiting their treasures, artifacts smashing on the ugly mosaic floor. He found one cache of crystals, danced his fingers lightly across them, but all they did was make him dizzy. No way home there.

Another alcove, a single crystal, red and ruined. As soon as he touched it he shouted in revulsion—because he recognized it. *Remembered* it. Could feel its echo in his mind. *This*. This *thing*. This *monstrosity* had begun the nightmare. Had reached from this temple into the starship, into *him*, and warped him. Tried to make him a murderer by compelling him to crash the ship. The stench of death was on it, even though it was destroyed.

Bail's voice, anger and admiration combined. *"Whatever hold the Sith had on you? You broke it. Just before we hit the ground. It nearly killed you, but you broke it. You pulled us out of our nose dive and you—did something with the Force."*

Fresh strength flooded through him. He snatched up the ruined red crystal and hurled it to the floor. The impact shattered it into splinters, and he almost wept with joy. But the ground buckled violently, as if in furious protest, and he lost his footing. Crashing down on his injured knee had him screaming aloud. Another wild tremor and more crystals fell, cracking like rotten eggs all around him. He groped at the nearest alcove for support so he could stand, keep on looking, and only run . . . try to run . . . at the last possible moment. His fingers closed on something cold and rough and awful . . .

. . . and a window opened deep in his battered mind. He could see across the galaxy as though across a crowded room. For a split second it was *wonderful* . . . and then darkness smashed him flat.

Die Jedi, die Jedi, die Jedi, die.

He dropped the black-and-red crystal, spitting bile, and tried to stand so he could continue his search. But the floor was heaving and the ceiling was breaking apart, like river ice at the great spring thaw it was cracking and crazing and if he stayed in here much longer the Sith would get the death he thought he'd denied them.

For the second time, as though it were meant, his fingers found that impossible device. The darkness shouted again, but this time he didn't let go. Instead he thrust the thing inside his tunic, tried to stand, and had to duck as a chunk of ceiling missed his head by a whisper.

Bail Organa appeared in the drunkenly swaying doorway. "*Obi-Wan!* Get *out* of here, *now!*" And then like a fool, like an idiot, just like a politician, convinced the laws of nature did *not* apply to him, he ran into the dying Sith temple.

"Are you insane?" Obi-Wan demanded as Bail reached him. "*You* get out!"

"You're welcome," Bail panted, dragging him to his feet. "So, it's run or die, Master Kenobi. Your choice—but choose now."

Oh, how typical, always striving for the last word.

Slipping and sliding, they bolted for safety . . . with the Sith temple throwing great jagged slabs of rock at them with every staggering step. They fell through the wildly swinging doors as the first of four walls bowed and buckled. Rolled over the heaving ground, flailed themselves upright and kept running.

With a thundering groan, with a rumbling roar like the death of some dark, ancient beast of legend, the Sith temple fell in on itself, ceiling, walls, and buttresses shattering to pieces. The impact knocked them to the dying grass like a glancing blow from a thug's fist. Obi-Wan heard Bail curse. Heard himself curse, as every bruise and cut and scrape and tear shrieked in outrage. As he felt a rib crack against the crystal shoved inside his tunic.

Silence. Blessed silence. One heartbeat. Two heartbeats. Three heart—

Die Jedi, die Jedi, die Jedi, die.

TWENTY-TWO

"No!"

Knocked flat and breathless, Bail heard the outraged, desperate cry and somehow scrambled to his feet.

It was Obi-Wan. Bloodied, half stunned, on his knees and screaming with fury at the red-and-black crystal clenched in his right hand. Clenched so tightly that blood seeped between his fingers.

He felt like screaming himself, felt like throwing himself to the ground again and hammering his fists against the hard uncaring dirt. *No, vape it, no. Isn't this over yet? Why can't this be over?*

But he didn't. It wouldn't help. Unsteady on his feet, he edged cautiously to the left until he could see the Jedi's face. It was bone white, smeared with dirt, smudged with bruises, the cut over his eyebrow clogged with grit and glued with blood. His eyes were wild and red-rimmed, sunk as deep as death. It was the face of a man dragged beyond his endurance.

"Obi-Wan?" he said warily. "Obi-Wan, what's wrong?"

Obi-Wan's head snapped around. "Get away! Get back! You mustn't touch it."

Halting, he raised both hands like a supplicant. Like a prisoner who wasn't capable of harm. "All right. I won't. What is that thing? Can it get us home?"

Obi-Wan didn't answer, just glared at the red-and-black crystal. "It's still whispering. In my head, it's all I hear. *Die Jedi.*"

"Then we'll get rid of it, Obi-Wan, whatever it is. We'll smash it. We'll—"

"Are you *mad*, Organa?" the Jedi shouted. Oh mercy, he'd become a crazy scarecrow of a man. "This device is going to save us! It's the *only* thing that can save us! But it won't stop *whispering*, it won't leave me *alone*!"

"Okay, Obi-Wan," said Bail, placating. "Then why don't you give it to me? It can't hurt me, I can't hear it. Let me keep it safe, like your lightsaber, and we'll figure out a way to shut the kriffing thing up." He took one cautious step. "How's that for a plan?"

"I said *get back*!" said Obi-Wan, and punched his right fist forward. Bail felt the blow in his chest, felt the Force wave take him. Felt himself flying, helpless, to crash spine-first into the rubbled temple some thirty paces away. The impact was far worse than when he'd been flung out of the ship's cockpit. Then, Obi-Wan had tried to control his compulsion toward violence.

But not this time. This time, the Jedi embraced it.

The impact woke every sleeping pain in Bail's body. He couldn't move, couldn't breathe, couldn't speak or even groan. His nervous system had shut down—the lightsaber was useless to him. All he could do was lie there and wait.

He said this might happen. He said he could turn. But I didn't believe him. I'm a fool. This time I really am going to die.

But Obi-Wan ignored him. Still on his knees, the red-and-black crystal was pressed to his forehead and his lips were moving. One word, over and over, soundless and desperate . . . but it seemed that nothing was happening.

"I can't *hear*!" he shouted. "*Stop whispering at me!*"

Taking advantage of Obi-Wan's distraction, Bail struggled to move, but still his nerve-shocked body refused to obey. And then just when he thought he might truly suffocate, his diaphragm spasmed and he could breathe. Wheezing, gasping, he flexed his arms, flexed his legs, terrified for one blind moment that he'd suffered some dreadful damage. He heard the slither and clink and chink of stone as the rubble began to slide and settle around him. That had him on his feet, heedless of all discomfort, imagining an imminent crushing beneath the crimson-black slabs.

And Obi-Wan sent him flying again.

He landed on open ground, hard on his side. Something tore— his left shoulder, already badly weakened—and white-hot pain flooded every insulted nerve and sinew. He sank his teeth into his split lip, strangling a shout. Dimly he heard Obi-Wan shout, too.

"Be quiet—be *quiet*!"

What the vape was he trying to do?

Who knows? He's finally lost his mind. He can smash his skull to pieces now, for all I care.

Except he didn't mean that. That was his torn shoulder talking. That was days and nights of strain and hunger and thirst and fear. Obi-Wan wasn't the enemy, he'd been viciously attacked by the enemy, and if he was—if he was—

How can a Jedi like Obi-Wan go insane? After all his years of training, after everything he's seen and done? He's a good man. He's a great man. How is this possible?

The dark side. The Sith.

I never knew I could hate someone like this. Hate so I can taste it. Hate so I could kill.

A long, thin shadow fell across his face. He looked up. Saw Obi-Wan standing over him like a nightmare spat out of the Nine Corellian Hells. He fumbled for the lightsaber, his fingers thick and clumsy. Couldn't unclip it. Couldn't find how to turn it on. Didn't dare turn it on anyway while it was attached to his borrowed belt.

It was over. It was over. Obi-Wan was a Jedi. He could kill with his bare hands. Bail braced himself—thought of Breha—and for the last time waited for the killing blow to fall.

Obi-Wan raised his hand, still clutching the red-and-black crystal. "No. No. Bail. Help me."

He felt his breath catch. Thought this was some kind of last-living-moments delirium. "What?"

"*Help me,*" said Obi-Wan. He sounded desperate. And then, as though he were hamstrung, dropped to the ground. Choked as his knees hit the dirt and dry grass. "Crystal is telepathic. It can reach Yoda, at the Jedi Temple."

One word. *Yoda.* He'd been calling for *help*? With a *rock*?

I will never understand these people. Their world is too arcane for me.

"I don't—I'm sorry, I—"

Obi-Wan pressed his fingertips against his face, trying to contain some pain beneath the skin. "But I can't—break through. The Sith whispering won't stop."

They'd destroyed the temple and everything in it, except for this one crystal, and *still* it wasn't enough? Still the Sith could kill them?

It's not fair. It's not fair.

"Obi-Wan," he said, sitting up slowly, shrinking from the fire in his damaged shoulder, "I don't know what you think I can do. I'm not telepathic. I can't broadcast my thoughts through that thing. And if you don't stop trying, it's going to burn out your mind." He held out his hand. "Give it to me. I can rig up a slab of that temple rock and smash it to pieces. You'll never have to hear a Sith voice again."

"*No!*" said Obi-Wan, and snatched the crystal to his chest as though it were precious. As though it were his child. "I can make it work. If you help."

Still moving slowly, feeling like he was negotiating with a ticking bomb, Bail eased himself to a crouch. "Me? What can I do? You're the Jedi, Obi-Wan. I'm just the politician along for the ride."

Obi-Wan's eyes were feverish. "My lightsaber, Bail. Pain clears my mind. Drowns out the dark side. The ravine. Remember?"

For a moment Bail couldn't make sense of what Obi-Wan meant. And then comprehension flooded him, and he was on his feet in a heartbeat, heedless of every scrape and bruise and tear. "*No*, Obi-Wan! Absolutely *not*! You really *are* out of your mind!"

Still on his knees, Obi-Wan's head lowered till his chin touched his chest. He breathed, just breathed, and it was painful to hear. Then he looked up. "You . . . have a wife, Bail. I am a Jedi. *We cannot die here.*"

He was going to be sick. His empty belly was churning. First the killings in the space station, and now *this*? Obi-Wan was crazy even to suggest it.

This is not happening. This is not my life. Senators from Alderaan . . . Princes of Alderaan . . . do not find themselves in this position.

Except today they did.

He swung about, so angry, so frightened. "There has to be another way."

"Would I suggest this . . . if there were?" said Obi-Wan. His voice was filled with a grim endurance.

Breha. Slowly he turned back again, desolate. "I don't know. Can't you think of—Obi-Wan, there has to be a different choice."

As though he'd run through the dregs of his strength, Obi-Wan folded in on himself until he was sitting on the ground. "There's not."

Fingers clenching and unclenching, longing for something or someone to punch, Bail stared at him. "And say I agree to this—this *insanity*. How am I supposed to—how do I injure you with a *lightsaber*?"

Obi-Wan's lips curved in the faintest, faintest smile. "Very . . . carefully, Senator."

He laughed. He couldn't help it. This truly was madness. Utterly surreal. "Obi-Wan—are you sure? *Really* sure?"

Obi-Wan nodded.

Oh mercy. He unclipped the lightsaber from his belt. Obi-

Wan's belt. Stared at its black-and-silver elegance as though he'd never seen it before. And in a strange way, he hadn't. At least not like this.

"I don't even know how to turn the kriffing thing *on*."

Obi-Wan held out his hand. "Here."

Bail watched him activate the weapon. Watched the mesmerizing blue blade leap from its hilt. Saw the apprehension . . . the resignation . . . in Obi-Wan's sunken eyes.

Taking the weapon back, he clutched it awkwardly. His hands were sweating. Shaking. His heartbeat boomed in his ears. "What now?"

"Coordinates," Obi-Wan whispered.

Coordinates? Oh. Of course. To the planet. He'd scribbled them on a flimsi before they'd left the starship. Kept the flimsi in his backpack. An act of faith, or wishful thinking? Both. Neither. It was all the same now.

He fetched it and returned, walking carefully, not daring to run with a lightsaber in his hand. Obi-Wan had stretched himself supine on the dead grass. Zigoola's sun, sliding down the sky, lay insubstantial shadows over his face. Holding the red-and-black crystal tightly in his left hand, with his right he took the flimsi then lightly touched the tear in his thigh.

"Here. No point making . . . new holes. Don't . . . stab. Lay the blade . . . against the wound. Not hard. Not long. I don't . . . want to . . . lose my leg. It's . . . a bit far to hop home."

He was joking. How could he *joke* about this? This wasn't funny. This was dreadful. "Do you want me to—to warn you? Shall I count to three first?"

Obi-Wan looked at him. *"Bail."*

Oh. Right.

He did it. An electronic sizzling sound. The sickening smell, mingled, of burning cotton and flesh. Eyes stretched wide, spine arching, Obi-Wan swallowed his distress and tried to send his

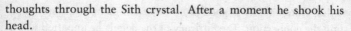

thoughts through the Sith crystal. After a moment he shook his head.

"No good. Again."

Oh mercy.

Beyond the boundaries of the Republic, on planets with no moral code, sentients tortured other sentients for power or greed. Sickened by the notion, he'd always wondered how anyone could do it. Deliberately, cold-bloodedly, inflict pain on someone else. Even derive pleasure from it. Or, conversely, feel nothing at all.

He wanted to vomit. He wanted to weep.

As the lightsaber burned him a second time, Obi-Wan's eyes went blank. A frantic pulse beat at the base of his throat. On a deep groan he tried once more to reach the Jedi Temple.

"No," he said, teeth gritted. "Again."

Dizzy, Bail pressed the back of his hand to his mouth. *This is it. This is the last time. I'm not doing this anymore.*

And to make certain, absolutely certain, he took a deep breath . . . and put some weight behind the bright blue blade.

The voice came through so faintly that at first Yoda, sunk deep in meditation, thought he'd imagined it. Thought he was dreaming, or committing the grave error of aimless hoping. He'd been waiting so long, with no answers, and had begun to fear the worst.

Then he heard it again, stronger. Vivid with pain . . . and stained with darkness. Obi-Wan's voice . . . his thoughts . . . unmistakable. Yet somehow the dark side was threaded through his Force presence. Yoda rarely admitted to alarm . . . but the bitter taste of Sith in their communication was a legitimate cause for apprehension. The echo of another, virulent voice . . . *die Jedi, die Jedi.*

Pushing the malevolence to one side, he descended more deeply than until this moment he'd ever dared to go, opening himself until he was virtually defenseless. Obi-Wan's thoughts poured into him, a desperate babble, as though he was terrified he could not maintain the connection. The intricacy of the details he imparted was as worrying as his fear, and that taste of the dark side; telepathy was hardly ever so precise. Feelings, impressions, yes. But pinpoint-accurate galactic coordinates? Precisely ordered requests? No. This communication was unwholesome. To the light side, abomination.

Then as suddenly as he'd made contact, Obi-Wan vanished. Not in death, but as though a holotransceiver circuit had fused.

Heedless of the late hour, Yoda woke Mace Windu.

"And you're sure it was Obi-Wan?" said Mace, after listening in focused silence.

Yoda nodded. "Yes."

Wrapped in a sleep shift, Mace slid off the end of his bed and paced to his window, where the night-lights of Coruscant played over his stern face. "Are you going to do what he asks?"

"No choice do I have. More Jedi we cannot risk. A death trap this Zigoola is."

"Yes," said Mace, turning. "But set by whom? Dooku? Or this mysterious Darth Sidious?"

"When attacks on the Jedi the Sith make, one is as the other. Important only is that they have failed."

"This time," said Mace.

They stared at each other, starkly aware of the dark side, creeping closer.

"To ourselves we should keep this," said Yoda, at last. "Until more we understand."

Mace nodded. "Agreed." Then he sighed. "You'll see her now?"

"I will," said Yoda. "For time to waste we do not have."

Slowly, reluctantly, he groped his way back to consciousness, guided by a familiar, urgent voice.

"Obi-Wan. Obi-Wan, did it work?"

He cleared his throat. The pain in his leg had reached obscene proportions. It was so appalling, so obliterating, really the only thing he could do was laugh.

"*Obi-Wan!*"

Oh dear. Poor Bail. He sounded quite cross. With an effort, he smothered hysteria and opened his eyes. "Yes," he said, his voice terribly altered. "It worked. Help is coming."

Bail swayed where he stood, then sat down, abruptly. "Here," he said, and almost threw the deactivated lightsaber at him. "Take this. *Take* it."

Moving only stoked the pain to newer, fiercer heights, but that was his lightsaber. He wrapped his fingers around its cool metal hilt. Felt the peace that came from being whole again.

Bail stared, his face haggard. "How long till we're rescued?"

"I don't know. A few days."

"A few days," Bail echoed. "We've got the supplies, if we're careful. But can you last that long?"

What an interesting question. A shame his only answer was another *I don't know.* "Perhaps."

"*Perhaps?*" Now Bail sounded offended. "What the varp do you mean, *perhaps*? I haven't gone through all this to watch you die now, Master Jedi. You're not going anywhere, do I make myself clear?"

Whispering, taunting, the persistent voice of the Sith, making itself heard even through all his bright pain.

Die Jedi, die Jedi, die Jedi, die.

"Senator Organa, it might not be up to you."

Bail looked at the red-and-black crystal, tumbled onto the dry ground. "Are you absolutely certain you got through to Master Yoda?"

"Yes," he said, remembering the touch of that ancient, disciplined, desperately sought intelligence. Feeling again the overwhelming relief.

"Then we don't need *this* kriffing thing anymore," said Bail, and snatched up the Sith's telepathic device.

Enervated, incapable of protesting or stopping the man even if he'd wanted to, Obi-Wan watched as Bail smashed the Sith crystal to powder between two slabs of collapsed temple stone.

The Sith's whispering fell silent, and even though the dark side still oppressed him . . . for the first time in days . . . in what felt like *years* . . . he was alone in his own mind. The relief of *that* reduced him to brief tears.

"Hey—*hey*!"

Bail again, alarmed. Squatting on his heels beside him, one hand on his shoulder. A warm, dependable, improbable presence.

Blinking away weakness, he made himself look at the Senator from Alderaan. Saw clearly, for the first time, what he'd asked the man to do. The price Bail had paid for the courage of his convictions.

Something of what he was feeling must have shown in his face.

"Don't," said Bail roughly. "It doesn't matter. We survived. The rest of it's nothing. Less than nothing. Just one more war story. The point is *we won*."

Was this what victory felt like?

May the Force spare me another victory like this.

"Hey," Bail said again. "How are you, Obi-Wan? Really?"

"Really?" Beneath his aching bones, the hard cold dirt of Zigoola. In his battered body, a fire that would not go out. "Really, Bail, I hurt quite a lot."

Bail shook his head. "Thought so."

"But it's better than being dead."

"Yeah," Bail said softly, and a slow smile spread across his thin, filthy face. "Yeah, you can say that again." The smile faded. "So. No more voices?"

"No."

"No more visions?"

"No."

"Then let's see what we can do about the pain. I've got drugs in the first-aid kit. Just don't argue with me, all right? I know where I can lay my hands on a lightsaber, and I'm not afraid to use it."

Obi-Wan looked at him. Anything he said would sound trite. Sentimental. Anything he said would only embarrass them both.

"Don't go anywhere, Master Kenobi," said Bail, patting his shoulder. "I'll be right back."

As the Senator from Alderaan withdrew to fetch the medkit, Obi-Wan let his eyes drift closed. For so many reasons, a Jedi's life was lived mostly solitary. For so many reasons, it was better that way. But sometimes . . . sometimes . . . they could make an exception. Sometimes . . . unexpectedly . . . they could make a new friend.

First Padmé, now Bail Organa. It appears I'm collecting politicians. Who would have thought it? Life is very strange.

Of all the beings she might reasonably expect to find in her living room at almost half past three in the morning, Jedi Master Yoda was at the bottom of the list.

Stunned silent, Padmé stared down at him. Only her years in public service saved her from betraying alarm. *Can it be Anakin? No. Why would he come to me for Anakin? It must be Bail and Obi-Wan. They've been gone so long now. Much longer than I thought.* She'd been covering for Bail in the Security Committee, but her excuses on his behalf were starting to wear thin. And she'd been getting more and more anxious . . .

Belatedly, she remembered her manners. "Can I offer you refreshments, Master Yoda? Threepio—"

"Thank you, no," said Yoda, and raised a hand to the droid. "Regret this intrusion I do, Senator Amidala, but on urgent business have I come."

"I gathered as much, Master Yoda, given the hour," she said, carefully noncommittal. Determined not to ask questions, but to see what he was willing to volunteer.

"A favor I would ask of you, Senator. Should you agree, in your debt would the Jedi Order be."

She pulled her robe a little closer to her body and sat on the nearest chair. "There can never be talk of debts between us, Master Yoda. What do you need me to do?"

Yoda leaned on his gimer stick. She thought he looked very tired. And at close to nine hundred years old, she supposed he had a right to be. "Word have I received from Obi-Wan Kenobi. Stranded is he with Senator Organa, on a planet called Zigoola."

For a moment she felt light-headed with relief. "They're all right?"

"They live," said Yoda. "But they have no ship, and send a Jedi to rescue them I cannot."

Relief chilled into foreboding. "Because it's a Sith planet?"

"Hmmm," said Yoda, his eyes narrowing. "Well informed you are, Senator."

"In this instance," she said calmly, refusing to be intimidated. "I take it you'd like me to fetch them, Master Yoda?"

And that put paid to his flinty disapproval. "Yes," he said, abruptly subdued. "The reason for my visit, that is. To ask for your assistance in this sensitive matter."

"Of course I'll assist you," she replied. "Always. Whenever and however I can."

Some great weight seemed to lift from his shoulders then. "In danger from the Sith you will not be, Senator Amidala. Deserted the planet is, save for Master Kenobi and Senator Organa."

Good. She'd had enough Sith to last her a lifetime.

"However," Yoda added, "clone troops will I send with you. In Wild Space is Zigoola. A dangerous destination, and from home a long way."

Wild Space? Wait till Anakin heard about this. She pulled a face. "It can't be more dangerous than Geonosis, Master Yoda."

"Independent you are, Senator, this I know well," said Yoda, severely. "But take the clone troops with you, you must. Unarmed is your private yacht. Protected you must be."

Anakin would say the same thing, if he were here. If she flew off into Wild Space without any kind of military escort he'd be furious . . . and worry about her even more when he was away fighting the Separatists, and the Sith.

The last thing I want to do is add to his burdens.

"Of course, Master Yoda," she said, and stood. "The Royal Yacht's one of the fastest ships on Coruscant, and it's ready to fly at a moment's notice. At top speed the clones and I will be there before Bail and Master Kenobi know it. Do you have the coordinates?"

Yoda took a data crystal from his pocket and held it out. "Plotted on here the fastest course is, Senator. Follow it, and avoid trouble with the Separatists you will. Also on it are life-sign signatures for Master Kenobi and Senator Organa. Easy will that make finding them, I think. The clone troops I will send at once to your private spaceport."

Anakin was wary of this ancient Jedi. For herself, she often found him obscure and aloof. But she had the knack of reading people . . . and in his eyes now she saw such worry. After what she'd seen in the cavern on Geonosis, she knew Obi-Wan held a special place in his heart . . . though doubtless he'd deny it until he drew his last breath. The Jedi, and their disdain for attachment.

"Master Yoda," she said, taking the data crystal, "I will bring Obi-Wan home to you, safe and well. On that you have my solemn word."

To her surprise he took her hand in his, and held it. "Thank you, Padmé. Upon me you must call if ever a service for you I can perform."

If he knew how she and Anakin were deceiving him, he wouldn't be grateful. He'd be furious. Somehow she managed a smile. "I'll remember that, Master Yoda."

After he left she got C-3PO to warn the spaceport to expect her and the clone detachment while she dragged on a flight suit, tossed some spare clothes in one bag and stuffed another full of official datapads, then sent a time-delayed message to her Senate office, logging a personal business absence.

Threepio was hovering anxiously by the apartment's front door. "Oh dear, milady. I'm afraid this sounds very dangerous. I do hope they're all right. I hope *you'll* be all right. Wild Space? This whole business sounds most alarming."

Chances were that *alarming* was only the beginning. *Obi-Wan. Bail. What have you been up to?* But there was no point encouraging the droid to fuss. "I'll be fine, Threepio. You heard Master Yoda. I'll have clone troops watching my back every minute I'm gone." She patted his golden shoulder. "You take care of things here, and I'll see you again when I return. All right?"

"Oh yes, yes, milady," said 3PO. "Don't you worry about a thing."

He might as well have told her not to breathe.

"I won't," she said, hefted her travel bags, and took her apartment complex's swift-tube to the parking bay and her private speeder.

TWENTY-THREE

AS PROMISED, THE DETACHMENT OF CLONE TROOPS WAS WAITING for her at the spaceport, heavily and reassuringly armed. Five soldiers and their leader, disconcertingly alike.

But only on the outside, she reminded herself. *On the inside, they are themselves.*

"Senator!" said their commander, saluting, bulky helmet neatly tucked under his arm. "Captain Korbel, reporting."

She didn't recognize his insignia. All she knew was they weren't from Anakin's company, the doughty 501st. "Captain. I'm pleased to meet you," she said. "And most appreciative of your help. I take it you've been fully briefed by Master Yoda?"

Korbel nodded. "Certainly have, Senator. We're all of us fully medic-trained, so that won't be a problem. We'll take good care of the general and Senator Organa."

She felt a punch of adrenaline burn through her blood. "I'm sorry. Medic-trained? I wasn't—I don't understand. Are you saying they're injured?"

"Oh," said the captain. Despite his rigorous training, concern touched his intense black eyes. "I thought you'd been fully briefed as well, ma'am."

"Apparently not," she said. "But that's no matter. Master Yoda was tired, and doubtless distracted." Or else, just as Anakin complained, he very rarely stopped to think about trivialities, like feelings. "Let's get on board, shall we? It seems we have no time to waste."

"Yes, ma'am," said Korbel. He collected his men with another nod.

Thank you so much, Yoda, she thought as she hurried to her sleek, swift starship. *Let's just hope there are no more surprises.*

Unnerved by the worry she'd seen in Yoda's eyes, dismayed by what Captain Korbel had told her, once they cleared Coruscant she poured on the speed and the yacht ate up the parsecs between home and Zigoola. If she'd been flying for any other reason than rescue, perhaps she'd have found herself excited by the prospect of leaving the Republic behind, the Outer Rim behind, and flirting with unknown, exotic *Wild Space.* Even if her destination was a Sith planet. But instead of excitement, all she could feel was apprehension. Bail *and* Obi-Wan injured?

Whatever happened, it must have been bad.

Captain Korbel and his men kept their professional, polite distance. Taking care of themselves, and her, too, with an efficiency that could only be admired. Korbel had been most complimentary about the yacht's medbay.

I wish I found that less alarming.

To distract herself, and because she didn't dare let herself fall behind, she plunged into the Senate work she'd brought with her. The course the Jedi had plotted for her was flawless. They didn't encounter a skerrick of trouble: no Separatists, no pirates, nothing to hinder their speed.

When at last the nav comp announced their arrival at Zigoola, and she dropped the ship out of hyperspace, she barely looked at the planet or the raging nebula behind it. Felt no excitement at the exotic location, just a pounding drive to *find them find them find them.*

Captain Korbel came up to the cockpit. "I understand Master Yoda gave you General Kenobi's and Senator Organa's biosigns, ma'am?"

"That's right," she agreed.

"Like me to scan for them while you're flying this sweet thing?"

Clone Captain Korbel had a most engaging smile. "Thank you, Captain," she said, smiling back. "That would be appreciated." Then she patted the helm console. "And she is a sweet thing, isn't she?"

Korbel nodded. "Sweetest ship I've flown in my whole life, ma'am."

And how long was that? Nine years? Ten? She pointed to one of the other cockpit seats. "There's the sensor array console, Captain. The biosigns are already programmed into it."

"Excellent, ma'am."

After she'd positioned the yacht in a geosynchronous orbit, Korbel took a seat and started running various sensor sweeps. It didn't take long to find their quarry.

"On the night side," said the captain. "And they're alone. Whole vaping planet's empty, pretty much."

It couldn't have been too empty, or Bail and Obi-Wan wouldn't be hurt. But she didn't voice the thought, just tied in the nav comp to the biosigns readout and kicked the yacht in a shallow dive down to the planet's sunless surface. It didn't matter about them being found on Zigoola's night side; the yacht's powerful floodlights could turn night into day.

"I'll return to my men," said Korbel. "If there's nothing else I can do here?"

"No, no, you go," she said, distracted, staring through the cockpit viewport, feeling ill with apprehension.

"Once we're down," Korbel added, "you should let us recce the area before you set foot on the planet."

She glanced at him. "But you just said they're—"

"Better safe than sorry, Senator," said Korbel with a shrug. "You're under our protection, ma'am. I'm aware of your expertise but I'd appreciate it if you'd humor me."

In other words, Yoda had warned them she didn't like being fussed over. But Korbel was a good man. She liked him, and he was only doing his job. So she swallowed annoyance and nodded. "Of course."

"Thank you, Senator," said Korbel, withdrawing, and she was left to land her sweet ship.

The first thing she saw in the floodlights was the edge of an enormous pile of rubble. Recent rubble, from the look of it: the stones showed no signs of weathering.

Boys, boys. What have you done?

The yacht settled like a lady on the barren plateau. She let down the ramp, rushed from the cockpit to the external hatch, then stood back to let Korbel and his men disembark for their recce of the immediate vicinity. Obeyed the captain's stricture to stay well out of sight and target range until he gave her the all-clear. It didn't take long.

"All right, Senator!" Korbel called up to her. "You're good to go."

At last. She leapt to the top of the ramp . . . and stuttered to a halt in the hatchway. Bail was standing at its base, waiting for her.

He looked . . . *appalling.*

"Senator Amidala," he said, offering an awkward bow. The contrast of courtliness with his truly ruffian appearance . . . dirt and stubble and dried blood and cuts and bruises and rags and *oh,* he'd gotten so *thin* . . . stopped her breathing for a moment.

His eyes were very bright.

Slowly, with great care, she walked down the ramp. She wanted to run to him, embrace him, but he looked so brittle she was afraid he might break. As well, Korbel and his men had formed up in close protection, and she felt suddenly conscious of Senatorial dignity. Instead she reached him, and stopped, and gave him a tremulous smile.

"Senator Organa," she said, her voice unsteady. "I understand you need a lift."

Bail laughed, but his voice cracked, and he looked down, breathing hard. "Only if you're going my way," he said, after a long pause, then looked up. "I wouldn't like to put you to any trouble."

Her eyes were burning. "No. No trouble. There might be a small fee . . ." And then she stopped. "Oh, *Bail* . . ."

To the Hells with dignity. Besides, he was married and so was she. They held each other like brother and sister. She could feel his shoulder blades like knives beneath her hands.

"I'm sorry," he muttered. "I stink."

Yes, he did. And she couldn't have cared less. "You're alive." Releasing him at last, she stepped back. "Where's Obi-Wan?"

The smile died out of his eyes. "Ah." He nodded toward the rubble. "Over there. Master Kenobi's a man of leisure these days."

Oh no. Oh no.

"It'll take a couple of men to get him in the yacht," said Bail gently. "He's . . . not well, I'm afraid."

"Captain," she said to Korbel. "I'll need you in a moment, but for now—hold your positions."

"Ma'am," he acknowledged. "Say the word when you're ready."

Bail took her over to the collapsed building, where Obi-Wan sat on a seat made of stone, wrapped in a tattered heat-seal blanket, the edge of the yacht's floodlights washing over him. And if Bail looked appalling . . . if Bail had gone thin and brittle . . .

There were no jokes. She had no banter. For this man . . . in this moment . . . she had nothing but tears.

"Padmé," said Obi-Wan, his voice as changed as the rest of him. "Riding to the rescue again." He smiled, and her heart broke. "It's good to see you, Senator."

She couldn't speak. Could hardly breathe. When she was sure of herself again:

"You . . . you . . . *reckless* Jedi," she said, walking forward, and when she reached him she dropped into a crouch. "Anakin is going to be *so cross* with you!" Her head lowered then, and she fought a private, losing battle.

"There, there," he said gently, and clumsily patted her arm. "No need to upset yourself. It's not that bad really."

She stood and stepped back, one hand dashing across her face. "Not that bad?" She pointed. "Let's start with the most obvious, shall we? What happened to your *leg*?"

It was stretched out in front of him, his right thigh crudely bandaged with strips torn from his tunic, the wound patently severe. When Obi-Wan didn't answer she turned to Bail . . . and caught the most peculiar, complicated look pass between them.

Then Obi-Wan sighed. "It's nothing. Truly. A lightsaber mishap."

"A *lightsaber*—" She stared. "What? *Again?*"

"Hey," said Bail, resting a hand on her shoulder. It felt like . . . a warning. "At the risk of being pushy, Padmé, I really want to get the vape off this rock. So can we . . . you know . . . go?"

There was a story here. There was a story. The air reeked of secrets. But this wasn't the time or the place to start digging for the truth. Not with Obi-Wan sitting there, so—so *reduced*.

"Of course," she said, then turned. "And Obi-Wan, you'll be pleased to know that Master Yoda handpicked these clone troops. All of them are medics. You'll be well taken care of, I promise."

With a careful tenderness that surprised her, Captain Korbel and one of his men carried Obi-Wan onto the yacht. She and Bail followed closely on their heels.

"Thank you, Captain," said Bail once Obi-Wan—beyond speaking—was settled in the comprehensively equipped medbay. "Give us a few moments. Then he'll be all yours."

Korbel nodded. "Sir."

"I'll get us out of here," Padmé murmured as the captain returned to the passenger compartment and his men. She touched her hand lightly to Obi-Wan's cheek. "Don't worry. We'll be home soon."

Then, leaving Bail to keep him company, she went forward to the cockpit and did indeed get them the vape off Zigoola. Good riddance, good riddance. Kriff the Sith and all their foul works.

Return course set for Coruscant, punched deliriously fast into hyperspace, she left the yacht to fly itself and made her way back to her rescued passengers. Lowered voices in the medbay stopped her outside, in the corridor.

"Well?" she heard Bail say. "Is it coming back?"

A long silence. Then: "Yes," said Obi-Wan. Padmé felt a new rush of relief. He'd looked so dreadful, as though he'd never speak again. She really wished she knew what they were talking about.

"See?" said Bail. "I told you the Sith couldn't stop you being a Jedi. Not forever, anyway."

"Yes, you did," said Obi-Wan. To her shock, his voice broke. Held such emotion. She'd never heard anything like it before. Not from him.

"You need medical attention, Obi-Wan," Bail said, after a moment. And he, too, sounded like a man overwhelmed. "You heard Padmé. Yoda's handpicked clone medics. So are you going to make a fuss or will you let them do their job?"

She heard Obi-Wan cough, a horrible rattling sound. "Has anyone ever told you, Senator, that you're really rather annoying?"

"In fact they have, Master Jedi," Bail retorted. "But not as many times as you've been told you're a pain in the butt."

There was so much affection in their voices, Padmé felt her throat close. She'd never imagined she'd hear Bail and Obi-Wan speaking like—like *friends*. Like two people who'd known each other for years. What had happened to them, back on Zigoola? She was desperate to find out.

"You want a painkiller?" said Bail.

"I believe I do," replied Obi-Wan.

Bail snorted. "Smart man. I'll go get Captain Korbel." A moment later he stepped into the corridor. Saw her and stopped. "Padmé."

Caught eavesdropping, she lifted her chin. "Obi-Wan's not the only one who needs first aid. We've got six medics on board, remember. One of them is yours."

Bail nodded. "That sounds good. But I'd like to sit for a while, first. Can we just sit, do you think?"

His eyes were shadowed with what she was sure were dreadful memories . . . and he looked ready to drop where he stood. "Of course," she said gently. "And if you want to talk . . . I'm here."

He shook his head. "Not now. Maybe later."

He'd have to talk about it eventually. For security reasons, if nothing else. But she could wait. She was good at waiting.

She patted his arm. "Anytime . . . my friend."

Yoda found Obi-Wan in the Temple's lush arboretum, sitting cross-legged under a waterfall, eyes closed, fully dressed . . . and perfectly dry.

Not quite a week had passed since Senator Amidala brought him home from Zigoola. He'd spent most of that time in a deep healing trance. Yesterday Vokara Che had pronounced him fit to leave the Halls of Healing, but had restricted him to the Temple precinct on pain of her most severe displeasure.

The warning was as effective as a Geonosian containment field.

Sensing his approach, Obi-Wan opened his eyes. Smiled. And extricated himself from beneath the waterfall. A wave of his hand started the water flowing freely again, and he bowed.

"Master Yoda."

"Master Kenobi," he replied. "Sit."

Obi-Wan sank to the cool grass. Only the slightest hesitation in his movement hinted that he might not be quite himself as yet. That and the fact he still needed to finish regaining the weight he'd lost in his battle with the Sith.

Balancing comfortably on his gimer stick, Yoda inhaled the fragrant arboretum air deeply. Wondered about the waterfall. Decided not to ask. "Eager the Council is, Obi-Wan, to hear of what happened on Zigoola," he said instead. "Ready to speak of it yet, are you?"

Obi-Wan's expression did not change, but the faintest of shadows touched his eyes. "I think so, Master Yoda."

"An affirmative answer that is not."

"I'm sorry, Master. It's the only answer I have to give you."

Yoda sighed. "Troubled you are, Obi-Wan. Understand I do. Time you need, and time you will have."

Obi-Wan plucked a stem of grass and considered it, his face grave. Stroked a fingertip down its blue-green length. Then he shivered. "Do you know, Master Yoda," he said, his voice very low, "there is more of the light side in this sliver of grass than I could feel in my whole body while I was on Zigoola. It was . . ." He exhaled, so slowly. ". . . the most empty, the most lonely, the most *bereft* I have ever felt. Worse even than all the deaths I relived, so many times, as though each time was the first." He let the blade of grass slip from his fingers, his gaze roaming across the arboretum. "That emptiness is what awaits the Republic if we should lose this war with the Sith. It is an outcome to be . . . *deplored*. And avoided at any cost, no matter how high."

Yoda felt the echoes of Obi-Wan's memories in the Force. Felt the touch of that dreadful bleakness, and a bitter sting of cold. "Agree with you I do. But dwell on this experience you must not, Obi-Wan. Survive it you did. Learn much you did."

Obi-Wan nodded. "That is true. And I shan't dwell, I promise."

"Tell me, can you, the most important thing you learned?"

"That I am a Jedi," said Obi-Wan simply, after a long silence. Simply, and with great joy. "And always will be."

Yoda smiled, then sighed again. "A great pity it is that the artifacts you discovered in the Sith temple were ruined beyond recovery."

Obi-Wan shook his head. "They were poison, Master. Steeped in the dark side. I think it likely not even you would have been allowed to touch them safely."

That made him stare. "Indeed?"

"Indeed," said Obi-Wan, and held his stern gaze.

"Hmmm." He poked the tip of his gimer stick into the ground and watched the soft soil give way. Smiled, not warmly. "Lost to us the artifacts are, it is true. But also to the Sith. A victory, that is." He looked up. "And what of this Senator from Alderaan? *Bail Organa*. Trust him can we, Obi-Wan, to keep our secrets safe?"

For the first time since his return to the Temple, Obi-Wan smiled an unfettered, unshadowed smile. "Oh yes, Master Yoda. We can trust Bail with our lives."

"Pleased to hear it, I am," he said. "And now leave you I will. Rest, Obi-Wan. Your strength you must recover. Need you we do, in this war against the Sith."

Obi-Wan nodded. "Yes, Master."

At the arboretum door, Yoda paused and looked back. Obi-Wan had returned to his seat beneath the waterfall. He looked . . . happy.

Despite his burden of worries and secrets Yoda smiled, with warmth this time . . . and left him to play.

Even though she knew what he was like about getting messages promptly, Ahsoka took a moment . . . just a moment, all right, several moments . . . to stand in the doorway of Allanteen VI shipyard's Hangar 9C and watch Anakin run through his Force-enhanced calisthenics. Barefoot, stripped down to his leggings, he used the whole empty hangar space to full effect. Powerful and effortless, in perfect tune with the Force, he performed—his execution flawless and very fast—seventy-five traveling double-twist backflips.

She counted.

And as he landed the last one, his breathing steady and undis-

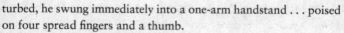

turbed, he swung immediately into a one-arm handstand . . . poised on four spread fingers and a thumb.

Eyes closed, he said, "What is it, Ahsoka?"

No one was ever going to play hide-and-go-seek with Skyguy. "Incoming holomessage from Coruscant, Master."

And then he was . . . on his feet, in front of her. And there was this moment—this tiny moment—again, as usual—when she could never catch how he got from *there* to *here*.

"Obi-Wan?"

She nodded. "Obi-Wan."

He shot her a cold look in passing. "You don't ever make him wait."

Falling into step behind him, walking fast, she cleared her throat. "Ah . . . Skyguy?"

He slowed. Turned. Cold was cautious now. He was coming to know her. "What?"

"I think he looks a bit . . . *wrong.*"

And then she had to run, to keep up.

He took the call in the chief designer's office, unceremoniously evicting the chief designer, his assistant, and two other shipyard execs. They were coming to know him now, so nobody said a word. They just left.

Ahsoka tucked herself into a corner and pricked up her ears.

"Obi-Wan," Anakin said to the hologram sitting on its desktop transceiver. "Sorry. I was training."

Master Obi-Wan's hologram looked Anakin up and down. *"Yes, I can see that."*

Anakin ignored the gentle sarcasm. "So you're back from your mission. At last. How did it go?"

"Moderately uneventful, thank you," said Master Obi-Wan. He did blandly evasive like nobody's business. *"I have a new assignment for you."*

Anakin folded his arms. "Yeah. That's great. Obi-Wan, what happened?"

"*Oh, it's far too tedious to get into,*" said Master Obi-Wan. "*How's your apprentice coming along?*"

Ahsoka scowled. What? They thought she was an idiot? So they couldn't discuss the mission in front of the Padawan. They could just *say* that. She wouldn't burst into tears.

"She's fine. Master, you're not looking well."

"*You're imagining things, Anakin. Now, do you want to hear about your mission?*"

"Yes," said Anakin, rolling his eyes. "But in case you think we're done discussing this? We're not. What's the mission?"

"*New intelligence has just come in. The Separatists have established a secret listening post. It could explain how Grievous took out the Falleen battle group.*"

"Any idea where it's located?"

"*Well, no,*" said Master Obi-Wan, dry as Tatooine. "*That would account for the 'secret' part of 'secret listening post,' Anakin.*"

"Ha ha," said Anakin. But he did smile, even though his eyes were still worried. "So, you want me to find Grievous's spyhole. Do I take the *Twilight*? And Captain Rex?"

"*You do. We've also picked up some partially triangulated chatter, which I'll have transmitted to your bridge. That should get you started on tracking down this mystery base.*"

"Thank you, Master," said Anakin. "Ah . . . don't suppose you'll be joining us for this one, will you?"

Master Obi-Wan shook his head. "No. I'm afraid I'm involved in an extensive mission debrief. Maybe next time. But I'll wish you good hunting, Anakin. Find that outpost. Things could get tricky for us fast if you don't."

The hololink disconnected.

Ahsoka waited, but Anakin didn't move. Instead he stared at the empty transceiver. "Extensive mission debrief my crippled old dewback," he muttered. "You're convalescent again, Obi-Wan. What did you do?"

Ahsoka stepped forward. "I guess he'll tell you when I'm not around," she said. "Skyguy, can I go find Rex? Let him know we're on a countdown?"

Anakin nodded. He was hardly paying attention. "Yeah. Sure."

"Thanks," she said, heading out. But in the doorway she paused and looked back. She knew him well enough now to know he really was worried. "Hey, Skyguy. He didn't look *that* bad. Whatever it was, I bet it was practically nothing."

Anakin spared her a startled glance, then a wry smile. "Yeah. I guess. Go tell Rex I'll come brief him soon. Okay?"

"Okay," she said, hurrying off to find their Clone detachment. Did a few backflips of her own, to celebrate. Another mission. No more boring shipyards. *Yes!* Life was finally looking up.

When Palpatine saw Bail Organa in the noisy Senate cafeteria, deep in lunchtime conversation with Padmé and that inept Gungan bumbler Jar Jar Binks, he suffered an actual, *physical* shock.

Organa was *alive*? He was *here*? On Coruscant? But that must mean *Kenobi* was alive, too. Because if *he* was dead, with Organa surviving to tell the tale, the Jedi would have mentioned it. If Kenobi was dead, neither Padmé nor Organa would be laughing so delightfully together.

When had Organa returned to Coruscant? And why had Mas Amedda failed to inform him of the fact? Was this *another* functionary he'd be forced to replace?

The recent extended absence of Alderaan's popular Senator had been noted. There had been some muttering. He'd been on the point of expressing concern and launching a discreet little investigation, which would then reveal the truth of Bail's tragic demise. *And* the tragic demise of a great Jedi hero.

And now they *weren't* dead?

How . . . disappointing.

Although . . . now that he looked closely . . . Organa did seem a little *worn*. So something must have happened. Perhaps Kenobi was a little worn, too. With luck he was a *lot* worn. He'd have to ask Yoda.

But worn wasn't good enough. He'd wanted them *dead*.

He was aware of rage bubbling beneath his surface. He had not bothered to pursue the Zigoola gambit himself. He had assumed . . . he had accepted . . . that Dooku would keep track of that. That was his *function*. That was his *purpose*. That's what an aging apprentice was *for*.

Housekeeping.

Did this mean Zigoola was compromised? Or worse, did it mean its treasures were destroyed? Priceless Sith artifacts, hoarded over centuries.

If this is true . . . if this is true . . .

With more of an effort than he cared to expend, Palpatine soothed his rage into affable cordiality. Smoothed his expression into one of genial goodwill. And set forth across the dining floor to engage Padmé and Bail and, if he had to, the regrettable Jar Jar Binks, in the kind of wistfully erudite conversation that had earned him so many, *many* friends.

And as he greeted them . . . as he joined them . . . as he asked about their day . . . beneath the affable surface, Darth Sidious's dark thoughts seethed.

This is a minor setback. A mere ripple on the pond. There are many other artifacts at my disposal. I still have Anakin. He still has Padmé. The war is worsening at every turn. Kenobi serves on the front lines. He could perish any day. Organa can be easily enough contained. And as for Dooku, I'll deal with him . . . when it's time.

This Republic will fall. I have foreseen it.